prey tell

USA TODAY BESTSELLING AUTHOR
AMANDA RICHARDSON

Prey Tell
Amanda Richardson
© Copyright 2023 Amanda Richardson
www.authoramandarichardson.com

Copyediting: Ellie McLove at My Brother's Editor
Proofreading: Michele Ficht
Cover Design: Moonstruck Cover Design & Photography
Cover Photography: Rafa G Catala
Cover Model: Aitor Ferron

BLURB

They say monsters are made, not born.
He was both...

Chase

As the second youngest Ravage brother, I've spent my entire adult life rectifying our tainted family name and keeping my urges behind closed doors.

Until my best friend's little sister shows up at The Hunt ready to play, and I lose control.

I tell myself it's *just a taste.*

Except, with her, I should've known a single taste wouldn't be enough.

And then the good girl I've known most of my life drops to her knees.

For me.

From that moment on, I knew she would only ever be one thing.

Mine.

Juliet

Presenting my brother's best friend with a pros/cons list of why he should take my virginity seemed like a good idea at the time.

I thrive on information, data, and lists, and it made sense on paper.

Until he rejected me and walked out of my life.

Now, eight years later, my life is falling apart despite my careful planning.

Tempted with an invite to Ravage Castle, I show up seeking answers to questions I'm not sure I can handle.

Except, a furious Chase finds me talking to another man.

Under *his* gilded, arched roof.

I soon learn that despite his controlled exterior, Chase seems to have one weakness.

Me.

Prey Tell is a full-length brother's best friend/billionaire romance with primal play themes. It is book one in the Ravaged Castle series. All books can be read as standalones.

Warning: This book contains a possessive, jealous antihero, explicit sexual situations, and strong language. There is no cheating, and there is a HEA.

There once was a castle, so mighty and high,
With large, gilded gates, it rivaled Versailles.
To all those below, it was splendid and lush,
But to those inside, it was ravaged and crushed.
Five Ravage boys born amongst old, rotted roots,
Their father ensured they'd all grow to be brutes.
Some said they were cursed, sworn off of desire,
But they turned into men and found what they required.
Forbidden, illicit, they had to work for that love,
They questioned that castle when push came to shove.
The curse and the rot gave way to unsavory tastes,
Dark proclivities and sick, messed up traits.
Five stories of five men with sinfully dark tales,
The Ravage brothers prove that love does prevail.

TRIGGERS

Triggers: BDSM elements (Dominant/submissive, consensual non-consent, spanking, primal play, predator/prey play, rough sex, use of riding crop), parental death (remembered), child neglect (remembered), coming out themes, and anxiety.

*Please note that Prey Tell is *not* a dark romance. Happy reading!

For all the girlies who want to be caught.

PROLOGUE
THE OFFER

Chase

Eight Years Ago

I'm just slipping the pink rubber gloves onto my hands when I hear a crash and subsequent moan coming from the front porch. Muttering under my breath, I walk over to the front door and throw it open.

"Parker," I growl, taking in her small, slumped body sitting on the large porch swing. She's fumbling with the straps of her heels as a string of curses leaves her lips. "Are you fucking drunk?"

She snaps her head up and glares at me. "I'm not drunk. I tripped on the stairs because these heels are trying to kill me." Her eyes swing to the gloves. "I never knew you were so domestic. Pink is undoubtedly your color."

I lean against the doorframe and smirk. "You always know what to say to make a man swoon."

She narrows her eyes at me before she continues fumbling with the tiny straps. "Why are these ankle straps so hard to unbuckle? I don't understand why we women constantly torture ourselves like this. For example, why are these holes so hard to find in the first place?" The instant the words leave her lips, she glares up at me. "*Don't* make some sexual innuendo right now, Ravage. I'm not in the mood to spar tonight," she says, using her nickname for me.

"Let me," I offer, snapping the rubber gloves off and shoving them in the back pocket of my suit pants.

Walking over to where she's sitting, I fall to my knees and pull her left leg up first, exposing one of her creamy thighs. I clear my throat and focus on the task at hand. Much to my chagrin, she's not wrong. The buckles are tiny and it takes me a solid minute to slide the thin strap off from around her delicate ankle. When I grab her other leg, it takes an inordinate amount of self-control not to run my fingers up her toned legs.

When I finish, I sit back on my heels and grin. "It wasn't that hard."

She blinks a few times and looks at something behind me, refusing to make eye contact. "Is Jackson asleep?"

"Yeah. Those toddlers will be the death of him one day," I mutter, standing up. I'm referring to the little crotch goblins he teaches every weekday. I'd been cleaning up after our dinner so that it was one less thing he had to do tomorrow.

She snorts. "Probably. But he'll love every second of

his hard-earned demise."

I hold the front door open for her as she walks inside before me, heels dangling from her fingers. I study the way she sets them down by the door neatly —the way she lingers and gazes around longingly. Pulling the gloves on, I walk over to the sink.

"So, rough night?" I ask her.

She hops up onto the counter next to me, crossing her ankles as her hands grip the edge of the countertop.

"No."

"Parker," I warn her, my tone low and intimidating. I pick up the first plate and begin the arduous process of cleaning up after her sloppy brother. "You know, I can always tell you're lying because your voice drops an octave."

She twists her lips to the side, looking so fucking *innocent.* Except she's endured more than any eighteen-year-old ever should.

"Fine, you caught me."

I start to load the dishwasher, knowing my silence is eating at her. "I also know you're lying about being drunk."

She scoffs. "I had two drinks. I'm hardly falling over my—"

"Front steps?" I finish, looking over at her as I quirk a brow. "Juliet Parker *actually* went to a party and indulged in... fun?" I tease.

She swats my arm. "I can be fun sometimes. It's rare though, so you better soak it all up now while you have the chance, Ravage."

I set my plate down and turn to face her. My eyes bore into her light-green ones, and then they perused her heart-shaped face, the dusty rose of her lightly freckled cheeks, before tracking down her slender neck. My mind memorizes the way her dress—which is too *fucking* short—clings to her smooth curves—the slim waist that flares into rounded hips. When I'm done, I meet her eyes again, but this time, her cheeks are tinged with pink.

She's playful tonight. I'm enjoying it, and it might be my new favorite version of her. Leaning closer, I can see the way her chest rises and falls at my perusal.

"Oh, I plan to savor it, Parker."

Something shutters behind her eyes and her lids lower slightly as she considers my words.

It takes me a second too long to realize I'm flirting with her.

Fuck.

Flirting with Juliet Parker? I shouldn't be entertaining the idea—and trust me, my mind *wanted* to entertain the idea numerous times over the past couple of years.

But her brother was my best friend. I'd known her for a decade. And even if that weren't the case, I was Chase Ravage, fourth son of Charles Ravage, also known as the billionaire who fucked over a bunch of people five years ago. The Ravage name is basically cursed, and Juliet is perfection personified. I'd drawn the line years ago. As tempting as she was—and she was *always* fucking tempting—I could never have her. *She* would never want me.

At least not in the uninhibited ways I wanted her to want me.

"Are you going to help me with these dishes or do I have to do them all myself?" I say quickly.

It seems to break the spell, because Juliet shakes her head and hops off the counter. "Why are you here anyway if Jackson is asleep?"

I shrug. I could tell her the truth—that seeing my best friend is the highlight of my Friday evenings, so I savor my time in this quaint fucking house. I could confess that my job at Ravage Consulting Firm is slowly eating away at my soul, and while my penthouse in downtown Crestwood is nice and big, I'd much rather be here because it feels more like home than anywhere else. Or I could confide that ever since her and Jackson's parents died two years ago, I feel obligated to take care of them.

Jackson Parker is the closest thing I have to a real family.

And Juliet comes with the territory.

It's why I knew she'd taken a cab home—because I'd given her access to my business account, and I'd seen a notification earlier that she was being picked up.

"Like I said, his kids wear him out. And though my father was a deplorable human being, he still taught me basic manners."

"I assumed you wouldn't know how to do dishes. You know, with your upbringing."

My jaw tics, but I don't indulge her with a response. "Grab a towel and help me dry."

She reaches for the towel on the counter, but then she notices my ring on the soap dish. Her finger brushes over the gold, the letter 'R' engraved in the middle. I watch her as she places it on one of her fingers, smiling as it dangles off.

"I always forget that you wear this ring."

"I don't."

"It looks like a relic." She places it back down on the counter. "Though it is quite pretty. It goes well with the pink gloves," she deadpans. Despite her teasing, I laugh. "If you hate your father so much, why do you wear it?" She grabs the towel as I hand her a large pot.

"To remind myself."

Drying the pot, her large, chartreuse eyes find mine. "Of what?"

A muscle quivers at my jaw as I hand her a wineglass. "That I never want to end up like him."

She dries the glass without asking anymore questions, but if I know her at all, I can assume she's formulating a response in that big brain of hers. Juliet is nothing if not practical, driven, and focused. In fact, if she weren't about to attend college, I might've offered her an internship at Ravage Consulting Firm. After five years, she could have been the goddamn VP. Though, that would mean she would need to be associated with the Ravage name, and I knew she was better than that.

Her arm brushes against mine briefly. Taking a step away, I don't let myself register the slightly dejected look on her face.

"Are you going to tell me why tonight was a bad

night?" I ask before she can hurl one of her Parker-isms at me. I know she wants to ask about my family. She always does. I swear my family is like some sort of science experiment to her.

"It's nothing. Just your normal teenage teasing."

I stiffen. "Was someone teasing you?" I ask, my voice lower than before.

Give me names, I want to ask.

"It's not a big deal, Chase."

My first name on her lips startles me. She hardly ever calls me that. Even when she was a wily nine-year-old, she referred to me as Ravage.

I wipe out the sink and she finishes drying the second wineglass. "Tell me."

She shifts uncomfortably. "It's really nothing."

I snatch the towel from her hand and twist it up. "Tell me, or I'll figure it out myself. I have connections."

She crosses her arms. "Why do you care?"

I shrug. "It got under your skin enough to have two drinks. I don't think I've ever seen you drink anything. Ever. Except your disgusting protein smoothies before a run."

She cracks a small smile before sighing heavily. "Okay, fine. But I know once I tell you that you'll get all protective and angry, so you have to promise to stay calm."

Her words cause me to bite the inside of my cheek. "I'm listening," I growl, setting the towel down and turning to face her.

"Well, a couple of the girls from my senior class

were talking about losing their virginity this summer so that they didn't have to go to college a virgin," she starts, her voice wavering a little bit with nervousness.

I don't like the sound of this. "And?"

"And then I realized I'm the only girl I know who is still a virgin."

Fuck.

I'd suspected and selfishly hoped it was the case, but again, I didn't have any claim over her, so it's not like I could ask.

Still, despite the fact that I *shouldn't* go there with Parker, I'm intrigued. The possessive beast I attempt to hide from almost everyone is roaring to claim her.

Double fuck.

I clear my throat. "What's wrong with going to college as a virgin?"

"Everything?" she retorts, her cheeks flaming. "I'm —I'll be the only one."

I narrow my eyes, mulling over her words. It would be so easy to take advantage of this situation, but it's *Parker*. She deserves the whole world. I wish she'd realize that. *Fuck* her friends for making her feel bad about it.

"So what? You think your virginity is something you should give up and discard on a whim?" My voice is harder than I intended it to be.

That stuns her. She pulls her lower lip between her teeth and *fuck me* she looks so goddamn vulnerable right now.

"You asked," she replies, her voice hard. "And I told you. It's a big deal to me."

"You're right. I'm glad you told me, Parker." She's still chewing on her bottom lip. She's not finished, even if she wants me to think she is. "And? What else happened?"

"One of the guys overheard and offered to take it there at the party."

I see red. Bright *fucking* crimson.

She's not mine. None of this matters. And yet...

Reaching up, I loosen the tie around my neck. "Who?"

It's an innocent enough question, but I practically snarl it.

Parker laughs. "Right, like I'd tell you."

My eyes turn cold and flinty as I assess her. Long, light brown hair. It's so fucking shiny it looks like polished brass. Pale skin, pink lips, and big, green eyes. She's small but not petite, and her body is... *fuck,* what I'd give to kiss her. Just once.

Maybe I'd even break my 'no kissing, no intimacy' rule for her.

I'd likely break all of my rules for her, now that I think about it.

And now I find out that someone else had the audacity to try and steal her virginity at a *fucking* house party?

"Fine. Don't tell me. But I'll find out."

She smirks. "Fine."

"So, that's it? You obviously turned his offer down," I growl.

"Of course I did. I'm not—that's not who I am. I want my first time to be with someone I trust.

Someone I care about, and someone who will be gentle."

"That's right," I tell her, pushing off the counter and turning toward the dishwasher, before I get in over my head.

Calm down, Ravage.

"Your first time should be with someone who will revere you," I murmur, popping in some detergent and then pressing start. "Someone who will make your toes curl and your eyes roll so far back in your head that you'll see white." I'm still facing the sink. I can't face her while I say this, but she needs to hear it. "Someone who will make you wonder what the fuck you've been missing out on. Not some guy at a party. Not in some random bedroom in a house you've never been to. Somewhere meaningful—with someone who will treat you like a seven-course meal."

When I turn around, I don't expect the look on Parker's face. It's almost... triumphant?

"I agree," she says, her voice clear and resolute. "Which is why I'm going to ask you to hear me out before you say no."

I narrow my eyes. "Okay..."

She clears her throat and pulls her phone out from the pocket in her dress. I want to laugh, because dress pockets are another Parker-ism I've come to adore. She refuses to wear dresses without them.

I've seen her pull out full-sized books from the depths of her skirts.

"Chase," she starts, pinning me with the same look she gives to anyone she expects will challenge her.

Standing straighter, she gives me a soft smile. "I've been thinking—since the party, that is—"

"Parker," I warn, not liking the sound of this one bit.

"I think you should take my virginity. Tonight."

I squeeze my eyes shut and rub the bridge of my nose. Exhaling slowly, I open my eyes again to Parker's hopeful expression.

"*What?*" I growl, crossing my arms.

I'd love nothing more than to knock her legs apart and wrap them around my waist while I fuck her into this counter, but there are *so* many reasons that can never happen.

Does she realize how *fucking* tempting she is? Always—not just tonight.

I've held Juliet Parker on a pedestal for years.

"Before you freak out, let me read off the list I created in the taxi earlier."

I groan. "Of fucking course you have a list. Leave it to you, Parker, to be the best at selecting the person to take your virginity."

She gives me a wry smile. "You know I have to be the best at everything. Why would this be any different?"

Sighing, I rub my mouth, trying to distract myself from the way every nerve ending seems to be firing off inside of me at once.

I think you should take my virginity. Tonight.

"Go on, then. I wouldn't want your list to go to waste."

She wastes no time—almost like she expected this.

"First, you're my brother's best friend. The stakes are high for you. You'd be gentle and caring because of Jackson. You'd never want to lose him."

I never want to lose you either, Parker.

I watch her as she continues her little list of reasons why I should fuck her. And with every word that leaves her lips, I lose another fraction of my resolve.

"Two, you come from money. Should our tryst end in an unexpected pregnancy, I know you could—and would—provide for me."

Fuck. Me.

I don't know what to say to that. My skin heats at the thought of pumping her full of—

No.

Fuck.

"Third, I trust you, and I like you. I also find you physically attractive," she states, as if she's reading from a textbook. "Fourth, I don't have any other options. I don't want to go to college as a virgin, and you're my only hope."

She lowers her phone, and my eyes roam over her pink cheeks and flushed chest. Her last point sticks in my head, though.

I don't have any other options.

She needs someone to pop her cherry. I'd be checking off one of the things on her list of things to do before college.

Too bad for her, though. She means more to me than that.

My jaw tics. "I assume—since you're always thorough as hell—that you also have a list of reasons why I shouldn't take your virginity."

She gives me a look that screams *of course I do* before glancing down at her list.

"You can't hold any of these against me, Ravage."

I shrug. "I promise you there's nothing on there that I don't already know."

She nods and begins reading. "One... your family." She winces slightly as she looks up at me for a second to gauge my reaction. I keep my expression indifferent. "We all know that the Ravage name doesn't have the best reputation. And while it doesn't matter for the purposes of taking my virginity, it could reduce the chances of a real relationship down the road."

I was wrong.

Her words *hurt*.

Real relationship...

She continues. "Ultimately, the pros outweigh the cons on this point. I only have two weeks before I start my first semester. Like I told you before, you're kind of my only choice."

"What else?"

"Two... we come from different social classes. I had to take your preferences into consideration, and it occurred to me that perhaps you might find me too common for you—"

"Jesus, Parker," I growl, glaring at her as I shake my head. "Seriously?"

She chews on her lower lip as her shoulders sag forward slightly. "I don't know. I've actually never seen you date anyone..." she trails off and her eyes go wide.

"Oh god." Her hand comes up to her mouth. "Are you gay?"

I smirk. "Definitely not gay, Parker," I tell her, my voice gravelly as my eyes wander down her body once. "Keep going."

"Three is sort of similar to two. I realized that your sexual preferences might be entirely different than mine—which are, as you know, nonexistent. I have no idea what I'm doing, and maybe you'd prefer someone more experienced."

I roll my tongue against my cheek as I peer down at the ground, trying not to smile.

Oh, Parker. If only you knew the depraved things I like to do in bed.

I raise my eyes slowly as my own list formulates in my head. So many cons for why I should decline her offer—and one giant pro.

Because I'd probably commit murder in order to be Juliet's first.

To ingrain myself inside of her consciousness—to *be* that person for her.

But I couldn't.

I'm nowhere near worthy of her.

As much as I want to be that person for her, I don't know how. I never learned how to be gentle. I never learned how to love. She wanted to know why I never dated? Because I didn't know *how.* Sure, I could fuck like an animal. I knew how to bed a woman—knew all the ways to make them scream. But love? No *fucking* idea. And Parker deserved to lose her virginity to someone she loved—and someone who could love her back.

That person would never be me.

"Are there any decisions you don't overthink?" I ask her softly.

She scoffs. "Of course not. I have to collect the data and analyze. It's the only way I know how to function."

I chuckle and place my hands in my pockets. My smile falls from my face. I dip my head in concession, though I wish I could tell her that I'd burn the world to get a taste of her.

Still, I'm putting my foot down.

I'm not worthy.

I can't be that person for her.

"Parker, it's not a good idea."

"Really?" Her quiet voice is tinged with hurt as her arms drop to her side. "You're rejecting me?"

Fuck.

"Look, it's not because I don't want to, okay?"

"Well, obviously it is, or you'd be—you would've —" She presses her lips together and closes her eyes. Shaking her head a few times, she opens them. Except where she was happy and chatty earlier, she's now cold and closed off. "You know what? It's fine. Of course you'd reject me. You're entirely out of my league. I'm an idiot, and I never should've—"

"Out of your league?" I ask her incredulously. "Are you serious?"

The fucking irony.

I reach out to touch her arm but she flinches away. "It's fine." Only then do I notice the splotches of red along her collarbone, her neck. The way her chin is dipped down slightly.

Not only did I reject her, but I embarrassed her. I open my mouth to explain, but she pushes off the counter and walks past me. Without thinking, I grab her wrist and tug her back.

"Listen to me," I grit out.

She pulls away. "You don't need to explain. It's complicated—with my brother, and who you are..." she trails off, still acting withdrawn.

"That's not it. Those things don't matter." I look into her eyes, but all I see is hurt. A wounded eighteen-year-old. And my stupid fucking ass was the reason for her pain.

This is why I don't do feelings, or dating, or love.

Because it always blows the fuck up in my face.

"Then what is it?" she challenges.

"It's hard to explain. I'm not sure that I could."

She rolls her eyes, trying to play it off, but I see the hesitation. The way she's angling her body away from me. The way she's fidgeting with the hem of her *too fucking short* dress.

"Forget I ever brought it up, okay?"

When she looks up at me, I swear my heart cracks in half. Her lashes are wet with unshed tears, and her brows are pinched together in anger. Aside from casual joking around, I don't think I've ever seen Parker angry at me.

I need to shut this down before she gets hurt.

She doesn't know it yet, but I know she'll be fine— soon, she'll have her pick of the lot. Men would fall to their knees before her. And though it made me blow a fuse thinking about that, I knew it was true.

"Okay. You should get some sleep," I tell her.

She looks like I slapped her—shocked and angry. Whatever friendship we'd naturally amassed over the years suddenly crackled and exploded around us. Parker was smart—but she was also fucking proud. Which meant she was unlikely to forgive me anytime soon.

Without another word, she glares at me before she walks away. I hear her bedroom door slam loudly. Wincing, I sigh and turn, resting my arms on the counter as I hang my head between my shoulders.

Fucking hell.

Did I make the biggest mistake of my life? What if I'd said yes? What the hell was she expecting me to say?

Sure, Parker. Let me bend you over and fuck you against the kitchen counter...

My cock twitches at the thought—at the mere idea of lifting her dress and exposing the backs of her creamy thighs.

Fuck.

Grumbling, I push myself up and finish cleaning the kitchen. When I'm done, I grab my ring and force myself to leave. I refuse to glance up at Juliet's window as I climb into the driver's seat of my red Maserati MC20 Cielo. In ten minutes—breaking *all* the speed limits—I'm pulling into my parking space. Locking the car, I take the elevator up fourteen stories to the penthouse suite.

I think you should take my virginity. Tonight.

Discarding my wallet and keys by the door, I walk into the bar area of my living room, pouring myself a large glass of scotch. It's something I'd normally savor, but tonight, I need to drown in it. Shooting it back, I pour another.

I don't have any other options. I don't want to go to college as a virgin, and you're my only hope.

By the third half glass of scotch, the telltale signs of numbness descend down my limbs, fogging my mind. Removing my tie, I walk to my bedroom, somehow feeling worse for doing the right thing.

God knows it took every ounce of decency to reject her.

She's going to hate me forever.

We all know that the Ravage name doesn't have the best reputation. And while it doesn't matter for the purposes of taking my virginity, it could reduce the chances of a real relationship down the road.

Maybe it's for the best.

Maybe she *should* hate me.

Because that would mean she stays far away from me. And though it kills me to think about it, I know it will allow her to find someone to love her in every way that I can't.

By the time I've showered and climbed into bed, I'm wholly convinced that Juliet Parker is better off without me in her life.

And I just gave her the push she needed.

CHAPTER ONE
THE SHORTFALL

JULIET

Eight Years Later

"Oh fuck. Yes, Dylan. Right there. I'm *so* close—"

I arch my back underneath my fiancé as he drives into me rhythmically. The bed squeaks with every half-hearted thrust, and my pelvic bone is beginning to ache from the way he jackhammers straight into me. A second later, he goes still—his telltale sign that he's about to come. Closing my eyes and turning my face to the side, I try not to groan with frustration.

Another day, another disappearing orgasm.

Dylan jerks on top of me a few times. He stays completely silent, mouth open, before he pulls out and falls onto the bed next to me.

"Fuck, Jules. That was incredible," he pants.

I withhold a sigh. "Yeah."

"Did you come?"

I never do.

"No, but it's fine."

He turns to face me, running a finger over my bare arm. "Do you want me to get you off?"

I bite my tongue. Why does he always offer to do it himself? We both know he means watching me as I use Wolverine—my handy black vibrator—to bring myself over the edge.

Most of the time, I don't have the energy to finish myself off, and tonight, I just want to go to sleep.

"No, I'm okay."

"You sure? I could try—"

I kiss his shoulder. "I'm sure. I'm tired."

Every time I suggest getting me off *before* inter-course, he loses patience. I've shown him what I like, how to move his fingers, his tongue, his hips... but it's pointless. He gives up after a few minutes. I'm not the kind of girl who can get off instantly. It takes me a long time. Sometimes I wonder if something's wrong with me. I know, logically, that it's normal. I've concluded that I'm one of the unlucky ones who doesn't climax during sex. I get close sometimes, like tonight—if I can touch myself, that is.

But it's never quite enough.

Sitting up, I shuffle to the bathroom in my robe and clean up while he lounges on the bed. Once I'm done, I walk back into my bedroom to find him snoring and asleep where I left him. I grimace as I close the door and walk into the kitchen. *How can one person be so satisfied after sex that they just... pass the fuck out like that?*

I wouldn't know what that's like.

My engagement ring knocks against the edge of the counter as I walk, and I hiss in pain as I glare down at it. The damn ring gets caught on *everything*.

"What's wrong?"

I spin around, only to find my brother lounging on the couch with his laptop. "You know, when I let you keep your key, that wasn't an invitation to waltz into *my* house anytime you wanted."

Jackson smirks as he types. "It's technically my house too."

"How long have you been here?" I ask, crossing my arms.

He cringes. "Long enough to know I'm going to need to gouge my eardrums."

Oh, God.

I grab one of the spare pillows and chuck it at him. "Go home."

He holds his arms out to defend himself and laughs. "I can't. Chase is having one of his parties, and I need the quiet to go over the production plans for next week. Rehearsals start tomorrow."

Clenching my jaw, I lean a hip against the back of the couch. "Yes, well, I don't know what you expected by moving in with *him*. You know you could've stayed here."

Jackson continues typing, wincing slightly. "Jules, as much as I love you, I'd rather not be the third wheel. Chase has plenty of room anyway, and it's closer to work."

I study him as he squints at the screen. Six years

my senior, Jackson Parker is a goddamn breathing, walking bleeding heart. A hopeless romantic, he's the only person I know who enjoys working overtime for tiny, little dictators. As a preschool theater teacher at Saint Helena Academy, Crestwood's only private school, he spends all of his time shaping impressionable minds. Truth be told, the kids are damn lucky to have him. If California had a Best Teacher award, Jackson would win. Ten times over.

With a quick glance at his computer, I can see that he's coordinating next week's theater productions.

"Right. When is the show next week again?" I ask, rubbing my eyes. It's late, and we should both probably be asleep.

Adulting is hard sometimes.

"Friday night. I already got you and Dylan tickets." He looks up from his computer and pushes his glasses up the bridge of his nose. His light brown hair is swept off to the side, and his sharp cheekbones mixed with amber-colored eyes make most adults swoon. "Two Friday nights in a row. Is your nerdy, introverted soul going to be okay?"

I snort. "Fuck off."

"Are you excited for tomorrow?"

I shrug. "It's just an engagement party. You know I hate when the attention is on me."

"Please tell me you're wearing white," he chides, goading me.

He *knows* how I feel about the whole virginal bride thing.

I pretend to gag. "No. My dress is black."

He hollows his cheekbones but doesn't say anything when he goes back to typing. I play with a loose thread on the sleeve of my robe, trying to ignore the hardness in my gut that's still lingering from earlier. I grab my laptop from the coffee table and take a seat on the opposite chair. Out of the corner of my eye, I see Jackson glance over at me.

"Jules, you should go to sleep. You look exhausted."

"Speak for yourself," I tell him, jaw hard. "And I will. I just need to do a bit of work before tomorrow."

When I look back up at him, I see a mirror version of myself. Hardworking, determined, passionate. While he's planning an entire production of *Much Ado About Nothing* for four-year-olds, I'm working on my dissertation which is due in three months. Sometimes I forget how similar we are—how we both go after what we want, like it's the only thing we can see on the horizon. How we learned to be self-sufficient and rely on our self-discipline like it was the only lifeline we had. How we both work hard to be the *best* in order to cover up our shortfalls.

Losing our parents so young meant that we needed to keep moving forward.

Keep our eyes on the prize.

But I'm not entirely sure the prize is what either of us expected.

My research has only gotten more complex over the last few months, and soon I'd need to stop compiling new data in order to collate a submissible piece of work. For any normal person, this was a natural part of the process. But my mind never stopped working, so I knew it was going to be a rough couple of months trying to figure out what I was going to include and what I was going to leave out.

It was like asking a toddler to choose their favorite candy.

Though I'd solidified my research questions and theories, my arguments needed work. I was *already* fretting about them.

It didn't help that I was getting a PhD in Human Sexuality.

Sexuality meant a lot of studies on orgasms and sexual relationships.

The irony was *not* lost on me.

Despite that, though, I didn't have room to complain. Dylan and I had our engagement party tomorrow. He'd be moving in soon, and I'd already had numerous assistant professorship offers from prestigious universities all over the country. In the world of academia, that was practically unheard of. But I'd made a name for myself in the human sexuality field over the years—publishing papers once a year, coauthoring several large studies which were all presented on, and serving as an assistant editor on several renowned academic journals.

Once I finished this fucking dissertation, my real life could begin. I'd been working toward this moment for over eight years, and everything was falling into place.

I was doing *just fine*.

"How was your date last night?" I ask absentmindedly as I format a new reference.

"Ugh. She was fine, but I didn't see a future with her, so I left early." He gives me a *look* and continues. "Before you ask, of course I was honest with her. I'm not an asshole, and I didn't want to waste her time or mine." He chews on his lip for a few minutes. "I'm beginning to think that something is wrong with me."

I glance up at him and take in his pinched, unhappy expression. My heart sinks.

Oh, Jackson.

I carefully weigh my words before speaking. "Was it something she said?"

He shakes his head. "No. There was no chemistry." Sighing heavily, his expression turns drawn. "I think I'm done dating for a while. It's too disheartening."

My lips pull downward. "Whatever you decide to do—even if it's forming a vow of celibacy—just know that I always support you."

His eyes soften as he looks over at me. "I know, Jules."

Half an hour later, I resign myself to my stinging eyeballs and perpetual yawns. Closing my laptop, I stand. "Okay. I give up. I need sleep."

Jackson nods and closes his laptop, too. Stretching, he groans when he looks at the clock. "Fuck. It's already midnight?"

"Tomorrow is going to be rough," I say without thinking.

"Jules..." he trails off, rubbing his face as he looks around, opening and closing his mouth a few times.

"Hmm?"

Giving me a half-clenched smile, he shrugs. "Never mind." He loads his computer and phone into his backpack, pulling the massive bag over his shoulders. "Guess we'll see if Chase's place is still crawling with women."

I wrinkle my nose. "I still don't understand how the two of you are best friends. He's such a manwhore. And don't get me started on the bachelor parties. The whole idea is so trashy."

Jackson sighs as his hand touches the handle of the front door. "I know he's not perfect, Jules. Trust me, he can be a pain in the ass. But he's my best friend."

I wrinkle my nose. "You can stay here tonight if you want," I offer, pointing to his old room.

He shudders. "And risk waking up to a naked Dylan making breakfast in the morning? I think not."

"That was one time."

He holds his free hand up as he opens the door with the other hand. "One time was enough, Jules. Night."

I lock up after he leaves, and then I lean against the door and sigh. I'm tired and I know I should go to bed, but instead I walk to the sink and pull on a pair of pink rubber gloves.

You should be with someone who will treat you like a seven-course meal.

I close my eyes and lean against the counter as the water runs.

The memory slams into me so hard that my throat

tightens. Rubbing my palm over my chest, I take a few deep breaths to dispel the memory. For being the single most humiliating night of my life, that memory sure does replay in my mind more than it should. I reach forward and turn the water off with more force than necessary as the familiar anger floods through me.

I should've known—should've seen the signs. I was a stupid eighteen-year-old. Chase Ravage was twenty-four, already two years into starting his successful company with his brother. An adult, who probably only thought of me as his surrogate little sister. And now? The last eight years had cut him into stone. He's now the fucking president of Ravage Consulting Firm—cold, businesslike, and hardworking. And because of him, I spent the better part of freshman year feeling like my whole world got turned upside down. I thought we were

friends—and sometimes, I wondered if we were more—but it was obviously a schoolgirl crush. He never thought of me *that* way. That night cemented the fact that I never really knew him.

And then he stopped coming over. I'd only seen him a handful of times since that night. Even now, when we happen to cross paths, he acts like he hardly knows me, or cares.

That's the part that hurts the most.

It was a lose-lose for me, and a betrayal. I trusted him enough to be honest, to open up. To go out on a limb and ask him if he would help me. It's not like I didn't notice the way his eyes lingered sometimes. I thought he'd jump at the chance. Instead, he acted like it was *inconceivable.*

The sting of rejection is still *so* potent, all these years later.

Fuck Chase Ravage.

I finish loading the dishwasher and then I scrub the sink out when I'm done.

A small smile plays on my lips when I remember witnessing my parents having a bubble fight as a kid over this very sink. The whole kitchen is wholly outdated, with dark wood cabinetry and avocado green appliances, but I love every square inch of it. I was born in this house, and I planned to die in it, too. Or, at least, I never wanted to sell it.

It was the only thing I had left of them.

I'd have to figure out a way to convince Dylan to stay, because he was adamant about finding a bigger place eventually.

I turn off the lights and climb into bed beside Dylan, who must've woken up at some point and pulled the covers over himself. He's snoring lightly, and I curl my back up against his chest. He unconsciously reaches around to my waist, pulling me close. I let myself relax against him, but the hardness in my gut persists. Dylan pulls me tighter, but I suddenly feel claustrophobic and *stuck.* I take more deep breaths, slowing my pulse and calming my breathing. Still, I toss and turn for hours.

Lots of women don't orgasm during sex.

Lots of people get post-engagement jitters.

Dylan Hall is everything a girl like me could want.

He's a PhD psychology student who wants to specialize in marriage and family counseling. We're currently coauthoring a paper that we've submitted to one of the top psychology academic journals, and I love how our disciplines overlap. He's intelligent, and he's been a great partner in every single way. Ever since we met during junior year of undergrad, he's been nothing but wonderful and supportive. It's rare to meet a guy who can match my intellect.

It's why I said yes to the extravagant ring, and the engagement party. It's why I approached him in our Psych 301 class all those years ago.

I turn over and study my sleeping fiancé, my mind moving a mile a minute as I recall the pros and cons list I made before I agreed to marry him over a month ago. I had it written down somewhere on my desk. I'd found the ring a few days before he proposed on the couch, so of course I made a list.

Pros: he's smart, we both want to work in academia, he's okay living in this house for now, we both want children someday, we have the same religious and political beliefs, he puts the toilet seat down every time, and he's independent.

Cons: he wants to buy a bigger house in five years, he can't make me orgasm, and sometimes I wonder if he's actually in love with me.

Dylan made sense in almost every way. And even in the ways he didn't, they weren't exactly deal breakers for me. Lists and analytics are my thing. The list speaks for itself. Emotions and feelings complicate things. Men and women in arranged marriages were onto something. At the end of the day, it all came down to data—my favorite four-letter word. Who would be the best person for you on paper? *That's* what matters when you're old and gray. The man who can provide for you and become a conversational companion outmatches anyone who can give you momentary fanny flutters.

Because the romance and the lust all go away. You get old. Your kids move out. You have to hope the man you married is going to make a good companion.

Dylan loves me.

And I love him.

We will be fine, because we make sense together.

My eyelids grow heavy a few minutes later, the same visions of my parents in the kitchen floating behind my eyelids. They were *so* happy together, it was almost sickening. You could feel their love. Still could, even now. It'd worked its way through the old house in ways that made me question every rational thought that I had.

They were the opposite of companions.

I still remembered the way my dad looked at my mom. He was the raindrop, and she was the flood. She overtook every single aspect of his life.

But that was rare.

And still, their lives were cut short one night in a car crash, so did it matter in the long run?

I couldn't hinge my future on waiting for my one great love. I'd realized long ago that life owed me nothing. Fate stole my parents when I was sixteen, and I had to claw my way to where I am today by my own two hands. I was smart and scrappy, and I would be happy, dammit.

I love Dylan.

And he loves me.

A minute later, my eyes drift closed as the hardness in my gut settles into a heavy stone.

CHAPTER TWO
THE CASTLE

CHASE

"Chase, come to bed," the brunette whines, rolling over onto her back. "I could go for round three. Or I guess technically it would be round four?"

I turn from my place at the window, watching as her hands come up to her breasts, squeezing them.

"That's not the name you're supposed to call me."

She smirks. "Are we still playing? Sir?"

The fact that she needs to question it, that she'd think I'd go against every term in our contract... my interest in her disappears completely.

"I have an early meeting. Your clothes are on the floor. You can show yourself out." Her mouth drops open in protest, so I saunter over to her with a cold smirk. "Don't misunderstand me. Last night was fun, but you agreed to the terms and signed a contract. I don't fuck the same woman twice."

"But—"

"What part of the terms did you not understand?" I ask, my voice low.

She pouts. "Yes, sir."

I watch her as she climbs out of bed and pulls her dress and underwear on. I'd already given her basic aftercare last night, and she'd fallen asleep, so I let her stay the night. I'm not a total monster, after all. I just didn't have anything more to give. It was all or nothing with me and being with these women meant nothing beyond satisfying a sexual urge. Still, I don't do anything by halves. She expected a Dom, so I would give her a Dom until the second she walked out of my door.

I am happy to play according to the rules of my contract—it's when they decided they wanted *more* that pissed me off.

I had rules.

Rules I didn't intend to break.

She snatches her purse up and looks at me with a stormy expression. "Can I ask why? Why only one night? Didn't you have fun?"

I cast her a quick glance before turning to the window. "I don't have time for romance. If that's what you wanted from me, I'm sorry to disappoint you. My contract is clear," I add, dismissing her.

She leaves in a huff without saying anything.

It was always one night. Not enough for any of them to get attached. And it provided variety. Still, most of the women I fucked didn't understand it. Despite making my intentions very clear via a contract,

NDA, and a rigorous vetting process, they still expected sweet, morning romps and romance outside of the bedroom—two things I never did.

It's a simple agreement, beneficial to both parties: they get a Dom who won't take advantage of them, and I get a sub who will provide a distraction for the night.

And yet, I somehow end up feeling wholly unsatisfied every time.

I run my hand over my face as the sun climbs over the horizon. Despite the tainted memories of growing up here, Downtown Crestwood can be beautiful in the mornings. The coral-colored sunrise reflects off the dark-blue water of the ocean in the distance, and the bright greenery of Hemford Park appears almost neon in the late spring light. It's a charming city, nestled right between Orange County and Los Angeles County. Being the third largest in California, it's a major tourist attraction, especially because of the large, picturesque bay.

And, of course, Ravage Castle—where I grew up.

My great-grandfather, Walter Ravage, started building the estate on five hundred acres of land overlooking Crestwood in 1912 when he was seventeen years old. It was completed in 1914—and then he was drafted into the first world war. By 1917, my great-grandmother had commissioned a massive upgrade, turning it into an actual castle with twin towers, three luxurious guesthouses, and over two hundred and fifty acres of gardens, pools, fountains, and mazes—not including the three thousand acres of forest behind the castle. When my great-grandfather returned from Europe, he'd brought with him an entire Spanish ceiling dating from the 1400s.

"A little history for the modern age," I recall him telling me when I was very young. He was 103 when he died, and I still remember the size of the funeral. It felt like the whole world turned up to see Walter Ravage off.

I grew up in Ravage Castle. My four brothers and I spent most of our childhood getting up to no good—parading around the stone columns, chasing swans and peacocks, tormenting the household staff. But there was also an undercurrent of darkness that surrounded my childhood. My father, Charles Ravage, was a cruel man. Unloving. A workaholic and unethical in every way. He took what my great-grandfather built and nearly drove it into the ground—similar to what his father did. Every generation since Walter was worse, like the grounds of the castle somehow tainted each heir a little bit more.

My brothers and I were still dealing with the aftershocks of our father's decisions, trying to right the wrongs of the three generations before us.

Miles, my older brother, and I had worked tirelessly over the last decade trying to improve our reputation.

Still, the Ravage name was corrupted—probably forever.

And it didn't help that my father had been a recluse for the last twelve years, incriminating him and ensuring the general public distrusted our family.

Most people viewed us as snobs. And as the saying

goes, you'd never find a Ravage holding a knife at the scene of a crime, but their fingerprints would be all over the handle. My father delighted in his power behind the throne, happy for others to do the hard work in order to capitalize on their successes—and their vulnerabilities. He influenced elections, bought major media conglomerates—most of which were sold after his major fuck ups—and treated people like they were less than.

We were all independently wealthy thanks to my great-grandfather and his luxury passenger ship business. None of us needed to work, but Miles and I decided to start Ravage Consulting Firm right out of college. People sometimes declined to work with us thinking we were spoiled heirs. However, we had money and power behind our name, despite our reputation. People knew that, and we did well for ourselves.

I am determined to bring the Ravage name into the goodwill of the general public. I have hope that one day, our name will stand out in a positive way.

Once I hear the front door slam closed, I walk out of my bedroom and pad down the glass stairs to my kitchen. My penthouse is large—two stories, four bedrooms, five bathrooms, and more living rooms than one person should have a need for. But the views of Crestwood are unbeatable. One day, I'd buy a place that felt cozier and less modern.

Jackson is making coffee when I walk into the kitchen. He turns to face me with bloodshot eyes, sporting his normal dark circles and shabby pajamas.

"Dude, you could've warned me. One second I was

grinding my beans, and the next, a woman was storming out looking like she was going to raze your place to the ground."

I grab a mug and scowl. "Sorry. I think she misunderstood the terms and expected a morning romp."

Jax laughs. "Ah, so she's dicknotized."

"What?" I ask incredulously.

"Hypnotized, but dick—"

"Yeah, got that part." I laugh.

He sighs. "Everyone's having sex but me."

"Yeah? Maybe you should remedy that," I joke.

"How was the party last night?" he asks, changing the subject.

"Same as usual." I look over at my best friend, who's looking down at his coffee with a furrowed brow. "One of these nights you should stay. I bet you'd like it."

He wrinkles his nose. "Thanks, but I'll pass. I won't pretend to understand the kind of sexual deviant shit you're into, and I most certainly don't want to find out."

I chuckle. "You'd be surprised."

"You do you. But I don't get it."

I arch one of my brows. "Maybe it's not about *getting* it. Maybe it's about finding the right person to try it with," I offer, watching his face as he considers my words.

Jax straightens and finishes his coffee. "Yeah. Maybe." He looks at the door. "*You* certainly have a type."

"Oh? Please do enlighten me, ye olde wise one," I tease.

He grins. "Small, brunette, feisty..."

"I've fucked all kinds of women, Jax. I don't have a type," I interrupt. Setting my mug down, I walk to the other side of the kitchen and grab a pan. "I'm making an omelet. Want some?"

"Sure."

I crack the eggs into a bowl and add cheese, sliced bell peppers, and mushrooms. Two minutes later, I'm sliding the perfectly cooked breakfast onto our respective plates.

Jax is staring into his second cup of coffee.

"Here." I slide the plate to him. "Eat. You're going to need your energy with those miniature tyrants."

"Fuck me gently with a chainsaw," he grumbles. "I'm so fucking tired. I need caffeine in an IV."

I smirk. "I can have that arranged, you know."

He gives me a withering look. "Fuck off, you rich bastard. I could sleep for twenty more hours. And I have to stay after work to help with the rehearsal for *A Midnight Summer's Dream,* and then Juliet's party..."

Fuck. Is that tonight?

I grip my fork tightly as my jaw clenches. Jackson must see my hesitation, because he sits up straighter and scrunches up his face.

"Hey, I've been meaning to say thanks—"

"Don't worry about it," I tell him quickly, suddenly too nauseous to eat. "It's the least I could do."

"You're a good friend, Chase Ravage. And a good person."

No, I'm not.

I give him a smile that's probably more of a grimace as I take our plates and load the dishwasher. I wish he were right. I wish I could wear my heart on my sleeve, like him.

But my heart is locked away behind barbed wire and chains.

Only one person ever had the key, and she was too good for me. I pushed her away before she could find out.

Because I'd never be worthy of that key.

I'm not a good person, despite Jax's insistence that I am. A small part of me often wonders if I inherited my father's ruthlessness. If our blood was tainted. Corrupted. *Cursed.* My other brothers were the same. Single, and dealing with their own fucked up bullshit, never settling down. We all had our personal... preferences. For me, I liked control.

Order.

Domination.

Honesty.

Raw instinct.

The tabloids certainly think we're all fucked up in the head, so they must be onto something.

"You've always thought too highly of me, Jax."

He leans back and bobs his head. "No, I just see the real you behind the brooding asshole."

"I'm not brooding."

He laughs out loud. "Right." He stands up and stretches. "All right, time to go change the world."

I snort. "You sure do think highly of yourself."

"Teaching is the most important job in the world," he replies, holding a hand over his heart as if I've physically wounded him.

"Whatever. You know the offer to work with me still stands."

"I'd rather choke on my own vomit before working in your corporate hellhole." He gives me a sardonic smile. "But I do promise to be out of your perfectly coiffed hair soon. Thanks for letting me live here for a bit."

"You know you can stay as long as you want. *Mi casa es su casa.*"

Jackson is the only reason I'm a halfway decent person. He latched on to me in ninth grade at Saint Helena and refused to let go, and we'd been best friends ever since.

Jackson rolls his eyes. "Thanks. I'm glad I gave Juliet some space. I definitely don't need to hear my baby sister having sex," he grimaces.

If silver could shatter, the fork in my hand would be dust on the floor right now.

Fuck me gently with a chainsaw.

"Didn't think the dude had it in him," I say carefully. I'm gritting my teeth together so hard that my jaw aches. "Dylan, right?"

I knew his name. I'd done my research years ago. An aspiring psychologist. He was "nice" and respected—my opposite in every way.

Parker deserved "nice."

"Yeah. You met him at the—"

"I remember," I growl.

How the fuck could I possibly forget last Thanksgiving? Giving into Jackson's demands, I'd invited Miles and Liam to the Parker's annual Thanksgiving potluck. We'd all crammed inside that tiny house, and I'd barely spoken a word to Juliet—or her boyfriend at the time.

I hadn't seen her in years.

And I couldn't get enough.

I had to get through dinner, watching as some other man touched her for all the world to see. As some other man *kissed* her. It turned me into something ugly and jealous.

I know I didn't deserve to feel like I had any claim to her, but I did.

I *always* would.

Needless to say, I'd left that dinner early.

I still remember the disappointment written all over Parker's face—the way she tried to persuade me to take some leftovers. The bolt of electricity when her fingers brushed against mine accidentally. The way I wanted her in that moment, and the way I envisioned sweeping everything off the dining room table and having my way with her... the way I *needed* her. And the way her eyes lingered on mine for a *fraction* of a second too long, like she knew...

I couldn't stop thinking about the night she asked me to take her virginity.

And I couldn't help but think I'd made the world's biggest mistake by saying no.

I'd barely made it to my car before I unzipped my pants, threw my head back, and came all over the white leather seats of my newly refurbished vintage Bentley.

With the slightest touch, she'd turned me on.

Enough to make me stroke my cock outside of her house. I shouldn't have been thinking of her that way. Like I always told myself, I didn't deserve her. And in that moment, I felt like a terrible friend to Jackson.

So, *no.*

I wasn't a good person.

And I remembered every single thing about Parker that night—her casual ponytail, and the way the small hairs clung to the back of her neck because of the heatwave, accentuating her long neck. The way her dark-green dress made her eyes look lighter somehow— almost reptilian. The dark red nails, the pink lips that tilted up in the corners, the high, pealing sound of her laugh...

"I hope she enjoys herself tonight. I'm worried about her. She's working herself to death," Jax offers.

I file that information away to dissect later as I glance at the clock. As much as I want to talk about Parker all morning long, I do have a meeting at eight.

"She'll enjoy herself."

I'd made damn sure of it.

He nods. "I hope so. I think we both need to let off some steam."

I pat him on the back. "See you tonight," I tell him, turning around and walking out of the kitchen. "Have a wonderful day with your small despots."

CHAPTER THREE
THE PARTY

JULIET

"Holy fuck," I murmur to Dylan, my eyes wandering over the—are those *swans?* And ice sculptures? Dylan drops my hand as we both take in our lavish surroundings. I suddenly feel thoroughly underdressed in my simple black dress. I knew the party was going to be at the Black Rose—which is one of Crestwood's finest dining establishments—but I had no idea of the extent to which Jackson had gone. As my eyes rove over the waiters walking around in black suits, the seven-tier cake adorned with—you guessed it—black roses, and the crystal champagne flutes in everyone's hand...

That's not taking the personal touches into consideration.

On one table sits a large, framed photo of Dylan and I in Ireland last spring. Black rose petals are scattered over the table, as well as pillar candles of all

heights. Each corner of the restaurant has an extravagant display of dark red dahlias, pink peonies, and
black roses, as well as candles and antique-looking
books. And on every table sits crystal vases bursting
with the same flowers, white pillar candles, and a stack
of antique books. The flickering candles all around add
a touch of magic to the atmosphere.

As Dylan and I fully enter the room, I glance over to
one of the tables to see white napkins monogrammed
with our initials—J&D. Custom-designed menus sit
atop fine, white china plates and more forks than I
thought possible for a meal. The opulence is... unset-
tling. I narrow my eyes at another table, realizing the
favors consist of individual boxes. I walk over and open
a few of them up. They're all filled with chocolates
shaped like Wolverine...

Wait a second.

My eyes dart around when I notice the ice sculptures are also shaped like the beastly man I am
obsessed with. *Did Jackson do all of this?* Hugh Jackman
as Wolverine was the reason for my sexual awakening
as a teenager. I even have a cardboard cutout of him in
my bedroom. My eyes prick with tears as I scan the
faces of the crowd for my thoughtful brother, but I
don't find him. Instead, I'm greeted by a quick nod by
Professor Landon—my old mentor. Shivers run down
my spine when his eyes linger a little bit too long on
my chest.

Creep.

Thank God I don't ever have to interact with him in
person anymore.

"A little over the top for an engagement party," Dylan mutters, looking uncomfortable.

Jackson had offered to pay for everything wedding-related. I had no idea how he was managing it on his measly teaching salary, but I still appreciated it nonetheless. I'd recently hit six figures of student debt, which meant I had *negative* money to my name. That would hopefully change this fall, when I accepted one of the professorships I'd been offered, but until then... this was *beyond* anything I could ever imagine.

"I think it's romantic," I argue, looking around. "He knows me so well. Look at the old books! And the candles! I mean, there's an ice sculpture of Wolverine!"

Dylan's brows pull into an affronted frown before his face softens slightly. "If you like it, that's all that matters."

Giving me a quick peck on the forehead before walking off to talk to someone he knows, I take in more of the surroundings.

The Black Rose is one of the only restaurants in California with three Michelin stars. The menu options alone would set me back half my monthly assistantship stipend. *How the hell did he pull this off?*

I'd only been once before, when I graduated high school.

There are several large, round tables with black tablecloths and modern, wooden chairs. Despite being early May, it's chilly tonight, and the fire is roaring in the grand fireplace. The bar at the center of the restaurant is fully stocked, the counters and shelves gleaming

brightly. I stop walking when I notice a chocolate fountain, pieces of fruit piled higher than my head beside it.

How the hell did...

My thoughts trail off as the crowd quiets. I spin
around just as five people walk into the room.

The last five people I ever expected at my engagement party.

Liam Ravage, the eldest Ravage brother, is wearing
a dark-green dress shirt and dark gray trousers.
Despite being dressed up, he looks like he came from
chopping wood in the forest. His dark brown dress
shoes could double as hiking boots. He's always been
rugged and enigmatic, a closed book. Kind of a recluse.

Next to him is Miles Ravage, the second oldest. As
always, he looks like he stepped out of a boardroom
meeting. As the CEO of Ravage Consulting Firm, he
always looks really fucking rich. Shiny watch, polished
shoes, and a suit that probably cost him thousands.
He's cutthroat and a little bit scary. I don't think I've
ever seen him smile.

To his left is Malakai Ravage. He's in a white dress
shirt with a black collar, black pants, and black
converse. I'm actually not sure what he does—I think
he's a priest or a pastor or something. Jackson
mentioned it at some point growing up, but I can't
remember now. I've always thought he seemed to be
the nicest of the brothers. The most *normal*.

My eyes wander to Orion Ravage—the youngest of
the quintet. Despite their mother leaving Crazy
Charles and remarrying when he was a teenager, he
seems to be the most unhinged of the Ravage brothers.

He's wearing a long, black thermal shirt, sleeves pushed up to his elbows. Dark tattoos snake down his right arm, and his face is full of dark scruff.

And next to him...

I stiffen when my eyes land on Chase, because his blue eyes are already on me.

Is it possible for people to become *more* attractive as they age? Is Chase Ravage selling his soul like Ariel sold her voice to Ursula? Because *fuck,* the way he looks should be illegal.

Which makes our history even more infuriating.

I could've had him, and he rejected me.

I press my teeth together and attempt to take him in without being obvious.

He's wearing a dark-blue, three-piece suit with slim-fit trousers and a notch lapel over a crisp, white shirt. The fit is sharp enough for me to know this suit is expensive, and Chase wears the hell out of it. A slim necktie the same aquamarine color of his eyes, gold cufflinks, and dark brown dress shoes complete the look.

My eyes track up to his face. A prominent chin, angular jaw, and day's worth of scruff surround his full lips. Straight nose, light eyes, and eyebrows that frame everything to make him seem more intense. His hair is a medium brown—currently combed back and parted to the side. His large hands are resting in the pockets of his trousers, and instead of a congratulatory smile or wave, he continues to glare at me.

He looks like he'd rather be anywhere but here.

Clearing my throat, I avert my gaze. Twisting

around, my hand shoots out to swipe a glass of champagne from one of the passing servers. I shoot it back in seconds, plopping the flute down roughly on the bar before I scan the crowd for Jackson.

I find him immediately, chatting up one of the male bartenders. He throws his head back and laughs. Seeing him laugh startles me. I hardly ever see him so carefree. I walk over and his face lights up.

"Jules!"

"Where the *fuck* did you find swans in Crestwood?" I ask, swiping another glass of champagne from the corner of the bar.

He chuckles. "You'd be surprised."

I shoot the second glass back, and my nerves start to feel decidedly calmer.

Much better.

"And the chocolate fountain," I add, wrinkling my nose. "Never mind. I'm not going to ask."

"Just enjoy it. You look beautiful," he interjects, beaming down at me.

"Thanks. You don't look so bad yourself," I tell him, taking in his white dress shirt and khaki pants. Turning to the bartender, I hold a hand out. "I'm Juliet. Jackson's sister."

I swear I see a brief relieved expression pass over the stranger. "I can see the resemblance," he says, looking between us. "I'm Mark."

Looking at Jackson, I nod once. "I'll let you get back to chatting with Mark. I just wanted to say thank you. For all of it. I don't understand how you possibly afforded it, but I won't be gauche and ask. The

Wolverine ice sculptures were a nice touch," I add quickly.

His brows furrow. "Oh, um, sure—"

"This is one of the nicest private parties I've ever worked," Mark says, his brown eyes twinkling as he looks around. "I mean, to book out a Friday night for a private event, the catering alone..." he whistles, rubbing two fingers together. "And I'm getting paid *triple* my normal hourly rate."

I narrow my eyes and glance over at Jackson, who is sipping his drink innocently. Bright red warning lights are flashing through my head. *Triple my normal hourly rate...*

One of the swans squawks nearby, and I jump.

"Oh? That's interesting." I glare at Jackson. "How the hell did you pay for all of this on a preschool teacher salary?" Looking at Mark, I frown. "Did he tell you that he's a preschool teacher?"

Mark laughs. "Yes, he told me. Sounds exhausting. He's a much better person than I ever could be."

When I turn to face Jackson, his cheeks are pink. It could be from the alcohol, or maybe the guilt that is very possibly eating him alive right now for lying to me.

"The swans are from a private collection," Mark adds, incriminating my brother further. "I mean, I didn't realize the Black Rose allowed animals, you know?"

Scheming son of a bitch. He had help. Of course he did. Only one family I know would have a private collection of *fucking* swans.

Anger blooms through me.

"How much did this party cost, Jackson?"

My brother shoots the rest of his drink. "Don't worry about it. Chase loaned me some money."

I'm such an idiot. I should've known—everything about this party screams Ravage money. It's extravagant, and bold, and the fucking *napkins* are monogrammed. The swans. The chocolates. The location. How did I not see it before?

"So, you're paying him back?" I ask hopefully.

"Um, yes?" He squeaks.

My jaw tightens and I let out a long, slow breath through my nose. "He didn't lend you the money, did he?"

"He wanted to help, Jules."

Truth be told, I'm not quite sure why the idea of Chase Ravage paying for my engagement party bothers me so much.

But it does.

It *really* fucking does.

I close my eyes and pinch the bridge of my nose. *Five breaths, four, three, two, one...*

Stay calm, Juliet.

"He offered to pay for the wedding."

I snap. "No. Absolutely not," I hiss, my voice venomous and deadly.

"He's basically family. I don't see what the big deal is," Jackson explains.

I give him a cruel smile as my temper rises to the surface. I know he meant well, but...

Not Chase.

Anyone but him.

"I really appreciate the party, Jax. But right now, I need to calm down before I say something I'll regret."

Turning around, I storm off, grabbing yet another glass of champagne from a passing server.

Now that I know about my secret benefactor, I can scrutinize the party through a different set of eyes.

The food—smoked salmon with caviar canapes, topped with perfect, purple edible flowers. The bottles of Dom Pérignon. Squinting, I look closer at the label. *Vintage.* And the year...

My birth year.

Growling, I pull my phone out and quickly Google the price. My eyes bug out. One bottle is worth hundreds of dollars. And the servers are walking around with an unlimited amount of flutes, refilling glasses, acting as if the dollar signs aren't adding up significantly with each sip.

Dylan was right.

It *is* over the top.

And it's fucking *dripping* with the essence of Chase Ravage.

Wonder and betrayal and hurt all slam through me at once, as do the butterflies that frequented my teenage years whenever he was around.

The room swirls around me—too much alcohol and not enough food.

It's over the top, yes, but... the personal touches. The vintage year. I can't deny how beautiful the whole party is.

But why?

Why would he pay for this, and offer to pay for my wedding? I know he used to help Jax out when I was in college. I figured out my junior year that the Uber account Jackson and I shared was actually Chase's. The mortgage on the house was also paid off my senior year of high school. I remember seeing the statement and assumed our mom and dad had left us the money to do so—now I'm second guessing what I thought I knew about that. And despite the fact that Jackson worked low-wage jobs in college, we always had food on the table, our bills were always paid, and, because he was my guardian after our parents died, Jackson somehow managed to buy me nice birthday and Christmas presents.

My entire life rearranges itself before my eyes.

My lavish prom dress.

My used VW Jetta that he *happened* to find a deal on.

My girl's trip to Ensenada my freshman year of college, that he insisted he pay for, because he wanted us to stay somewhere safe.

His insistence that I not kill myself by working during grad school, instead opting to fund my life. I wasn't irresponsible with my money, but I'd stupidly assumed he could afford it. Or, at the very least, that our parents had left him a small nest egg to take care of me.

It *all* makes sense.

I was only sixteen when they died, so I didn't understand their will when it was presented to me. My mind was still clouded with grief. Money was the last thing on my mind. That week—and the months after—Chase was over nearly everyday.

Helping Jackson.

Picking me up from school, or sending his driver when he or Jackson was unavailable.

Unloading groceries into our refrigerator when Jackson was having one of his bad days.

And the expensive, private tutors...

Everything in my life has been touched by him.

Chase was *there* for us in more ways than I could ever imagine at the time.

And I suppose he still is.

My jaw unclenches a bit as my anger abates slightly. I'm still pissed, but Jackson is also his best friend. They've been inseparable since ninth grade. I've always considered Jackson to be the bleeding heart, but perhaps Chase was a bit of one, too. We *all* knew about the Ravage family growing up. You couldn't grow up in Crestwood, or California for that matter, without knowing about Crazy Charles and the ways he scammed thousands of people out of their money when I was in middle school. He was still around somewhere, a crazy recluse, because of course the justice system rewards the people who can afford the top lawyers and have the money to bail them out of jail. The castle is still owned by the family, too, and I believe Miles Ravage still lives there.

My skin flushes as I grab a nearby canape. I've never had caviar, but as I process the salty, umami taste... *dammit.* Okay, that's not bad. I grab another one before snatching a flute of champagne from a passing server. Might as well indulge, and really squeeze Chase for all he's worth. Once I'm done chewing, I walk around and give everyone a nice smile, trying to hide how tipsy I am.

Tipsy, grateful, confused, angry... an emotionally lethal combination.

My eyes land on Chase, who is talking on the phone in one corner of the party. He's scowling, the frown lines between his eyes deep and making him seem so authoritative.

Why? Why did you do all of this?

After rejecting me—

After making himself scarce—

After *completely* ignoring me at Thanksgiving last year—

And now he has the audacity to pay for this wonderful party?

No.

I'm not his lifelong charity case.

I'm not someone he can pity from afar, paying for my engagement party without me knowing about it.

He offered to pay for the wedding.

A new batch of anger fires through my nerves, making my nostrils flare and my skin burn with fury.

Because maybe it's not the fact that he paid for all of this.

Maybe it's because he so very *clearly* doesn't want me, and never would. If he had any issues with me getting married, surely he would not have gone to such lengths to plan this gorgeous evening. I have no idea what the alternative is, and it's not like I expect him to stop me from getting married and professing his love for me. He doesn't think of me like that.

Or does he?

That little, persistent feeling that has followed me around for over a decade creeps up again. Why else would he do this? Why else would he care so much about his best friend's sister? And if it *was* all for show, how fucking dare he?

He deserves to know that he is really fucking confusing. He should know that he ought to back off from my life if he insists on disappearing from it because it isn't fair to me.

My feet are moving before I can think.

At the movement, Chase looks up from his phone call, and his expression doesn't change as he watches me cross the room of the most beautiful party there ever was, heading straight for him.

And I'm sure I look pissed as hell, too.

Good.

He needs to know that none of this is okay.

He wants out of my life? *Fine.* But he can't pick and choose. It's all or nothing, and quite frankly, if I have to tell him to get lost and to take all of his money with him, I will.

Just as I reach him, I see him end the call. His arm reaches out for mine, and he drags me away, looking angrier than I feel.

Oh, the fucking nerve.

CHAPTER FOUR
THE BET

CHASE

"Don't make a scene, Parker," I growl, and her outraged expression *almost* makes me want to smile. I nod my head as we pass surprised onlookers. I'm sure the last thing she wants is for her guests to wonder why she's so angry at her engagement party, though a small thrill works through me when I think of how it was *me* who worked her up so much. I open the first door that I see —an office—and pull her inside before closing it. Once we're inside, I let go of her arm and take a step back. "Now, are you going to tell me why you look like you're about to go postal on me?"

She scoffs, and being this close to her, I can smell her perfume. *Is it perfume?* It's light and floral, subtly smelling like roses and fresh cut flowers. No, it must be her shampoo.

"I think you already know," she accuses. Her

cheeks are flushed pink, and her breath smells like champagne. *Ah.* Liquid courage, then. This should be fun.

"Why don't you enlighten me?" I ask, keeping my lips straight. If she suspects how amusing this is to me, I might not make it out of this office alive.

"The *swans*," she hisses.

My lips twitch. "You have a problem... with the swans?" I ask lightly.

She makes a half-assed attempt at shoving me back, but I don't budge.

"*Yes, the swans,*" she says cruelly. "And the champagne from my birth year, the caviar, the whole ordeal, really... it's so fucking over the top, Ravage."

Her use of my old nickname sends a thrill through me. I rock back in my heels as I place my hands in the pockets of my pants. "Are you surprised that it's over the top? You know I don't do anything half-assed, Parker."

Especially when it comes to her.

Is that why she's mad?

Because I went too far?

Her eyes narrow. "I don't know," she admits, her voice still huffy and tense. "I don't know anything about you anymore."

I don't know what to say to that, so I go with the next best option: pushing her buttons.

"Okay, then I think we're done here," I goad, taking a step toward the door.

"Oh no," she growls, baring her teeth and pulling me back by the front of my suit jacket. "You're not

going anywhere. Not before I tell you how inappro-
priate this all is."

Damn. She's as feisty as I remember, but my urge
for control wins out. The last thing I want to do is stay
in this office with her. In such close proximity. Not
being able to touch her. Especially because she's
engaged to someone else.

"With all due respect, if you'd like to continue
yelling at me, I think I'll pass. When you're ready to
thank me, you know where to find me."

I step back again, and I realize within half a second
that my response was entirely the wrong thing to say.

"*You,*" she seethes. "You don't get to come into my
life on what's supposed to be one of the happiest
nights of my life. You were supposed to stay in my
past," she adds, her voice softer.

"One of the happiest days of your life?" I ask, my
jaw hardening. "Then tell me, Parker, why you look like
you're going to a fucking funeral?" I let my eyes slowly
peruse her body, and *fuck* if that dress doesn't fit her
like a glove. My eyes bore into hers as I raise my
eyebrows in a silent question. Her mouth opens and
then closes. I close the distance between us. "Or would
you rather elaborate on why it's *supposed* to be one of
the happiest nights of your life? Supposed to be... the
way you worded that tells me everything I need to
know."

Her fists curl at her side.

Okay, maybe I'm provoking her a bit unfairly.
Spurring her into admitting what I want to hear. But I
can't help but wonder why my financial help and my

presence here tonight are making her practically foam at the mouth. As always with her, I am straddling the line between wanting to push her and mold her to my whims until she's saying all of the pretty words, and wanting to ensure she stays far away from me for that very same reason.

"I want to know why," she says simply, looking more resigned now.

I shrug. "I have all this fucking money and nothing to spend it on. It's the least I can do for my best friend's sister."

She rolls her lower lip between her teeth as she looks off to the side. Her hands uncurl and she crosses her arms.

"You didn't need to do all of this," she says tightly. Her brows are pinched when she looks back up at me. "I'll find a way to pay you back. And you are *not* paying for my wedding."

I hold my hands up in silent surrender. "Fine. Whatever you want, Parker."

"Fine," she huffs.

Sighing, I rub my mouth. "He makes you happy?" I ask.

"What?" she asks, suddenly angry again.

"Declan."

"It's *Dylan*," she hisses.

"You didn't answer my question," I tell her sternly.

Her mouth parts and she looks like she doesn't know what to say. "Yeah. He makes me happy."

And I know—*I know*—I shouldn't ask her this question. *Let lying dogs lie, and all of that.* But I have to know. Some small, twisted part of me needs to know.

"Does he treat you like a seven-course meal, Parker?"

She shifts her weight and looks away.

I've spent years studying body language. Due to the nature of my extracurricular activities, I have to ensure that the women I'm with are enjoying themselves. I've taught myself to read every inhale, every muscle jerk, every expression imaginable. When my subs are too into a scene to speak verbally, I can decipher what they're thinking through body language. We use verbal and non-verbal safe words for a reason. It's a useful tool—one that certainly comes in handy in times like these.

And Parker? She's so fucking easy to read.

I school my face into indifference as she sucks in a breath of air.

"Yep. Seven-course meal," she says quickly.

Little liar.

I mindlessly play with my ring as I study her. She's not going to open up to me tonight after hardly speaking to me for eight years. But for some *damn* reason, I want her to admit her farce. And not just because I don't tolerate lying. Juliet is not my submissive. But because I want to be *right*.

About why she pulled me aside tonight.

About why she cares so damn much.

I hate myself for it, but I *want* her to want me.

Though I'm totally and utterly fucked if she does.

"Really?" I ask, studying her face.

She looks down at her shoes. "Yes."

My jaw feathers. "All right, Parker. We can continue this conversation when you choose not to lie," I say quickly, turning around and reaching for the door handle.

"Wait. You're right—I lied before."

My hand stills inches from the brass handle. *She admitted her lie so easily. Would she submit just as easily?* I'm suddenly fighting an internal battle—be the respectful man she thinks I am, or bend her over this desk and show her how badly I want a seven-course meal. One part of me wants to shield her from me, from dirtying the Parker I've known since childhood. But the other part is *so* curious to see how she'd react.

My lips curl briefly before I turn around and glare at her.

"Why did you lie, Parker?"

Her cheeks flush as she digs the toe of her shoe into the wood floor. "Before I tell you, I need you to answer one question."

I widen my stance and cross my arms. "Okay."

"Why are you still trying to take care of me?"

"Parker—"

"I'm not finished," she interrupts, eyes gleaming with rage and... something else. Something vulnerable. Her honesty always astounds me. "I don't need you to save me, Ravage. Not tonight, and not ever. I asked you once to take care of me, and you rejected me."

Fuck.

I know better than to speak until I know she's done. Her eyes go a bit wild before she drops her hands to her side and blows out a long, steadying breath. It's then that I realize she's trying to hold back tears.

"Dylan doesn't—I don't—" she trails off, her voice breaking. She gulps. "I'll have a PhD in Human Sexuality in a couple of months, and I feel like a hypocrite because I have no idea what sexuality actually *means*," she finishes. Her eyes are glassy as I take in her confession. Why is she telling me this? Why is she always so fucking *forthright* with me? Does she have any idea how much I admire her for something I wish I could do as easily as she does?

"Jesus, Parker," I sigh, rubbing my mouth. "I really wish you hadn't told me that."

Her eyes go wide as she sniffs. "It should've been you that night," she says quickly. "I wanted it to be you." Her neck is flushed, and she looks at the ground. She can't look me in the eye for this. *Hmm.* "I've tried to make it work—with Dylan—but he can't—and it's fine, because we're so compatible in every other way," she adds, stumbling slightly. *Fuck, how much has she had to drink?* I want to refute her words, but I know she's had just the right amount of champagne to tell me everything I know I shouldn't want to hear.

I shouldn't want to hear this.

I can't give Juliet what she wants.

And I need to shut this down before it goes any further.

I place my hands on her arms, hoping I can convey how much this hurts me.

"You should get back to your fiancé, Juliet."

Maybe it's the way I used her first name, or the way I'm touching her, but her pupils blow out slightly.

"You didn't answer my question," she counters.

Why are you still trying to take care of me?

I drop my hands from her arms. Under normal circumstances, I'm able to maintain control. Nothing —and I mean *nothing*—can penetrate the hard shell I've created for myself.

Except Parker.

For whatever reason, she's always been exempt from every single rule I've ever implemented for myself. Every time I interact with her, she slowly, *efficiently*, breaks down every wall I've ever erected. It always takes me ages to build them back up, too.

"I wasn't lying when I said I wanted to help my best friend's sister," I growl.

"Bullshit."

She's purposefully provoking me now.

"You think you know me better than I know myself?" I ask, my voice cold.

"Of course not," she retorts. "You made damn sure I wasn't around you enough to know *who* you are, Ravage. But I know you're not telling me everything."

My jaw feathers. "You want to know why?" I ask. The familiar flush of anger rises to the surface of my skin, and everything is *too hot*. "Because I wanted you to have the best engagement party money could buy. Because I want you to be *happy*."

"Why?" she asks softly. "It almost sounds like you have something to gain from it. Need I mention the Wolverine ice sculptures?"

My lips quirk to the side. Of course I know she's obsessed with Hugh Jackman as Wolverine. I know she likes to read. I know she likes black roses because they remind her of her mom, and mood lighting. Everything about this fucking party is *for her*. I was around her everyday for nearly a decade. She thinks she's changed since she was a teenager, but she hasn't. Not really. I can still read her like a fucking book.

I run my hand through my hair. "It doesn't matter, Parker," I tell her, clenching my teeth together to keep from saying more. "You're engaged."

"Admit it, then. You wanted me. The night I wanted you to take my virginity."

Sighing, I look her right in the eyes—the eyes of a woman who is engaged to another man. Who sleeps in another man's bed. Who lets *someone else* touch her. So fuck it. After tonight, it might be another seven months before I see her again. Or longer.

"You caught me. Are you happy now?" I tell her, my voice low and threatening.

She lets out a tiny gasp. "Then why did you say no?"

Fuck. Guess we're doing this now, then.

"Jesus. You're relentless."

She smirks and gives me a cocky, little smile. "Is that why you paid for this party?"

"No. I did that for Jackson."

Now I'm *the liar.*

Her eager, hopeful expression makes me uncomfortable. And not in a bad way. Because something inside of me is singing at the notion of her *wanting* me to want her.

No.

I have to shut this down.

"Listen to me closely," I demand. She snaps to attention, spine straightening, which doesn't help a single fucking thing. *Would you submit to me, Parker?* "You weren't the right fit for me. There are things I like to do..." I trail off, looking away like a coward. *How is it that she can completely undo me like this?* "You couldn't handle it. And you're too good for me."

Her eyes sparkle. *Fuck.* I know that look. When Juliet gets an idea in her head, there's no talking her down from it.

"I *wasn't* the right fit? The way you worded that tells me everything I need to know," she says, throwing my words from earlier back at me.

And *fuck...* her face is full of expectation, like she expects me to do the right thing. But I'm not a good person, so of course I won't.

No.

I have to shut this down.

I push her against the desk, my hands on either side of her hips. She inhales sharply as I press into her.

"You're not the right fit for me, Parker. Present tense. You can't handle me."

Lifting her chin, her light green eyes bore into mine. "Bet."

"Parker," I growl, my eyes fluttering slightly when I get a whiff of her skin.

"What could *possibly* be so bad that you want me to stay away, back then and now?"

"You think you could handle it, huh?" I ask softly.

"Try me," she says, her voice low.

This is the closest we've ever been. My face is inches from her. For good measure, I take my knee and slide it between her thighs. She moans.

God—

Fuck.

"Try me," she repeats.

And then she does something that shatters every resolve I have. Every single fucking wall, brick by brick, that I've put up since I learned to fuck the way I do. She writhes against my thigh. Just once—and she's biting her goddamn lip again as I stumble back.

I'm so hard that my cock is straining against the thick leather of my belt. Shaking my head, I rub the back of my neck.

She is offering everything I've ever wanted on a gilded fucking platter.

"You think you can handle it? *Fine,*" I growl, glaring at her. "It's your fucking funeral, Parker." She crosses her arms. *Fuck it. It's not like she'll actually show up.* "My apartment. Two weeks from today. Nine p.m."

Her eyes go wide, and I want to laugh. She looks unsure. Scared. Apprehensive. Like she regrets challenging me.

Juliet Parker is a good girl. High achieving, smart, prim and proper.

She'll never actually go. But at least it'll get her off my back.

"Is this one of your stupid parties?" she asks, rolling her eyes. "Thanks, but no thanks."

My lips tug up. "My point exactly." I look at the door. "Now, you're going to go back out there to your doting fiancé. You're going to plan the wedding of your dreams. And you're going to live happily fucking ever after, yeah?"

She nods. "Of course."

I take a step back. "And you forgive me for this *over the top* party?"

She shrugs. I can't read her right now, but I think I see respect in her eyes. "Don't think you can buy my forgiveness that easily, Ravage," she teases.

Good. We're back to calling each other by our last names.

I crack a rare smile. "I'll earn it, then."

She nods. "Have fun at your *party*," she says quickly, her cheeks turning red. "And thank you. I think you're right. I've had too much to drink."

Good girl.

"I'm glad you're thinking clearly now. You'd never be caught dead at a party like that in a million years."

She pushes off the desk and walks past me, brushing my shoulder as she goes. "Thank you for the party, Chase. But I won't be taking another cent of your money. Now excuse me as I go back to my *fiancé*."

CHAPTER FIVE
THE RECKONING

JULIET

They say monsters are made, not born...

Chase Ravage was both.

And his words have a way of sinking their claws into the darkest recesses of my mind over the next week.

After our little tête-à-tête, I'd managed to maintain my composure for the rest of the party. Though I didn't see him again, I could feel his eyes on me the rest of the night. The tingling, hair-raising feeling persisted until I left with Dylan—and I made sure to show Ravage just how *happy* I was all night. I'm not sure why, but I felt like I had a point to prove. Maybe seven-course-meal sex was overrated, you know? How long did that sort of thing last in the real world? Kids, jobs, old age... the *connection* was the most important part. Compatibility. Stability. A smiling fiancé who kisses you chastely on the cheek when you cut the seven-layer cake.

And that night, I rode Dylan until he came—and a few minutes later, I came using Wolverine, pushing all thoughts of Chase's thigh out of my mind.

I slept restlessly that night and the next six nights.

Does he treat you like a seven-course meal, Parker?

The question haunted me.

I'd turn to face Dylan, studying his face as though it held the answers. I *loved* him. There was no denying it. We were six years into our relationship. It was normal not to feel that rush, that sense of euphoria when he was close.

Had I ever felt it, though? Even all those years ago?

I can't remember... which makes me think I hadn't.

Still, like I told Chase, it wasn't the most important thing. Just because Chase's close proximity turned my knees to jelly, and caused me to stumble over my words, it meant nothing. Nor did the fact that I had to squeeze my legs together when we were arguing. And his thigh—how he so expertly maneuvered it between my legs, indicating that he knew *exactly* how he affected me... it all meant nothing at the end of the day. And so what if I'd moaned? Sure, it was bold of me to do that, but I wanted to prove a point. He was underestimating me, and it made me angry.

He was and still is the *only* person who can make me feel silly. I am a confident, accomplished woman. I give lectures most weekdays. I completed a full marathon last year. I am well on my way to being a tenured professor in a few years if I do my job well and accept the right job this fall. I have a handsome, caring fiancé. Things are good. No need to rock the boat.

So, on the sixth night of tossing and turning, I throw the covers off me and walk to my dresser. I can't think straight. My mind is swirling with work, Dylan, Chase, the upcoming wedding...

Yesterday evening, during office hours, I'd had the strangest reaction to a compliment one of my students had given me.

"Ms. Parker, you're going to be famous one day."

I sit back and study Cara, my favorite student. "Is that right? And what will I be famous for?"

She begins to pack up. Narrowing her eyes as if it's an obvious answer, she stands up and holds her computer against her chest.

"Your academic work, of course. People will be citing you for hundreds of years."

She meant well.

I'd smiled and waved her out, and then I'd slunk back into my desk chair, feeling uncomfortable, perplexed, and unsatisfied.

My academic work? That's *it?*

Which, in hindsight, is a silly question. I *wanted* to go into academia. Of course it should be a compliment that I would be remembered in that way. My chest starts to tighten, and I stand up, shaking off the impending panic attack. *Inhale, exhale...*

My academic work.

What if I wanted to be remembered for more than that? What if I wanted a fulfilling personal life, too?

After pulling on my running shorts, I throw a

sports bra and t-shirt on before tugging my long hair back into a ponytail.

And then there was Dylan. Even *he* seemed like he was a part of some grand plan. It had all gone so smoothly—a first date, a third date, exclusively dating, moving in together, getting engaged... nary a disagreement or a fight. We always got along splendidly.

I rub my chest and sit down on the floor, massaging the dull ache that's settled just below my throat. With shaking hands, I pull my running shoes on, and then I glance at my watch. Half past four in the morning. *All right, so it's early. Who cares?*

I close my eyes.

Everything feels like it's unraveling. The control I've held on to when it comes to my life is unspooling slowly.

This is the trajectory I worked so hard for.

This life is the one I dreamed about for years.

So then, why do I feel so unsettled?

I've made more lists in the last week than I ever have in my life—scribbling furiously between classes, pulling over on the side of the road, sending myself voice memos. I was trying to crunch data that wasn't there—trying to prove some hypothesis or formula that didn't exist.

Because no matter how many times I wrote and rewrote the *fucking* list, I always came to the same conclusion.

Dylan made complete sense on paper. *My life* made complete sense.

But I could never quite figure out why it always felt like the wrong conclusion.

Dylan stirs in bed.

"Jules? You're going running *now*?" he says, his voice croaky.

I bite my lower lip. "Want to have sex?" I ask.

What the hell is wrong with me?

He shifts. "Yeah, okay." He pulls the covers off him, showing off morning wood. "Come lie down."

You weren't the right fit for me. There are things I like to do... You couldn't handle it.

"Can you just, like, bend me over and fuck me?" I ask, my voice squeaky. God, why is this so awkward?

Dylan snorts. "Right. Because that's respectful."

Pressing my lips together, I let out an angry huff. "Maybe I don't want you to be respectful," I say defiantly.

He sits up. "Jules, come to bed."

I shake my head, digging my heels in. "No. I—we— I want you to *fuck me*, Dylan. Maybe choke me a little bit. God, something," I tell him as I close my eyes.

I hear him get out of bed and walk over to me.

He places his hands on my face. "Jules, what's wrong?"

Does he treat you like a seven-course meal, Parker?

"I don't know," I tell him honestly.

"Do you want to give me a blowjob?" he asks, his lips quirking up.

Now, you're going to go back out there to your doting fiancé. You're going to plan the wedding of your dreams. And you're going to live happily fucking ever after, yeah?

Yeah.

Happily *fucking* ever after.

I drop to my knees, withholding the tears that threaten to spill out of my eyes. A few minutes later, after Dylan comes, I leave the room and run out of the front door as tears stream down my face. Three blocks in, I have to stop. I'm crying too hard and I can barely breathe. Resting my hands on my knees, I take several steadying breaths as I look around the suburban neighborhood. It's dark, but the streetlights provide enough light for me to feel safe. The sky is a navy blue, teetering on sunrise. I place a hand on my throat as I cry, wondering what's wrong with me.

Where did I go wrong?

Why am I not bursting with happiness?

The list makes sense. It *all* makes sense.

I slowly jog back to my house, leaving the front door open as I climb the stairs two at a time. Dylan is walking out of the bathroom when I get to the bedroom.

"Where'd you go, babe? I was just—"

"Are you happy?" I ask, panting.

He shrugs. "Yeah. Why?" He studies my face, taking in the swollen eyes, the tear-stained cheeks. "Fuck, Jules. Is this about the blowjob?"

I huff a laugh. "No, Dylan. I'm trying to figure out if we ever had that electric chemistry everyone always talks about."

Dylan opens and closes his mouth. "I don't think that's real. Is this about your dissertation?" he asks hopefully.

I shake my head.

He takes a step toward me. "I'm guessing by the way you phrased that question, that you never felt that electric chemistry everyone always talks about?" he asks, his voice low.

I cross my arms. "I—don't know."

His brows slant down into a frown. "What are you saying, Jules?"

I throw my hands out. "I don't know. I was supposed to be happy."

"Supposed to be," he says glumly.

"Are you *in love* with me?" I ask him. "The kind of love that makes your heart skip a beat? The kind of love that makes you fall asleep with a smile on your face?"

He scoffs. "You're acting weird. Of course I love you."

"I didn't ask if you loved me. I asked if you were *in* love with me."

"Jules, I don't know why you—"

"*Answer the question,*" I hiss, my heart beating a million miles a minute in my chest.

His face falls, but I know his answer.

Because it's the same as mine.

I let out a quiet sob, covering my mouth with my left hand. Which reminds me—

Reaching down, I pull the engagement ring off. He looks as shocked as I feel.

"Here's your ring back, Dylan." I pry his fingers open and place it into his hand.

"What? Are you breaking up with me?"

Am I? I didn't realize I was, nor that this would

happen today. But the instant he says it, all I can feel is relief.

Relief that I won't be stuck in a marriage where neither party is in love with the other.

"I think so," I say quietly.

He nods once, still looking shell-shocked. But... he's not fighting it. Not denying it. In fact, I think I see a hint of a smile on his face.

"Well, I never expected this," he says slowly, rocking back on his heels. "But I respect your decision."

"You do?"

I don't know what I expected. Him to fight for me, maybe? I'm not sure.

"Yeah," he says quietly. Looking around, he sighs. "I guess I should move out."

I narrow my eyes. This seems almost too easy. But then again, everything about Dylan is too easy. He's *nice*. That's his fatal flaw. I don't want *nice*. I want him to fight for me, to beg me to change my mind. Because that would mean he actually cares.

"I'm—um—going to finish my run," I tell him, sniffing. "I need to clear my head. We can talk when I get back."

He looks over at me, and it strikes me that he doesn't seem sad. "I need some time too, Jules. I'll be packed up by the time you get home."

"Okay," I whisper.

That was... what *was* that? Did we just call off the engagement? Could it possibly have been that easy?

"And Jules," he says, as I turn toward the bedroom door. I spin around to face him. "Maybe you're right."

"About what?" I ask.

"About not being *in love*." He shrugs, and the hardness in my gut—the same one I've been carrying around for weeks—dissipates completely. "I hope we can still be friends. I don't want to lose you."

I nod, thoroughly dumbfounded. "Of course."

I walk down the stairs and swipe at my already-dry cheeks. That was... the easiest breakup ever.

I should feel *something,* right? I should be sad. I should be crying. Instead, all I can feel is relief. I jog out of the front door—the one I threw and left open only a few minutes ago—and jog down the block lighter than I have in months.

———

I should've taken the day off, but I suddenly have the urge to throw myself into my work. Dylan was gone when I got home after a ten mile run. I don't normally run that far, but I wanted to give him time to pack his things—not that he ever had much. He'd arrived with a suitcase when he moved in, as if this house was a temporary stop between the apartment he rented with his friends, and our future house. His other things were in storage.

I'm such an idiot.

All the signs were there. They'd been there for years. I was so convinced my life was perfect from every angle... except the angle that mattered.

And as I shower and get dressed, I feel more level-headed than I have in months. He was never *in* love with me. I was never *in* love with him. Maybe we were once, but I can't remember a time. It was always so easy. Effortless. But I'm now wondering if love is supposed to be like that—or, at least the love that I think I want. Because I can't deny the way Chase made me feel. The way my whole body responded—the way my nerves sang when he was close to me.

I drive to the University, sitting in silence the whole time. Twenty minutes later, I'm walking into my student office. I have office hours again today, so it'll be an easy day of guiding people—mostly undergrads—through their coursework. I open my work computer and debate opening the Google can of worms, deciding to do it anyway. Today's already been a shit show.

"What does the internet have to say about you, Chase Ravage?" I ask.

I've Googled him before, but I've never gone on a deep dive like this. Thousands of articles pop up. I stare at the tabloid headlines.

Ravage Heir Loves to Dominate, Says Secret Source

Chase Ravage, California's Hottest Bachelor, On the Prowl Again

"He Made Me Feel Special, and Then He Kicked Me Out": Is Chase Ravage a Playboy? Or is he Protecting His Heart?

I click on the first one, but it's some garbage about how *someone* claimed she acted as his submissive. Having signed an NDA, no one could confirm or deny her claims.

"It's all conjecture," I say out loud.

Besides, BDSM is everywhere now, thanks to a

certain book. A lot of people are into it. There's no way *that's* his secret. It has to be something different. Something more obscure.

Could This Be the One Sweet Story We Ever Print About the Ravage Brothers? Keep Reading...

I click it quickly. And then my mouth drops open in surprise. Ravage Castle had a menagerie of animals when I was growing up. I remember my parents talking about a panther being on the loose in Crestwood at one point. But when Crazy Charles moved out, all the animals were confiscated. Well, all except a few of them. Rumor is, each brother took an animal for themselves.

I smile. What kind of weird animal does Chase Ravage have at his fancy penthouse?

Pulling my phone, I text my brother the article and ask him if it's true. He responds in seconds.

> *rooster emoji*

> But you did NOT hear that from me. It's on the DL. The damn thing doesn't even crow.

> Huh. Would've pegged him for a cheetah or tarantula kind of guy.

> Like I'd ever move in here with a tarantula. Really, Jules...

I laugh.

> Are you free for lunch? I want to talk to you.

I'm going to have to tell him about Dylan sooner rather than later. Maybe Jax will be delighted to know that he can move back in with me.

> Sure. Can you be here around 12:30?

I oftentimes travel to meet Jackson since he has roughly twenty-five minutes of a break between mitigating play yard fights between his mini lords.

> Yeah, that works. Chipotle?

Again?

> What? I like their rice.

Fine. The usual for me.

And I mean it about the rooster. Don't ever let Chase know that you know. He's oddly protective of it.

> Does it have a name?

I mean, this is Chase we're talking about. He's like the least paternal person I know.

Smiling, I'm about to respond when my first student walks in through the door.

All thoughts of Chase leave my mind for a blissful three hours.

———

"So, he just left?" Jackson asks, taking a gigantic bite of his burrito. I have no idea where he packs it all away, either. I, on the other hand, was not blessed with the same metabolism.

I nod as I eat my burrito bowl as quickly as possible. This is how our lunches go—me rushing across town to spend twenty minutes with the brother I see nearly everyday. We're probably closer than most siblings, and most definitely co-dependent.

"Yup. He was gone by the time I got back."

"And he *actually* woke you up to tell you that he wasn't in love with you?"

Okay, so I might've embellished what happened this morning.

"He said maybe. That he was *maybe* not in love with me. There was no confirming nor denying."

"Fuck that," Jackson mutters. "If I wasn't such a pacifist, I'd go over to his apartment and kick his ass."

"Jax, it was mutual." I look over at him. "And really? You kicking someone's ass? I've seen you move *ants* outside so you don't have to kill them."

He huffs a laugh and a piece of rice flies from his mouth and over his desk. "Just because they're small doesn't mean they're not important." He swallows and looks over at me. "Can I be honest?" he asks.

My mouth is stuffed with charbroiled chicken, so I only nod.

"I never really understood why you guys stayed together."

I stop chewing. "What? Really?" I ask, my mouth

full. I finish chewing quickly. "Why didn't you say something?"

He shrugs. "I don't know. I guess I thought that maybe you'd be ready to admit it in your own time."

I study my brother as he picks at his burrito. The same could be said for him, I suppose.

"Well, it was bound to happen. He could never get me off."

Jackson chokes on his food and sets his burrito down, making a disgusted noise. "Jesus, Jules. There is such a thing as too much information," he adds, grimacing.

I smirk. "It's true."

Scraping the last of the delicious rice from the cardboard bowl, I stand. "You have about thirty seconds before the bell rings," I warn him, looking at the clock. "Thanks for having lunch with me. And for understanding."

"Of course. I'll think about the offer to move back in. I kind of like living at Chase's apartment."

I wrinkle my nose. "Really?"

Jackson laughs. "Yes. But I'll think about it, okay?"

"Okay."

"Don't be late tonight. Show starts at five."

Fuck. I'd completely forgotten. "Yeah, I'll be there."

"I'd gotten Dylan a ticket, but I've since rescinded my offer. Oh, and I invited Chase," he adds casually.

I freeze, but before I can fully take in what he said, the bell rings, indicating the end of Jackson's lunch break.

"Okay. See you tonight. Love you."

I walk out of Saint Helena in a daze. I'd contemplated his invitation for next week, but now, I would be seeing him again tonight, and I wasn't sure how that made me feel. I throw myself into work instead, and it's only when I'm entering the large, ornate auditorium of Saint Helena Academy at four forty-five that my nerves get the best of me.

Breath, Juliet.

I look down at my seat number, walking past rows of chairs until I find my seat. Of course, the seat directly to my right is empty, and I can only guess who will be taking it. I fidget until the show starts, ignoring the way my body slackens with disappointment as the lights dim. It's probably better that he doesn't show up. Sitting next to him in the dark for an hour is asking for trouble, anyway. Plus, I'm sure the very last place he wants to be is here, watching a bunch of elementary-school-aged children butcher the classic Shakespearean play. Just as I lean back and get comfortable, a warm hand brushes my shoulder.

I jump at the contact, looking up to see Chase scowling down at me.

"I believe you're in my seat, Parker."

"Oh—sorry," I tell him, but before I stand, he moves in front of me, placing a hand on my other shoulder as he scoots past my legs and sits down in the seat to my right. I slyly take in the dark gray suit, the gold-flecked tie, and the gold cufflinks as he props his left foot on his right knee, which turns his body toward mine slightly.

I say the first thing I think of as I face forward, skin heated. "You're late."

Out of my peripheral vision, I see him glance at his gold watch. "Am I? I thought it started at five."

Swallowing, I scoot away from him slightly. Just as I open my mouth tell him that it is, in fact, two minutes past five, the music starts. I focus on not breathing too loud, grateful for the high-pitched voices on the stage to drown out the sound of my heart slamming against my chest. I could *smell* him—the smoky scent he always wore, that wasn't perfume but his natural musk. Like a smoker who didn't smoke. Every minute or so, the hair at the back of my neck stands up. I'm grateful for how dark it is here, because my cheeks burn every single time. *Is he looking over at me?*

It doesn't help that Chase's arm is hogging the arm rest, and mine hangs limply at my side, my sweaty palms dampening my jeans. I have to wipe them a few times to dispel the moisture, and at the same time, I take a few calming breaths. When there's a break in the music, I feel—and hear—Chase lean down close to my right ear.

"Nervous, Parker?"

I nearly gasp. "No. Why do you ask?"

My eyes are still on the stage, but I don't hear or register a single thing happening. The only thing I can register is his breath on the side of my neck, and the way his shoulder is practically touching mine. My skin burns at the contact.

"You're fidgeting."

The deep timber of his voice sends an electric shock

through me, straight from my right ear and down between my legs. I shift in my seat slightly, ignoring the pulsating sensation at the seam of my jeans. *God, Juliet.*

Get.

A.

Grip.

"Am I?" I ask innocently.

A few seconds pass where he doesn't answer me, so I tear my eyes from the stage, only to find him watching me. His gaze wanders down my face to where my hands are resting in my lap before snapping his eyes back to mine.

"Maybe you should stop staring," I tell him, emboldened.

Even in the dark, I see how his eyes narrow slightly at my words. "Am I? Turnabout's fair play, Parker."

Something white-hot zips through me at his words. I open my mouth to retort, but another swelling of music overpowers the theater.

I turn back to the stage, hoping beyond hope that he can't see how flushed I am, or how much I'm trying not to pant at his words.

Halfway through a cringe-worthy monologue, one of the older kids says something that makes Chase chuckle.

"*I will live in thy heart, die in thy lap, and be buried in thy eyes.*"

"What's so funny?" I whisper, looking over at him again.

"Am I not allowed to laugh?" he asks.

I open and close my mouth to tell him that I don't understand why he's laughing, but he beats me to it. Leaning close to my right ear again, his breath slides all the way down my body again. My eyes flutter closed briefly, my skin tingling.

"In Elizabethan slang, 'to die' was a euphemism for an orgasm," Chase purrs. His hand comes to the side of his thigh. He's an inch away from my thigh since our seats are so close, and I nearly gasp at the almost-contact because of the way the heat is radiating off him. He must sense my energy though, because the second I swallow, he moves his hand away. "Benedick just told his lover that he will 'die' in her lap."

"Oh," I whisper, feeling feverish.

"It should also be noted that the title of the play—*Much Ado About Nothing*—is a dirty pun. 'Nothing' was an Elizabethan euphemism for a woman's..." he trails off, and when I snap my eyes to his, he's smirking.

Why is it so hot in here?

The play continues in the same fashion—with Chase leaning down to whisper into my ear every few minutes. Things about the play itself, or Shakespeare. Suddenly, the play ends, and I spy a beaming Jackson on stage grinning as Chase waves at him nonchalantly.

I gather my things, intent on exiting the auditorium without my underwear getting any wetter, but Chase has a different idea.

He follows me out of the theater, hand on my lower back like a gentleman as we wait for Jackson. People disperse and walk to their cars, but Chase hangs next to me as I try not to 'fidget.'

"How's work?" he asks, hands in his pockets.

I shrug. "Fine."

He huffs a laugh and looks away. "Just fine? What's the problem? I would've thought Human Sexuality to be of interest to you."

I look up at him as his blue eyes pierce into mine. "It is interesting."

"But..." he murmurs, taking a step closer.

I look around the empty school, realizing that I'm standing in front of Saint Helena Academy alone, with Chase Ravage. The parking lot is cleared out now, and the dusty, orange sky makes his eyes seem gold rather than blue.

Not that I'm noticing his eyes.

"But," I huff, crossing my arms. "One of my students said something to me yesterday that I can't stop thinking about."

He arches a brow and inclines his head, waiting for me to continue. *Why am I telling him about this?*

"She said that one day I'd be famous for my academic work. But I don't want to *only* be remembered by that." I look down at the concrete. "I'm twenty-six, and it's just now occurring to me that I haven't *really* lived at all."

Chase opens his mouth to respond, but as he does, Jackson pushes through the front door of the building, and I get distracted by the way Chase's face crinkles with delight when he pulls away from hugging my brother. I always forget how close they are—how comfortable they are around each other.

I give Jackson a quick hug and we all walk toward

the parking lot together. Jackson gets in his car and drives off, leaving Ravage and I alone with our two cars two spaces away from each other—his a thousand times nicer than my used VW Golf. So much so that I can't decipher what kind of car it is.

I turn to face him, expecting a quick goodbye, but instead, he leans against his car and watches me as I attempt to unlock my door.

"It gets stuck sometimes," I mumble, twisting the key and trying to quell my shaky hands. "Come on, you piece of—"

"Allow me."

I inhale sharply when the front of his body presses against my back. My body shudders once. His hand comes around mine, working the key out slightly, before turning it again.

The doors click open audibly, but Chase doesn't step away. He's directly behind me, and I have to close my eyes to steady my shortened breaths. His hand squeezes mine, and it takes me a second to realize that he's pulling the key out of the lock. Still, he doesn't move, except for a soft swipe of his thumb against the top of my palm.

"Chase—"

He steps away—several steps, actually. When I turn to face him, his expression is slightly bewildered, but then he snaps back to his usual, steely self—like he's closing himself off again.

Clearing his throat, he gestures to his car. "I should go. Goodnight, Parker. Give Duncan my regards," he adds, practically growling the last sentence.

Watching as he drives away, I wait until he's out of sight to gulp in some air. I hadn't realized I was holding my breath. Duncan... did he mean *Dylan?* I suppose he doesn't know about the fact that we broke up. If he had, would he have stayed longer? Suggested dinner? Pressed himself against me harder?

Maybe that was the reason behind his multifaceted expression as he pulled away. He felt it too—but he thinks I'm still engaged to Dylan.

Climbing into my car, I stare at my steering wheel for several minutes.

I should go next week—to Chase's party.

I should go and enjoy myself.

It didn't make sense. It went against everything I ever thought I wanted, or thought I knew. But maybe that was the point.

I'd never done *anything* strictly for myself, and look where it had gotten me?

I quickly make a mental pros and cons list. This one is different from my last hundred or so, because instead of running the data against Dylan, I run it against Chase. Data never hurts, and in this case, it can only help me, right? Data never lets me down.

As I weigh the pros and cons of both choices, the answer clears and the fog lifts.

Pros: Curious about Chase's extracurricular activities, I can snoop around his apartment, I need to meet more people that aren't scholars or grad students, I am newly single, Chase will be there, I *want* to go, I can't keep wasting time in a life that hardly feels like mine anymore

Cons: Nervous, What if it's something weird like scat play? (maybe I'd be into that? Or maybe not?), I've recorded X-Men to watch next Friday with my favorite ice cream, I could get hurt, or I could get murdered.

I'd be an idiot not to see this out. I'm *so* curious. He *touched* me in a way that sent everything into flames—

Maybe I can look at it as research. And also maybe it can be a big *fuck you* to Chase Ravage. This is what he gets for underestimating me. He said I couldn't handle him?

Fucking bet.

CHAPTER SIX
THE LIST

JULIET

Okay, so maybe this was a stupid idea.

I had the taxi drop me off in front of Chase's apartment building ten minutes ago, and I'm pacing back and forth nervously like a pig going to slaughter. I keep going over the pros and cons list. Obviously I have nothing to lose by taking the elevator up to his penthouse. I've been here before—multiple times—so this isn't new territory. And I know for a fact that Jackson isn't here. He's at my house, probably watching *my* recording of X-men and eating *my* ice cream. I wasn't entirely sure if he bought my excuse of attending a last minute work dinner, but he didn't say anything as I raced out the door twenty minutes ago.

I pretend to play on my phone, loitering by the closed front door of the building in downtown Crestwood. Several people have walked inside. They look normal. Nice dresses and suits. A few of them are carrying bags which is interesting. *What's inside? Giant dildos, or something crazier?*

Shaking my head, I pretend to text someone on my phone as a large group of young women giggle their way through the front door. They give their names to the security guard at the front desk. *Fuck.* Is my name going to be on the list? Am I going to be turned away before I'm able to ascertain what the hell kind of kinky shit Chase Ravage is into? I feel like a sleuth as I watch them all sign something on a clipboard. *Interesting.*

Maybe I should've come up with a fake name?

I look down at my outfit of choice. I'm wearing a dark red velvet dress that's about five inches too short. It's cute for a night out, but it's not fancy, and now I feel underdressed. My black-heeled boots also feel ridiculous and way too casual.

Fuck it.

I am the queen of overthinking. If I think about this for any longer, I'm going to back out, and then that $24 cab ride into the city will have been for naught. I run my fingers through my hair and walk toward the front door, pulling it open and walking confidently to the man sitting behind the desk.

"Juliet Parker," I tell the guard. "I'm on the list for the party in the penthouse."

His eyes scan the list and then he shakes his head. "I'm sorry. You're not on the list."

Fuck.

"Chase invited me," I tell him. "Chase Ravage," I

emphasize, my eyes scanning the elevator behind him as if to drive the point home.

"Sorry, miss. If you're not on the list, I'm under strict orders not to let you in."

I sigh and pinch the bridge of my nose. "Okay, can you call Chase—"

"She's with me," A voice says from behind me.

I spin around to find an unfamiliar man standing in a suit. He's a few paces behind me apparently watching this all unfold with bemusement. He's handsome—older, tan complexion, white teeth. Probably in his late thirties. I look at the guard.

"I'm with him," I say excitedly.

The guard looks over my shoulder and gives the man behind me a simpering smile. "Of course, Mr. Hearst." He holds out two forms over the marble stand, and I glance over the standard NDA before signing. The man behind me does the same.

The guard gestures to let us through to the elevators. I nearly skip inside an open one as the man follows me through the double doors.

"Thank you," I tell him as the doors slide shut, and he presses the button labeled, 'P' for penthouse.

"Of course," the man says, coming to my side as we smoothly glide up several stories. "What kind of gentleman would I be if I left a beautiful woman like you outside in the cold?"

I smile even though it's 74° right now. Definitely not *cold*.

Before I can thank him again, he bends down and speaks directly into my ear. "I assume you like to play?"

Chills run down my spine. "Um, play?" I ask, keeping the fake smile plastered on my face as the doors open at just the right moment.

My eyes widen as we walk into the living area. I've been here before to visit Jackson, but only a handful of times. I was always hesitant to run into Chase, so I kept my distance. So while the room we enter into is familiar, I also notice the details that aren't so familiar. Like the black roses on every table, the candles, and the fact that the entire party feels more like a glitzy soiree rather than whatever the hell Chase was hinting at two weeks ago. I expected women in chains, maybe even a fire-breathing lion tamer or something.

You couldn't handle it.

Yeah fucking right. I can handle a fancy party just fine.

My eyes dance over the familiar-yet-unfamiliar room, and the man guides me through the crowd until we're walking onto a large balcony I've never seen before. It's three times the size of my house, the walls are open to the air, and I can see all of downtown Crestwood glittering below. There are high tables and chairs, a full bar, soft music, and a few people dancing in the center of the patio to the music playing softly through invisible speakers.

"Yes. Play. You said you know Chase Ravage, so I can only assume you're one of his subs."

Subs. Right.

"Just an observer tonight," I tell him.

He chuckles, pointing to the bar. "Point taken. Can I at least buy you a drink?"

I shrug. "Sure. Why not?"

He walks away, leaving me to explore by myself. I hold my gold clutch at my side as I walk to the balcony, leaning over slightly to take in the view. It's dark out, but the city is all lit up. From this vantage point, it looks like any other large city, but I know that Crestwood is different. Smaller. Wholesome. A haven of independent shops, cafés, and restaurants. There are only a few high rises, as the rest of the city is made up of old, Victorian houses, brick buildings that somehow weren't damaged during the recent earthquakes, and greenery. It's not perfect, but it's home. I turn around as the man walks over with two cocktails.

"I hope you like vodka martinis," he says suavely, handing me a crystal coupe.

I try to hide my grimace. "Thanks."

"I'm Ben Hearst," he says, holding his hand out.

"Juliet Parker," I tell him, shaking his hand firmly.

If there's one thing I've perfected being a woman in academia, it's a firm handshake.

"So, *Juliet*," he drawls, sipping his martini. "If you're just an observer, why are you here?"

I pretend to sip the vodka. "I was curious," I tell him honestly, leaning against the glass railing.

"About BDSM, or about primal play?"

"Both," I answer without thinking.

What the hell is primal play?

My heart is racing as he smirks and sets his drink down on the steel banister. "Oh, so you're new."

My cheeks flush. "Yup," I say quickly, taking a sip. "Care to enlighten me?"

Ben chuckles again. "I'd love to." He takes another sip of his drink. "Primal play is a type of BDSM that focuses on... natural impulses and urges," he says slowly. "Raw feelings, raw actions. That means something different for everyone." He sips his martini. "Sex with little-to-no restraint."

So that's what Chase is hiding?

My whole body heats at the thought.

"I see," I answer, looking out over the city.

"The more consuming the primal urges are, the more consuming the play will be."

"And what, exactly, does playing entail?"

Ben grins. "I'm very glad you asked, Juliet."

Before he can explain, several servers walk around with trays lined with black, velvet masks. They efficiently offer the tray to people, and I notice that not everyone takes one. I watch as a woman places one over her face. They're bigger than a regular masquerade mask. It almost looks like a cat face—large, almond-shaped eye holes, pointed ears and a catlike nose, ending above the mouth and extending out to the sides of her face. With it on, you can't make out any part of her features other than her chin. When the waiter walks over to us, Ben grabs two masks, handing one to me.

"What are these for?" I ask, my stomach clenching nervously.

He grins. "I'd put it on. Otherwise, you're fair game."

"Fair game?" I ask.

He snaps his on, but I hesitate to put mine on.

What is this? Why are only some people wearing one and not everyone?

"Welcome to the hunt, Juliet. Do you want to be the prey or the predator tonight?"

Just as he says it, the lights dim and turn a reddish color. And then everything descends into chaos as the music gets louder. A few people scream with delight as they start to run, both across the expansive balcony and into the apartment. *No wonder Jackson doesn't want to be here during these parties.* The woman I was watching a second ago chases the man she was talking to, and then Ben's hand wraps around my forearm.

"Put the mask on or leave," Ben urges.

What the...

"That's not..." I trail off, snapping the mask in place over my face.

"The NDA," Ben explains, murmuring into my ear. "You didn't read it, did you?"

My blood turns to ice. And yet...

And yet...

My pulse thrums beneath the surface of my skin with anticipatory excitement.

As a human sexuality student, this fascinates me. The notion of turning into animals like this, chasing, hunting... but rather than devolving evolutionarily, people have *fun* with it. There's no shame associated with it—which is wonderful. Assuming the NDA grants consent, it's actually an amazing concept. These people are higher-ups, upstanding citizens of Crestwood, and they're partaking in something that is the complete opposite of their normal lives. Something that allows them to run on pure instinct and primal urges in a world that's driven by competition, ambition, and logic.

There's *so* much more to a person's sex life than I realized.

I make a mental note to do more research on this for my dissertation—and also perhaps to learn a few things from these people. Maybe everything and everyone doesn't fit into a certain type of box.

"I must've skimmed that part," I tell him honestly. "This is fascinating though."

"Fascinated enough to play with me, Juliet?"

I turn to face him, and he reaches out to run a hand down my arm. Cocking his head, he leers at me from behind the mask. My smile drops from my face.

Fuck.

"Oh, um, actually—"

He tugs me closer. I place my palms against his chest to try and push him away, but he only holds me tighter. He bends down so that his lips are next to my ear.

"Let me teach you."

His tongue barely grazes the edge of my ear when the music stops and he lifts his head in confusion. I look over my shoulder to see a masked man enter the veranda. Several people freeze and stop what they're doing. I push against Ben but he doesn't let me go. He watches the man stalk across the room, coming directly toward us. I can't see his face, but I'd know that hair anywhere. The fluidity in the way he moves.

Chase.

His shoes click loudly against the stone floor. *Too loudly*. Like every step down is made with fury and intention. I can tell his blue eyes are trained directly on me. The hairs on the back of my neck rise. *How is it that I can always feel his gaze on me?*

Chase doesn't pay attention to anyone else as he gets closer. A masked woman reaches out for him, but he ignores her, brushing her off with zero hesitation as he moves through the crowd with brutal efficiency.

I stop breathing.

His black suit is tailored perfectly to his body, like always. Simple black dress shoes. White shirt. Gray tie. Even with the mask, he looks deadly.

When he's close enough, he reaches out and grabs my wrist, tugging me out of Ben's hold. All the air and sound in the area is suddenly sucked away. Deadly silent. No one speaks.

"You shouldn't be here, Parker," he snarls through his mask, releasing my wrist now that I'm away from Ben. As if he can't stand to touch me for a second too long. I open my mouth to respond but he looks over at Ben and speaks before I have a chance. "Get out."

Ben's face blanches. "Excuse me?"

Chase's jaw feathers as he narrows his eyes. "I can assume by the way Ms. Parker was trying to get away from you that you didn't ask for consent, and knowing your history, I'm going to be looking into why you were even allowed inside."

Ben huffs an arrogant laugh. "I'm on the list because your company struck a deal with mine. I'd be careful about your next words."

Through the mask, I can see the way Chase's eyes glitter with anger. "If it wasn't abundantly clear by now, the deal is off. You're a liability. As a dominant, you should know that consent is paramount. You are no longer welcome here, and you are no longer a client of ours."

Ben's face hardens as he looks between us, and then he walks away. A guard escorts him out of the courtyard.

A few people begin to murmur, and Chase flicks his hand as if to tell them to resume their game. Suddenly, the music starts up again.

Just as I twist around to ask Chase what the hell just happened—did he really dissolve an entire business deal over a single, innocuous touch? —he removes his mask and tugs me into his body, looking down at me with utter fury.

"You shouldn't have come," he says, his voice a dark purr.

"And why not?" I ask, my voice resolute. "Why *shouldn't* I be here, Ravage?"

He lets out a low growl. I feel it more than hear it. He takes a step forward and grips my chin between his index finger and thumb. My knees wobble at the sudden contact. His eyes scan mine for a second, and my heart thumps quickly against my ribs. Surely he must be able to feel it—how it's beating erratically by being so close to him.

I pull out of his grasp, angry at his non-answer. Nothing makes sense. *He* doesn't make sense. He can throw away an entire business deal over another man touching me, but he can't admit why he doesn't want me here?

Twisting, I walk away, but before I get far, his hand comes to mine and he tugs me back, twirling me so that I have to place a hand on his chest to stop my body from colliding with his. He looks down at me, and his heart is pounding underneath my hand. With darkened eyes, he looks down at me like he's angry too, but it's more than that.

It looks like he's possessed, and the devil won out.

"Fuck," he whispers, grabbing my mask and pulling it off roughly.

And then he crashes his lips against mine.

I'm too stunned at first to do anything. I hear my mask clatter to the ground at his feet. He smells smoky, like always, and also like something sweet—butterscotch? But then my whole body descends into an inferno, and I moan as goosebumps erupt along my skin. *So soft... his lips are so soft.* He drops his hand and grabs the front of my dress, tugging me into his body as his tongue moves into my mouth. He groans before pulling away quickly.

"You idiot," he growls, his hands cradling my face.

I open my mouth to protest, but he pushes me against the glass railing and kisses me again. The kiss before may have been exploratory, but this kiss is rough and heated.

A claiming.

He doesn't take his time. Instead, he pushes my lips apart with his tongue as he grips my hips. He presses himself against me and I claw at the back of his suit jacket.

"Not in my apartment," he murmurs against my lips.

"What?" I ask, suddenly dizzy and hot.

"He touched you. Not in my *fucking* apartment, Parker."

My stomach drops at his words, and my clit begins to pulse as he watches me with swollen lips and a deranged expression.

My hand comes up to my mouth. I can still feel him kissing me—still feel the hardness of his muscles pressing into me from beneath his suit.

"I want to play," I tell him.

His lips curl as his eyes narrow dangerously. He grabs my arm, dragging me away. "Not tonight."

Anger blooms through me as he pulls me through the balcony until we get to the living room next to the elevator. It's quieter here, the lights are normal colored, and it's not full of running or gyrating people.

I pull out of his grip. "You can't kiss me and then still want to protect me."

He widens his stance and rubs his mouth as he studies me. He still looks pissed off.

"Oh, yes I can. It was a momentary lapse in judgment."

His words sting, and I look away as the events of the last few minutes plow through me.

"Did you come here with him?" Chase snarls.

"Who?"

He sighs and looks away, as if I'm playing games. "Ben Hearst."

I laugh. "Are you serious?" His jaw clicks. *Oh.* He is serious. I try to hide my smile, try to quell the butter-flies dancing around inside of me at the thought of Chase Ravage acting possessive and jealous. "No. He let me in because, despite your invitation two weeks ago, I just so happened to be excluded from your exclu-sive list." I glare at him. "Which is very rude, by the way. It makes you a take-it-backer."

His jaw is still tensed, but it loosens some at my childish retort.

"Of course you weren't on the list, Parker. I didn't think you'd actually show up on my fucking doorstep." He looks away for a second. "Ben Hearst is what we call a fake Dom in this community. Men who seek out submissives, thinking that being a Dom means being domineering and foregoing consent. He took advan-tage of your newness. Trust is a massive part of play-ing. Unfortunately, not everyone understands that." Looking back at me, he still looks pissed off. "You should get home to your fiancé."

I look down at my boots. "We broke up."

When I look up at Chase, he's watching me like the predator that I now know he is. "And *this* is where you decided to sow your wild oats?" he asks.

Shrugging, I wrap my arms around myself. *I wanted to see you.*

"I don't know. I didn't—I had no idea about the... all of this," I say, cheeks flaming.

"The what, Parker?" My eyes snap to his. He's

testing me. "What *is* all of this?" he adds, placing his hands in the pockets of his dress pants. He looks more amused now than irate, which I suppose is a good sign.

"The hunt," I say softly. "I'm intrigued. I want to stay."

"Fuck that," he mutters, reaching for my hand, but I pull out of his grasp. His nostrils flare as he glares at me, but I don't care.

"I showed up tonight because I was curious. And maybe a little desperate. I can't remember the last time I did anything for myself. Dylan and I, we..." I trail off as fresh tears sting my eyes. "I was complacent. And I'm trying to *feel* something again. Anything. I won't let you take that away from me."

His jaw hardens as he considers my words. And then he laughs.

"Sorry, but no. This isn't the place for you to discover yourself. One, it's not safe for you. And two, there are things you need to know before committing to something like this. I'm walking you out of this damn building myself, right now, or I won't hesitate to call security."

CHAPTER SEVEN
THE RULES

CHASE

I've barely contained the pure wrath at the idea of Ben Hearst *touching* Parker. I'm not sure why he was on the list in the first place, and I make a note to check with my security team. It's possible I added him months ago, when we struck our business deal. He's notorious for his red flags. And now Juliet tells me she's no longer engaged? I never expected her to show up, let alone to be interested in all of this. It makes me feel so many things at once. I don't know if I should be proud, furious, protective, or relieved.

I'm erring on the side of protective and furious.

Primal play and BDSM are things she should be taking seriously. She's a good girl. An academic who is smarter than anyone I know. I'm sure she's scrutinizing all of this in that analytical brain of hers, trying to deduce and compute what's happening, and maybe she needs a rebound. That's all. I'm another lab rat to her. She's curious. Too bad I'm not her teacher. This is not something she can research in a day. It's innate; a primal need. The complete opposite of what she's used to. If she really wants to know, she can put that doctorate degree to good use. However, a part of me wonders if she'll ever be able to turn that part of her off completely. If she wants to learn about this, she's going to need to figure out how.

My eyes flick to her lips briefly before the elevator dings, and we walk inside.

That kiss...

Fuck. I'll be thinking of that kiss for the rest of my life, and it's taking every fucking ounce of strength I have not to savor her tongue inside of my mouth again. As the doors slide closed, I think of the little, breathy moans she made against my lips. The way I could feel her heart racing, knowing I affected her like that... knowing it was just a kiss, knowing I could make her scream if I ever got the chance to offer her more.

I'm distracted the entire elevator ride down, and when the doors slide open, I place a hand on her lower back, guiding her to the front door of the building. I nod at the security guard as he scowls at Parker. Walking her over to my driver parked right outside, she twists out of my grasp and looks at me with a pinched expression. My eyes scan the streets of downtown Crestwood briefly before I turn them back to her. It's quiet tonight. No cameras or an audience, which is good. The last thing I need is for people to overhear our conversation.

For her *brother* to find out we were together tonight.

"Why don't you want me here?" she asks. I stop and stare at her. *What the fuck do I say to that? Of course I want her here. But that in and of itself is the issue. I want her here too much.* Luckily for me, she saves me the embarrassment and continues talking. "I don't know how I got to this point in my life." Her voice sounds so small. Crossing her arms, she leans against the black SUV. "Sex is so complicated sometimes." I stiffen. Where the hell is she going with this? "Did you know that Dylan never made me come?"

I blink. "Never?"

"Never," she confirms, looking away. "Not once. And the guy before him? Nope. The guy before him? Not even close. And the—"

"Jesus, Parker," I murmur, shaking my head. "I do not need to hear about all of your sexual escapades." She smirks as she looks up at me and *fuck me.* I don't regret kissing her. But I do regret waiting so long. "Have any of them made you come?" I ask tentatively.

She shakes her head, and my cock instantly hardens.

Not a single one.

I could be the first.

Something dark and possessive rips through me at the thought. Of my head between her shaking legs, feeling her body quiver underneath me, being the first to feel how tight her cunt would grip me...

The only indication I give her is a tight curl of my

fists. Besides, how the hell is that possible? Parker is...
she's fucking stunning.

She's been playing with mere boys. I suck my
cheeks in as I glare down at her. "I gave you one piece
of advice all those years ago, and you didn't even take
it?" I tease.

She grins. *There she is.* I relax instantly as we drop
back into our normal charade.

"I don't think Dylan was ever in love with me," she
adds, biting her lower lip. "To be fair, I don't think I
was in love with him either—"

"Hold on a second," I growl. "He's not sure if he's in
love with you? Parker... the man you choose to spend
the rest of your life with should be shouting his love
from the fucking rooftops." I rub my mouth and sigh.
"Not sure if he loves you... fucking hell. Listen to me," I
tell her, suddenly filled with the desire to *show* her how
it should be—even if I can't be the one to give it to her.
"You deserve someone who will make damn sure you
know that you hold his heart in your hand. Someone
who will love you with every cell in his body. There
should be no question. *Ever.*"

She cocks her head as she assesses me. "Do you
ever take your own advice, Ravage?"

I let out a dark chuckle. "I'm not looking for love,
Parker. I'm looking for a good fuck."

It's true. Even if I wanted to be that man for her,
I'm not capable.

And I certainly don't deserve her.

Her pupils darken at my words. "Is that what all of
this is for you? Just a good fuck?"

"Yes. Usually."

She considers my words as she continues to bite that damn lip. "Why do you still call me Parker?"

Her question comes out of left field, and for the first time in a long time, I'm stunned. I know I should get her inside the car so that Diego can drive her home, but I'm torn between wanting to leave her be, and wanting to see where this goes. I reach a hand out, wanting to touch her face, but then I drop it to my side.

"Because it reminds me of who you are. Because it reminds me that your brother is my best friend. It's a constant reminder of *who* you are to *him*. And I can't lose him, because he's the only person who sees me for who I am, and not for the bloodline I was born into. Calling you Parker keeps me grounded. It keeps me from doing something utterly stupid."

"Like what?" she asks, her voice tight and breathy.

As much as I love to see how I affect her, I can't give in. "There are so many stupid things I want to do to you, Parker," I growl.

Her lips part as she stares up at me. "So do them."

Fuck.

She's going to be the death of me.

"It's time for you to leave," I tell her. My voice is gentle, but stern.

She crosses her arms. "Fine. I'll go. But I have one more question."

I tip my head. "All right."

"Let's say I was here as a regular guest. Can you explain what all of this was?"

I shift my weight. I really didn't want to have this

conversation now, but if she's curious, I can give her enough fuel to go home and do the work herself. A jumpstart, if you will.

"I'm glad you want to know more."

"You are?" she asks, surprised.

I huff a laugh. "You have no idea, Parker." Her cheeks flush, and I continue. "If you were a regular guest, and I wanted to pursue you, I would've bought you a drink. I would've asked—*explicitly*—what your limits were and what your safe word was. I would've gotten enthusiastic consent. Did you see the clock?" I ask, already knowing the answer.

She shakes her head, and I make a *tsk*-ing sound with my tongue.

"It's a countdown."

"For what?"

"The Hunt."

Her cheeks turn a brighter red. "Okay. And that is?"

"People who are masked want to play. Predator and prey. The hunt and the catch. It's not usually a free for all, but if you signed the contract and put on the mask, people might assume you are willing to play. Though most of my acquaintances are fellow Doms or subs who wish to have a little fun at the end of a busy work week. You don't normally play with someone until you trust them. You need consent. Limits. A safe word. Are you understanding why Ben is so dangerous?"

She nods.

"Good. Stay away from people like him."

"What do I need to do?" she asks. "If I wanted to explore it."

My eyes drill into hers. *Calm down, Ravage. She's just curious.*

"A hell of a lot of research. You'd need to know your limits. That means knowing what you like and dislike. Sexually. And you'd need to find someone you trust."

Her eyes glitter as they bore into mine.

I continue, "You need someone you trust, because it will be akin to running from an actual predator. Except you *want* to be caught. There is no greater freedom or trust." I lean forward a couple of inches. Juliet lets out a tiny gasp, and I hold back a smile. *It's so easy to wield my Dominance with her, because she naturally submits to me.* I noticed it at her engagement party, too. "Many people have trouble acting on instinct in bed. There are so many protocols and things that are considered taboo or uncouth. That leads people to overthink. Unable to relax. Unable to enjoy themselves. Unable to come," I purr. She visibly shivers. "With primal play, we act on physical desire and raw emotion. It's messy. Gritty. Rough. Not for the faint of heart. And," I add, placing my hands on her shoulders. "It's not for beginners. It's an intense experience, and there needs to be a foundation of trust before anything else."

Before she can respond, I knock on the window. Diego lowers it, and I take a step back from Parker.

"Please escort Ms. Parker back to her home."

I look at Juliet, and she's watching me with something I can't decipher. "One more question," she says quietly.

I press my lips together. "Make it quick."

"Give me examples of what you'd do. In this kind of scenario. What could I expect?"

The corners of my mouth tilt up into a small smile. "You really want to know?"

She nods enthusiastically. Maybe telling her explicitly what happens during these types of games will steer her away. Because as much as I want to explore this with her, I also know she *really* needs to want it. It's serious, and it can be dangerous. The thought of someone hurting her makes me want to burn the world to ashes. Also, like I told her during her engagement party, I'm not sure she can handle it. Not because she's not brave. But because men like me are simply patient hunters waiting for their prey. Juliet doesn't understand how intense it can be—how my world will fall away, how I act on pure instinct, how I'm not the man she knows, but a beast in disguise.

And with her... I worry about how *much* I want her.

"Consensual forced submission. Consensual non consent. Scratching, biting, hair pulling, spanking, and chasing, which you saw tonight," I add. "Among other things."

She swallows. As she nods, I reach behind her to open the door of the SUV. Her hand comes up to my shoulder, and I flinch away, taking a step back.

"Thank you," she says, giving me a small smile. "For explaining."

I give her a curt nod. "Have a good night, Parker."

I turn around before I can change my mind. Because though it goes against every single moral code I have, I want to drag her back to my party.

I *want* to show her.

But I can't. Because she's Jackson's sister, and she deserves someone who doesn't have the inclinations that I do. Someone without my past, without my cursed history. I've known it my whole life, and tonight was the second time I had to convince her of it.

As the car drives away, my control grows thin. The control I've worked so hard to cultivate. One more feel of her hand against my chest—one more heady glance up into my eyes—and I might snap. *Break.* Bend myself around her, just like I wanted to all those years ago when she came to me that night.

She may think I hurt her all of those years ago. She may even tell herself that I hurt her tonight by refusing her—again.

But I don't think she understands that she has the capacity to *ruin* me.

That maybe she already has.

CHAPTER EIGHT
THE RESEARCH

JULIET

The next two weeks go by at a sluggish pace. I keep myself on an identical routine every day, even going so far as to work over the weekend to keep myself busy. The good news is, I manage to distract myself enough during the days that I hardly think of Chase, or the party, or the things he told me. And despite the one encounter with Professor Landon in the library—and how *sorry* he was to hear that Dylan and I had broken up—the days fly by. I meet up with Dylan to discuss the paper we're coauthoring, and it startles me to see how well we work as peers and friends—and how much we might've been forcing a romantic relationship. And after I get home each night, I grab my favorite ice cream, my computer, and I research.

First, I analyze the *whys* of how a partner could never make me come in bed. It wasn't that they didn't know how. But I realized, after pulling up articles on the topic of orgasming with a partner, it all came down to trust. *Had I never trusted Dylan, or the other couple of guys I'd slept with?* I thought I had at the time, but the deeper I dug, the more I realized that it wasn't intrinsic trust people were referring to, but rather the trust of handing your pleasure to another person. Apparently, it's a skill that not everyone naturally has.

Of course, *that* revelation led me to researching how, exactly, one begins to trust their partner to handle your pleasure. Which then naturally led to Dominance and submission. Or, those were the aspects I'd focused on. From an objective standpoint, it made complete sense. The whole underlying current of BDSM was giving your power to someone else. *Submitting* to them. *Trusting* them to keep you safe as they brought you pleasure. Sometimes, even through pain.

Every single night, I watched YouTube videos from experienced submissives. I took notes. I pulled articles up from my university library. I even went so far as to bookmark certain studies to use in my dissertation. The psychology behind primal play makes sense, too. People strip everything away to appeal to their primal selves. Biologically, we *are* animals, after all. Other mammals reproduced in similar ways, acting on pure instinct. It would make sense that humans, as primates, were aroused by acting like the animals. It's completely natural.

Truthfully, I wasn't expecting to agree with the research I found. At first, the notion that Chase was into BDSM terrified me. Chains, whips, bondage... *was* I into that? I wasn't sure. But the researcher in me didn't want to give up. The *PhD* student wanted to see this through, to analyze all of the data once I had it to make an educated decision.

And I couldn't deny the pull of using only my primal urges. Of trusting my instincts. And *that* led me to the only conclusion I kept coming back to.

It was worth trying.

But only if Chase would be my Dominant.

Which meant, I needed to convince him.

My reasons for this were three-fold, and eerily similar to the list I made asking him to take my virginity.

Pros: I trusted him. He was Jackson's best friend. He would be gentle, caring, and understanding. After learning about the levels of trust needed, I was terrified of choosing the wrong person and having that trust abused. I also found Chase attractive—*obviously*. I'd read that that was very important with primal play. The smells, the taste, the appearance of your play partner all had a huge impact on your ability to listen to your intuition. *And,* though this was on the cons list eight years ago, I now knew he was attracted to me, too. Why else would he have kissed me? And, for the purposes of this experiment, though he did come with family baggage, it didn't bother me.

Cons: Chase might want someone more experienced as a submissive.

All in all, it's a short cons list, which is wonderful. *And* it is something I can fix by pouring myself into research—which is exactly what I do for two days straight, only emerging once I realize I haven't left the house in forty-eight hours.

I text Jackson, glancing at the clock. It's just before six on a Thursday night, so he likely hasn't eaten yet.

> Want a burrito for dinner?

It's like you can read my mind.

I work my lower lip when I realize I'm about to suggest going over to Chase's apartment.

> Ok. I'll be over in 30.

Can you get an extra burrito?

For Chase, presumably.

> Of course.

I take a quick shower and throw on jeans and a hoodie when I'm done. Slipping into some sandals, I head out, priding myself on not dressing up for Chase. I'm almost always in clothes that are comfortable, being an over-committed graduate student, so I don't see any reason to change that aspect of myself. Besides, I'm not even sure he's at the apartment. All the other times I'd gone to *The Penthouse*—as I liked to call it—he hadn't been there. I pick up the three burritos and pull into the fancy garage, parking next to Jackson's car. My eyes glance over the line of shiny cars absentmindedly, wondering if they're all Chase's. *Does one man really own that many cars?*

Frowning, I walk back to security and show my ID. The building is exclusive, as I'd learned the hard way two weeks ago, but Jackson had me placed on the approved visitor's list when he moved in.

Obviously, they use an entirely *different* list for Chase's infamous parties.

Once I'm given the go-ahead, I take the elevator up sixteen stories to *The Penthouse,* trying not to think of the way a certain pair of shoes clicked against the marble floors two weeks ago. The way a certain pair of eyes gleamed with fire when they roved over my lips, my neck...

The doors slide open. I take a calming breath and walk through the marble foyer.

"Jax?" I call out.

There are voices coming from the kitchen, so I steel myself and stand up straighter as I walk toward them, my eyes flicking over the lux furniture, abstract art... and black roses on the bookshelf of the formal sitting room.

I stop, narrowing my eyes. I'd seen them two weeks ago at the party, but I assumed it was a coincidence. Just a way to give the party a moodier vibe. But here they are, again. Fresh, if the perfect, smooth petals are any indication. *Interesting.*

I turn the corner, only to see Jax sitting at the island of the kitchen sipping a beer, and...

"Hey, Juliet."

Miles Ravage gives me a tight wave before continuing to glare down at his phone.

My heart sinks. *Not* that I'd been hoping to see another Ravage brother.

"Hi!" I chirp, setting my purse down. I glance at Jackson. "Extra burrito?" I ask, pointing at Miles.

Jackson nods.

Be cool, I tell myself. *It's better that Chase isn't here.*

"I'm starving," Miles says, grabbing one of the bags and walking over to the couch. "How much do I owe you?" he asks, tossing the burrito between hands as he shuffles away.

"Don't worry about it," I tell him.

Truth be told, I hardly know Chase's other brothers. Jackson knows them from school and from being best friends with Chase, but I'd only ever met Miles a few other times.

"A Ravage always pays his debts," he says. Is he always *so* serious?

Jackson and I follow him to the expansive, U-shaped couch in the casual living area off the kitchen. The rug on the ground is made of fake animal fur, and the TV is massive. The couch is a rich, chestnut leather. Now that I know what I do about Chase, the fur checks out, though I'd never noticed it before. I hadn't been to this part of *The Penthouse* two weeks ago.

"Did you just compare your family to the Lannister's?" I ask Miles.

He unwraps his burrito. "We're basically the same, minus the blonde hair. Everyone hates us."

"Not everyone," Jackson interjects, chewing. "Only some people." I snort as I take a sip of beer. My brother can be so oblivious to social cues. I blame it on working with kids. He's brutally honest—he has to be.

Jackson turns to me. "How was your weekend, Jules?"

I shrug.

I spent it researching shibari and flogging.

Coming to terms with my existential crisis.

Making a million pros and cons lists.

Considering celibacy.

"Fine. Just busy with my dissertation."

He nods as he continues eating.

I love when my academic work can be used as a scapegoat. It's one of the pros of being in academia— no one else really gets it unless they're in academia, and I can get out of—or into—almost anything if I weaponize it in the right way. But of course, I'd never really taken advantage of that, because I enjoyed following the rules.

"How have you been, Miles?" I ask politely.

"Fucking busy," he says, leaning back with his beer. "The company is doing well, though."

I hardly know anything about Ravage Consulting Firm. All I know is that it's located in the fanciest building downtown, and there are signs everywhere with their logo—a simple 'R' with a 3-pronged crown on top. Both Chase and Miles work there as the president and CEO, respectively. As far as I remember, they're an investment firm.

He clears his throat and leans forward. For the first time since I've known him, I notice the edge of a thick, jagged scar running up the left side of his neck, ending just below his jawline. Even now, on a Sunday evening, he's wearing a silvery dress shirt and dark gray slacks. Does the man own any casual clothing?

"You're a doctor, right?" he asks me.

I shake my head. "No. I mean, yes. *Technically.* I'll have a PhD, but I won't be an MD. You wouldn't want me volunteering as a *medical* doctor anytime soon," I add, smiling as I tell him what I've told hundreds of people before him.

"Too bad," he mutters, standing up and finishing his beer.

I let out a surprised laugh. "Why?"

"He's looking for a fake wife," Jackson says through bites.

I raise my brows conspiratorially. "Do tell."

Miles walks back into the kitchen and throws his burrito wrapper away. "There's nothing to tell. Your brother already said too much," he grumbles, glaring at Jax. "Our PR team thinks bringing fresh blood into the Ravage family may help our image. Ergo, a fake wife. But she has to be normal."

I open and close my mouth, looking at Jackson. "Normal?"

"Likeable. Someone to give the Ravage name a new reputation. Potential clients aren't interested because of his last name. He thinks if he can bring a wife to the table, it might help his image," Jackson explains.

I narrow my eyes. "Ah. I see. Sorry I couldn't be of more help?"

Miles washes his hands and shakes his head as he dries them off. "I didn't mean you. No offense." My eyebrows pinch together. "Chase would never let me get within ten feet of you."

The instant he says it, the room goes quiet. Jackson looks over at me with raised brows.

Oh god, are my cheeks bright red? They must be.

Luckily for me, Miles' phone rings and he steps into the other room, his voice emanating importance to the person on the other line.

"Good burritos," I say quickly, hoping my brother will forget what Miles said.

Jackson nods, completely oblivious. "The best." His eyes rove over my face briefly. "You've been distant," he says mid-chew, looking over at me. "Everything okay?"

I nod as I pick at my tortilla. "Just post breakup blues."

He mumbles something unintelligible as he finishes chewing. I take two large swigs of my beer, because I'm not sure I'm brave enough to admit what I've been doing with all of my free time. Jackson and I are close, but Chase's involvement complicates things. So, for now, I decide to stay mum on the subject. I don't need to give him any more fuel than he already has, thanks to Miles.

"How's work?" I ask.

"Fine. Though I did have to clean vomit out of a pair of shoes earlier," he says, smirking.

I wrinkle my nose. "Gross."

He laughs. "I don't mind it. I love my kids this year. I'll be sad to see them move on next month."

I snort. "And I'm sure you'll bake your infamous farewell cake?"

"Of course."

"They're lucky to have you," I tell him, and he gives me a small smile before I decide to pry a bit further. "What did you end up checking out with my library card, by the way?" I ask.

He stills for a second before setting down his burrito. Earlier this week, Jackson had asked to borrow my library card so that he could check out a book that Mark—the bartender from my engagement party—had recommended.

"Oh, just this nonfiction book about teachers in America. It's very enlightening."

I nod once. "That's great. And I'm glad you've made a new friend," I tell him gently, wrapping up my burrito.

"Yeah. I mean, I've only hung out with him a couple of times," he says quickly.

"He's nice. I really liked him when I met him at the party," I add, choosing my words wisely.

Jackson looks over at me. "He has good book recommendations, and good taste in coffee." Leaning back, he stares down at his bottle. I continue eating and watching him from the corner of my eye. Good books and good coffee are the way to my brother's heart. Jackson's jaw tics as he peels the label—one of his nervous habits.

"It was nice of him to recommend a book to you about your job," I add, treading carefully. "He must know how much it means to you."

Jackson turns to look at me. "Yeah, he's observant."

I slowly set my beer down on the black stone coffee

table. Just as I open my mouth to reply, Miles walks back into the kitchen.

"Sorry, it was Chase."

Don't ask, Juliet. Don't ask—

"Where is Chase, anyway?" The words slip out of my mouth before I can balk in horror at my obviousness.

Miles' eyes narrow as he studies me. "He's away for the long weekend."

I nod as I look down at my old jeans, picking at one of the holes. "A business trip?"

Oh my god, Juliet. Shut. Up.

Miles chuckles, and I snap my head up. It may be the first time I've ever seen him smile. His eyes flick over to my brother briefly before they turn back to me.

"No. Not business. He's hunting at the castle."

Shivers run down my spine at his words, because I *know* he's not talking about the kind of hunt a normal person would think of. My research this week has been extensive, and I'm now pretty well-versed with the predator/prey games people play in the primal community.

I know I should keep my mouth closed, but after two full weeks of neck-breaking research, I am *so* curious—and possibly turned on—at the notion of Chase *hunting.*

Those blue eyes, pinning me to the spot...

Those large hands, running over my naked body...

Those taut muscles, pushing me into the ground...

I shake my head to clear my thoughts.

"The Castle?"

Miles nods once. "The woods behind the castle." His serious expression falters for a second, and then he's turning away.

"I can't for the life of me picture Chase *hunting*," Jackson says, scoffing. "But he goes every few months, so I suppose anything is possible."

Yes, it is.

I look at Miles, and he's watching me with interest. Something tells me that Miles knows about my history with his brother. And if he doesn't, he seems like the observant type.

"I have to get back to the office for a bit," he says quickly, pulling his wallet out and dropping money on top of my purse. "Thanks for dinner, Juliet. Lovely to see you. See you later, Jackson."

He turns and walks to the elevator.

My head is spinning as I wrap the rest of my burrito up. Suddenly, I'm no longer hungry.

"I recorded *X-men: The Last Stand* if you want to watch it with me?" Jackson asks, sighing as he leans back.

"Sure. Just going to use the restroom. Where is it, again?"

"Down the hallway," Jackson tells me, texting on his phone. "I'll be here."

I scurry down the hallway, studying the art and the design aesthetic of the house through fresh eyes. Chase certainly has a very... masculine... style. Lots of earth tones, blacks, silver...

I close the bathroom door and lock it behind me.

Pulling my phone out of my back pocket, I Google

Hunting + primal play + Ravage Castle and pray something comes up.

"Aha!" I say gleefully, staring at the top search result, which is an Instagram story shared earlier today by a profile with the name The Domme Group. Clicking on it, my heart races as I watch it, realizing it's an exclusive invitation unboxing. A sleek black envelope —stamped with gold wax—is opened, and then the profile is pulling out an invite in gold ink on fancy parchment. I pause the video to read the text.

*Welcome to The Hunt: three days of connecting with our primal selves. If biting, scratching, and howling is your thing, join us for a night or for the whole weekend. Safely learn to focus solely on language via movement, sound, touch—and **play**. Primal games expected.*

Where: Ravage Castle

Hosted by the Domme Group.

*This event is 18+. **Invitation only.***

We play by RACK (risk aware consensual kink), safe words <u>will</u> be utilized, and intake forms are required.

My heart thumps against my ribs as I watch the video four more times. I click over to the profile and read their bio. *The Domme Group is a collective of fierce femme-identifying Dommes headquartered in Southern California who are dedicated to the BDSM lifestyle and community.*

There's nothing else about The Hunt on their profile, but before I can think, I shoot off a message about obtaining a ticket as a single submissive.

What the hell am I doing?!

After using the restroom, I walk back into the living

room, sitting down next to Jackson as we watch the movie, and I scroll through my phone. An hour later, I received a response.

Apologies, but we actually don't manage the invitations, and the event is invite only, unfortunately.

I chew on my lower lip as I think.

About Chase. About The Hunt. About how I can obtain an invite at the last minute.

It starts tomorrow, so if I'm going to do this, I'll need to figure it out.

When the movie ends, it's like coming out of a daze. Jackson is asleep, so I pull a blanket over him and lower the lights before leaving.

My heart is racing as I exit the front of the building, heading into downtown Crestwood and walking toward Ravage Consulting Firm. *Will Miles still be there?* At this point, he's my only hope. I'm risking a lot by showing up—possibly outing his own brother. Does he know about Chase and what he does in his free time?

I hesitate in front of the glossy door, glancing inside of the building to see a security guard at the front desk. I curl and uncurl my fists. If I'm going to do this—if I'm going to explore my submissive side—it's going to have to be with Chase. He told me to educate myself. To do my research. To know my limits. He thinks I'm not serious. But what better way to show him I'm serious than showing up at this event?

Many people have trouble acting on instinct in bed. There are so many protocols and things that are considered taboo or uncouth. That leads people to overthink. Unable to relax. Unable to enjoy themselves. Unable to come...

My thighs squeeze together as my skin tingles.

I want this. And maybe I *need* this.

I march forward to the desk, quickly smiling at the security guard, who looks entirely disinterested in my presence.

"Here to see Mr. Ravage," I mumble. "He—uh—is expecting me."

The guard gives me a glum smile and waves me toward the elevator. "Go on up."

Hmm.

I thank him and press the button for 'RCF,' taking the elevator up five stories. When the doors open, I march straight through the office, though I've never been inside. Quickly taking in the modernity and warmth, my eyes adjust and a minute later, I find Miles inside one of the large offices, his feet propped up on his desk as he types on his computer.

"Ms. Parker," he drawls, giving me a stern look. "To what do I owe the pleasure, for the second time tonight?"

You can do this, Juliet. Just ask.

I clear my throat. "Right. I, um, was wondering if you—if the hunting was—" I stumble over my words and take a deep breath. "If I were to be interested in hunting at Ravage Castle this weekend, how would I go about getting a license?"

There. It's innocuous enough that I can play it off if he doesn't know anything about it.

Miles' eyes twinkle as he removes his feet, leans forward, and reaches into a drawer in his desk. He slides a black envelope toward me, and when I gape up at him, he shrugs, arching a single brow.

"You didn't get this from me. Got it?"

I nod quickly and grab the invitation before twisting around and walking out of his office.

By the time I get back to my car, I've already run through the list of pros and cons five times, and I'm mentally preparing myself for a long weekend at Ravage Castle.

CHAPTER NINE

THE CONTRACT

JULIET

For the second time this month, I'm wondering what in the ever-living-fuck I've gotten myself into. Only this time, I'm standing in front of the infamous Ravage Castle after having been dropped off by a taxi. The opulent manor is larger than I remember as a child—not that I'd ever been inside. Since it was considered a private residence, no one was ever allowed inside, but anyone who grew up in Crestwood or the surrounding area was well aware of the looming estate. I knew the general history—we'd done a module on it in school. Built around the first world war, it had passed down from generation to generation, with the current occupant being Miles Ravage.

I gawk up at the ornate monstrosity of a building, visible through the gate. It's *gorgeous.* Stone frescos, similar to gothic, European buildings, two towers, built on a hill looking directly over Crestwood... I think I remembered learning that there were over forty bedrooms and hundreds of acres surrounding the building—including the mountains and forest behind the castle.

It feels so out of place in Southern California. Then again, I suspect that's the point.

I walk up to the small security stand. "Hello," I say, my voice overly friendly as I show the elderly guard the invitation. "I'm here for the long weekend."

I glance down at the black envelope in my hand. There were a few additional notes on the back, including the dress code (which is flexible) and conduct policy. It's all pretty straightforward. Rooms are gratis and available for the long weekend upon check-in for each participant. The limit is ten couples. An *intimate* experience. Single submissives are also allowed, but the limit is three.

I have to quell my racing heart when I think about where that puts me, and if Chase will already have a submissive picked out for the weekend.

It also makes me wonder if he only allows three so that he can have a different girl each night. But I can't think about that right now, or I'll never find the courage to walk through this gate.

"Just yourself?" he asks, cross-checking with a list he has before him.

"Yes," I answer nervously.

Please, please, please—

"Name?"

I swallow. "Juliet Parker." For a second, I wonder if I should've used a pseudonym—

"Right." He hands me a gold skeleton key. "This will grant you access to most of the castle for the weekend. The key is programmed electronically, so all you need to do is swipe it over any of the door handles. The east wing is off limits, but all other areas are open to guests for the weekend. Luna, our guest relations specialist, will greet you once inside." He smiles as I take the key from him. "Have a great weekend, Ms. Parker."

I nod as the iron gate begins to creak open, I debate turning around and going home. Forgetting I was ever here. Wasting away in orgasm-less existence. What am I doing here, anyway? Two weeks of research is nothing. Chase doesn't know I'm here, and I have no idea what I'll do if he says no. If he turns me down—*again.* I'm too curious to go home, yet everything hinges on him *not* turning me down. That image keeps replaying in my mind—of Chase pinning me down with his strong hands. Of giving into my needs. Of letting him do whatever he wanted to me.

I want that.

I want *him.*

I'd been attracted to him my entire adult life, and while I don't know him as well as I used to, he's my brother's best friend.

He's not some stranger. He's *Chase.*

And that kiss two weeks ago... the way he described what would happen if I *played*...

Suddenly, my lust-addled brain is convincing me to

pull my heavy suitcase behind me to the front door of Ravage Castle. I'd packed way too many clothes for three days, but I had no idea what to expect. The invitation was vague, and I wasn't sure what, exactly, I'd be expected to wear. *If* I was allowed to stay.

I'd canceled my office hours on Monday and told Jackson that I had a sexuality convention to attend this weekend—which, *technically*, was not a lie. Taking a deep breath, I swipe the gold key in front of the handle on the large, arched front door. It clicks open, and I step inside.

I am suddenly intimidated. I am inside of Chase's childhood home. I know Jackson had been here a few times, but Chase was over at our house ninety-nine percent of the time. He always cited preferring our house to his, which... I am now wondering why, because it might be the most beautiful foyer I've ever seen, made up of a tall, arched ceiling with mosaic tiling. The floor is pure, white marble. My eyes adjust to the glittering wealth as I walk further inside—a theater, several living areas, a study, a library... I'll have to sneak off and explore it later. I bet the Ravage family has first editions of my favorite books.

"You must be Juliet?" I swing around to face a woman in a pencil skirt, blouse, and heels.

She's small with long black hair. Her uptilted brown eyes are studying me apprehensively. "I'm Luna, the guest relations specialist," she says warmly. "Would you please follow me into the Blanca study? We can get your room sorted now if you'd like."

"Sure. Thank you," I tell her. "I'm here by myself," I blurt, unsure if she actually needs that information.

She smirks, her red lips quirking up. "Not for long. I'm sure someone will eat you right up. Figuratively and literally."

I swallow. "How does that—I'm unsure of the protocol," I admit, hoping I'm not being too obvious.

She lets out a light, lilting laugh as we walk toward a room toward the back of the castle. I guess a palace of this size would need two studies.

"Right. Pardon me, where are my manners? Since you're here as a single submissive, we can look over your intake and limits form, securing a dominant match for the weekend."

Nervous butterflies dance around in my stomach, and my palms are sweating so much that I'm afraid I'll drop my purse.

"Sure, that all sounds good."

Just as we arrive at an unmarked door, Luna turns to face me. "I promise that you're safe here. We're compliant with RACK—" Her eyes widen as they look at something over my shoulder. I turn and follow her wide eyes gaze to the other end of the ground floor.

Chase storming toward us.

And this time, he doesn't look pissed. He looks downright *wrathful.*

My pulse speeds up as he gets closer. He's wearing a white button-down shirt and navy slacks. I wish I'd thought to wear something other than my old leggings and gray crew neck sweatshirt. I look down at the floor instinctively, and then he's right in front of me, breathing heavily.

"Hi," I say quietly.

His light-blue eyes are a dark, stormy navy now—and he glances at Luna briefly, nostrils flaring.

"Oh. Do you know Mr. Ravage?" Luna asks, though I hardly hear her. My heartbeat is whooshing in my ears.

"Yes. He's my brother's best friend," I explain.

"Lovely," she chirps. "Explains the invite, then." Winking at me, she glances up at Chase. "I was about to get Ms. Parker settled."

Chase's jaw twitches and his tempestuous eyes don't leave mine as he speaks to Luna. "Excuse us for a minute, please, Luna."

She nods once and walks away, her heels clicking against the marble.

I turn back to a fuming Chase. "I'm about to check in—"

"Like fuck you are," he growls.

I sigh. "Look, I know you're trying to protect me. But your party opened up a whole new world to me. I've spent the last two weeks researching and educating myself." I look into his eyes. "I want this, Chase."

Just as he opens his mouth, a group of people walk into the lobby. My eyes rove over to the people behind him briefly. They're all dressed nicely, and I see Luna usher them in the opposite direction of Chase and me. Two men, two women—and one of the men reaching into his pocket as his phone blares—a loud crowing sound. It takes me a second to realize this stranger's ringtone is a crowing rooster. I cover my mouth as I burst out laughing.

"Would you care to enlighten me as to what's so funny about this situation?" Chase chastises, glowering down at me.

"Oh my god," I say between gulps of air. "He has— a rooster ringtone."

Chase slowly looks behind him as the man's phone rings again, the noise resounding through the entire castle. Turning back to me, his eyes are glittering with rage.

"I don't understand."

I compose myself and stand up straighter. "A rooster."

"What?" he grits out.

"A *rooster.*"

He shoots me a venomous look as his tongue rolls along the inside of his cheek. For a second, I think he's going to berate me, but then the darkness in his eyes dissipates. Placing his hands on his hips, he lets out a quiet, genuine laugh as he rubs his mouth.

"Of course Jackson told you."

Thank god for Mr. Rooster, the real MVP. Unknowingly, he totally broke the tension, because Chase's eyes go from dangerous to mirthful in a matter of seconds. The lines around his eyes soften, and he sighs heavily.

"Do you really want to do this, Parker?"

I cross my arms and look into his eyes. "Yes. Look, if you don't want to be my Dom, that's fine. But can you at least help me choose someone safe? Everything you said about Ben sort of freaked me out. But I want to do this. I'm committed now, and I'm not leaving. I won't force you to do this with *me*, obviously. Consent and everything. Luna said she could set me up with another Dominant, so I can always find someone else." He huffs a laugh and looks away. Anger blooms through me. I put myself out there like that and he's *laughing?* "What?" I exclaim, irked by his mocking response.

"Yeah, that's not happening."

"Why—"

"*Find* someone else? You really think I'd let you go find another Dom who isn't me?" His words cause my skin to pebble, and his narrowed cerulean eyes pierce into mine as he takes a step forward. His gives me a dark, layered look—and there's a distinct hardening of his expression. His nostrils flare as he brings his face within an inch from mine. His eyes dip to my lips briefly. "There was never a question of if I *wanted* to be your Dom, Parker, but rather if you could *handle* it."

I swallow as my whole body heats at his words. "So, you'll do it?"

His nostrils flare. "Yes. Since you asked so nicely," he murmurs.

"Are you sure? I don't mind finding someone else—"

"You're *mine*," he growls.

I snap my mouth shut. The synapses in my brain are firing off in different directions.

You're mine.

"If we do this, we're going to do it the right way," he adds, taking another step closer. The front of his dress shirt brushes the front of my sweatshirt. "First things first, you'll be in my room for the duration of the hunt." I keep my mouth closed, nodding once as excitement builds inside of me. *Don't talk back.* "You'll sign my standard contract, and you'll disclose your limits. Oh, and you'll need to choose a safe word." He looks at me with narrowed eyes. "Since you're new, I would suggest we abide by the traffic light system. Red means stop, yellow means slow down, green means keep going," he purrs.

"Okay," I reply. My mind is spinning, but I can't ignore the thrill building inside of me. Placing a hand on my lower back, he takes my suitcase and leads us away from the lobby. "Don't I need to check in with Luna?" I ask as we walk toward a pair of shiny gold elevators.

"I will let Luna know of our predicament," he growls.

Predicament. I get the feeling I am going to be an unintentional thorn in his side.

My eyes take in the rest of the first floor. It's cozy yet glamorous. Brown leathers, natural colors, lots of gold and crystal, and luxuriance.

"Who runs The Hunt?" I ask.

"I do," he says, pressing the button to go up.

"And who are The Domme Group?"

"Business partners. They help me with my events and ensure everything is compliant." Turning to face me, he cocks his head as he studies me briefly. "You did your research."

I nod. "I did. I've done nothing but research for the last two weeks."

He purses his lips and looks away. When he looks back at me, that same easygoing, mirthful expression stares back at me. Arching a brow in surprise, his eyes wander over my face once again.

"And you think that makes you an expert in being a submissive?"

I shrug. "I guess we'll see, won't we?" I flick my eyes up to his, and something dark passes over his expression.

Fuck.

Is it hot in here, or is it me?

The elevator dings, and the doors slide open. Chase and I step inside, and he presses the number '3'.

"I'm willing to learn more. And I know my limits now. I've gone through each and every thing that could possibly come up this weekend, and I know where I stand," I explain. My eyes drift down to the large suit-case. "I brought a lot of clothes," I blurt, feeling the word vomit creep up as I babble nervously. "I wasn't sure what I should be wearing, if anything. I know some Doms prefer their subs naked, so I suppose we can discuss—"

"Parker."

I snap my eyes to his, and then I nearly gasp. His eyes are doing that dark, brooding thing they do some-times. The last time he looked at me like that...

The doors glide closed, and the next thing I know,

Chase's hand is around my neck and he's pressing me up against the elevator wall.

"Fool," he mumbles, staring down at me. "You're a fucking fool, Parker." And then he crushes his lips against mine roughly. I moan as his tongue pries my mouth open, fisting his shirt, pulling him closer. Every calm thing inside of me shatters with the hunger of his kiss, and a low, dangerous swooping sensation drops down to my core, straight to my clit. He growls into my mouth. "I shouldn't want this so much," he sighs, his breath hot on my lips.

"Why?" I ask, nipping his lower lip with my teeth. "I thought primal play was all about listening to your instincts?"

He pulls away and looks at me as if I've electrocuted him. Smirking, he grabs the back of my head and bends down to give me another demanding kiss while pressing his body against mine.

"Fuck," he says, his voice shaky. His lips brush against mine with his words, and it sends another shiver straight through me.

I moan as he fists my hair tightly, as his mouth moves to my neck. I hear him inhale—smelling me—and my knees shake as he grips my hair harder. He unconsciously bucks his hips against me.

The elevator dings and we suddenly spring apart. I touch my lips when I look up at him. He's panting and watching me with amusement glinting in his eyes.

"Let's go before I get carried away."

And then he turns and walks out of the elevator, dragging my enormous suitcase behind him.

My heart is still racing as I follow him down a dark hallway lit up with actual candle-lit sconces. There's a dark-green patterned wallpaper lining the walls, and at the end of a hallway are two double doors. I glance at the sign outside of the door.

The East Royal Suite.

Of course.

My mind dances back to the conversation with the security guard.

The east wing is off limits, but all other areas are open to guests for the weekend.

Is this wing off limits because it's where Chase lives? Where does Miles live, if Chase is here? Is Miles here this weekend? Likely not...

Even still, it sends a skittering of nerves down my spine when I realize I'm being given access to a side of the castle that is off limits to other guests.

Once inside the room, I stop walking as I take it in. It's... jungle themed. A sitting room with two chairs, a formal dining table next to a large window, and a couch facing a massive TV are the first things I see. There's leopard print, zebra print, a few palm trees, and a large birds of paradise plant in one corner. The furniture is all made of bamboo, and the textiles are bright and vibrant. Further on, past the kitchen, is a bathroom and a closed door. *His bedroom.*

I turn around once, taking it all in. *Even his fucking living quarters are bigger than my house.*

"Did you already have a submissive picked out for the weekend?" I muse, my finger running over the stone mantle of the large fireplace. There's a large, framed painting of a cheetah sitting atop the stone.

"No," he says, opening the bedroom and depositing my suitcase inside. *First things first, you'll be in my room for the duration of the hunt.* "I hadn't chosen one yet."

I set my purse down on the couch and cross my arms as I study him.

"Do you normally play at these events?"

He mimics me, leaning against the doorframe of his bedroom and crossing his arms. "I don't play here. Normally. But I do usually take a sub."

Ignoring the way the idea of Chase being with other women makes me feel downright murderous, I tilt my head.

"Why don't you play here?"

"I prefer more of an... urban setting."

"Like The Penthouse."

His lips twitch. "Yes."

My eyes scan the living quarters again as I try to quell the nervous butterflies fluttering around inside of me. Wiping my sweaty palms on my leggings, I look at Chase.

"So, what now?"

He nods to the dining room table. "Sit."

Something hot flashes through me at his command, and I walk over to the wood table and sit down in one of the chairs. I watch as he moves across the room to the large safe. Entering a code, he pulls the door open. I crane my neck to see what's inside, but his stupid, hulking body is in the way. He closes the door of the safe before I can get a better view. Walking back over at me with a black, leather folio, I admire the way he walks. Slow, deliberate, smooth. Like he's trying to unnerve me.

"We need to discuss limits," he says, his voice low and businesslike.

I try not to smile. "Okay."

Unzipping the folio, he pulls out several pieces of paper.

"These are mine, if you'd like to educate yourself."

Dom's have limits? I nearly shake my head at the thought, because of course they do.

I greedily read the form—which is basic in nature. At the top is a space to check either Dominant/Master/Top or submissive/slave/bottom. I see Chase has selected the first, obviously. Under that is experience—Beginner, Average, or Extensive. He's marked extensive. Under sexual orientation, he's marked straight. And under relationship preference, he's marked monogamous. *That* surprises me, but I file it away to ask about later.

"If there are any limits you don't understand, ask me."

I look up and nod, continuing my perusal into his sexual preferences. He's marked 'prefers to wear suit.' *Hmm.* I glance up at him briefly, and his eyes pierce me with their intensity. Looking back down at the form, I see the next part is a list of activities, with a 'Have you participated?' with a yes and no option, and next to that column, options for your interest in participating. My eyes widen when I flip through the pages. Chase has participated in nearly every single activity. And his list of interests... most of them are checked 'Yes'. There are a few he's indicated 'maybe,' and only one hard limit.

Sharing.

Chills run up my spine when I look at him. He's chewing on the end of a pen, one leg resting over the other.

"Questions?" he asks, setting the pen down.

"No. Yours is pretty straightforward."

He nods and slides what I assume is my version of the checklist across the table. I pick the pen up—the one he was just chewing on—never breaking eye contact as I pull the papers toward me.

Looking down, I check my answers off. Submissive. Beginner. Straight. Monogamous. Under the 'prefers to wear' section, I look up at Chase.

"What do your submissives normally wear?"

Chase leans back. "What do they normally wear? Or what do I prefer you wear?"

"Well, you. Since you'll be my Dom."

"I want you to be comfortable. So answer honestly. We can discuss what I expect you to wear, among other things, as we move forward."

My core swoops low again and I write 'Anything.'

The list is next, and my cheeks burn as I mark 'no' for almost everything. In fact, I only mark 'yes' for five things.

"I don't have a lot of—"

"It's fine," Chase interrupts, glancing down. "It doesn't matter to me, Parker."

I nod. Then I go down the list, marking off my hard

limits first. *Definitely* no golden or brown showers. Catheterization. Enemas. Infantilism.

I look up at Chase. "If you don't share, neither do I," I tell him, checking it as my last hard limit.

His pupils darken when my eyes find his again. "Fair enough," he murmurs, rubbing his mouth.

I go down the checklist until I have an answer for most things, saving my questions for him for last. Luckily, my research was extensive, and I know what most of the items are. I'm also self-aware enough to know that while I think I might not think I'll enjoy certain things on paper, I'm willing to try anything other than my hard limits.

"Cock worship?" I ask, arching a brow.

He smirks. "Exactly what it sounds like. It's when a sub enthusiastically gives their Dom a blow job."

I mark 'maybe.'

"Orgasm denial?" I ask tentatively before clarifying. "I mean, I know what it is." Clearing my throat, my pen hovers over the 'Yes' box. "I want to be sure if I mark this that you won't deny me an orgasm for too long? Like as a form of torture. Because honestly, that sounds horrible."

Not like I haven't been living with that all my life with partners.

He cocks his head. "If you mark yes or maybe, I'll deny you for as long as I want, Parker."

I shouldn't be turned on by his answer, but I am.

I swallow nervously and mark 'Yes.'

"Last one. What is twenty-four-seven?"

Chase's eyes twinkle as he gives me a small smile. "A relationship where protocols are in place 24/7."

I narrow my eyes as I decide. I mean... if it's Chase... I'd probably let him control me all weekend. As I study his face, it occurs to me that I'm far less nervous than I probably should be. But because it's *Chase.* He's Jackson's best friend and roommate. I've known him since I was a child. I'd be experiencing this in a completely different way if it were anyone else.

I mark 'Maybe.'

Sliding the form back to him, I watch as he inspects my answers.

"I know I briefly mentioned earlier that we could use the traffic light system as a safe word. Red means stop. Yellow is used when you're nearing a limit or you can't take any more, but you don't want the scene to end. An example of this is switching from a paddle because you're struggling with a whip. It can also be used to signal something needs changing such as a position or restraint. Green means keep going. Because you're so new, it's easy to remember red, yellow, and green. However, if you'd like to use another word, please let me know."

I shrug. "What about rooster?"

Setting my limits down, he glares at me. "I can't tell if you're serious or if you're being snarky. If it's the latter, you should know now that I don't tolerate brats."

Something white-hot coils in the pit of my stomach at his disciplinarian tone.

"The traffic light system works for me," I acquiesce.

He nods. "I'll use the same one for myself. For non-verbal, I suggest you think of something you can do with your hands tied up and your mouth otherwise occupied."

I lean back and try to cool my overheated body. Why am I having this reaction? Is it because he's being all domineering? Is it because I'm thinking about doing all of this with him? Or am I *that* orgasm-deprived that a silly list is making me hot? Luckily, I already have an answer for him, thanks to my research.

"Humming the theme song from Wolverine?" I suggest.

His gaze cuts to mine, and a million butterflies begin to dance inside of me at his penetrating look.

"Okay," he says, writing it down on the page of my limits as his lips threaten to twitch into a smile. Then he pulls out another couple of papers. "I will utilize the safe word if I need to stop the scene for any reason—including your safety or mine. I know you've done your research, but please understand that you shouldn't hesitate to use the verbal or non-verbal safe word. *Ever.* It's there to keep us both safe." His low voice rumbles out and reverberates through my body.

"Got it."

Continuing, his eyes look down at the other piece of paper. "This is my contract. It includes an NDA and my requirements. Once you fill this out and sign it, we'll be ready to begin." He slides the papers over, and I glance down at the top of the contract.

Chase Charles Ravage and (submissive's name) agree to the following, effective from (date) to (date), at which

time this contract will end or be renegotiated. Any partici-
pant may also choose to end this contract before that time,
for any reason...

I fill it out slowly. It's extensive, going into my
medical history as well as my mental health history. I
list out my safe words as well as my hard limits. It also
asks for my birth control method, and I write down
that I have an IUD. It asks for equipment, and I hesitate. *Was I supposed to bring equipment?*

"Umm," I mumble, and Chase glances down at the
words my pen is hovering over.

"I have everything we'll need," he says coolly,
looking away.

I am *so* tempted to ask, but I decide it's a question
for another day.

There's a section for my behaviors and responsibil-
ities, and I slide it over to Chase. He fills it out,
speaking as he writes. Something about him filling out
this section for me makes my skin tingle.

"Mealtimes will be discussed every morning. I
generally expect my submissives to eat with me to
ensure they're well nourished. You can wear whatever
makes you comfortable. If that changes, or I'd like you
to wear something specific, I'll discuss it with you
ahead of time. Appearance and grooming are fine," he
mumbles. "I have had a recent negative test, and
assume you get regular checks as well?"

I nod, but then remember he needs to hear me
agree to all of this verbally. "Yes."

"Good. I prefer to go bare."

My chest flushes at his words. *Bare.* Before I can

ruminate on why his words are causing me to feel like I have a high fever, he continues. Looking up at me, his eyes darken slightly as he speaks his next sentence.

"Though I normally encourage masturbation, for this weekend, I'd like for you to abstain."

What?

My cheeks flame. "Okay."

"As for public conduct, I will introduce you as my submissive to those here for the weekend, unless you prefer I introduce you as Juliet." I nod, and he continues. "You will call me sir during a scene, but all other times, Chase is fine. Like I said, I normally don't play at the castle, but since you are here and willing to learn, I think it would be best to start slow. Since we are discussing the event and only the event—which is a primal play event—we need to come up with a signal that starts the scene."

I look down at the table. I wish I'd done some research, maybe asked Miles what this was all about, because aside from what Chase told me two weeks ago, and my own research, I am wholly unprepared.

"It depends where we are, I suppose," I say, shrugging. Hopefully my answer will be vague enough for him to understand that I have no fucking clue what I'm doing.

"An indicator I've used in the past is rolling my shirt sleeves up. So, if we're out there and I roll them up, what does that mean for you, Parker?"

I swallow thickly. *Think, Juliet. You're a smart girl.*

You need someone you trust, because it will be akin to

running from an actual predator. Except you want to be caught.

"It means I run."

His expression clouds as his eyes grow hooded. "Good girl."

Oh boy.

I resist the urge to physically fan myself, instead choosing to take a few steadying breaths.

We quickly go over the rest of the contract—ending a scene, which entails Chase putting a shirt back on or rolling his sleeves down. Then there's punishment. I agree to spanking—with his hand to start—telling him we'll start there and work our way up. This earns me a genuine smile. Last, the signatures. Chase withholds the pen from me as he looks me in the eye.

"I need you to understand what you're agreeing to, Parker," he murmurs.

"I do," I tell him, reaching for the pen.

He holds it out of reach. "It's three days of hunting. Of chasing you. Consensual non-consent. It will be messy, intense, dirty, and probably confusing for you. Do you understand?"

I nod.

"I need to hear you say it."

"I understand," I answer.

"Good. You are aware that for the purposes of this event, you are the prey, and I am the predator?"

Full body chills.

"Yes."

"And you realize that you are stuck with me for the

weekend, yeah? You're mine for three days. This could change everything. I need you to understand that, Parker."

His voice is softer, and I bite my lower lip as I take in his words. I'm not sure if he means our relationship, or his relationship with Jackson. His eyes skim down to where my teeth are pressing against my lip.

"I understand," I whisper.

"There is no holding back for me once you sign this."

"I don't want you to hold back," I tell him, looking at him through my lashes.

He shakes his head, looking away as he lets out a small laugh. "Fuck, Parker. You make it really hard to stay away from you. Do you know that?" I smile, and he hands me the pen. "Last chance."

"I'm not afraid of you," I tell him defiantly.

He chuckles and leans forward, pinning me with a gaze that reminds me of the big, bad wolf. "You should be."

"Why? I know you, Chase. None of this scares me. Stop pushing me away."

His jaw tics as he leans back. "Correction: you used to know me."

I place the tip of the pen on the signature line. "What are you so scared of?" I ask him.

He looks away. "I'm scared I'll break you. And I'm scared you'll hate me for it."

My heart pounds inside of my chest as I take in his words. Is this why he rejected me all those years ago? Because he was scared of unleashing himself on me? Is that what all of this is about? The warnings to stay away... the rejections...

He wants me, but he's afraid he wants me *too much*.

My clit flutters at the notion of him finally *taking* what he's always wanted.

"Well, too bad for you. Because I'm a consenting adult, and I decide when I break. Besides, I could never hate you, Ravage."

"Doubtful," he murmurs.

I sign the contract and pass it to him. He signs it as well.

"I'll have Luna email you a copy." His eyes flick up to mine. "You've probably had a busy morning. Why don't you go rest for an hour in the bedroom?"

"Do you normally share your bedroom with your subs?" I ask before I can think to keep my mouth closed.

His jaw tightens. "Not normally, no."

I don't play here. Normally.

He stands up and walks back to the safe, essentially dismissing me. Showing up uninvited. Invading his bedroom. Forcing him to play. Maybe I truly am going to be a thorn in his side.

CHAPTER TEN
THE HIKE

CHASE

Have fun hunting, little brother. I hope you catch something worthwhile. ;)

I swirl the scotch in my glass as I stare down at my phone, re-reading my brother's text from last night. I should've caught on when he sent it. Miles has always been a meddler—always scheming and planning. Despite being the quiet one, he likes to stir shit up, but only if that shit has nothing to do with him. He is the epitome of the meme of the little girl smirking while the area behind her is on fire. It's what makes him an amazing CEO of Ravage Consulting Firm. He's always observing, always digesting the world in a way that keeps him separate from it. Because we deal with investments, his marketing brain is always thinking up ways to get our name out there. Always thinking of how we're seen by others. Always adjusting our business strategy according to his examinations of the world.

Unfortunately, he saw Parker and I sneak off together at her engagement party and put two and two together. He asked me about it no less than a dozen times.

Though his interests lie elsewhere, he knows I like to play. We are close. And we spend way too much time together at the office for him to *not* notice. And I know from my Ring footage—as well as the front gate visitors notification—that Juliet had been in my apartment last night.

It didn't take a genius to figure out that he'd said something to her.

Fucking Miles. He's like a serious, grumpy version of Lady Whistledown.

I finish my scotch.

I don't normally drink this early in the day, but my whole body is thrumming with need. I feel like a caged animal, ready to pounce. The second Parker signed her name away, I knew I was a goner.

Three days.

I can restrain myself for three days, can't I? The problem is, normally my submissives are strangers. I don't get tangled up with people I know personally. I didn't go over the list of available subs for the weekend —assuming I'd try a few different ones out over the course of the long weekend. Everything about this situation with Parker goes against my own rules. Three days. Which means three nights. I've never slept with the same woman for more than one night. That's when things get messy. But I couldn't resist Parker. I couldn't resist the way she blew back into my life.

Willing.

Interested.

Maybe it's not the worst thing. I can be a guide for her—teach her what she needs to know.

I pour myself more scotch as I lean back on the couch and rub my eyes.

I can show her. I can educate her. And on Monday, we'll go our separate ways. She wants to be a part of this community? Fine. I'll guide her as much as I can. Maybe at the end of this, she'll know how to choose a man who can give her the pleasure she needs.

Grimacing, I take another sip.

Thinking about another man touching her like I want to touch her—

Fuck.

I am royally fucked.

And Juliet is so... good. Open. Approachable. *Vulnerable.*

Why? I know you, Chase. None of this scares me. Stop pushing me away.

Her words from earlier startled me. I'd spent my entire adult life pushing people away. Women, mostly. Never getting too close. It's easier. Relationships are uncontrollable. Being in love, specifically, makes you do stupid things. I need the control. It's the only thing I can count on, besides Jackson and my brothers. I am an all or nothing man. This is the only way I can guarantee that control without half-assing anything.

It's why I got into this lifestyle. I saw what happened to my parents and decided at a young age that I would do *everything* in my power to control the situation. Especially after what happened to Miles when we were kids... I vowed to never let something like that happen again.

But Juliet? She's not afraid to throw herself into this. She's completely up front about her feelings. She always has been. She has these lists and arguments that are ironclad, and she isn't afraid to tell you why you're wrong. I smile when I think of how thoroughly she went through her limits—limits I'm sure she researched extensively.

And her feelings for me? She's not afraid to admit them. Not afraid to pursue me. To tell me that she wants me as her Dom. Which is... completely foreign to me.

She's not forward—she's *honest.*

She doesn't hold anything back.

It makes me want to relinquish all of my control, all of my self-imposed rules.

Juliet has always been special to me. With other women, I have no desire to emotionally connect with them. It's easier to keep them at an arm's distance. But I *want* to give her everything. I *want* to spend time with her. I wasn't kidding when I said she had the capacity to ruin me.

I rub my chest and stare at her signature on the contract. Large, swooping letters that make everything inside of me flare with heat. Will she regret signing it by the end of today? By Monday?

I am in control.

I can keep my feelings in check. I've never let that side of myself show. Not since I was a kid. Not in that way.

As long as she understands my limits, we will be fine.

My bedroom door clicks open, and I look up to see her watching me from the doorway.

"What should I wear today?"

"We'll be hiking," I say gruffly. "Wear something comfortable."

Her eyes widen as she nods, closing the door.

I hear the shower in my en suite turn on a minute later.

Running my hands through my hair and over my face, I try to calm the way my cock throbs at the idea of Parker naked in *my* bathroom—though I hardly come here anymore except for these hunts. We each had our own living quarters, and this one was mine. Miles was on the other side of the castle, and if I hadn't kicked him out of his house for the long weekend, he'd be here too. Instead, he's at my place in the city.

The shower turns off.

I've been so adamant about keeping her at a distance, but I've already let my guard down. Because my interest in Parker precedes everything I know. It goes back over ten years, back to when I was a fucking kid. She hasn't broken down any of my walls.

She was already inside.

I run a hand over my face.

Fuck it.

She's here, so like I said earlier, I guess we're doing this. Though, I can't deny the excitement that courses through my veins.

I suppose I should start acting like this isn't everything I've always wanted.

———

A few minutes later, I'm scrolling on my phone when Parker walks into the living area wearing dark red leggings and a matching sports bra underneath a denim jacket.

Sinful.

Also, fuck my life.

She's holding black trainers in her hands. "Just need to put my shoes on."

"Let me get changed," I add, walking into the bedroom.

My eyes scan my bed—her things scattered over my duvet. Her suitcase propped open, clothes overflowing out of it and onto the ground. I see an assortment of toiletries sitting on my bathroom counter, and my lips twitch with the hint of a smile. Both her and Jackson are quite sloppy. I'd forgotten.

I quickly change into a t-shirt, jeans, and lace-up boots. Grabbing a flannel and throwing it on, I walk back out into the living room.

Her eyes rake over my outfit quickly before she

smirks and raises one eyebrow, as if she approves. *As if she thinks she has a say and not the other way around.*

I grab two water bottles from the fridge across the room. "Leave your phone here," I tell her, handing her one of the bottles.

She looks up at me, mouth parted. "Why?"

I cock my head. "Because I said so. We're starting today off with an exercise in listening to our instincts, and I don't want any distractions."

I expect her to fight back, but if she's displeased, she doesn't show it. She sets her phone and wallet on the coffee table.

"Let's go."

I hold the door open for her, inhaling her scent as she passes me. She smells like fresh cut flowers and heaven. *I truly am royally fucked.*

She presses the button on the elevator. Her hair is pulled back into a loose ponytail. The doors slide open, and she walks in, turning around and facing me as I enter the elevator with her. As the doors slide shut, I slowly take a couple of steps so that I'm right in front of her. I bring my hand to a loose piece of hair, tucking it behind her ear.

"I'm not going to do anything sexual today, Parker. I want you to learn how to listen to your body." I run a finger down her jaw. I smirk when she visibly shivers under my touch. "A big part of primal play is listening to your animal side. And while you might claim I don't know you anymore, I think I know you well enough to suspect that foregoing logic is hard for you. For this to work, you're going to have to let go of everything you think you know."

She swallows, and I watch the delicate skin along her neck move with the motion. Tracking my eyes back to hers, I take a step away.

"You're right," she says quietly. "I mean, you know how I am. I have to research everything. I think I've scared my intuition away."

I chuckle. "Not possible. I'll show you, don't worry."

"I'm serious, Chase. I overthink *everything*. Even what I'm going to eat for breakfast."

I cock my head and take another step backward. "You have to trust me. Okay?"

The elevator door chimes as it slides open. She studies my face for a second before nodding.

We walk past the kitchen, where a couple of professional chefs are preparing lunch. Past the library—her head nearly swivels all the way around as she glances inside—and then we pass the study, the formal sitting room, and finally, the back patio, which leads out into the back garden. Since I like to keep these hunts exclusive and small, that means that Parker and I will be joined by a few other couples, single submissives, and a couple of dominants that I've pre-approved—including the three ladies who make up The Domme Group.

The plan for the weekend was supposed to be casual fun, but the second Louis texted me about a 'Ms. Parker' at the gate, I knew it would be anything but.

Though I host the event, I don't interfere. People

stay in various bedrooms we've set up with anything
and everything they could need, and aside from Parker,
every single one of them was invited personally by me.
They are free to play however they want. The invite I
send Miles is always a joke, and I should've known
better. But Juliet is here now, and Miles will get a
tongue-lashing the next time I see him.

Once we walk outside, I turn to the right—away
from the Olympic-sized pool—knowing the stone path
will lead to the back of the house and into the forest.
It's foggy today, despite it being Spring, and it gives
everything an eerie feeling. I haven't been back here in
years—since everything happened as a kid. But Parker
needs to learn how to let go, and I need to give her the
full experience. An hour in the woods is nothing.

The trees behind the castle extend for miles. My
great-grandfather wanted to ensure we could build a
hundred more castles if needed, so he snatched up the
land behind the house I grew up in. The stone path
weaves around the side of the house, past a large fountain, and then we walk through an iron gate that leads
to the woods beyond. I have to use my key to get us
through. From there, the path weaves deeper into the
thicket of trees, and Parker continues walking at my
side silently. The noise of the fountain disappears after
a few minutes, and soon, the path disappears, leaving
us to walk over the uneven dirt. The sun beats down on
the cool earth, causing a thin layer of fog to pool along
the ground.

"Do you know where we're going?" Parker asks,
stopping as she turns to face me.

No. I have no fucking idea.

Of course I used to play back here all the time as a child until the accident. Until the thought of being back in the woods sent me spiraling. However, my goal today is to get Juliet away from the lodge. From other people. From anything that can distract her. I want to unnerve her a bit. Bring her out of her element. *Show* her how to listen to her body, her breathing, quiet her thoughts to avoid overthinking.

"Do you want to go back?" I ask her, intentionally not answering her question.

This is a challenge for me just as much as it is for her.

An opportunity to throw all my fucking caution to the wind to help her.

Besides, I know that eventually, fifteen miles from here, there is a road that intersects the forest completely.

I won't get lost again.

I've spent *years* pouring over the maps after the incident. I never make the same mistake twice, and I'm not about to start now.

She presses her lips together and looks back toward the castle. "Haven't you ever seen those shows where the people get lost in the forest and die because they eat poisonous berries?"

My lips twitch, but I don't let myself smile. It's a valid fear. "I have. Are you afraid we'll get lost?"

I fucking hope not.

She nods. "Or run out of water. Or food. Or—"

"Parker," I growl, stepping closer to her. "We've

been walking for five minutes. Forget those shows. They use scare tactics to draw in viewers. Stuff like that works the same way as drugs or sugar. They pull you in, giving you an adrenaline rush so that you crave more. Humans nowadays are used to about one hundred times the adrenaline we're supposed to experience," I mutter. "Between click-bait news, social media pushing scary stories in front of our faces, and people not allowing themselves to relax—ever—it's a wonder we're all still functioning."

She opens and closes her mouth, looking around.

"Can you do something for me?" I ask.

"What?" she asks.

"Lie down."

"In the dirt?" she asks.

I nod. "Yes. Lie down on your back and close your eyes." She looks down at the ground. "It's just dirt, Parker."

She eyes me warily as she drops down onto the floor, finding a comfortable place to lie down flat and close her eyes. I let my eyes skim over her body for a few seconds before I lie down next to her, and I hear her sharp inhale.

"What next?" she asks.

"Nothing," I say calmly, closing my eyes as I lace my fingers together over my chest. "Just... listen."

"To what?" she asks.

I huff a laugh. "To the sounds. To your pulse. To your breathing. I want you to listen to what's happening to your body. Don't think of your job, or

Jackson, or me. Just pay attention to the things you can see, feel, hear, taste, and touch."

"Taste?" she asks.

"Don't be mouthy."

"Fine. I will try it."

I smirk. "Good."

"How will we know an hour has passed without a phone?" she asks.

"Maybe it'll be forty minutes. Maybe it'll be an hour and a half. Let go of the concept of time."

I can practically hear her squirming next to me, but I let her calm herself down as I rest my eyes.

Truth be told, I have no idea what I'm doing. Sure, I can act primal during a scene, but in real life? It's all new to me, too. I'm the goddamn president of Ravage Consulting Firm. We're not exactly leading meditation groups on the daily. But Parker needs to learn how to *relax*. If this is going to work, she's going to need to ignore her lists and rational thought. Most primal play is *irrational* to people like her, but once she lets go, it will start to feel completely natural, exactly like it did for me all those years ago.

Parker huffs a few little sighs from next to me. Then come the jerky movements—and the way she moves slightly to get more comfortable.

She's the opposite of relaxed.

"I feel like there are ants crawling all over me," she says, her voice resigned.

I smile. "Maybe. Ignore them."

"Ignore *ants?*"

"You heard me," I retort.

"I'd like to see you ignore ants crawling up your vag—"

"All right, stand up, Parker."

I get to my feet and reach down for her hand as her eyes study me. She takes it and brushes herself off.

"I'm sorry. I tried. It's not the way my mind works."

I study her face. "Let's try a different tactic."

Arching a brow, she crosses her arms. "Honestly, I wasn't expecting to learn about *nature*. I was expecting —" She clamps her mouth shut and looks away.

"What were you expecting when you came here?" I ask her, watching as she shakes her head.

"I don't know."

Her cheeks redden, and I take a step forward. Her eyes find mine as I place my hands on her shoulders.

"Close your eyes," I murmur.

Her pupils dilate slightly before she does, and then I wait a minute before I begin.

"What do you hear?" I ask.

She shrugs. "Your breathing. My breathing. Some weird bird sound in the distance."

"Good. And what do you smell?"

"Your cologne."

I laugh. "I'm not wearing cologne."

Her lips twist to the side, but she keeps her eyes closed. "Of course you aren't."

"What else?" I ask.

"The dirt. The trees." She inhales. "Water? Or something mineral-y."

"Okay. And what do you feel?" I ask.

"Your hands," she tells me, her voice low.

"What else?"

"My clothes. The breeze against my skin." I lower my hands and lace my hands with hers. Then I brush the underside of her wrist with my thumb. "Your thumb." Her voice is hoarse.

"And how does my thumb make the rest of you feel?"

"I—what?" she asks.

I do it again, ignoring the electric current shooting up my arm.

"My heart," she whispers. "It's beating really fast."

"Good. Tell me more."

"My skin. I have goose bumps."

I don't say anything as I reach one hand up, running it through her scalp as I pull her hair band out. I push back the light brown hair, inhaling the intoxicating scent of her shampoo. Moving it all to one side, I can see the way her pulse is jumping in her neck, can feel it beneath my other hand on her wrist. I watch her, study her, take in everything all at once. I don't know if I've ever been this close to her for this long, and I want to cherish it.

What I would give to run my lips along her neck. To *taste* her.

Soon.

One of my fingers lightly traces along the delicate skin of her neck, and I watch as a tremble ripples down her whole body.

I let out a low chuckle as I continue teaching her, relishing the way my low laugh seems to make her shiver.

Her face is flushed as I give in for a second, bringing my lips within an inch of the space just under her ear.

"What else, Juliet?" She's panting now, her skin pebbling where my breath touches her. She trembles once more. "My breath made you tremble. Imagine what my tongue can do," I add, smirking arrogantly. "Any other reactions?" I ask, my voice a deep purr.

"Yes, but since this is a non-sexual excursion, I'm not sure I should tell you."

My cock pulses. "Tell me."

"Okay. My nipples are hard. Every movement you make against my skin sends pleasure down my spine straight to my clit."

Fuck.

"What else?" I ask, whispering straight into her ear.

"When you talk into my ear... it makes my..."

"Tell me," I beg her. "Tell me how it makes your cunt feel, Parker."

She's panting now. Her skin is fully flushed, and her palms are sweating as she squeezes my hands tightly.

"Every time you whisper in my ear, or touch my wrist, it makes my cunt clench around nothing."

I run my nose along the side of her neck, inhaling and trying to gather my thoughts. I am keeping everything leashed for now—for today. But being here with her, *smelling* her, when my body knows damn well that she's my one weakness? It's a test of my control.

"Before I ask you the next question, I don't want you to overthink. I want you to listen to your body.

Ignore what you *think* you should do and let it happen. Trust me to stop us before it goes too far, because I'm not going to fuck you today. Okay?"

"Okay," she whispers.

"Last question. What do you taste?" I run a hand to the back of her neck and pull her face close to mine. We're an inch apart. "Lick me, Juliet."

CHAPTER ELEVEN
THE KISS

JULIET

I want to open my eyes. I want to see how Chase is probably looking at me—his blue eyes probably searching mine.

Lick me, Juliet.

Don't overthink.

Just *do* it.

I stick my tongue out and find his neck, licking the stubble. His skin is salty, and the musky scent makes me moan as I place both lips against his pulse point. He's staying completely still, but when my tongue flicks against his skin again, his hands clamp down on mine. Three senses assault me all at once. Taste, smell, touch. I suck gently and hear him inhale. Four senses.

It overpowers me.

His heart races beneath my tongue, and that

feeling of *knowing* this is affecting him as much as it's affecting me is... *intoxicating.*

All of my other thoughts drop back somewhere inaccessible, and all I can think is *Chase, Chase, Chase.*

"What else do you want to do, Parker?" Chase asks, his voice low and rough.

I want you to listen to your body. Ignore what you think you should do and let it happen. Trust me to stop us before it goes too far, because I'm not going to fuck you today.

With my eyes still closed, I reach up to his face, pulling him to my face for a kiss.

The dam breaks, and the instant his tongue probes my lips, I growl, fisting his shirt and pulling him roughly into my body.

"I want you," I mumble against his soft lips.

"You have me," he mutters.

Finally.

White-hot heat explodes through me. I am possessed as I nip at his lips, licking them and clawing at his shirt. Our lips are still locked as I remove his flannel, tugging it down his shoulders. I want to feel his skin against mine, so I take my jacket off, too. He doesn't stop me.

"Keep going," he says, his voice uneven.

I moan as his warm hands come to my back. I tug his shirt off, breaking away from him for half a second before I'm mauling him again.

Without thinking, I jump into his arms, and he grabs my thighs, hoisting my legs around his hips.

My hands drag down his bare back and chest, his

smooth, muscled skin...

I run my nails down his upper back, and he groans into my mouth.

"What do you want, Juliet?" he asks.

"Everything," I tell him honestly.

I hadn't felt him walking, but he must've moved us to a nearby tree because something rough presses into my back. I wrap my arms around him as I kiss him, as our lips move against each other, as my thighs squeeze his hips. I want to *consume* him. Drink him, eat him, taste him...

I pull away, eyes still closed, and his mouth finds my neck.

I didn't have to ask him.

I cry out when he sucks on the sensitive skin between my collarbone and neck. He lets out a low growl, dragging his teeth against my skin, barely grazing me.

"Bite me," I ask him.

His teeth clamp down on the perfect spot, and my pussy contracts several times as I open my mouth in a silent scream.

"Again," I pant. He bites harder, and I scream. "Please, God, more—"

One of his hands comes to my bra, his thumb brushing over my taut nipple.

"That's it, Parker. Tell me what you want."

"Your mouth. On my nipple," I gasp.

He pulls my bra down, exposing one of my breasts. I don't care. I'm so hot that nothing else matters. Just his lips on me. I buck my hips against his hard erection, and he growls again, suctioning my nipple into his mouth.

I cry out. *Holy mother of...*

I throw my head back as my whole body tenses up like I'm about to—

Wait.

"Chase, I'm going to come soon."

I work my hips against his hard shaft, the roughness of his jeans spurring me on. My mind is racing and slowing down all at once. This has never happened before. Someone *else* is going to make me come—

"Not yet, Juliet."

He pulls away and lowers me, holding me up and securing my bra back over my exposed nipple. I'm dizzy and disoriented, and cold air skirts over my skin, making me shiver. Every little touch gives me goosebumps and makes my core tighten around nothing. I touch my lips—which are sore from his stubble—and look up at him.

He doesn't look any more composed than I feel.

His hair is wild, his lips are swollen, and I can see the red lines from my nails all over his arms, torso, and neck. His bare chest is... I hadn't realized I was scratching him so hard when I was in the moment. Some of them look like they're bleeding. My neck flushes as I stumble back. *I went too far. I was overpowered by his scent. I didn't mean—*

"Parker." My eyes snap to his, and he's watching me carefully. He steps closer. "That was good. You did well listening to what your body wanted." My eyes survey his chest, and he reaches out, grabbing my chin between his thumb and index finger. It's not rough. It's almost... tender. *Why do I love when he does that?* "It can be overwhelming at first," he murmurs, his eyes searching mine. "But you need to know that everything that happened was completely normal."

He lets go of my chin and grabs his shirt, throwing it back on.

"I'm sorry about the scratches."

He chuckles. "I'm not."

"But I hurt you," I say, pulling my denim jacket over my shoulders.

"And I have our safe word, Parker," he murmurs, looking at me. "I know we weren't in a scene, but if anything had gone too far, I would've stopped it."

"Okay," I say unevenly.

We walk back to the castle silently. I'm not sure if I passed this first test—was it a test?—or failed. He said everything I did was normal, but then... why did we stop?

Chase, I'm going to come soon.

Not yet, Juliet.

He must be reading my mind because he clears his throat as we walk.

"If we're really going to do this, you have to trust me," he says sternly. "That includes trusting me to stop if either one of us is uncomfortable."

I nod. "I do trust you. I told you."

"Good. And I need you to trust that I will give you what you need. It may not be what *you* think you need, but again, it comes back to that trust."

"Then why did you stop when I wanted to keep

going?"

He shoves his hands in his jeans pocket. Seeing Chase wearing casual jeans—even if they are fitted perfectly and probably cost hundreds of dollars—does something funny to my brain.

It's like I can't compute it. I've had him in a box for years—one that labeled him as off limits, cold, serious —and now my brain needs to rewire around all of this new information.

"Because you aren't quite ready. It won't benefit either of us if we jump right into playing together. Do you trust me enough to know when and how to give you what you want?" he asks.

How the hell am I supposed to respond to that?

"Of course."

"But..." he trails off, looking at me and smirking.

I huff a laugh. He knows me too well, even after all of these years. *God, am I really that predictable?*

"But... I guess I'm trying to understand what's in it for you. You're going to *teach* me and give *me* pleasure. You say you're going to give me everything I want. But what about you? What do *you* get out of all of this?"

Chase stops walking, and I realize a few paces too late. I turn around to find him watching me with an incredulous expression.

"Do you really not understand?" he asks. The way he asks is not mean, or cruel, or condescending. It's more... disbelieving. "What do I get, Parker?" He steps closer. "I get you."

"You could've had me at any point," I blurt. "I was always here. Always a willing participant."

He thumbs his lips as he takes another step closer. "Yes, but were you ever willing to give up the control you so badly crave? Until this week, would you have signed a contract like the one you signed this morning? You're asking me what's in it for me? Control. I get off on receiving that control from you so that you can let go. So that you can *submit*. Your pleasure is mine."

Holy...

Fuck.

"Is that not why you're here?" he asks, cocking his head. "To relinquish your control and to trust me to give you that pleasure no other man could give you?"

"Yes," I whisper, suddenly hot again.

Why is it so fucking sexy when he talks like that? He's not worried that he won't be able to give me what I need, or the notion of failing. It's like he already *knows* he's won, already *knows* he'll accomplish it. And I'm not sure if it's confidence or something darker, something more demanding, but it comes from someplace deep inside of him. He doesn't ever falter or lose control. Even before, pushing me up against the tree, he was listening to *me*, guiding me, showing me how to do it. Seeing him like this, seeing how much control he has over himself... it's both terrifying and exciting.

Except, he did lose control.

Twice.

With me.

Once at his party, and once in the elevator.

But I know he's still holding himself back. I can feel the power, the domination, rolling off him in waves.

When will you snap, Ravage?

"Okay. Then let me take care of you, Parker. Would you still like to move forward with the Hunt?"

"Yes."

He nods once, his expression closed again. "Good. Let's get back."

The rest of the walk is silent as I think over his words. If I'd relinquished control years ago... could I have had him? All those nights I thought about *what if*... and all I had to do was sign over my control? But no. Dylan. I'd been distracted. I'd been playing by the rules. I'd been studying, working, and being a doting girlfriend and sister. And he'd been... doing this.

I spare a glance at Chase as we get back into the lobby. His jaw is set, but not in an angry way. He's wearing his *President of Ravage Consulting Firm* face. Serious, determined, commanding. I'm about to ask if we have any further plans today when he reaches into his back pocket and pulls out his key. It's identical to mine, but it has a gold disc accompanying it. I glance down at the words.

VIP.

"This will get you into the east wing. I've already let the staff know you are with me. Please head back to the room. I'll meet you there in a couple of hours." I take the key from him and open my mouth to argue, but he continues, looking over my shoulder, before I can respond. "Order some food. You can contact any of the staff, including my personal chef, using the iPad by the door. The passcode for it is 1124. Help yourself to anything." His eyes finally land on mine. "Understood?"

I take in all of the information he's throwing at me
—VIP, iPad with a code, personal chef, and then—

My heart stills.

1124.

November 24th.

My birthday.

I suck in a few mouthfuls of air. I'm still reeling
from what we did, and this is... it's almost like my brain
is shutting down. For so long, he was inaccessible.
Unattainable. And now he's throwing keys, and
contracts, and private access, and passcodes my way
like he hardly gives a damn.

And his room... is it a part of the game? Am I
supposed to go and *wait* for him? Is this what he
expects of me this week? I'm about to ask when he
reaches out and places a hand on the side of my face.
It's oddly gentle. Romantic, even.

"I assume you have some work to do with your
dissertation. And I need to meet with The Domme
Group to finalize some things for The Hunt tomorrow."

Oh.

I nod. "Yeah, that's fine." He's not wrong. I am
woefully behind on my dissertation since every ounce
of free time over the last two weeks was spent
researching all of this. "So we're not..." I trail off.

The corners of his lips twitch, but he doesn't smile.
"I said no sex today. And I am a man of my word.
Everything else, however, is on the table."

He turns and walks away, leaving me to contemplate his words until I see him again.

Everything else, however, is on the table.

CHAPTER TWELVE
THE SCENE

Juliet

I spend nearly twenty minutes cleaning the dirt out of my hair in the shower—because yes, lying in fresh dirt meant that I needed to shower again. I try not to over-think about the fancy shampoo and conditioner in his shower, the expensive skincare, the two sets of robes. Chase did say he hadn't selected a submissive yet, but I can't help but think that all of these nice things were meant for someone else.

After I'm done applying the toners and masks and lotions, I spend the next two hours too nervous to eat as my eyes scan an article about the central nervous system and its effects on human sexual behavior. *Ha.* It takes me way too long to pull quotes to use in my dissertation, and once I'm done formatting the refer-ence, I pick through the rest of my saved articles. Every noise and creak makes me jump.

After nearly three hours, I start to get impatient. I close my laptop and pull out one of my newest library finds—a new adult college romance about a girl who makes a deal with the campus bad boy. I hardly have time to read for pleasure, but when I do, it usually entails something delicious and smutty. I still haven't changed out of the massive bathrobe after my shower, and it occurs to me that perhaps I should've.

Just as I'm about to stand up to change, I hear the electronic beep of Chase's door unlocking, and then the whirring sound of the lock opening. I stare down at my book and pretend to read as Chase walks into the living room in my peripheral.

Don't look up.

Don't be obvious.

I read the same paragraph five times, deciding to cross my legs and pretend to be invested in the paperback that, of course, has a half-naked man on the cover.

Pretend.

Don't let him think you've been waiting three hours for him like a sad puppy dog.

My eyes skim over the same paragraph a dozen more times. I want to look up, but I also want him to think that I don't care that he was gone for three hours, wondering what he was doing.

"How long are you going to pretend to read, Parker?"

My eyes snap up from the book, and I realize he's leaning against the wall, watching me.

"I'm not pretending—"

He slowly rolls the sleeve of his flannel shirt up. My mouth falls open as his lips tilt up into a cocky smirk.

An indicator I've used in the past is rolling my shirt sleeves up. So, if we're out in public and I roll them up, what does that mean for you, Parker?

"I'm going to ask again. This time, try not to lie." He rolls the other sleeve up to his elbow, and I swear I think I might be drooling at his commanding presence. "How long have you been pretending to read?"

"Since you walked into the room," I tell him honestly. "Sir."

The instant the word leaves my mouth, his eyes narrow, and I swear I see the hint of a smile play on his lips.

He nods once like he expected this answer. "I want to play a game. I'm going to count to thirty, and you're going to hide."

"In this room?" I ask, looking around.

He pushes off the wall and puts his hands in his pockets. "We have the whole third story to ourselves."

My eyes widen. "The whole third floor?"

He shrugs. "I've been trying to tell you this for years. I don't half-ass anything. I'd have reserved the whole damn castle to play if I'd known you were the one I'd be hunting."

My body tingles at his words, and I chuck my book onto the side table before standing. My mind runs through his expectations, reeling with the idea of playing with Chase. Of going through a scene together. *Finally,* my mind sings.

I open my mouth to confirm what we're about to

do when Chase walks to the opposite side of the room, grabbing a crystal tumbler and pouring himself some scotch.

"You remember the safe word, yeah?" he asks, not looking at me.

"Yes, sir."

His eyes snap up to mine, and they're... dark. Foreboding. My body shivers as his eyes run over and assess me.

Like a predator.

"Twenty-nine," he says slowly, taking a sip of his scotch without breaking eye contact. He swallows, and I watch his throat bob as he swallows. "Twenty-eight..."

It takes me another second to realize he's already counting down.

"Twenty-seven..."

It means I run.

I turn and walk to the door of his living quarters, pulling it open and staring out into the empty hallway. The dark wood. The green wallpaper. My heart is racing, and a small smile breaks out on my lips. I count down in my head so that I know how long I have until he comes to find me.

I continue walking quickly down the hallway, my eyes scanning the other doors. Some of them are open, though most of them are closed. *Hmm.* Did he premeditate this?

I push one of the doors open randomly, closing it quietly behind me. I still have eighteen seconds left, according to the timer in my head, but I don't want to risk him hearing anything. As I turn around, I am met with a view of a standard bedroom. It's nice—but small. I tug on my lower lip and look around as I wipe my palms on my robe. Where the hell am I going to hide?

But more importantly... what the hell is he going to do to me when he finds me?

And you realize that you are stuck with me for the weekend, yeah? You're mine for three days. This could change everything. I need you to understand that, Parker.

I exit the room as my eyes scan the other rooms. Twelve seconds left. On the other end of the hall, there's another suite, but that might be too obvious. Instead, I turn to the door next to the elevators, marked 'Stairwell.'

I remember reading that Ravage Castle was one of the only manors of this size to have been built with an elevator. But of course, there was still a grand staircase at the front, and a small, back staircase for emergencies.

Smirking, I pull the stairwell open and step inside. Technically, he told me I had the whole floor. While it wasn't a bedroom, I am giddy with the thought of him searching every room before he finds me.

Giddy and... turned on.

I'm not wearing underwear. I focus on the slickness between my thighs, and the rough fabric of the robe grazing my taut nipples. I take a few steadying breaths and close my eyes as I lean against the wall behind the door.

There is no holding back for me once you sign this.

I open my eyes and push all rational thoughts to the back of my mind. Instead, I focus on my breathing —on the noisy inhale and exhale. On the way my heart is pounding so hard, and how my whole body is pulsing. How my clit is already swollen and sensitive. How the adrenaline is coursing through my veins, causing a whooshing sound in my ears.

I'm scared I'll break you. And I'm scared you'll hate me for it.

I want him to find me.

I want him to unleash himself.

I want to be caught.

Three...

Two...

One.

CHAPTER THIRTEEN
THE PUNISHMENT

CHASE

I give her an extra five seconds.

The beast inside of me wants nothing more than to cheat, to find her sooner, to relish in hunting her. But I know the longer the wait, the better the gratification. And finding Parker, running from me... *hiding* from me? It's a decade of pent-up frustration, need, and desperation seeping out of my pores. The gratification of catching her could very well make everything inside of me implode.

I'm still not planning on fucking her.

This is our first little game.

Cracking my neck and then my knuckles, I grab my key and slide it into my back pocket as I exit the living quarters. My boots pad on the carpeted hallway, and I scan the doors for signs of Parker. The thing with hunting *anything* is about getting in the right mindset.

Parker isn't going to choose any of these random bedrooms. They're all the same. They all offer the same kinds of hiding places. She's too analytical for that. No, she'll find somewhere different. Because deep down, Juliet wants me to find her.

You could've had me at any point. I was always here. Always a willing participant.

I can smell her—the floral scent of fresh cut flowers. My eyes track the carpet, and I see small footprints. *Oh, Juliet. So, so easy.*

My blood thrums inside of my veins as I eye the wooden door of the stairwell. I told her the entire floor was hers. Of course she'd find the one place that's not explicitly *only* on this floor. Pushing buttons, testing boundaries. Maybe this is my chance to teach her a lesson. Her first lesson. My body sings at the notion of bending her over and spanking her.

There's nothing like the high of a chase. Especially when you close in on your prey. I am unhinged as a human when I'm playing. *Bloodthirsty.* Everything else sort of falls away.

And Parker? She's the ultimate chase. My endgame.

This is the hunt I've been waiting my entire life for.

I push the door open and turn to find Juliet grinning at me from the shadows behind the door. Without speaking, I reach out for her waist and grab her, lifting her up and hoisting her over my shoulder.

"Hey! Ravage! My ass is hanging out—"

I reach up and slap the upper part of her thigh as I carry her back to our room. "Maybe you should've worn something less flimsy, Parker."

This shuts her up.

In less than thirty seconds, I'm back inside the living quarters. After tossing my key onto the coffee table, I set her down on her feet. Her face is red, and her hair is wild as she glares at me. Her nostrils are flaring as she pants, fists clenched. I grind my jaw as I go to sit on the couch. Once I'm seated, I pat the tops of my thighs.

"Come here."

She slowly prowls over to me. The tie on her robe is loose. With one tug—

No.

I will control myself.

She goes to sit down, but I use my strength to flip her over onto her stomach, so that her ass is face up on top of my lap. She lets out a tiny gasp when my hand trails up her soft, lithe thigh.

"Ravage, what are you—"

I smack the back of her thigh with my hand. "That's the second time you've called me Ravage. Are you really going to disobey me this early on into our scene?"

She is shaking on top of me. I smooth over the spot where I slapped her lightly, rubbing it with a circular motion.

"Sorry, sir. Please continue."

"Why did you choose to hide in the stairwell?" I ask, moving the hem of the robe up to the top of her thigh. Thumbing the crease between her ass and her leg, my body hums when she gasps again.

"I wanted somewhere different—"

I smack the back of her thigh again, this time harder. She whimpers this time. "Did you forget that I can always tell when you're lying? Your voice drops an octave. Remember? Now, tell me why you chose the stairwell."

"I don't know, I—"

"Stop thinking about what you think I want to hear. There is no right or wrong answer. Why did you choose the stairwell?"

She is shivering on top of me, and with each sweep of my thumb against her crease, she jerks slightly. Her hair is fanning down her back, and when I look over at her head, she's resting her face on her forearms, facing away from me.

"I wanted to be caught."

"Good girl." I bring the bottom of her robe back down over her thighs, though I want nothing more than to bite them. When I don't do anything else, she cranes her neck to look at me.

"Is that it, sir?"

Hmm. I don't normally like brats. I don't tolerate them. But with Juliet, it sparks something inside of me. Something that makes me want to punish her— something that makes me think she *wants* me to punish her.

"Stand up and remove your robe."

She inhales twice in quick succession before she pushes up and stands. I steeple my hands as she faces me, her hands on the loose front tie. When I look up at her face, I realize she's flushed. Her hair is tangled, and her lips are wet—like she's been licking them. And her eyes... they're a dark, emerald green. Three shades darker than they normally are.

Juliet Parker *likes* this.

The beast inside of me snaps. I jump up and tug her into my body, using the ties of her robe.

"When I ask you to do something," I grit out, sliding the soft cotton material apart. "I expect you to do it."

"Yes, sir." Her voice is breathy, but her smirk is one-hundred percent *brat*.

The robe opens slightly—just enough for me to see a sliver of abdomen and a patch of hair between her thighs.

Fuck, fuck, fuck.

I've dreamed of this for so long—so *fucking* long. I use my hands to widen the gap in the robe, getting a full view of her body as the weight of the thick cotton falls off her shoulders. Finally, Juliet Parker is standing naked in front of me, and it's so much better than my dreams. Her light brown hair falls over her narrow shoulders, and my hungry eyes take her in. Narrow waist, soft stomach, wider hips, a small patch of trimmed, light brown curls, muscular thighs, and her breasts... they're fucking perfect. Pert, light brown nipples. Everything about her is perfect. *Beyond* perfect. My eyes snag on a tiny tattoo on her lower left hip bone. On anyone else, I would've found it distasteful. I don't care for tattoos, but on her? It's so fucking sexy. Especially because I know the significance.

My fingers brush over the single black rose and the stem that forms the initials of her parents' first names.

My fingers linger a little too long, and I feel her skin tense beneath my touch.

Her skin pebbles the longer I stare at it, as I take in the fact that *I* know what happened. I was there. I was the one she came to for comfort. She was a fucking kid at the time, and I treated her as such. *Broken.* She was broken. The black flowers were her mother's favorite flower. Halfeti roses. She imported seeds from Turkey as the flower was rare and only grown there. Of course, the roses aren't actually black—they're really more of a deep purple, but I know how much the flowers meant to Parker.

It's why I'd spent a fortune importing Halfeti roses for her engagement party—and why I'd been special ordering the seeds from Turkey for years, growing them at the castle as well as my apartment so I could have them around.

My eyes snap up to hers, and she's watching me with a hooded, anticipatory expression. I realize I've been raking my eyes over her body silently for at least a minute. I'm sure I've unnerved her.

"Beautiful," I murmur, running a hand along her neck to the back of her skull. Fisting her hair gently, I tilt her face up. "So fucking beautiful, Juliet."

Her hand comes to my arm, small fingers curling around my bare forearm. I almost pull away, but instead, I take a step back and drop my hold on her.

"Walk over to the dining room table," I tell her, my voice gruff.

"Yes, sir."

She turns and walks over to the wood table, her

back to me. My eyes memorize the small dimples on her back above her ass, the way her hips are slightly dipped, the smoothness of her strong thighs, the way her hair falls down to past her waist.

"Bend over," I growl.

She immediately bends at my words, placing her hands flat on the table. I study her there—prone, vulnerable, waiting.

Trusting.

She's all new to this, and yet, she trusts me completely. She must, or she would've used her safe word. Which reminds me...

"Safe word?" I ask, rubbing my palm over the smooth muscles of her ass cheek.

"Red for stopping, yellow for slow down..."

"Good. Use them if this becomes too much."

"Okay," she whispers. Her fingers curl into a tight fist. "What will you be doing, sir?"

I cock my head as I take her in some more. My cock has been hard since before I went to hunt her down, and now, seeing her here, submitting to me... I bite the inside of my cheek, restraining myself. What I wouldn't give to pump her full of my seed. To fill her completely. To watch my cum drip out of her cunt, to press it back inside of her with one finger slowly...

I won't fuck her today. Not until The Hunt tomorrow. But I can do so many other things.

"Did you think you could show up here and not be punished, Parker?"

She lets out a tiny gasp. "But—sorry—*sir*—we signed the contract, and you said—"

"You're correct. But you left me with no choice."

"I am perfectly capable of finding another Dom. Sir."

A muscle quivers angrily at my jaw. "We both know I don't share, Juliet."

Pink splotches appear on her upper back. She's nervous. A small thrill works through me.

If this is ever going to work between us, I need to be consistent and set clear boundaries. Juliet has a bratty side. I am willing to offer her guidance, as she will probably need a lot of it. My goal is to help her become confident in her role as a sub. Well-adjusted. Relaxed. She's pushing my boundaries because she's a natural leader. I love that about her. I love that she challenges everything to the point of exhaustion. But right now? During a scene?

I'm going to have to enlighten her as to why people call me sir.

CHAPTER FOURTEEN
THE REWARD

J<small>ULIET</small>

I can hardly breathe. The anticipation is killing me. Each step sends an echo of his boot through the room —and each time, it sounds a little bit closer. My whole body is on fire—from humiliation or arousal, I'm not sure. Probably both. I mean, I'm bent over a table in front of Chase Ravage, my bare ass exposed to him. *What is he looking at?* God, what if he doesn't like what he sees? Can he see how wet I am already? From just spanking?

I hear him shifting behind me, the rustle of fabric. Each noise sends excitement and fear skittering down my spine, and I'm suddenly aware of everything my body is doing. I clench and flex my hands to give myself something to do. The cool wood of the table is a balm to my heated cheek, and my nipples are burning from being pressed down into the hard table—

I gasp as his cool fingers trace up my spine. He mutters some kind of praise, but I can't hear him over the whooshing in my ears. My heart is hammering hard in my chest. I'm sure the table must be pulsing with my heartbeat. He presses me down further into the table, and I feel the edge dig into my stomach. I squeeze my eyes shut.

"Hold on," he says, amusement playing on his lips. Something hot and heady flashes through me at his words.

And then he spanks me, and I let out a loud gasp. It hurts, but not as much as I expected. My stinging flesh tingles, and at the same time, my core lurches, a curious swooping pulling at my insides. He does it again—and like last time, I feel my cunt contract around nothing. *Huh. That's... interesting.* I let out a whimper after the third one, mewling as my nipples press into the wood. Awareness floods through me, and my vision tunnels. Like earlier, I take note of everything happening to my body. The way the bottoms of my feet are starting to sweat, how my toes grip the rug so that I don't slide. How my hair is sticking to the back of my neck. How my mouth is open slightly, how I'm panting like a dog in heat.

He spanks me a fourth time, and I cry out as my pussy pulses three times. *There's no way I'll come from this, is there?*

Chase's hand comes to my ass, rubbing small, gentle circles over the area he's spanking. My skin has permanent goose bumps, and when I open my eyes, I train my eyes on the wall so that I can concentrate on something.

"Good girl. We're halfway there. Are you doing okay?"

"Yes," I mewl. "Keep going—please. Sir."

He chuckles and spanks me a fifth time, and I let out a low groan.

"How many was that, Juliet?"

God, I love the way he says my first name. It sounds so reverent on his lips.

"Five," I whisper.

"I want you to count the last three. Are you ready?"

"Yes," I tell him quickly.

He slaps me, and this time, it *really* fucking hurts. My whole ass cheek is on fire, and I claw at the table as I open my mouth to cry out. But before I can, he spanks me again, and I scream.

"Six, seven," I warble.

I am drenched. I can feel it leaking down the inside of my thighs. The only thing I can think about is how badly I need the friction between my thighs, something to graze my swollen, needy core. How one slow swipe of his fingers through my slit might be enough to get me to explode. Chase runs a cool hand over my burning skin, soothing it again. *Fuck, that's nice.*

"You're doing so good," he purrs. "After we're done, if you're good, you get a reward."

Yes, yes, yes.

He spanks me one last time, and my whole body jerks as I scream again. I can't tell if I'm crying or laughing. It all feels so confusing—the spanking hurts, but my core is fluttering around nothing, one feather-light touch away from shattering and convulsing. *Pain and pleasure.* Through my clouded senses, I remember that from my research. How they're connected. How pain can *be* pleasure, too.

I am gasping for air as I speak. "Eight," I say, feeling the sweat that's making me stick to the table, the way my hands and legs are shaking, the way I can't seem to catch my breath.

All of my blood is flowing to the wetness between my thighs, and Chase kisses my ass before running a smooth hand over the tender area. Everything is on fire —every surface of my skin. I am *burning.*

"Not so bad, right?" he asks, his voice low.

"No," I say softly.

"I never dole out pain just to hurt you, Parker. When I'm punishing you, I want you to get something out of it. I want it to bring you closer to whatever it is you're craving."

"I don't know what I'm craving," I tell him honestly.

"Are you sure?" he murmurs. "I don't think that's true. I think you know exactly what you want," he adds, running his hand up my spine again. I shiver and he chuckles. He roves lower, coming to my ass again, and I hiss in pain when his fingers brush over my sore backside. Though, the sensation makes my insides contract again—especially when his hand comes to the crease between my thigh and ass. I stiffen. *Surely, he must feel how wet I am, right?* It feels... incredible. "I think you want the same thing you've always wanted from me."

Everything is hot. Everything is pulsing. His fingers are *just* on the edge of being where I can get some friction, and I shift so that I slide him closer to the spot I need him.

It makes me feel like a harlot. Wanton. I'm still panting, still *so* wet and aroused. I could probably get off with one stroke. I am *aching* for him to touch me. I'm in a fog of sorts. Like someone could come marching through the hotel door, and I wouldn't care as long as I could hump Chase's hand until I climaxed.

"Tell me," he commands.

I inhale deeply, exhaling slowly, trying to get a grip on this feverish feeling.

Subspace.

The word clangs through me as soon as the fog clears a little bit. The floaty, detached feeling that subs sometimes get during a scene.

"Tell you what, sir?" I ask, my voice uneven.

"What you want, Juliet."

"I want to come," I tell him. "Please."

He lets out another low chuckle. "Since you asked so nicely," he growls, grabbing my hips with both hands and pulling me off the table and into his arms. Setting me down on my back, I gasp when I see how dark his eyes are, how he's clenching his jaw in concentration. How he looks completely manic and frenzied, how his nostrils are flaring every time he breathes, how he's scanning my face like he's silently telling me that he's about to devour me. He looks so galvanizing, his eyes raking boldly over every inch of my body, that it sends a tremor through me.

"Lie down, Juliet."

I do as he says. He spreads me wide with his hands, and I blush as his eyes rove over my exposed pussy. Cool air hits me, reminding me of how my arousal is more than evident.

"Fucking beautiful," he murmurs, running one hand down my thigh. "I'm going to make you come. Your orgasm is *mine*. Do you understand? Your first by another hand. And tomorrow, we will play some more. Tomorrow, you need to be prepared. This is just a small taste, but it is still mine. Understood?"

I nod vigorously, my chest rising and falling as he slides one finger down my wet seam. I arch my back and let out a throaty moan as that same finger dips into my folds. I buck my hips, which causes his long index finger to slide in all the way. I snap my eyes to his —maybe I was too overzealous—but his eyes are twinkling as he inserts another one. I gasp as he curves them, as the signet ring on his pinkie finger presses into the inside of my thigh. I squirm and whimper as he holds his fingers still—and then slowly begins to massage my inner walls. *Oh, that's—*

"So fucking wet," he mutters, bending down so that he's hovering over me. His face is right above mine, his right hand next to my head as his left hand works me closer and closer. He shifts his hips against my spread thighs.

Is that—

He moves again, telling me that it is his thick erection against my leg.

I squeeze my eyes shut. This is... too much. Knowing he's turned on—how I must look right now, needy and shameless...

He removes his fingers, sliding them up and down my slit. My eyes snap open, and he's smirking.

"Do you know how hard it is not to feast on your cunt right now, Parker? I've been waiting *years* to taste you."

I keen as he inserts both fingers again, rocking my hips against him. I reach up and grab the top of his shirt. He sucks in a shaky breath as I touch the front of his neck, the skin hot beneath my fingertips. The muscles in his neck jump at the contact. I softly brush them against his skin again, feeling his cock twitch against my calf. I lower my hand down to the seam of his jeans.

"Parker," he growls in warning, working his hand faster.

"Let me touch you," I beg. "I've been waiting for years, too."

The words leave my mouth before I realize I'm saying them, but I'm too worked up to care about how they come across. He *must* know by now how long I've had feelings for him. He'd be stupid not to see. Something passes across his features, softening them slightly. Some kind of understanding. He nods once as my fingers graze up his shirt, his neck, running over his throat, the stubble on his jaw, the sharp lines of his cheekbones. He closes his eyes briefly.

"More," I beg. "Please, sir. I need more."

His eyes snap open, looking down at me. "This is the part where you trust me to give you what you need, Parker. I know you're used to trusting that big brain that got you here. But right now? Let me take over. I'm not the kind of man to dole out scraps, letting you take what you need, making you work for your pleasure without a second thought. I. Will. Give. It. To. You."

His words slam through me as he removes his fingers again, sliding them up and down my slit. *He's right.* I trust him. And I know he won't let me down. For the first time in my life, I let go completely, leaving my pleasure in his hands fully. He slides his calloused fingers up my slit again, and I moan, adjusting my hips so that I get the friction I need. *He's right.* I've never gotten this close with someone else. He moves subtly, but I find myself pinned beneath him, unable to move any more. After giving me a wicked smile, darkened eyes gleaming, he inserts both fingers again—and then he uses his thumb to circle my clit.

"That's a good fucking girl," he grits out. "Don't you think I know what you need to get you off? Tell me, are you worried about coming now, Juliet? Because the way your pussy is squeezing my fingers, I'd think you were"—he flicks my clit hard—"Almost there."

I go mindless. My muscles go taut suddenly—like I'm careening off the side of a road unexpectedly and quickly.

"Oh, god," I mewl, feeling everything pulling, pulling, pulling down between my thighs, coiling tightly—

"What I wouldn't give to sink my cock into your tight cunt right now," he says through clenched teeth.

He's enjoying this—

It's the last thought I have before he skims over my clit again, and something sparks inside of me. I'm seconds away—

"Please," I whimper, feeling my hips jerk uncontrollably. The word slips between my lips. I'd done the research. I knew I needed to ask to come during a scene. Still, it's too much—it's all too much. "Please, sir, can I come?"

"Come for me, Juliet. Let me be the first."

His words cause my whole body to shiver. Everything releases. The muscles that had contracted in my pelvis begin to quiver, and my orgasm explodes through me, shattering every cell, every nerve ending. I buck against him as the blinding ecstasy sends white-hot flashes of pleasure through me, my heat gripping his fingers tightly as I convulse and writhe on the table. I hear him growl as he moves his fingers slowly inside of me, extending my orgasm for several more seconds. *Stars.* I see stars. My eyes are squeezed shut as the last of it leaves my body, and I sag down into the table.

When I open my eyes, I see Chase stand up and place those same two fingers into his mouth. Sucking gently, he smirks at me as he watches my reaction.

"You did well, Juliet," he murmurs. "Are you okay?" I vaguely register him rolling his sleeves down—his cue that the scene is over. Something cold slices through me. Not disappointment—but something else. Like all the warmth is suddenly gone.

"I—yeah—um—"

He chuckles, reaching down for my hand. I wince when I sit up, and he pulls my body to his, procuring my robe and wrapping it around me. I didn't realize how cold I was. I feel dazed. Limp. Like I have the chills. Shivering, he tightens my robe and takes my hand, walking us both to his bedroom.

"What did you eat for lunch?" he asks, directing me to one side of his bed.

Oh, fuck.

"I—um—forgot to eat," I admit. Maybe that's why I feel so terrible?

His blue eyes cut to mine. "You *forgot* to eat?" he asks, his voice low and dangerous.

Before I can respond, he's grabbing his phone from the living room. When he walks back in a second later, he's holding it to his ear as he gestures for me to sit down.

"Luna. Yes, everything's fine. How quickly would I be able to get some food sent up to my room?" He glares at me as he nods. "One of everything. I have a feeling she's ravenous."

After he hangs up, he walks over to where I'm sitting—rather uncomfortably.

"Lay down on your stomach," he commands. I hesitate, and his jaw clicks. "Let me take care of you, Juliet."

"I'm fine—"

"You're shaking," he growls. "It's normal. It's called a sub-drop. The adrenaline causes a crash in your endorphins. Please, lie down. I assume your research was thorough enough to include the importance of aftercare, yeah?"

"Okay," I acquiesce.

I lie down on my stomach, and then I hear him walk into the bathroom and rummage around for something. A minute later, I hear him unscrew a lid, and then the bed next to me sinks down. My eyes fall closed automatically, and he moves the hem of my robe up high enough to see where he spanked me.

"This should help," he says softly, and I grit my teeth as he rubs some kind of lotion into my skin. But then... it begins to tingle. The pain numbs a bit, and it feels nice. *Soothing.* "Vitamin E to help the healing process, and calendula to help with the burning. You will be sore for a few days..."

His voice drifts off. My body relaxes into the bed further, and I feel my legs fall open slightly before he carefully pulls my robe back down over me. The curtains in his room are mostly closed, and that mixed with the smell of the lotion, the warm bed, and the feel of Chase's warm body next to me lull me into a relaxing nap.

———

I wake up with a start, pushing up onto my arms and looking around. The light coming from behind the curtains is pink, and when I take in the unfamiliar bedroom, the memory of earlier slams into me. Sitting up quickly, I wrap my robe tightly around myself and wander out of Chase's bedroom. I expect him to be gone—to be ashamed of what we did—even though we signed a contract. However, he's sitting on the couch, bare feet propped up on the coffee table as he types something out on his computer. It's oddly domestic, and it does something funny to my stomach.

"Sleep well?" he asks, closing his computer and setting it off to the side.

I lean against the frame of the bedroom door and cross my arms. "I was told there'd be food," I tease. "One of everything, if I'm not mistaken."

His lips quirk up, but he doesn't quite smile. Instead, he stands and stretches, and I wonder how long I'd been asleep.

"Yes, well, the food came… and went. I'll order more. Still like cheeseburgers?" he asks, pulling his phone out.

"Sounds perfect."

He orders two cheeseburgers, and I look around the living quarters. A few pieces of paper are scattered over the dining room table. His flannel is laying across one of the chairs. His shoes are lined up by the door. *Has he been here the whole time?*

When he hangs up, he walks over to where I'm standing.

"I thought you would've been gone…" I trail off, realizing how silly I sound.

"Where else would I be? I wanted to be here when you woke up."

His statement is oddly sentimental and sweet.

"Why?" I ask, my voice smaller than I intended.

He gives a half shrug as he shoves his hands in the

pockets of his jeans. *This* Chase—rumpled, wearing jeans, smirking like a cocky asshole—*this* is the Chase I remember as a teenager.

The notion makes my heart beat wildly in my chest.

"It's part of my aftercare. I never leave, and I never make my submissives leave before they fall asleep if they're tired. It's important that we check in with each other."

Oh.

Right.

I open my mouth to ask him if he does this with every submissive, but he sighs.

"No, actually, that's a lie," he admits, raising his hand and rubbing the back of his neck. "I don't always care about checking in emotionally. And to be fair, it's not always needed in casual play."

"He Made Me Feel Special, and Then He Kicked Me Out": Is Chase Ravage a Playboy? Or is he Protecting His Heart?

I furrow my brows. "So, the gossip articles are true, then?"

He huffs a laugh. "I guess. Sometimes. I don't usually invite my subs to my house for that reason, but when I do, I don't kick them out. But I also don't invite them to breakfast."

I look down at my feet. "But you have me for three days," I tell him.

He nods. "Unprecedented." His eyes rove over my face, a hint of worry etched into his features. "The whole thing is unprecedented for me, Parker."

My stomach swoops at his words, but before I can ask him what he means, there's a knock on the door.

"That'll be the food," he says, giving me a wry smile. "Care to join me at the dining table?" he asks, a glint of something wicked in his eyes as he walks over to the door.

Once we're done eating a few minutes later, I lean back as Chase pushes his plate away.

"What happened before... is that normal? Was that subspace?"

He rubs his mouth with his hand. "Not quite, but I think you were well on your way there. Subspace is most often experienced when there's a lot of trust," he starts.

"I trust you," I tell him, sitting up straighter.

He nods once. "I know. But you think very analytically, which prohibits you from entering subspace fully. You were on the edge—like a pinpoint focus on the endgame." Smiling, he looks at me. "Don't worry. We'll get you there."

Oh, boy. I'm in trouble.

CHAPTER FIFTEEN

THE CONTEMPLATION

CHASE

I excuse myself after checking in with Parker one last time, heading downstairs to the study to finish some work for Ravage Consulting Firm. Right now, we're looking to purchase an important property, and though our assistants handle most of the paperwork, I still have to go through the numerous clauses I added in, and their counteroffers. There's one clause specifically that I won't budge on, and the seller's hesitation is evident in their correspondence. I send an email that's probably a bit too surly, telling them that without this clause, they will not receive the money they need to continue functioning.

After, I call Miles so that he can get me up to speed on anything else happening with the business. Our PR team has been on our asses to show ourselves at more public events, and though I'm considered a lost cause, Miles has somehow been slated to be the next eligible bachelor. Probably because he doesn't have women breaking their NDAs and flapping their lips to any tabloid that will listen.

"I wish there was a service for this," he mutters, and I hear him tapping his fingers on his desk back in his office in Crestwood. I glance at the clock on my computer. It's past nine in the evening. "You can join discreet dating services. Why doesn't anyone have a service for—"

"Finding a wife?" I ask, laughing as I lean back in one of the office chairs.

He chuckles on the other end. "You know what I mean. Business arrangements."

"I'm sure you'll figure it out soon."

"Yes, well, you know how important our public image is. Hopefully I can get this taken care of sooner rather than later."

"Jesus. It's like you're talking about a root canal instead of a marriage."

He's quiet for a few seconds, obviously off in crotchety Miles-land, before he changes the subject.

"How's the hunting going?" There's a lilt of amusement in his voice. "Catch anything interesting?"

"Fuck off," I grumble.

"So, you're telling me that Jackson's mention of Juliet being away at a conference this weekend is a coincidence?"

I grind my jaw. I hate when he pushes my buttons. I think of Parker lounging on the couch with chocolate cake, watching TV, and looking at home in her bathrobe. Knowing she's safe, knowing I have her all to myself for two and a half more days... it brings me a weird sense of accomplishment.

"I have no idea what you're talking about," I tell him, voice clipped.

"Okay. Well, I hope you have a good night's sleep. See you Tuesday. Don't forget about the thing on Friday night."

I rub my face. *Fuck.* I'd forgotten about the party at the gallery.

"Are you bringing a date?" he asks, chewing something on the other end.

"I haven't thought that far ahead."

"Right. Well, it might help our image if we have dates. Just saying."

"Yeah, yeah. I get it. I'll figure something out."

"I'm sure you will," he adds, his voice serious. "Night, Chase."

He hangs up, and I stare at my computer screen for several seconds before I close it and rub my eyes, mentally preparing myself for tomorrow.

Though tomorrow is the official first day of The Hunt, and the Dominants are supposed to use today as a warm-up of sorts for their submissives. There's no formal hunt or event—it's merely a space for people to play however they want to, in a safe, inclusive setting. Unlike my other parties, there would be no masks or timers unless required by a Dom.

Each couple would choose how they spent the weekend.

And tomorrow, I knew I'd want to play with Parker.

I stand up and grab my computer as well as the amended business contract I've been pouring over. Work can wait until next week. I sent the email I've been dreading—the email that lays out our terms and reiterates that we wouldn't budge on one of our terms. It's possible they'll walk away from the deal, but it's done now.

They can take or leave our money, and something tells me they'll take our money after making me sweat a bit.

They need me.

And I was willing to exploit that need until I got what I wanted.

I trek upstairs and unlock the door to my living quarters, finding the living area empty. The bedroom door is closed, and the light appears to be off. I glance around the tidied suite, no evidence that she was laid out on the couch with cake before I left to work. I set my computer down on the dining room table and remove my shoes. Walking over to the bar, I pour myself a small finger of scotch, sitting on the couch.

Juliet did well today. Extremely well. I'm proud of her. I wasn't sure she'd be able to hand over her power, to transfer the power she's so used to, but she did it. I think of the way she stiffened in that broom closet at her engagement party. How her eyes fluttered slightly at my command. Perhaps she's a natural submissive. The thought makes my blood heat, causing the burn of the scotch to send another wave of arousal to my aching cock.

We didn't speak much as she ate, but I could tell she was tired and wanted to decompress. Being a Dom means that I need to be able to read my subs well, and with Juliet, I knew she wanted to relax, so I left her alone. I could tell by her relaxed posture that she felt safe. I didn't want to push, either. We covered a lot of bases today, and I wanted to give her time to adjust. I would move at her pace, and that meant knowing when to pull away.

I wasn't lying when I told Parker that this whole thing was unprecedented for me. I'm losing track of the rules I'm breaking for her, but I'm finding that with each encounter, I care about that less and less.

I've wanted this, *her*—both unconsciously and consciously—for a decade.

In fact, I vowed not to touch myself tonight so that when I have her tomorrow, it would be as explosive as possible.

Years of pent-up tension, of holding myself back, of being careful and choosing my words around her.

But not anymore.

Tomorrow would change everything, and I still fully expect her to walk away from all of this—and *me* —at the end of the weekend.

But she has to learn for herself.

She's desperate to see the kind of sex that I liked, and I would show her.

But she might hate me for it.

Or, maybe she'll like it.

That small inkling of hope—the same one that

sparked through me when Louis told me she was here
—sputters to life again.

If she does like it, if she decides to continue...

It would end with every wall—every boundary I'd
ever erected—crumbling down around me.

And that thought *fucking* terrified me.

CHAPTER SIXTEEN
THE ANTICIPATION

Juliet

I sleep like the dead. Better than I have in weeks, in fact. After Chase left to get some work done, I devoured my cake and then started to get drowsy. I'd fallen asleep within seconds of falling onto his lush mattress. Between my good night's sleep and my nap, I wake up feeling refreshed and rejuvenated. He's not in the bedroom, nor did I hear him come in last night, so I decide to take a quick shower and wash my hair. When I walk into the bedroom, my phone chimes. *Jackson.* He must be up getting ready for work.

> Just wanted to make sure you got to your hotel okay. How's the conference?

> Enlightening.

Helpful for your dissertation, I hope?

I roll my lower lip between my teeth as I contemplate my answer. I obviously can't elaborate, but I also don't want to lie to my brother. Still, I can't outright tell him about all of this. Not without talking to Chase.

Of course. I'll call you later, okay?

I'm busy tonight, but maybe we can talk tomorrow?

I smile. I secretly hope he's going out with Mark. I wish I could ask him, but I don't want to push. He's my brother and my best friend. I know he'll tell me if it turns serious.

Sure. Love you.

Yeah, yeah. Love you too, Jules.

A wave of guilt washes over me. Here I am in a skimpy towel, shacking up with his best friend behind his back, letting said friend do such unsavory things like spank and finger me...

I need to tell him. Not today, but soon. We don't have secrets, and I'm not about to start keeping things from him.

I change into a pair of black jeans, a cropped, white tank top, and grab my denim jacket as well as my white sneakers. When I walk into the living area, Chase is sitting at the dining table with his laptop, sipping a cup of coffee.

An identical one sits at what I presume to be my place.

I sit across from him, but he doesn't look up at me. I blush when I think of yesterday—of what he did to me on this table.

"Thanks for the coffee," I mutter, taking a sip. "How'd you know that I like my coffee strong and bitter?" I ask, holding the cappuccino in my hands.

He glances at me over the rim of his screen. I see his dimples deepen, but he doesn't quite smile.

"If you recall, I made it for you every morning of your senior year of high school."

"And you assumed my order wouldn't have changed over the last nine years?" I ask playfully.

He closes his laptop and steeples his hands as he studies me from across the table. His eyes scan over my face, my mouth, my exposed neck... I swallow audibly as he looks back into my eyes.

"You drink cappuccinos because you're no-nonsense, Parker. You don't have time for lattes—they're too milky. And yes, there's an extra shot in there, because I know you enjoy being over-caffeinated. It helps you think," he adds, tapping the side of his head.

I open and close my mouth. I don't think anyone has ever summarized me so succinctly.

"Well, I appreciate it."

He pushes a plate I hadn't seen before over to me, and I take in the eggs, bacon, and toast.

"You should eat. I want to go over a few things with you before we start."

Anticipation stirs inside of me as I eat my breakfast. Chase continues working, his eyes flicking back and forth across his screen in concentration. He looks so... serious. Commanding. It intrigues me.

"What are you working on?" I ask, biting into my toast.

I assume he'll brush me off, but instead, he sighs and rubs his temples. Despite being well-rested, he looks tired. I quickly glance over to the couch. *Did he sleep there last night?*

"Important client," he mutters, blue eyes finding mine.

"How important?" I ask, chewing.

"Very. To me, at least."

"And what is it that you do, again?" I ask, smiling.

He huffs a laugh. "Investments and consulting mostly. Some real estate."

"And this job is important because..." I trail off, waiting for him to shut me down. Close me down. Just like he's been doing for the last eight years.

Instead, he smirks and leans back in his chair, snatching a piece of bacon from my plate.

"Saint Helena Academy is in trouble financially. I found out and offered to fund them fully. To buy them out, basically. It's a good investment. Tuition is high enough to show a return of our money within a few years."

I nearly stop breathing. Saint Helena Academy is Jackson's school.

"But?" I ask, watching his face.

"But... I had some issues with their mission statement. There are certain clauses they've had since they opened in 1901 that need revamping."

I pick at my eggs. "Is it normal for an investor to negotiate something like that?"

"Well, technically, I would be the new landlord, and as their landlord, I have certain stipulations."

I swallow, knowing exactly where he's going with this. My whole body heats under his gaze.

"What kind of stipulations?" I ask softly.

He clears his throat and looks over my shoulder. "Certain clauses in their employee discrimination clause. All businesses in California as a whole can't discriminate against someone's sexual orientation or gender identity," he starts. I wipe my palms on my jeans as he continues. "Legally, an employee at Saint Helena is protected under the California law. However, I wanted to ensure it was ironclad should that policy ever be overturned. I told them that they would need a fair non-discrimination policy on the basis of sexual orientation, among other things, which they didn't have before. Also, I want it in writing that an employee of Saint Helena can't ever be fired over their sexual orientation or gender identity or for any other discriminatory reasons."

I look down at the table, willing myself not to cry.

"To add to that, we both know that because they are protected legally doesn't mean they won't face discrimination. A recent study found that over half of LGBT employees said religion was a motivating factor in their workplace discrimination experiences. Seeing as Saint Helena Academy is Catholic, I figured I'd make sure their discrimination policies were ironclad before funding them. I can't protect every single person from everything, but I can ensure that *if* any employees are ever let go over something like this, they could wipe Saint Helena off the map with a massive lawsuit."

"I see. And why would you do that?" I ask carefully, looking up into his eyes.

He gives me a sad smile. "Like I said, it's personal in nature." I take a sip of my coffee, about to outright ask him, when he interrupts my thoughts. "He's my best friend, Juliet. I want him to be happy, and those kids make him really fucking happy. For whatever reason."

My eyes prick with tears. "That's really nice of you, Ravage."

I pick at the rest of my breakfast, sneaking glances at Chase every minute or so. He's still working, brows drawn together in concentration. Once I finish my coffee, I stand.

"What are the plans for today?" I ask.

He glances at my empty chair. "Sit, please," he adds, closing his computer and pushing it away. I sit and realize there are a few scattered pieces of paper on the table. A quick glance at them tells me they're a copy of my limits. "I want to make sure you understand the limits you marked as 'yes,' as they may come up today."

I nod. "I researched all of them, Chase. Anything I marked as a yes or maybe is fair game," I tell him.

"Even this one?" he asks, pointing to *consensual non-consent.*

My cheeks heat. "I understand the general concept,

yes. It means I give you consent now even though during the actual act, I may not be able to give you explicit and enthusiastic consent. Besides, that's what the safe word is for, correct? To stop anything that's too much for me?" His eyes widen a bit, and I feel my lips pull into a teasing smile. "I may be new to primal play, Ravage, but I wasn't born yesterday."

"And this one?" he asks, pointing to *brute force.*

I roll my eyes. "Yes, Chase. I consent. To all of it. Enthusiastically." His eyes darken when I roll my eyes, and some masochistic part of me wants to see what will happen if I snark some more. "But I guess these things only apply if you can catch me."

His nostrils flare delicately, and the paper in his hands shakes as he grips it tighter.

Bingo.

"Careful, Juliet. I already told you that I don't tolerate brats."

I cock my head. Something about the way he says it tells me that perhaps he's not being entirely truthful.

In doing my research, and after taking a few quizzes online, I'd come across the terms brat and brat tamer. Pushing Chase like this comes naturally to me. It's fun to push him, and I enjoyed submitting to him yesterday after he won.

I enjoyed the challenge of him *earning* my submission.

His dark eyes continue scanning my neck, and I have to wonder if he's ever been challenged like this. *Questioned.* Do the other women bend over backward for him?

Pushing back is fun. Being punished... *even more fun*. It doesn't feel like I'm defying him. In fact, though he says he doesn't tolerate it when I talk back, the glint in his eyes tells me that perhaps he's never had someone like me as his sub.

It feels like we're playing a game—a game I have no intention of winning, of course, per the contract.

But damn. I can't wait for the rush of domination and submission when I lose the battle.

I guess a small part of me finds satisfaction in doing something he would never allow another sub to do.

The whole thing is unprecedented for me, Parker.

He stands up and excuses himself to the restroom, saying we will head downstairs when he returns.

I walk over to my purse and leave it where it is. I don't want to risk losing it. Instead, I tuck the gold key into the back pocket of my jeans. Chase comes into the living room again, and I take in his outfit. Like me, he's dressed casually in dark jeans, lace-up boots, and a black thermal. He leaves his phone on the coffee table, grabbing two water bottles and handing one to me again.

"It will help to stay hydrated," he says, placing his key in his front pocket. "Ready?"

If I didn't know him like I do, I might brush off the way his eyes peruse my face before looking away, the way his fingers are gripping the water bottle so tightly that the tips of his fingers are white. The way his jaw is feathering.

He almost seems... nervous.

Like he's waiting for me to back down or change my mind. Though I'm not quite sure what to expect today, I trust him. And I tell him that.

"Isn't that the most important part of all of this?" I add, watching as his brows furrow slightly. "Just think of me as another one of your women," I say casually, knowing that I'm playing with fire.

He shoots me a death glare as he opens the door and gestures for me to go ahead. As I pass him, I feel his breath graze my ear.

"Somehow, I have a feeling it will be impossible to ignore who you are to me, Juliet."

I go still at his words—at the way it makes my whole body tingle. But before I can act, he places a hand into my lower back and gently pushes me out of the suite.

The elevator ride down to the first floor is silent, and I wipe my palms on my jeans. Once we get to the first floor, I glance around the empty space. I brave a quick glance at Chase, and he looks down at me with darkened eyes.

"Last chance, Parker," he growls.

I cross my arms. "You really think I'd come this far to back down now?"

He bobs his head as people shuffle out of the room. Then he rolls his sleeves up, and my mouth waters.

"No, but I know you're proud enough to see this through."

"And that's a bad thing?"

He releases a cruel-sounding laugh. When he looks back at me, his eyes—now the color of dark denim—

bore into mine. Once he finishes rolling his second sleeve up, he cracks his neck before turning his gaze back to me.

"All right. I'll give you a ten-second head start." His voice is deadly soft. Something shifted in the last minute. He went from Chase to... someone else.

Something else.

My skin tingles with anticipation as my heart hammers against my ribs.

"What do you—"

"*Run,* Parker."

CHAPTER SEVENTEEN
THE PREDATOR

CHASE

My eyes focus on the way Parker's throat bobs, the way her eyes widen like she's a deer in headlights. It only reinforces the notion of *prey* in my mind. I clench my fists at my side as she turns and runs. The pull I feel to run after her immediately is potent, and my cock hardens as I watch her slip away from me, as I close my eyes and take a deep inhale, counting to ten. My heart pounds through my veins, beckoning me forward. When I get to nine, I open my eyes, and when I get to ten, I start after her.

I pass a couple of people lounging in the formal living room, but otherwise we're alone. I don't pay them any attention. Right now, my focus is on one thing, and one thing only.

Juliet.

I see her small form slip through the back door of

the kitchen, and I clamp my jaw in displeasure. *Of fucking course.* I shake it off and follow her out of the door. She's about a hundred feet away from me, and I jog as she runs. She glances over her shoulder, a look of pure excitement on her face.

Having fun, Parker? Well, that won't do.

I want her scared. *Terrified.* If she wants to be caught, I don't want to see it. It's all a part of the game —all a part of why I play.

Twigs snap under my feet as I follow her past the pool, past the garden, and into the wild forest. She veers off the trail immediately, pushing past bushes and weaving between large trees. When she looks back over at me again, she looks a little less sure of herself. I grind my teeth as I slowly jog after her. She'll tire herself out before I have to use my full speed.

And then she'll be mine.

I push away all the doubts I had prior to this moment.

She fucking wanted this.

She wants *me.*

And I want her so fucking much that it hurts.

My cock strains against my jeans when I think of catching my prey. When I think of showing her how rough I like it and what I can do to make her fucking scream. Of claiming her in every way I physically can.

I prowl closer.

I can hear the little pants of air escaping her lips as she continues. Her endurance is impressive, but of course, it is. She's a runner. She's probably able to run through this forest for miles. She can try, but I'll always outrun her.

She turns and sprints through a clearing, heading toward a set of concrete stairs that leads away from the trees, toward the lagoon. A prickle of unease runs through me, but I push it down. Breathing heavily now, I focus on my target.

She takes the stairs two steps at a time, slowing considerably. *Amateur.* It tells me one of two things— either she doesn't train laterally, only running on flat ground. Altitude is the quickest way to slow down a seasoned runner. Or... she wants me to catch her.

My nails dig into my palms when I think of the latter.

When I think of what she's allowing me to do.

She crests the top of the hill, tripping before stumbling up and running some more.

Come on, Parker. Let me catch you.

She looks over her shoulder, and all excitement is gone. Her face is pinched with worry, and her cheeks are pink from exertion.

Let me catch you.

Let me catch you.

I'm going to catch you.

I let out a low growl when she speeds up.

She's going to make me work for it? She wants to taunt the beast? *Fine.*

I move my legs faster, panting fully now as we weave through the trees. We must be half a mile away from the castle now. Something sparks in my chest when I think of how far we're going, but I shove it deep down. *Not now. Not when I'm so close to having her.*

Fucking finally.

I run faster, a few feet from her now. I can hear her gasping for air—likely due to adrenaline rather than exertion. And then she trips—falling over a loose patch of dirt—and suddenly, she's right in front of me. Then she scrambles up, and I grab the back of her jacket, tugging the back of her body into mine.

"Got you, prey."

CHAPTER EIGHTEEN
THE PREY

Juliet

How is it possible to be so turned on from being chased? Some vital part of me must love the rush of it all, because when Chase pulls my back into his hard body, I feel myself go limp—giving up the fight completely.

He notices, his hot breath on my neck. "Giving up so soon, Parker? You ran so fast and so far, and now you're putty in my hands?"

His deep, authoritative drawl makes me whimper. He wants me to keep fighting?

I twist out of his arms and take a step back, looking up into his eyes. His pupils are blown out so that his eyes are nearly onyx. His hair is slightly disheveled, but otherwise, aside from his panting, he seems completely put together.

In his element.

As for me... my jacket is hanging off one shoulder, both knees have scrapes that I'm pretty sure are bleeding—as does my cheek. My lungs are burning, and everything feels electrified. My fingers itch to touch him, but of course that's not what he wants. He doesn't just want sex. He wants to dominate. And my job as his sub is to *let him.* Because I know with that comes my pleasure—and everything I never knew I wanted until yesterday.

I'm terrified. And... devastatingly aroused.

I take another step back, and he takes a step forward.

Come get me, I think. The sounds and sights all around me become sharper as he prowls closer. With each step, the muscles in his abdomen contract, and I lick my lips as he gives me a small, lopsided smile.

Do I keep running? Or do I surrender now?

I take a third step back, but he must be done playing with his food because he sighs and lurches forward, pinning me against a tree.

I let out a sharp breath as he chuckles. I close my eyes as he presses his body into mine, as he runs his nose down behind my ear, inhaling.

And *moans.*

"You smell so fucking good."

When he raises his head and looks down at me, his eyes are burning with need. Alluring and petrifying. *What the hell is he going to do next?*

Fear bubbles up my throat and my skin pebbles. He gives me that monstrous smile again, and it's like Chase is gone, replaced by some kind of beast. He's *fully* primal. I'm not sure he could form coherent sentences right now. And the thought makes me *burn* so fucking hot.

It makes me want to taut him. To *push* him further into that beast form.

I wasn't lying when I said I wanted to see him at full capacity.

I want to see *everything* he has to offer.

Placing a hand on his chest, I shove him backward. *Hard.*

And then I run.

I'm able to run several feet before I feel his fist in my hair, jerking me back. I fight it this time—whipping my arms around as he wrenches me against his body.

His erection presses against my ass, and one arm comes to my hips, bending me forward.

"I'm going to fuck you, Parker," he growls.

"Yes, sir," I moan, feeling him gyrate against me. I arch my back further, moving my hips against him once, twice—

"Fucking *stop.*" He fists my hair tighter, and his commanding baritone makes me go completely still.

And then he pushes me down and flips me over so that my back is on the ground. His nostrils are flaring with every inhale, and he looks *crazed.*

I feel everything else fall away as Chase quickly removes my shoes and then unbuttons and unzips my jeans. I almost move to help him, but the way he's looking down at me makes me think that he likes to work for it.

He yanks them down my legs, his eyes catching on

my bright red underwear. Growling, he fists my shirt and tugs it roughly until I hear fabric ripping.

My eyes widen as he drinks in my matching bra.

"Did you wear these for me?" he asks, leaning over me as his thumb brushes my taut nipple. "Bright red, like you fucking *want* to be caught? Like you're a *target*?"

I stifle a moan. "Yes, sir."

He hums, reaching down and peeling my underwear off slowly before he reaches around my back and unhooks my bra. He jerks it off my chest, and suddenly, I am bare before him again. I feel the dirt digging into my back. My pulse is beating against my veins. As he sits back on his heels, I let my legs fall apart, and his jaw hardens as he watches me.

His eyes are coal-colored and hooded—and glowing with a savage inner fire.

My hand moves along my stomach, reaching down, *taunting* him, and as I get to my glistening seam, he snatches my wrist in his hand in one swift motion, grabbing my other hand and holding them over my head. His face is inches from mine, and I see a flash of red before he begins tying my wrists up with my panties.

"Be a good girl and stay still," he murmurs, his voice deep and rich like velvet.

I nod, assuming he's going to unbuckle his belt and have his way with me, but instead, he grabs my legs and drapes them over his shoulder.

"What are you—"

"Quiet, prey."

I tremble at his words, already so fucking wet. Already so fucking ready. He trails his mouth down my stomach, and my hands twitch, wanting to come down to his head and pull him down to me.

Before I can register what he's doing, he grabs my hips, pulling my core up to his face, and licks down my slit once, his nose brushing down my center as he audibly inhales.

"I can smell how aroused you are," he mumbles, his lips against my opening. "You smell like roses, do you know that?" he adds, and I moan.

His teeth graze the inside of my thigh, and he bites down. I cry out, lowering my bound-up wrists instinctively. He growls and in one violent jerk, pins my hands above my head again.

Heat blisters through me, and I buck my hips, needing him, needing the friction of his tongue, his lips.

He grips my ass as he pulls me up slightly, and then he dives back in, laving his tongue up and down roughly.

"Oh, fuck," I whisper, my voice shaky.

He goes slow at first, the low purrs coming out of his mouth giving me goosebumps. And then he speeds up, adding one finger, and I feel myself clench around him.

"So eager," he mutters. "So wet. I can't wait to sink my cock deep inside of you, Parker."

I moan. *Such a filthy mouth.* If I'd known... all these years...

I push the thoughts away as everything in my

vision blurs around the edges. As Chase's tongue rolls against my swollen nub, flashes of pleasure shoot through me, and his finger massages the perfect spot, using just the right amount of pressure. And then he squeezes my ass with his other hand, right over the area he slapped yesterday, and I keen.

"Holy shit," I hiss, feeling my core flutter around his finger.

He spreads my legs further before inserting a second finger between my folds.

I can feel something wet sliding down my ass, but I have no idea if it's me or his spit. His nails dig into my ass again, and I let out a throaty groan, seeing stars.

Everything clouds around me, bringing my focus to him and only him.

I can feel myself breathing heavily, can feel my heart racing in my chest, against my cunt as Chase pulses his fingers in and out.

"Can you hear how wet you are, Parker?" he asks, looking up at me briefly.

I prop myself up on my elbows to look at him, ignoring the pinch of dirt against my skin, and I know my eyes are half-lidded as I take in his wet mouth, his dark eyes. He moves his fingers inside of me, and my eyes roll into the back of my head. "Your cunt is *weeping* for me."

Fuck.

I feel my core squeeze his fingers as they crook upward on every pull out, as he swipes my clit with every push in. His forearms flex with every movement, and it suddenly occurs to me that this whole thing will give me a fetish for forearms.

His signet ring digs into my inner thigh, and I whimper when I think of how dirty this is—fucking his hand on the floor of the forest, him fully clothed, screaming with pleasure... and waiting for him to take me roughly, no holds barred.

Everything coils tight, ready to explode.

I whine and blubber something unintelligible, squirming under him as he watches me climb right to the edge of my orgasm.

"Don't come, Juliet."

I whine as he pulls his fingers out of me. My legs tremble on his shoulders.

I want to scream. *Beg.* My whole body is shaking, on the cusp of something powerful. I roll my lower lip between my teeth as he gives me a cocky smirk. Like he's *waiting* for me to talk back.

"Yes, sir," I tell him, trying to keep my voice from quivering.

"My one regret," he says slowly, lowering my legs and working his belt quickly, "is that I didn't have my cock inside of you when you came yesterday. Feeling you squeeze me. Knowing I was—*am*—the first to make you scream."

My breathing hitches as he unbuttons his jeans. He slides the zipper down slowly. It's *torture.* I want to see it—I want to *feel* his cock. I'm aching for it.

He shoves the waistband of his boxers down, unsheathing his cock, and fuck. It's perfect, because of course it is. Long, thick, already hard and seeping with precum...

"You're drooling, Parker," he teases, running his hand over it once.

"Chase," I whisper, feeling desperate.

"Do you really think I'd go through all this trouble and *not* fuck you, Juliet?" His words send a shockwave of warmth through me. "No, I've been waiting too long for this."

"How long?"

The words leave my lips before I realize what I'm asking.

He reaches forward, inserting two fingers into my pussy before pulling out and using the wetness as lube on his shaft. His throat bobs, and his mask slips for a second. Instead of the dark predator, I see my friend. His eyes get bluer, and his expression is almost anguished.

"Too long. Too long to control myself, Parker," he whispers.

I swallow. "I don't want you to control yourself. Give me everything."

His eyes darken again as he nods once, spreading my legs and crawling on top of me. I feel his thick head press against my core, and he angles himself to drive into me.

"You fucking asked for it," he mutters.

And then he roughly slams into me, burying himself to the hilt.

I gasp, throwing my head back, but his hand snakes around the back of my hair, tilting my face up to look at him. His mouth is open, and he pulls out before sinking into me again.

"Look at me," he commands.

I nod, but it's too much. He's stretching me in the most amazing way. *Perfect.* It burns, and then it doesn't, giving away to an ache that scares me. An ache that's a precursor for something that's never happened to me before.

"Juliet," he whispers, running another hand down my neck.

He's not asking me anything—he's saying my name—and *this* is what I wanted all those years ago. This connection. The way our bodies fit together perfectly. He hitches one of my legs higher, allowing him to sink deeper, and I fight the urge to squeeze my eyes shut.

"Chase," I moan.

He quickens his pace, and I see the darkness slide over his pupils again. He's fighting it—the predator and my friend are clashing. It occurs to me that perhaps I've always been something more to him. Growing up. The engagement party. All of it. This is everything for me, but maybe it is for him, too.

He pulls slowly out, and then he plunges into me. An inferno of red-hot heat sweeps through me, and white stars dance in my vision. He does it again—rougher this time—so that the dirt underneath me scrapes into my skin. I hiss, but it doesn't hurt. Not when he's doing this to me.

He quickly pulls my hitched-up leg fully over his shoulder and places both of his hands near my shoulder. He's relentless, going deeper now, and I hum my satisfaction. *Loudly*.

"Such a good fucking girl," he growls. "Taking my cock so well. Tell me," he adds, his voice rough. "How long?"

I know what he means instantly, and I fight to close my eyes. My hands move to his back, and I scratch him —*hard*. His eyes flutter closed briefly before he opens them again, fucking me into the ground with abandon.

"Since before my parents died."

He stops moving for a second—just enough for me to read the expression on his face. I thought he looked anguished before, but now?

He swallows once, jaw ticcing, and then he huffs a laugh. "We're both fucking idiots."

I open my mouth to retort when he places both hands on my hips, pulling my ass off the ground a couple of inches. He digs his nails into me, and I briefly notice the way his ring is pressing into my skin.

Like he's branding me.

The change in angle sends me flying, and I feel everything inside of me go taut as he rocks into me.

"Fuck," he whispers, letting out a tormented groan.

I open my mouth to scream, but then I remember the rules.

"Please, sir, can I come?" I ask, tilting my hips more to get the friction I need.

"Beg for it."

I gasp as he continues his relentless pace. With every hard thrust, he knocks the breath from my lungs. *Fuck*.

"Please," I whisper. "Please, Chase. Please let me come. I need your cock. I need you to fill me up."

He squeezes my hips harder with his rough fingers, and a small part of me realizes he's going to leave bruises. And possibly break the skin where his nails are cutting into me.

"Fuck," I whine. "Please. I want to feel you cum inside of me."

He lets out a pained growl, pulling out and slamming back in. "I know you do. Your greedy little cunt keeps squeezing me. I want you to come for me, Juliet."

Just like yesterday, one hand comes to my clit, and all it takes is three rolls of his thumb over my aching bud for me to shatter around him.

Chase's words flutter in and out of my consciousness as my back arches, as my core grips him over and over and over. Something about *dying for my cock for years* and *going to fill you so full of my cum*. My eyes roll back as my hips jerk and stutter, as electricity shoots through me, making my fingers and toes curl as I tremble underneath him. I go boneless, feeling something slick between our bodies. Did I just—

"Such a perfect girl," he murmurs, pushing his cock into me slowly as he watches where we're joined. "Fuck, that felt so fucking good."

I look up into his eyes, and he's rocking into me slower now. *He's close.* I can feel by the way his hands on my hips are trembling slightly. The way his mouth falls open when I smirk and clench my inner walls around him. Jaw tight, his lips twist into a threatening scowl, and he stops moving.

And then one hand comes around my neck.

My body instantly heats up again at the possession written all over his expression.

"Don't try me right now, Parker. You're going to come again for me before I do."

His words reignite the maelstrom. "I don't know if I'll come again," I tell him honestly.

His eyes blaze into mine. "Is that a challenge?"

"No. I'm being honest."

He squeezes his hand tighter around my neck at my defiance. And I realize... I've placed him in the same box as the other guys. Unable to get me off like the rest of them. He snaps his hips roughly, and I see white spots in my vision as he chokes me harder. But instead of being scared, I feel myself awaken for him again.

Even *I* can't get myself off twice in a row. It takes too long. It—

"I felt that. I felt you get wetter the instant I tightened my grip." I groan, and he chuckles. "What have I been telling you? Trust me, Parker."

His words send me flying somewhere I've never been—almost like an alternate universe where he knows my body better than I do. Because he does—every single interaction with him has been amazing. And that trust? It clicks right into place, more airtight than before. *Unbreakable.* Like he's always been the one inside of me.

My vision swims in front of me, and I feel that needy, frenetic energy flow into me again. *Subspace.* I feel my whole body relax further, feel myself give into him fully. It's done fighting. The only thing I can focus on is the feel of his cock sliding into me. The feel of his calloused fingers around my neck, squeezing. The feel of his other hand, and his ring, painfully pressing into my skin.

"Do you know how long I've been waiting for this?" he mutters, and I watch him as he lowers my leg, allowing himself to crawl further on top of me. He dips his head and licks my neck. I rasp his name. "How long I've been dreaming of sinking into your pretty, little pussy. How long I've wanted to mark you with my cum. Watch as it spills out of you. Knowing you were *mine*."

I whimper, feeling the familiar tug of all of my muscles coiling tight inside of me. I want it. I want his cum, want all of it. He fucks me with punishing strokes, bringing both of my knees higher. The sensation is exquisite, and I feel my cunt flutter around his cock. He's fucking me so hard that we've moved a couple of feet from where we started. My back is burning from being pressed into the dirt, but I like it. I want this.

He presses a thumb against my clit, electrocuting me and making me jerk as my orgasm begins to build. I'm keening now, scratching his arms as he pistons into me. He doesn't move his thumb—allowing the movement of our bodies to get me off.

"Oh fuck," I whisper. "I'm—so—"

"Now," Chase hisses. "Come with me. *Now*."

I unravel at his words, undulating under him as he clenches his jaw. And then his face slackens, and I scream, feeling my orgasm claw through me quickly.

I'm lighter fluid, and he's the match. My whole body tingles and sparks, sputtering and jerking. My nails break the skin on his arms. His cock goes taut and curves inside of me, and he hits my cervix with every rough jerk of his hips, ensuring he stays as deep inside of me as possible. His fingers grip me firmly as I shake, as I moan, and ride out my release.

Finally, he goes still, resting his forehead against mine. I'm not sure if I'm the one shaking or if it's him. Either way, we both twitch with aftershocks. When he pulls away, his eyes are blue again as he looks down at me, and his face and neck are glittering with sweat. The front part of his hair is wet, and I can see his pulse jumping in his neck. He's trying to catch his breath, his fingers working in slow circles over my hips.

"Juliet—"

I reach up to his head and pull him down, kissing his mouth quickly before moving down his jaw. Sucking, *licking*, tasting him. Tasting how hard he worked to bring us both pleasure. *God, I'd do anything for him. Right now, I'm completely at his mercy.* I continue laving my tongue up and down his neck, moaning when my tongue is met with the taste of salt and musk. His cock twitches inside of me when I suck, squeezing my legs tightly around him at the same time.

I feel feral. I want to lick him all over, want to touch and pull and maul him. He must be able to tell, because I feel him chuckle on top of me.

"As much as I want your tongue all over me, Parker, I need to make sure you're okay."

"I'm fine," I grumble.

He pushes off me, pulling out of me at the same time. I expect him to stand up, but he puts his still-hard cock away and sits back on his heels, looking down at me bared before him. His eyes close as he inhales once, running a hand down his face before he looks back at me and exhales.

"Do you know how *fucking* long I've been waiting to see my cum drip out of your tight, pink, overly-fucked cunt?"

Something sharp and sweet lances through me at his words.

Even though he hasn't rolled his sleeves down, I assume the scene is over, so I smile as he stares down at my wetness.

"Just think... you could've had me eight years ago."

His eyes narrow slightly as he brings his eyes to mine. "Watch your tone, Parker. The scene isn't over."

"It isn't?"

He chuckles, reaching forward and pressing a finger into my sensitive core, pushing his cum back inside of me. I moan when he does, and his eyes go dark again.

"Not even close." Once he's satisfied it's deep inside of me, he removes his finger and licks it slowly, keeping his eyes on mine the entire time. "I must confess, Juliet," he drawls, his voice a low purr. "I held myself back, and I still need more of you. Of this. Of feeling you squeeze my cum out of me." I try not to gasp, but my breathing stutters at his words. I open my mouth to reply, but he shakes his head. "Right now, however, I want to take care of you."

My chest aches at his words, and he sits me up, walking around to my back and gently dusting me off. I hiss when he runs his warm hand over a sensitive spot that I'm pretty sure is bleeding, or close to it.

"Fuck," he says through gritted teeth. "Maybe I didn't hold back as much as I thought I did."

I swallow. "It's fine. Sir."

I feel his head snap up, but I don't turn to look at him. He helps me stand, brushing me off and offering muttered curses any time he sees the slightest blemish on my skin. When he comes back around to my front, he studies my neck for a second too long, and I know it's already bruised from where he choked me. His eyes skirt down my breasts to my hips, and then he's reaching a hand and touching something on my lower hip. I follow his gaze, seeing the telltale 'R' of his signet ring forming a purple bruise below my hip bone, almost on my inner thigh.

I hear him emit a low growl as he traces a finger over it, and then he looks back up at me. Something greedy and covetous passes over his expression.

"You're mine," he growls.

I notice he doesn't say *today,* or *for the duration of this scene,* or even *this week.*

His.

But for how long?

He helps me into my underwear and bra, and when I scowl down at my ripped shirt, he chuckles and pulls his thermal off, offering it to me.

I try not to audibly inhale as I pull it over my head,

but I can't help that the smell of him makes me dizzy with desire.

I step into my jeans and shoes, and then I look up at him. Shirtless. Waiting. What's his next move? Just as I open my mouth to ask, he cocks his head toward the trail ahead of us.

"Let's go on a walk, Parker."

CHAPTER NINETEEN
THE WOODS

Chase

We walk deeper into the forest, and I blame the haze of fucking her for losing track of time, for not keeping tabs on where we're going, or how long we've been walking. I pepper her with questions about her dissertation under the guise of her Dominant. I know she's still sort of in subspace—so I'm probably taking advantage of the situation when I inquire about Dylan. When I ask about his inability to get her off. When I probe her for information about her other partners.

I try not to act jealous when she tells me about them. About having her, about the first guy to ever fuck her, not even ensuring she was ready. *It hurt.* That's what she tells me.

I make a mental note to find out who he is, but before I file it away for later, she stops and looks at the ground.

"At least I got an A in his class."

I stop walking as blood rushes in my ears. "*What*?" I hiss.

Her large eyes dance and skate over mine with apprehension. She looks so fucking small in my shirt. Vulnerable. Innocent. I'm suddenly filled with self-loathing, but I take a step toward her.

"He was my professor freshman year. He felt exotic because he was fifteen years older than me. We all went out for drinks one night after the class ended for the semester, and I'd had one too many drinks—"

"Are you telling me that your professor took your virginity?" I don't mean to growl the words, but they come out harsh. Accusatory. She flinches at my tone. I reach for her hands and pull them to my mouth, kissing the inside of each of her wrists once. "Tell me."

She shrugs and steps into me, and I pull her into a tight hug. "He took me back to his place. I was drunk, but he didn't take advantage of me. Don't worry. I wanted it. I was a freshman. I wanted to get it over with. As you may remember from... that night with you."

I grit my jaw against her scalp. "Jesus, Parker. I told you, seven-course meal—"

"I wanted it to be you. I pretended—I pretended it was you."

My fingers fist the material of her—*my*—shirt. I pull her closer, inhaling the scent of her hair. Wrists, cunt, hair—my three favorite scent markers. They all smell different, but they all smell like *her*.

"He was at the engagement party, actually. He works in my department."

I drop my arms and step away. My jaw is clenching uncontrollably, and I'm afraid I'm going to break my teeth from grinding them so hard.

"He does?"

She nods, looking unsure. "Yeah. Professor Landon. Fate brought us together again last year when he was assigned as my mentor. But he's not anymore." Her eyes crinkle at the corners, but she doesn't smile. "I was with Dylan though, one of his star students, so he never—it was never an issue after that first time."

I inhale and rub my jaw. "Okay."

She looks at me skeptically, almost like she's unsure that I'm actually dropping the subject. *Ha.* If only I could drop it. I file his name and this conversation away to deal with when I'm back in Crestwood.

We continue walking, and she tells me more about her work. It's fascinating. I watch the way she lights up when she talks about her dissertation, about the academic journals she works on, about the papers she plans to write once she's settled into a job this fall. I try to look casual as she continues babbling about moving to whatever university will take her, and again, I file that tidbit of information away. Perhaps someone like Liam Ravage—my eldest brother and a creative writing professor—needs to make some calls to local universities.

I shake the thought away. *Two days.* That's all we have.

I have no claim on her, despite everything inside of me screaming to possess her.

"And, anyway, I don't know what I'll do about my house. I'd planned on selling it after Dylan and I were married, but—"

"Sell it?" I ask, surprised.

"Yeah. Dylan didn't like it. He thought it was too small."

Fucking hell.

If I'd been anyone else, I might not know about how much that house means to Juliet. How it reminds her of her parents. How the kitchen is basically crumbling, but she refuses to renovate because it's the last thing she has of them.

She cried for a week when I installed a new dishwasher three months after they died.

"Did he know how much you love that house?" I ask carefully.

"Of course. But it *is* small, and I wanted him to be happy—" she prattles, walking ahead of me.

I tug at her elbow, pulling her back. "Add this to your stipulations for future partners then," I growl, and her light green eyes bore into mine with surprise.

"Stipulations?"

I nod once. "I know how much you love a good list." I smirk.

Her cheeks flush, and *fuck,* she's so goddamn beautiful.

"One, they must treat you like a seven-course meal." Her breathing hitches, and I love the way her throat bobs, the way her chest stutters whenever I talk dirty to her.

"Two, do you remember what I told you when you came to the party at my apartment?"

She nods, but I tell her anyway.

"You must *know* that you hold his heart in your hand. You need someone who will love you with every cell in his body."

She swallows, and I place a hand over her throat, my thumb brushing the impossibly soft skin there.

"Three," I add, my voice gentler. "They must be okay living in that house until the day *you* decide to sell it. And maybe that's never. And they have to be okay with that. Am I making myself clear?"

Her eyes search mine, and I can tell she's coming to her own conclusions. *Not me, Parker. I wish I could. I wish I could give you everything that you want, and more. I'd give you the whole fucking world.*

"Okay," she says finally.

When she takes a step backward, she trips and falls before I can catch her, yelping as she goes down. In a heartbeat, I'm crouching down next to her, helping her up. A cold sweat breaks out along my skin when I see the blood trickling down her temple.

"Fuck, Juliet," I hiss, pulling her closer, my eyes frantic as I take in her glazed eyes. "Are you okay?" I reach up and push her hair back, seeing the deep red gash on her hairline. "You hit your head," I murmur.

"It's fine. I'm fine, Chase—" She practically falls into my arms when she tries to take a step.

I look down and feel the blood draining from my

face. "You hurt your ankle," I growl, dropping to my knees and gently pulling the hem of her jeans up. "It's already swollen. Fuck," I mutter, standing up as I run a hand down my face.

Bile rises up my throat when she turns to face me, face bloody and eyes glassy. I look around. We must be a couple miles from the castle at this point. No phone. No way to call for help. My chest rises and falls rapidly as I walk to a nearby rock, closing my eyes to ward off the panic creeping up.

"Chase?"

Her voice is far away, lilted with worry. I'm such an ass. She's the one hurt, and I can't get a grip. *Fuck. Fuck. Fuck.*

Just like when I was a kid.

Just like when Miles almost died.

Just like *my worst fucking nightmare.*

I take a couple of steadying breaths.

This is different. I know this land now. Made it a priority to learn it in case my father decided to leave us in the woods again. Rationally, I know we're a few miles from the road that intersects the forest, and that the castle is behind us. If we don't turn up, Luna will send someone to come find us. Jackson will organize a search party. This *won't* be like last time.

It *can't.*

"Chase?"

My arms go out to Juliet's shoulders. Through the panicked fog, I know how to take care of her. I pull her gently into my body, using her small form to calm myself. *Inhale, exhale.* I feel my fingers grip her tightly.

Hear her murmur something comforting as my heart races inside of my chest, as my stomach lurches, threatening to spill my breakfast all over the ground. *Inhale, exhale.* Her scent is comforting. *She* is comforting.

"What's wrong?" she says, and her voice cuts through the panicked fog. Slices right through it. Clear, resolute. "I'm okay. I promise."

Inhale, exhale.

I quickly and gently pick her up, holding her in my arms and close to my chest. She's lighter than I thought she would be.

"I can walk," she mutters, smirking.

But all I see is the blood—dripping into the dirt on the ground. I take another steadying breath as flash-backs whip through me.

"It's fine. You hurt your ankle," I answer roboti-cally. *Calm the fuck down, Ravage.*

She looks up at me with an unsure expression as I walk back in the direction I *think* we're supposed to go. But then she nods and rests her head against my chest as I carry her through the forest like fucking Tarzan.

Never again.

I told myself I'd never go into the forest again, and here I am, breaking all of my rules for her.

CHAPTER TWENTY
THE BLUFF

JULIET

Chase is quiet as he carries me through the woods. I try to adjust myself in his arms so that he can carry me easily. I'm a runner, but I'm not the lightest or smallest person ever. However, each time I move slightly, he grips me tighter, as if he's trying to hold me as close as humanly possible. Whenever I sneak a glance up at him, he's scowling and staring at the trail ahead, his jaw rigid and his eyes taking on an empty, faraway look.

I have no idea why he reacted the way that he did. Why he seemed completely spooked when he saw the blood that was currently drying. When he inspected my ankle—which is still throbbing with every movement.

I *would* trip over myself and sprain my ankle. Juliet Parker... ever graceful.

I contain my smile as we continue walking. I don't know if we're still in the scene. If I should initiate small talk. I let out a giggle at the thought of asking him about the weather.

"Something amusing, Parker?"

Despite carrying me and walking at a brisk pace, he doesn't seem winded at all. It puts my fitness to shame —and I run twenty miles a week.

"You're so brooding and quiet."

He frowns but doesn't look down at me. "Brooding?"

"Yeah. I'm okay. In fact, I'm pretty sure I could walk back—"

"Not happening."

I open and close my mouth a few times, deciding on my next course of action, when he begins speaking.

"Your brother said the same thing about me. That I was brooding."

I grin. "Of course he did." And maybe it's because I may have a concussion, or because we had sex—*God, I'd nearly forgotten*—but I blurt out the first thing that comes to mind. "He's the exact opposite of you. I never understood how you two became friends."

This elicits a rumbling chuckle from him. "He's never told you how we became friends?"

"No. I mean... I was young. Nine, I think, when you met."

"You were. I remember meeting you. You didn't look up from whatever book you were reading on the couch. Your parents were cooking, and Jackson and I had come inside from playing football outside. You had on these pink cat ear headphones..." he trails off.

My heart pounds against my ribs as a thousand emotions claw through me. "You remember that?"

"Of course I do."

I bite my lower lip so that I can ruminate on his words for a minute, but he continues talking.

"I remember you and Jackson were new to Saint Helena," he starts, adjusting his hands under my knees as he walks.

I snort. "We were so out of our league. But my parents had come into some money and wanted us to have the best education."

"I was sitting in algebra class, trying to ignore the taunting from the other kids. Something about my driver, about my father being too drunk to drive me to school," he says, his voice low. I swallow thickly. "And in walks this gangly, happy-go-lucky guy with thick, horn-rimmed glasses. He was *so fucking* sure of himself. I wasn't paying any attention to him. I assumed as a new student, he would be trying to fit in and he wouldn't want anything to do with me. But then he sat down in the seat next to me, introduced himself, and when I said my name, he looked completely unfazed."

I go completely still as he continues his story.

"And then he followed me out of class, and I turned around and told him that he didn't need to put on a show. That he must know who I was, must know the story of my father, of our family. But Jax cocked his stupid head and said, 'Yeah. I know who you are. You're Chase.'"

I huff a laugh. "Sounds like him."

Chase chuckles again. "Anyway, despite my suspicions, he hung out with me day and night. Standing up for me. Welcoming me into his family, which, at the time, was completely different than mine in the best way possible." He stops walking for a second, and I look up at him as his brows flicker with uncertainty. He looks down at me. "You asked me earlier why I was taking on Saint Helena Academy as a client. It's because of Jax. Because I have the capital and the resources to change his environment. Whether he chooses to utilize the new clause or not, it's there for him. I did it all for him."

My eyes prick with tears as he walks on, and we're quiet for the rest of the walk.

Thirty minutes later, we're entering the back door of Ravage Castle. Chase sets me down on a stool and walks over to the iPad charging on the counter, tapping a few buttons.

"I'll have Luna call for a doctor," he mutters, tapping the screen.

"Chase," I warn, sighing. "I'm fine."

He ignores me, bustling around the industrial kitchen shirtless as he grabs a bottle of water for me.

"Drink," he commands. "I'll get some food for you."

I take a few sips, but then I shake my head, which makes me wince. "I'm not hungry."

He turns to face me. "Are you nauseous?"

I shrug. "Kind of."

He bends down and props his elbows on the island, running a hand over his face.

"Fuck. You probably have a concussion."

Just then, Luna bustles in, wearing an elegant jumpsuit and red heels. She stops when she sees me.

"Oh dear." Walking quickly over to the pantry, I see her pull out a first-aid kit. "Dr. Hatchens is on his way," she tells Chase, and he nods tightly. His fists are balled at his sides. His eyes scan my body quickly before he continues making me a plate of food. Luna walks over with rubber gloves, a disinfecting wipe, and a piece of gauze. "Tilt your chin up," she says, and I hiss when she cleans the blood off with the wipe. "I don't think she needs stitches. The gash is shallow."

Over the next few minutes, Chase pushes a plate of crackers, gourmet cheese, and fruit over to me. I eat slowly as Luna finishes cleaning me up. Dr. Hatchens arrives, and it's decided that I don't have a concussion, but that I should be resting for the next forty-eight hours. He examines my ankle, too, and tells me to stay off it. I try not to pout when I realize that means no more running through the woods this weekend.

The entire time, Chase is leaning against the wall furthest from me, looking like someone gave me a goddamn death sentence.

By the time I finish eating, Luna offers to help me to the east wing, but Chase picks me up, thanks her for her help, and carries me to his living quarters.

After he sets me down on the couch, I see him walk over to the large window. My eyes skate over to the coffee table, and I quickly check my phone, responding to one of Jackson's texts. By the time I look back up at Chase, he's watching me with crossed arms.

And though the scene is presumably over, he still has a wild look about him—his eyes are scanning me, but in a different way this time. His face is completely closed off—his expression is emotionless as he sighs, running a hand through his hair.

"What's wrong?" I ask.

It jolts him out of whatever dark trance he was in. "You're hurt."

My lips quirk up. "You heard the doctor. I'm going to live," I add, rolling my eyes.

He takes a step forward. "Listen, maybe we shouldn't—"

"Stop," I beg, already knowing where this is going. "Don't use this as an excuse to push me away. I tripped on a rock. It's not like you threw me down onto the ground and—"

"I could have."

I swallow and take a deep breath before answering. "I tripped. What you did—what *we* did—it was incredible. I'd like to continue with the weekend as planned."

He huffs a laugh. "I don't think that's a good idea, Juliet."

My skin begins to tingle, and I grind my teeth together as I try to keep my voice calm and level. "You can't be serious. You heard the doctor. I can't run, but that doesn't mean I can't do other things."

He inhales sharply and turns to the window. *Stupid, brooding man.*

"Do you know where the name Ravage originated from, Parker?"

His question catches me completely off guard. "No."

I see his shoulders straighten as he continues gazing out of the window, facing away from me. "It's a French term. Originated in the 1600s. It means to desolate by violence. To commit havoc or devastation. To spoil, to plunder. To *consume*."

His low murmur sends shivers down my spine. "Okay. And?"

He turns around, his eyes still wild and dark. "Isn't it obvious? I ruin things. It's literally my namesake. We all do. It's like the name haunts us."

Everything clicks into place slowly. "You mean you and your brothers, right?"

He nods, thumbing his chin. "Yes. My family ruins things. And you..." His throat bobs as his eyes scan the bandage that the doctor placed over my gash. "You're like a rose that got tangled in a bed of thorns."

My breathing hitches at his words. "I see where you're coming from, Ravage." A look of surprise passes over his face before he goes back to sulking. "But I think you've forgotten that roses have thorns, too."

His jaw tics as he looks away. "That may be true, but I do still think it's best if you leave."

My pulse races through my veins, and everything feels hot and cold all at once. I stand up a bit unsteadily, and Chase twitches before I hold a shaking hand up. He wanted to continue playing games? *Fine.* I could play his game. I was always capable of playing his game, but he's always too busy underestimating me to notice.

"Okay. I'll go pack my things."

I swear I see his face pale a bit. His stiff posture breaks for a second, like he's about to reach out for me, but then he presses his lips together and nods.

I'm about to turn toward the bedroom when an idea forms in my mind.

"Can you please help me change clothes?"

He stiffens but nods, walking over to me and helping me into his bedroom. Before he can react, I pull his shirt over my head and toss it into the corner. When I turn to face him, his eyes are not on my face.

"Pants too, please."

Did you wear these for me? Bright red, like you fucking want to be caught? Like you're a target?

He steps forward, and I exaggerate my limp as I meet him halfway. His hands move to my waistband, and when his thumb grazes my sensitive skin, I let out a tiny moan.

He goes completely still, and I watch the way his chest is rising and falling. "Juliet," he warns, glaring down at me.

"Are you going to help me out of my jeans?" I say, completely ignoring his warning.

His nostrils flare as he unbuttons and unzips them, tugging them down my legs. As he goes lower, I place a hand on his shoulder and take the tiniest step forward so that his face is inches from my core. I step out of them slowly, and I don't exaggerate the wince that leaves my lips when he gently pulls my bad ankle out of the leg hole.

He's standing in the next second, taking a step back.

"Thanks," I mumble, my eyes catching the stiffness in his pants with a satisfactory smirk. "On second thought, I might take a quick shower." When my gaze moves to his, I see both sides of him warring each other as he looks away from me, scantily clad in my bright red bra and underwear. The side that thinks he wants me to leave... and the side that *really* fucking wants me to stay. "Do you think you could help me so that I don't fall?"

His expression is deranged when he looks up at me.

Marching forward with determination, I yelp when he pushes me roughly against the wall, somehow managing to lift me slightly so that I don't hurt my ankle.

"I know what you're doing, Parker. I can see right fucking through you."

I narrow my eyes as my hands wrap around the back of his neck, as my legs come up and wrap around his waist.

"And I see right fucking through you, too, Chase."

His eyes flicker back to blue briefly before darkening again. "And what is it that you think you see?" he growls. His calloused hands come to my hips, running along the curve of my ass.

A breathy moan leaves my lips. "Stop with the idle threats. They mean nothing to me. I know you want this. I know you want me, so stop trying to make me walk away."

His chest is rising and falling rapidly as his eyes bore into mine. "Fine."

"Fine," I acquiesce.

"You would've walked out of that door just to prove a point," he says, something akin to amusement dancing over his features.

"Damn right, I would've." I lift my hands to his neck, and he tilts his head slightly, leaning into the touch. My right palm comes to the side of his face, resting against his scruff. *God, he's so fucking beautiful.* "I told you before. You don't scare me. I can see you. *All* of you."

"Parker, you don't know the first thing—"

"Stop underestimating me," I grit out. "Yellow. Red. Whatever. Look at me as *Chase*. Not as my Dominant."

He lets out a shaky sigh and rests his forehead against mine. "Fine. You win, Parker."

"And what have I won?" I ask, trying to keep my hand from trembling on his jaw.

"Everything."

Something victorious and hot flashes through me, but I can tell he's being serious. "So tell me. Tell me why you got all spooked in the woods. No lies. No deflecting."

He nods, quiet for a minute before he starts to speak. "I was nine. My parents had been having a particularly bad fight, and my mother was staying elsewhere—if she'd known, she would've—" He closes his eyes. "Anyway, one morning after breakfast, my father tells us to put on our shoes and a jacket. Liam, my oldest brother, was the only skeptical one. He was sixteen then, seven years older than me. And Orion, my youngest brother, was five. He was a fucking baby."

My stomach sinks as he continues.

"He loaded us all up in his Range Rover and we went out into the forest. I don't know how long we drove for. He intentionally zig-zagged through the trees to throw us off. Finally, he hands Liam a large backpack, tells him there's enough water for a week, and that if we try to come home before the week is over, he'll drive us back out here until we learn what it means to be a man. Or some bullshit like that."

My heart is racing as I listen, as he idly traces patterns into my bare thighs. He sucks in a breath and keeps talking.

"I think we were all in shock. He'd always been volatile, but he'd stooped to a whole new level with that. Liam and Miles took it upon themselves to set up our camp. Our father had been *kind* enough to provide the bare essentials, including a tent," he snarls. "I was too young to really grasp the gravity of the situation. Orion was ecstatic—he thought we'd be camping. And Malakai was sort of hovering between worry and playfulness."

"So, he left you all there? In the woods?"

Chase nods. "For a week. And honestly, it was fine. Somehow, Liam killed and skinned rabbits. He made a fucking slingshot out of sticks and a rubber band. He was our forager, coming back with berries and mushrooms that we would grill up over a fire. We had to ration the water, but we were fine. But two days before the week was up, we were all sleeping when we woke up to the tent on fire."

I suck in a sharp breath. "Fire?" I whisper.

"We got out, thanks to Miles and Liam. The Santa Ana winds had caused an ember from our fire to spark on the tent, and it went up like a flame on lighter fluid. Anyway, we got out, but Miles got burned. It was pretty bad. And needed emergency attention. So we packed everything up and headed home, but we got lost. By the time we made it back to the castle, Miles was barely alive. The burns were infected, and the doctors told us he would be lucky if he survived."

I wrap my arms around his neck and nuzzle into his skin. "That must've been so terrifying as a child."

Chase nods. "Do you know the worst part?"

"What?"

"We all lied for him. For my father. When the doctors took us aside, we said that we'd been begging him to camp out by ourselves. That Liam was old enough to watch us. That it was an *accident*," he bites out. "They never charged him with anything. But that week changed us. It rewrote the fabric of our souls. It was... horrific. Especially those last two days. We thought our brother was going to die."

My mind is racing as I think over Miles's serious persona, the way he throws himself into work, the way he's more closed off than Chase. And the scar I saw snaking up his neck a couple of days ago.

"I'm sorry your father did that. I can't imagine

being little and not being able to trust the one person you should be able to count on."

My mind is racing. I'd grown up knowing about Charles Ravage and how ruthless he was. And he was still alive, living in seclusion somewhere—Paris, I think. I knew from Jackson that the only person to ever visit him was Miles. Their mother, who remarried, had died a few years ago. I'd sent Chase a fruit basket. But this whole thing puts everything else into perspective. It explains *so* much. Chase and Miles starting Ravage Consulting Firm. Chase becoming a Dominant— learning control and setting boundaries. Never playing in the woods. Never letting anyone get too close. He's resourceful because he had to be. Because he experienced something horrible.

Of course he grasped on to something that offered him total control.

Something that allowed *him* to be in control.

And I know from my basic child development classes in college that if a child isn't shown love, if they are left to feel unwanted or neglected, it can have a lasting impact on their future relationships. Anything from fear of commitment, jealousy, control...

I pull him closer, relishing in the way he squeezes me back.

It's very possible that Chase needs this connection as much as I do.

CHAPTER TWENTY-ONE
THE POSSESSION

CHASE

I reluctantly pull away from Juliet and look at her. Instead of pity, like I expected, I see something else. Understanding. Compassion. Her expression is open and approachable. It startles me, and I lean down and place my lips on hers. My hands come up to grip her hips, and then I slide them up until they're on either side of her face. She moans when I suck gently on her lower lip, and my cock twitches against her hot core.

"Thank you for telling me," she mumbles against my mouth.

My brows furrow slightly when I pull away, expecting her to make an excuse to leave or possibly change the subject. I know it's not easy to talk about. And in my rule book, I avoid hard conversations if I can help it, so I wouldn't blame her. Especially because I unloaded fucking *everything* onto her when this was supposed to be three days of casual fun.

But her green eyes are still so fucking open and kind. I lean down to kiss her again, but she pushes against my chest.

"Chase," she says, her voice low. "We need to talk about why you keep wanting to push me away."

Do we? I wince slightly and lower her to the ground, ignoring my stiff cock. "Of course," I say sternly, walking over to the bed and sitting down.

Limping over to the bed, clad only in those bright fucking red panties and matching bra, she takes a seat next to me, turning to face me.

Fuck...

She looks so vulnerable.

I swallow as she gives me a small smile. "I want to be here. *With you.* When you rejected me eight years ago, it took me *months* to recover," she starts, and I feel something crack inside of me.

"Fuck, Juliet," I say quickly, running a hand down my face. "I didn't mean to hurt you."

"But you did," she says slowly. Except, she's not mad or disappointed. She's stating a fact. Which is classic Juliet Parker. "I was sad, angry, and embarrassed. I barely paid attention to my classes for weeks, and I was constantly hounding Jackson for information about you." She bites her lower lip and leans her cheek on my shoulder. "I missed you."

I am the world's biggest asshole.

I wrap my arms around her, and something inside of me feels a little bit lighter. "I'm sorry," I tell her.

"I've forgiven you," she says quickly. "I need you to know that for me, this isn't just an experiment. This is everything I never knew I wanted."

Fuck.

Me.

I close my eyes and inhale the scent of her hair, the feel of her soft skin in my arms. Juliet *fucking* Parker. She's so honest. Open. It's startling to hear her come out and talk about all of this, but it shouldn't be. She's always been someone to tell you exactly how she feels.

Maybe I could learn a thing or two from her.

Especially since I'm fighting every reflex to make a sarcastic retort, pushing her away. My instinct is to put distance between us—to get her as far away from me as possible. But what if I didn't? What if... I tried to be better? Just for this weekend?

Before I can prove it to her and myself, she continues talking.

"At the engagement party, I was mad at you. Not for paying—though it was a bold move, Ravage," she says, and I chuckle. "I was mad because I *knew* you felt something for me. I knew eight years ago that you were attracted to me. And yet, you weren't fighting for me. I *wanted* you to fight for me. I wanted you to *show me* that you still cared, and when I found out you offered to pay for the wedding, I assumed it meant I'd been wrong. But then you pulled me into that office..." she trails off, snaking an arm around my waist. *Fuck, it feels so fucking good to be touched like this. To hear her say these things.* "I think I knew I was ruined. You ruined me for anyone else," she says softly. "The second you pushed me against that desk, I knew I would stop at nothing to get you."

Something significant cracks in my chest, and I twist her, pressing her down on the bed as I hover over her.

"You think it was easy seeing you with him?" I ask, feeling out of control. *She* makes me feel out of control. All or nothing—and I want to give her every single fucking thing. Why am I telling her this? Her cheeks flush, and I continue, reaching down to move her underwear to the side, pressing a finger into her wet, warm cunt. "You think I *enjoyed* seeing you two together? Hearing about your engagement to *another man* from my best friend?" She arches her back, and I don't wait. I *can't*. I unbuckle my pants, but I don't touch myself yet. I want to savor this.

I want to savor *her*.

Kissing her, I speed up the ministrations with my fingers. I lower myself onto her so that she's pinned beneath me and the mattress, settling between her legs.

I press my palm against her clit, and she gasps.

She was my prey before, but right now, she's Juliet.

"Finally," I mutter gruffly, bending down to her neck and kissing her. "Fucking finally."

Juliet moans as I suck on her skin, and I feel her pussy flutter around my finger. Adding a second, I keep my palm pressed against her clit, ensuring my ring is digging into the inside of her thigh. *Marking her as mine.* Her mouth drops open when I curl my fingers, when I brush them against the spot I know will make her see white.

"Be a good girl, and come for me, Juliet."

I feel the cords in her body snap, feel the way her cunt grips me frantically, and I moan as she comes all over my hand, contracting around my fingers. I press kisses into her forehead. She convulses as she comes down slowly. I draw it out, keeping my fingers curled, gently pressing against her. She pants underneath me. I stroke her hip with my free hand until her eyes flutter open.

"That was..." she trails off, smiling. I smirk as I roll my hips against her, watching as her eyes flutter with her evident desire. "I want all of you. I need it, Chase."

I fist my cock before pressing into her. We both let out low moans as I sink in deeper.

"*Fuck,* Juliet. I've held you on a pedestal my entire life. No other woman has ever..." I trail off, watching as her eyes roll back into her head. Closing my eyes, I relish the way her velvet folds wrap tightly around my cock. *Fuck.*

"Chase," she whimpers, placing her hands on my face. "Remember what I said yesterday? I see you. All of you."

I groan as I slide back into her, as her nails trail down my back, as her eyes flutter closed. Something deep inside of me snaps, leaving a burning, possessive ember in its wake. I drive into her, gritting my teeth as she screams, as her pussy clamps down on my cock.

Mine.

She's mine, and she always will be.

I don't hold back as I fuck her—as I bend her knees and press them against her chest, as I thumb her clit and make her toes curl. *Fucking god, she feels incredible.* Made for me. Perfect in every way. My throat constricts as she comes again, as she screams my first name. A second later, my balls tighten, and my cock bows inside of her, spilling my cum as I roar and collapse on top of her.

I would fucking do anything for her.

I press kisses to her temple, her neck, her collar-bone as I twitch inside of her.

Juliet *fucking* Parker.

Calling my bluff, pushing my boundaries... she's not fucking messing around.

She found a crack and took a hammer, breaking straight on through to a place I haven't ever let anyone else before.

And while she might be happy about it, I know she's in a dangerous place now. I hoard the things I cherish—my job, my brothers, Jax... and now her.

I know myself well enough to know that I won't ever—*can't* ever—let her go.

I drag her to the shower, fucking her as I press her against the white marble wall.

I feed her, take care of her, tend to her.

Eventually, after a large dinner of steak and a salad, she falls asleep.

In *my* bed.

Realization sets in a few minutes later, and I walk out into the living room, pouring myself some scotch. I glare at my bedroom door, though I'm not mad about her being here. I'm mad that I have to share her with the world.

Swirling my scotch, I lean my head back and stare at the ceiling. Ravage means to consume... but Juliet has consumed *me*. I already know we won't be joining the rest of The Hunt. I can use her head and her ankle as an excuse. And despite fucking her several times, my cock is hard now as I think about her.

I'm suddenly insatiable.

Like I've given myself permission to have what I've always craved the most.

Whatever the fuck happened earlier today cracked me right the fuck open, and now I'm contemplating ways to keep her all to myself.

I'm thinking up places to show her in the castle— places I loved as a child.

I'm dreaming of taking care of her—of dominating her. Of pushing her down on her knees and fucking her mouth, her throat, and every place she'll have me.

I finish my drink and set it down on the coffee table.

I have one and a half more days with her, so I have to make it count.

CHAPTER TWENTY-TWO
THE FOOL

JULIET

I've awoken a beast.

We spend the next day and night barely leaving the bedroom. Barely surfacing for air. Waking up to Chase curled around my body two mornings in a row is a dream, and though I'm sore all over my body, he continues to find ways to drag the pleasure out of me. Sometimes as my Dom—by rolling the sleeves of his robe up—and sometimes as Chase. Both ways are toe-curling and mind-blowing—with the latter being slightly more intimate. I'm exhausted, sore, bruised, and I don't want to go home today, because I like the sex nest we've created.

I haven't worn real clothes since I hurt my ankle—which feels much better now.

The morning I'm supposed to leave, I'm finishing my shower when Chase walks into the bathroom.

Smirking, I turn the water off and take a step out of the enclosed waterfall room, grabbing a towel and wrapping it around myself quickly. Chase stalks forward, wearing nothing but pajama bottoms. Without breaking eye contact, he kicks off his pants and prowls closer. I swallow nervously and back up a step. He looms over me, his erection bobbing between us. Slowly, he fists the fabric of my towel and rips it away violently. Adrenaline courses through me, and I bite my lower lip in anticipation. I fucking *love* this Chase— the one with blown-out pupils. The one who pushes the boundaries of consent and non-consent—though I would always give him consent anyway.

The one who *takes* what he wants without any hesitation.

"Get the fuck back in the shower, Juliet."

I smirk. "You haven't had your fill yet?" I ask, teasing him. I can because I know we're not in a scene. And I love that he allows both sides of me to play.

"No. I haven't filled you properly since an hour ago."

My mouth drops open as he shoves me back into the shower and turns the water on. I've come to find that Chase has a fascination with watching his cum drip out of me—and making sure it stays inside of me for as long as possible. Even yesterday, when I dropped to my knees as his submissive and tried to suck him off, he threw me back onto the couch and impaled me once before coming inside of me. Afterward, he cleaned me up with his tongue.

He presses my back up against the wall, the water

spraying down on us. I gasp when he knocks my knees apart and slides inside of me, groaning as he sheaths himself fully.

"Fuck," he says, his voice shaky. One hand is on the wall next to my head, and I see his fist curl as he closes his eyes. His other hand comes to my hip, fingers digging into my flesh. "I'll never fucking get over the feeling of being inside of you, Juliet," he murmurs.

My legs tremble as I moan, as he quickens his tempo, fucking me hard enough to lift my feet off the ground.

"Oh god," I whimper, wrapping my arms around his neck. I throw my head back, and the force against the marble makes me see stars. I yelp, and suddenly Chase's hand is behind my skull, cushioning it as he looks down at me with a fierce expression.

"Say *my* name," he demands, speeding up his tempo. His fingers grip my hair.

"Ravage," I taunt, smirking.

His nostrils flare. "You sure you want to be cheeky right now, Juliet?" He pulls out of me, and I stare at him as he takes a step back.

"Chase," I say, and as the word leaves my lips, he gives me a breathtaking smile—and it nearly makes my heart stutter.

He twists me around, and I yelp with surprise as he spreads my legs wide.

"Hands on the wall, Juliet."

I place my palms flat as he nudges his cock inside of me. I pant as he slowly pushes all the way in, and then he doesn't move. I'm about to turn around to look at him when one of his hands comes around my stomach, roving lower, slipping in to swirl around my swollen clit.

"Now," he growls, his breath on my neck making my tight heat contract around him. "Say my name again."

"Chase."

"Again," he commands, rubbing my bud gently.

"Chase," I mewl.

"Once more, Juliet."

"Chase," I mutter, feeling my orgasm beginning to build.

"Good," he murmurs, working his fingers faster. Feeling him there, massaging me as I'm full of his cock... "Get used to saying *my* name. No one else's."

He smacks my core once, and my back arches as I scream out.

"Oh g—"

He takes his free hand and slaps it over my mouth before the rest of the word can escape my lips.

"Who?" he growls. "Who is bringing you this pleasure? Me, or God?"

"You," I whimper, my knees beginning to shake. "Chase," I beg, rolling my hips so that I'm getting the friction I need from his cock.

"Good fucking girl," he says, groaning when I speed up. "That's so good. Fucking my cock so perfectly."

I let out a sharp cry as he smacks my core again, and I'm moving my hips quickly on his hard shaft.

"That's right," he grits out, his voice rough. "Keep doing that, and you're going to make me come."

That's all it takes—his gravelly words and his fingers sliding across my overused clit. I shatter, my hips jerking on his cock as I see stars. He growls, pulling me closer as he pulses his seed into me. My mouth drops open as we stand there, completely still except for his hand, which is slowly running up and down the top of my slit. I'm gasping for air as one arm comes under me, holding me up as my knees threaten to give out.

"Such a good girl," he murmurs, pulling out and dropping to his knees.

I gasp when he inserts a finger, pushing his cum back inside of me as he emits a self-satisfied chuckle. Twisting me back around to face him, he picks me up and carries me to his bedroom, dropping me down on the bed and quickly drying me off.

"I keep telling myself the sex can't possibly get better, and then it does," I joke, bending my knees and holding my legs together.

Chase lies down next to me and gives me that earth-shattering smile again. "I'm only getting started, Juliet."

I tilt my head as I look at him. "You don't call me Parker anymore."

He shrugs. "I don't see the point. Would you prefer it?"

"I liked it. You were the only person who called me that."

He dips down and kisses my neck, a hand running over my stomach. Ever since he told me about what his father did to him and his brothers in the forest, he's been so affectionate. Touching me, kissing me, watching me... it sends shivers down my spine.

Sometimes it feels like he's already claimed me, and I've yet to catch on.

Not that I don't feel the same way—I do.

But his intensity is startling. It's so different from the man who walked into my engagement party. Distant, cold, mysterious...

Chase Ravage is becoming less and less of an enigma by the hour.

"I can keep calling you Parker," he says lightly.

"Yes, please," I hum.

"Let me clean you up, and we can get ready to go."

My heart sinks as he walks into the bathroom. I hear him run the water as I prop myself on my elbows, watching him when he comes back into the bedroom. Sliding the warm washcloth between my legs, his eyes find mine as he runs it gently over my sore areas.

"I'm not going to be able to sit down for days," I say, laughing as he helps me up and helps me discard my bra.

"Good," he murmurs, stepping into his boxers. "I want you to think of who made you sore every time you move or walk. Who was between your legs all weekend."

My breath hitches as I get dressed for the first time in two days, distracting myself from what his words make me feel.

I wince as I pull my foot through the leg hole of my leggings. My ankle is tender, but I can put my weight on it and walk with a small limp. Guess all the "resting" in the bedroom has helped. And the cut on my head is hardly noticeable—especially since Chase has been tending to it whenever he can. I decide to wear sandals, and then I pull a cropped T-shirt on without a bra. Comfort is key, and it's not like I'll be seeing anyone but him. Once I'm dressed, I pull my hair into a wet bun and walk over to my purse, checking my phone.

"Jax is at the apartment," Chase says, zipping up his leather overnight bag. "You won't have to worry about him seeing me drop you off."

I shake my head. "I wasn't worried." *He's going to find out one way or another.*

"Ready?" he asks, donning faded black jeans, a black blazer, and a crisp gray T-shirt.

I shrug, feeling glum. "I suppose. I didn't get to tour the library."

Chase grabs my suitcase and hauls his bag on top before walking out into the living quarters.

"You are welcome here anytime. I mean that, Parker. Luna lives on site, so she can give you a tour of anything you want to see."

I nod, but I don't answer him. As we exit the living quarters and walk down the hallway, Chase looks over his shoulder and glances down at my feet.

"Are you okay to walk? I can carry you."

I *almost* lie, but then, being carried like a blushing bride before I have to say goodbye to him probably isn't wise. Especially since I have no idea if we're continuing whatever it is that we're doing.

"I'm fine."

The elevator ride down to the ground floor is quiet. When I look up at Chase briefly, he's staring at the wall over my shoulder, his jaw tight as he rubs his lips.

Once we're outside, I see a pristine vintage yellow convertible. My mouth drops open.

"It looks like a toy," I joke, and Chase scowls as he loads the trunk up with our bags.

Once it's closed, he walks around to the passenger side and opens my door, glaring at me with those piercing blue eyes. His lips quirk with the hint of a smile as he pops a pair of black Ray-Ban aviators over his eyes.

"It doesn't drive like a toy, Parker."

I climb inside as he shuts my door, and I study the vintage interior as he climbs into the driver's seat. Tracing my fingers over the shiny, polished silver and the black leather, I cock my head and turn to him.

"What kind of car is this?"

"A 1960 Ferrari California."

"Of course it is," I mutter, watching as Chase turns the key and the engine purrs to life. His muscled forearm works the clutch as we lurch forward. "How many cars do you have?"

"Right now? Five. Liam helped me restore this one last year."

I nod. "Liam. Your oldest brother. Does he live in Crestwood?"

Chase chuckles. "He prefers a more rugged setting. He lives north of here in a remote house that isn't connected to the internet."

I laugh. "He sounds fun."

Chase shrugs. "He's a good brother. Professor of Creative Writing. Never been married, so he keeps himself locked up in that massive house of his like a fucking recluse when he doesn't have classes."

I'm quiet as I digest this information. I hardly know any of the other brothers—only vague recollections from what Jackson tells me in passing.

"So, what animal does he keep as a pet?"

Chase laughs. "What?"

"You know exactly what I'm talking about. The menagerie. Which animal did Liam take?"

Chase glances at me as we come to a stop at a light. "You'll have to ask him yourself. We're all sworn to secrecy."

I grin. "Why a rooster for you?"

He shrugs. "I don't know. It was better than the other options. I've formed quite an attachment to him, though."

Just as I'm about to ask about his other two brothers, Chase makes a sharp left, and we merge onto the freeway. It's too loud to talk, and I laugh as the wind runs through my hair. Taking my hairband out, I shake my hair out and raise my hands as he speeds down the 405. It feels amazing, and I close my eyes, relishing in the feel of the warm air whipping around me. We drive like this for a few minutes, and every time I look over at Chase, he's watching me with a smile.

Finally, he pulls off, and we head toward my house. I manage to sort my messy hair out—at least it's dry now—and then we're pulling up to my house.

I'm not ready to say goodbye.

Chase must be thinking the same thing because he doesn't turn the car off. Instead, he removes his sunglasses and turns to face me.

"This weekend was fun, Parker." Giving me a small smile, he exits the car before I can say anything else.

That's it?! Is he breaking it off with me? Are we... done?

He pulls my door open, and I climb out with the help of his hand. I know I should say something, but what can I say? *Hi, hello, I'd like to continue being your submissive even though we signed a contract stating that we would only fuck for the weekend?*

He pulls my suitcase to my front door, and I suddenly start to panic.

Will I see him again soon, or is it truly over? Have I been reading everything wrong this whole time? Maybe he only ever meant for us to be together temporarily? I mean, it's obvious that he cares about me, but he clearly does things his own way.

I meet him at my front door, and I fumble for my keys.

"Parker..." he trails off, looking away.

Here it comes.

I should say something. I should tell him how I feel.

"Can we continue?" I ask, blurting it out before thinking. He quirks his brows questioningly, and I continue. "I mean, can we continue... with the Dom/sub thing? It can be casual if you want. I know we were only fooling around—"

He huffs a laugh and presses me into the side of my house, interrupting my babbling mouth.

"I don't do casual. I don't fool around."

My heart sinks. "Oh. Okay, that's fine. I thought—"

He presses his body into me, and I let out a small squeak as his lips graze my ear. "Are you blind, Parker? Do you really expect me to *fool around* with you?" I open my mouth as his hand comes to the back of my neck. He grips me tightly, and a pleasant sensation runs down my spine as his warm hand squeezes my flesh. "I'm not a fool, nor is this a casual fling. I meant it when I said you were mine."

Fuck.

"But the contract—"

"Fuck the contract," he growls. "We need to discuss a permanent one anyway."

My heart is beating so hard, I'm positive he can feel my skin pulsing underneath his fingertips. My eyes flick across his face, trying to swallow his words as they make everything buzz inside of me.

I meant it when I said you were mine.

"Okay," I whisper, placing a hand around the back of his neck and pulling him down for a soft kiss. He doesn't fight me—he delicately kisses me back, squeezing the back of my neck once. My skin pebbles, and I visibly shiver as the sensation rolls through me again. "That feels amazing," I murmur, feeling almost sleepy.

"You hold a lot of tension in the occipital area of your skull," he says softly. "I noticed it the first day. Don't worry. I'll make sure to relieve the tension when I can."

My chest aches when I turn to look up at him.

We've only been *not fooling around* for four days, but it feels like he knows my body better than I know it.

"Thank you."

"Are you busy Friday?" he asks, smirking slightly. "I have a work party, and I need a date."

I feel my lips pull into a grin. "I'm not busy."

He bends down and kisses me before releasing my neck and taking a step back. "Be ready at six."

I nod and touch my lips as he waves and walks away. I quickly open my door so that I can swoon in private, depositing my suitcase inside so that I can watch as he drives away.

After he's gone, I stare at the house I grew up in—taking everything in with a fresh set of eyes. Smiling again, I collect the mail and bring it over to the dining room table. My eyes catch on one of the envelopes, and I quickly tear it open, staring at the words before me.

Dear Juliet M. Parker,

We are pleased to inform you that your student loan(s) referenced below have been paid in full. Please keep this letter for your records as proof of payment for this student loan. We've enjoyed having you as a customer and wish you the best in the future.

I grab my phone and call Jackson before the letter hits the floor.

"Finally! I was starting to think you'd met some hottie on your work trip and—"

"Did you pay off my student loans?" I ask, my voice shaky.

He laughs. "I wish I was rich enough, Jules, but no. Why? Did someone pay them off?"

My hand is shaking as I stare at the letter on the ground. "I had six figures of debt. I'd accounted for that, budgeted for it for the next twenty years, and now it's just... gone?"

Jackson laughs on the other end of the line. "Yeah, and? Why do you sound unhappy about it? Maybe it's a glitch."

"It must be a mistake," I tell him, but the instant the words leave my mouth, I know it's not. "Fuck," I mutter, sitting down on one of the dining room chairs. "I have to go."

"Wait, aren't you going to update me on your trip? How was it?"

Right. Work trip. "Good. Learned a lot."

"Want me to bring over some dinner tonight?"

I nod even though he can't see me. Truth be told, I'm still reeling from the letter. "Sure. Sounds amazing."

After we hang up, I stare down at my phone. I have Chase's number from when we were younger, but I realize now that I don't know if he still has the same number. I didn't think to ask—it felt so insignificant compared to what we shared over the weekend. Pressing the call button, it rings a few times before Chase answers.

"Miss me already?" he purrs. He must still be driving, because I can hear the wind.

"Did you pay off my student loans?" I ask, my throat catching because I already know the answer.

"Of course I did. Didn't you read the contract?"

I squeeze my eyes shut. "There was nothing about paying off my loans—"

"Actually, there was. At the bottom. Check your email—Luna emailed you a copy, remember?"

"Thank you," I force out, trying to rationalize the multitude of emotions welling up inside of me.

"You're welcome." He clears his throat, and I hear a car door open. "I'll see you Friday, okay? My assistant will be dropping something off this week."

"What?" I ask, my voice soft.

"You'll see. Get some rest before Friday," he adds, his voice a low growl. It sends a spark of something hot through me. I don't need to ask him what he means— my body understands.

"Have a good week," I say numbly, and then I'm hanging up and staring at the front door for several minutes before his words slam back into me.

Check your email—Luna emailed you a copy, remember?

I pull open my email, wincing at the multitude of neglected emails. I don't think I've ever gone this long without checking my university email, but I digress. I find the email from Luna, and it's all very professional. I have to enter my birthdate to open the file—I certainly appreciate the discretion—and then my eyes scan over the bottom portion of the contract, written in fine print.

The Dominant unconditionally and irrevocably agrees to pay off any and all debt accrued by the submissive according to the terms and conditions as detailed in Exhibit A, line 5.

My eyes wander up to Exhibit A, and my heart flutters when I see the line.

The Dominant agrees to care for the submissive to include tending to the physical safety and emotional and mental wellbeing of the submissive as long as he owns the submissive.

I set my phone down as I smile, place my face in my hands, and cry.

CHAPTER TWENTY-THREE
THE DRESS

JULIET

Since the week is short, it goes by quickly. It doesn't hurt that Chase checks in with me every day—enough to remind me that he's thinking about me but not enough to satiate the intimacy that I'm craving now that I've had a taste. *Thank God for Wolverine.* Still, the week is impossibly busy catching up on my dissertation and my classes. I don't sit down except to sleep, and by the time Thursday afternoon rolls around, I am more than happy to unwind with some pizza and beer, courtesy of Jackson.

That is, until a mysterious delivery appears, and I have to hide my embarrassment as the delivery driver hands me a bouquet of black roses and a large black box with a black velvet bow. I stumble back inside as Jackson's eyes widen.

"Oooh, the plot thickens," he says, giving me a wry

grin. "And who's the lucky man? Or is it men? Why choose when you can have them all?"

"Shut up," I grit out, walking quickly to my bedroom.

Closing the door behind me and trying to quell my pounding heart, I place the roses on my dresser and walk over to the box. Untying the ribbon and lifting the lid, I gasp when I see what's inside. A midnight-blue velvet dress—vintage, by the looks of it—and stunning. I lift it out delicately and hold it up to myself in the mirror. Just as I scan the vintage label—Victor Edelstein—Jackson raps against my door. I quickly fold the dress and place the lid back on before opening the door and ushering him away from the incriminating items.

I sit and continue eating my pizza, looking anywhere but my brother's eager face. Finally, after finishing my beer, I sigh and resign myself to giving him a half-truth. I'm going to need to tell him something now that Chase is being positively blatant about things.

"Fine. I'm seeing someone. I'm not ready to talk about it because I don't know what *it* entails, but yeah. Can we move on now?"

Jackson snorts as he texts on his phone. "I won't stop until I know, but sure. I'll stop for tonight."

"What about you?" I ask casually, watching as Jackson's cheeks redden. "Any hot dates lately?"

"Yeah, actually."

When he doesn't elaborate, I clear my throat. "So? Spill the beans."

Jackson wipes his palms on his jeans and leans forward. "I should go. But maybe we can have dinner on Saturday? There's something I want to talk to you about."

I hide my smile as I nod. "Of course. I'll clear my busy social calendar."

He narrows his eyes as he stands, stretching as he yawns. "Hopefully you can squeeze me in," he jokes, wincing as his hips crack. "I swear, every year I teach gets harder and harder. I'm sore in places I never knew existed."

I laugh. "I told you those kids would kill you one day."

He cleans up—and by cleans up, he shoves the empty pizza boxes into my tiny recycling receptacle—and then walks to the front door.

"Whoever he is, I hope he makes you happy," Jackson says, opening the door as he pulls on a blue cardigan. "Truly."

My throat constricts. "He does." Just as Jackson walks across the threshold, I turn to watch him go. "Same with you. Whoever they are." His wide eyes meet mine from the darkness of the porch, but then he nods once and closes the door behind him.

He'll tell me soon. And if he doesn't, that's fine too.

———

By the time six o'clock rolls around the next day, I am a wreck. The dress is tight—almost too tight—but I'm able to get it on. I need Chase to help me zip it up. It's stunning—and familiar—but I can't put my finger on why. I decide to do very light makeup, and though I didn't notice before, inside the box were vintage Prada stilettos. They're tall, but not enough to break my neck. I have my hair up in a low chignon, accentuating the way the dress sits off my shoulders and hugs my body like a glove before fanning out at my knees. Just as I grab my black clutch, there's a knock at my door, and I pull it open to see Chase in a matching, midnight-blue suit.

"We match," I say nervously, pointing between us.

What an idiotic thing to say.

Chase's eyes darken as he reaches forward and tugs me into his body. "Not quite. I don't look anywhere as spectacular as you do, Parker."

And then he kisses me—slow and sensual at first, but then more urgent, more demanding as it progresses. I feel him reach back and zip up my dress. I hadn't asked him to—he just knew.

"We should go," I murmur against his lips, pressing against his chest.

"I haven't seen you in days, and yet I can't get the smell of your cunt out of my mind. I'm starting to go crazy."

"How much time do we have?" I ask, panting.

"Not enough for that," he growls, pulling away and looking rather reluctant about it. "When I fix my cuff-links later, take it as the signal that the scene is about to start, Juliet."

A flash of anticipation blazes through me, and I

nod once as he walks me outside to his waiting car. This time, it's a black vintage car.

"And what kind of car is this?" I ask, tilting my head as I admire it.

"A 1957 Bentley S1," he says as if I know what that means.

Opening my door, I sit carefully as he shuts it and walks around to his side.

"And my dress?" I ask, running my hand along the dark-blue velvet.

"Probably worth more than my car," he says casually, winking before popping his aviators on.

My mouth drops open as I take in the beautiful vehicle. There's no way...

"Chase," I say slowly, my hands resting on my thighs. "Tell me about the dress."

He pulls out onto the road. This car is definitely slower than the yellow one, but it still runs smoothly for an old car.

"The designer is Victor Edelstein," he says smugly.

"Yeah, I gathered that from the label."

"In 1985, Princess Diana saw this dress in burgundy and asked Victor to make one for her in blue. She then wore it to the White House for a gala. It's famous. People call it the Travolta dress, because there's a famous picture of her dancing with John Travolta at that gala."

My pulse thrums inside of me as we merge onto the freeway. I barely hear him over the whooshing in my ears when he continues speaking.

"She donated it before her death, and it passed into

many different hands before my mother—a lover of the royal family—bought it ten years ago."

I'm stunned. Deceased. My mind is both screaming at me and deathly quiet as I take in his words as I look down at the iconic dress. *I'm wearing Princess Diana's dress.*

Swallowing thickly, I look over at Chase, who looks completely nonplussed.

"What if I spill something on it?" I say quickly, my voice panicked.

"Don't worry. It's insured for over a million dollars."

I slap my hand over my mouth and close my eyes. "Oh my god," I mutter, and Chase laughs as we fly down the 405.

"Parker, when are you going to learn that I don't do anything—"

"Half-assed, I know," I mutter, running my finger along the fine velvet.

I am wearing a dress that is quite literally in history books. One of the most sought-after dresses of all time. This dress should be in a museum. Not pulled snugly around me, someone at least two sizes bigger than the infamous original owner. I'm still in awe when Chase's hand comes to my knee, and he grips it tightly.

"You're radiant, Juliet. Stop doubting yourself."

I take a deep breath before I respond. "Where are we going tonight, anyway?" My eyes dart to the signs on the freeway, indicating that we're heading toward downtown Crestwood.

"Work party at one of the local galleries in town"

"Potential clients?" I ask.

He nods. "New clients, actually. They host exhibits from marginalized groups—showcasing newer artists, mostly. Tonight is the opening night for the gallery."

I pull my lips to the side. "Sounds amazing."

"We won't be staying long. But Miles thought it might be good to show our faces."

"Maybe Miles will have a brand new blushing bride at his side," I murmur.

Chase chuckles. "Maybe. So you know about that?"

"He told me the night I was over with Jackson. My question is, why can't he make a good name for himself without a wife? It's not like marrying someone will magically gain him new clients."

Chase shrugs. "I have a feeling our father is behind the ploy."

"Does Miles still talk to your father?"

"He does. He's the only one of us who is still in contact."

Interesting.

Before I can ask more, Chase pulls off the highway and pulls his car to the valet line a few minutes later. Walking around to my side, he opens my door and helps me out. Now that I know I'm wearing a famous dress, I'm more nervous about splitting the seams or falling over and tearing the fabric.

"Stop worrying, Parker."

I smirk. "How can you read me so well?" I ask as he takes my arm and leads us to a nondescript door—though the gathering of people tells me that this is the party.

And I am most certainly *not* overdressed—everyone is wearing a ballgown. At least I won't stand out in that regard.

"I've always been able to read you well," he murmurs into my ear.

A few camera flashes go off as he tugs me into the gallery. It's a large space. An open warehouse of sorts, with brick walls staggered evenly to create the illusion of separate rooms. The art is stunning—everything from oil paintings to photographs to sculptures. I take everything in quietly as Chase's hand comes to my lower back.

"What would you like to drink?" Chase asks, peering down at me once we're inside.

"Oh, um, maybe some of that fancy champagne from my engagement party?"

His eyes flash. "We're starting early with the snark, are we? Very well. Stay here. I'll be back."

He walks off, and I'm left to admire the art by myself. There are others around, of course, but it's a large space, and I soon find a pocket of solitude next to a sculpture of a breastfeeding woman sitting on a chair. The statue is made of dark clay, and there are flecks of gold interspersed along the curves of the mother's body, highlighting the stretch marks on her thighs, her stomach, her breasts. Highlighting her nipples and the apex of her thighs. It's *gorgeous*. I read the description. *Goddess: Mother. The beginning of everything.*

I'm smiling when I feel a hand on my shoulder,

spinning around to tell Chase how much I love this piece when my words fall flat.

"Professor Landon?" I ask, unable to hide the surprise in my voice.

"Hello, Ms. Parker." His smile doesn't reach his eyes. "Fancy seeing you at a party like this."

"I'm here with a friend," I say quickly, hoping he'll leave me alone. I've always hated the way he looks at me—especially after we slept together—but lately, despite not being my mentor anymore, he's been visiting me during my office hours. Standing too close, touching me without permission, sending me emails asking about my day... now that everyone knows Dylan and I called off our engagement, he's been much more present in my life.

"Oh? A friend who has access to one of the most exclusive galleries in Southern California?"

I open and close my mouth. "I could ask the same of you," I tease. "Surely professors don't normally find themselves at these exclusive parties," I barb back.

He chuckles. "Surely not. Except my wife owns this gallery."

My mouth drops open. "You're married?"

He nods once. "Thirteen years, to be exact."

How did I not know? How did this never come up? Thirteen years means...

He must see the wheels spinning in my head because he leans down. "Yes. And I'd do it again, if you're amenable. My wife and I have an... arrangement."

I think of the way his tongue slithered into my

mouth that night after I'd had one too many drinks. How easy it was to go along with it. I never said no—it was consensual. But it wasn't good, and I never wanted to repeat it.

"I'm seeing someone, actually," I tell him firmly. Using Chase as a scapegoat feels slimy, but I want him to leave me alone. I don't think he'd resort to pushing me to do anything untoward, but still. He'd backed off when I was with Dylan. It makes me mad that I feel the need to lie about being in a relationship so that he doesn't leer at me from across the auditorium. "But even if I wasn't, I'm not interested. Please leave me alone."

Professor Landon smirks. "Do you think I'm stupid, Juliet? I know you requested to be placed under me as your mentor." I shake my head. *No.* I never did that. I open my mouth to tell him that he's wrong when he continues, cutting me off. "But if you want to play hard to get, I'll wait. You know where to find m—"

"Is there a problem here?"

Chase's low growl slices through the room, low and menacing.

Professor Landon looks over my shoulder in surprise. "Mr. Ravage. Thank you for hosting this fabulous party for my wife. We were honored to receive your funding offer."

Chase walks up to us, slinking an arm around my waist and tugging me closer to him. He looks between us as something registers in his mind.

"Ah. I should've put two and two together. Of course, you work at the same university as my Juliet," he says, his voice still tainted with something threatening and violent.

My Juliet.

Professor Landon looks between us. "He's your date?" Professor Landon asks me.

I nod. "He is."

"Now, if you'll excuse me, I'll be dragging my date into the bathroom and making her scream so loud that she forgets every other man who's ever been inside of her."

Professor Landon mutters something, but I don't hear it as Chase drags us away to an abandoned room.

I turn to face Chase with a shy smile as he hands me a glass of champagne. "Thank you for rescuing me," I say, sipping my bubbles.

"You don't need rescuing, Juliet. But I'm more than happy to stake my claim."

His words cause shivers to slide down my spine. I tip my glass to his, and we both take a sip without breaking eye contact. He opens his mouth to say something when someone walks up behind him.

"Fuck, there you two are. I need saving," Miles says, straightening his tie.

I arch a brow as I take in his disheveled look. "Hello, Miles. I've been dying to ask if you've swindled a poor, innocent soul into holy matrimony."

Chase snorts as he sips his champagne, coughing once to cover it up.

Miles glares at me as he tilts his head, giving me a brittle smile. He looks so much like Chase—except where Chase is soft, where his lips are round and plush, Miles is all cut angles and a long, sharp nose. Still handsome, but in a more ruthless way. Where Chase is fire, Miles is ice.

"You've got yourself a witty one," Miles bites out, glancing at his brother before looking back at me. "Nice to see you again, Juliet. Twice in one month... must be my lucky night." He winks as his words sink in. *He hasn't told Chase that he's the one who gave me the invite to The Hunt.*

"Nice to see you as well, Miles."

"And no, still no fake wife. Just an angry date who didn't appreciate my swift proposal."

Chase's eyes flick over his brother's face. "You look like you've been mauled."

He gives Chase a wan smile. "Unfortunately, yes. Though I am discovering that the whole primal thing is very much not my thing." His eyes scan mine. "No offense to the two of you."

I bark a laugh and cover my mouth. Well, there goes the question of if Miles knows about Chase's proclivities.

He adjusts his collar, and I get a glimpse of warped skin underneath his starched collar. His light-blue eyes —so similar in shade to Chase's—narrow as he covers his scars back up.

Right, the fire. I'd nearly forgotten.

"Well, I'll leave you two lovebirds to it. Have a good night." He nods at me once before walking away, smoothing his hair as he goes.

Chase pulls me into another exhibit room, and neither of us speak as we go from piece to piece. The air is heady and tense thanks to what Chase said to Professor Landon, and I want to ask if he meant what he said—about dragging me into the bathroom and making me scream. I have to rub my thighs together to dispel the ache. Chase is reciting something from one of the descriptions, and when he looks over at me, he takes in my flushed chest and neck. He continues reciting meaningless words and names, his voice low, and I try to follow his train of thought. The champagne is making my head feel light, and I want nothing more than to feel him inside of me again.

"Are you paying attention, Juliet?"

His commanding tone snaps me out of my lust-filled daze. I look up at him and nod. "Of course."

He holds a hand up, adjusting his cufflink as he stares down at me.

When I fix my cufflinks later, take it as the signal that the scene is about to start, Juliet.

His eyes don't leave mine as he adjusts the cufflink on his other sleeve. I swallow as my eyelids grow heavy, and I set my empty champagne glass on a passing tray held by a server.

"Did you hear anything I said?" he asks, his voice clipped.

I shake my head. "No. Apologies, sir. I was distracted."

He cocks his head and places his hands in his pockets. "By your professor?"

I nod. "Yes. And what you said to him."

His lips twitch. "Because he's the one you fucked." It's a statement, not a question.

I nearly gasp at the caustic way he says it. "Yes, sir."

Chase rubs his mouth and looks away. "Wonderful. Luckily, I only have to deal with his wife, otherwise I'm not sure I could handle funding the man who took something that was supposed to be *mine*."

I actually gasp this time, my body turning molten. "I did ask you first," I whisper. "Sir."

Wrong thing to say.

His nostrils flare as he stares down at me with nearly obsidian eyes. Without another word, he grabs my elbow. It's rough but not painful. Dragging me to the other side of the building, he brushes people off and briskly walks us over to the dark area that houses the single bathroom. I open my mouth to protest, but he pushes me inside and kicks the door closed, locking it quickly.

It's a small, modern bathroom with black and white tiles, but I hardly have time to observe our surroundings before Chase is on me. I whimper as he presses me against the cold tile, gasping as I felt him rucking up my dress. *The* dress.

"Remember your safe word, Parker." His voice is dark and venomous.

At first, I register it as a question, but then he presses up against me, at the same time, the sound of a belt buckle peals from behind my hips.

"It would be quite a shame to sully this beautiful dress, don't you think?" he growls.

"But—"

"Do as I say, Parker," he murmurs.

A flash of something akin to fear—or maybe excitement—rolls through me as one hand wraps around my neck, the other one grabbing on to my hip. I feel his thick cock press against my aching core. He tightens his grip on my neck, and black spots float in my vision as he thrusts into me. *Roughly.* I rise onto the balls of my feet from the sudden stretch of accommodating him with no foreplay, crying out as he pulls out and slams back in, squeezing my neck harder.

"How many times do I have to fuck you to make you forget all the other men before me?"

"Chase," I wheeze, reaching up to claw at him.

"That's it. *Say my name*," he says, his voice a low rumble.

His right hand digs into my bare flesh, pulling me onto his cock with zero abandon. I feel our pelvic bones slamming against each other with each snap of his hips. Though he wasn't necessarily gentle with me last weekend, this is still the roughest he's ever been. His hand roves to the back of my neck and he tugs my head back by grabbing my hair, and I cry out as my pussy squeezes him.

"You like it rough, don't you?" he purrs. He lets go of my hip, and at first I think he's bracing himself against the wall until I hear the sharp slap of a hand against skin. Until I *feel* the sting of his palm. "He may have been your first, Juliet, but I intend to be your last."

His words ricochet around the bathroom as he spanks me again, and this time, I see stars. I feel myself flutter around his cock, on the brink of a cataclysmic orgasm.

"Chase," I gasp out, and he slaps me again. This

time, I scream out loud, and I have half a mind to hope that the hallway outside is empty.

"My girl's a screamer," he hums, caressing my sore ass. "Did you scream with all of them? Or just me?"

"Just... you..." I moan, feeling hot tears sliding down my cheeks unconsciously.

"Good girl," he says, his praise like a balm to my frayed soul. He relaxes his hold on my hair and brings his slapping hand around to my clit. "I want you to come for me, Parker. I want you to milk my cock for all it's worth."

"Oh, fuck," I wheeze, the sudden pressure of his calloused thumb sending me over the edge.

"That's it," he says, his voice almost frantic. "Come for me. *Only* for me."

I shatter around him, feeling my whole body pulse as I squeeze his hard shaft. My vision goes white, and my body pulls taut uncontrollably, snapping and shuddering beneath him as the most powerful orgasm I've ever had runs through my veins like wildfire. He groans and presses into me as he finds his release, pulling my hair each time his body twitches. It sends aftershocks through me, and though I'm not screaming anymore, I can still hear the echoes of my cries against the tile.

After a few seconds, he pulls out. I hear him walk to the sink, and I assume he's going to clean me up—*the* dress, after all. Instead, when I look over my shoulder, he's splashing water on his face.

"I know what you're waiting for, but I'm not cleaning you up," he says. After buckling himself back into his pants, he walks the two feet to me, turns me around to face him, and reaches down between my legs. When he pulls his finger away, I see the sheen of his cum on the tip of his index finger. Opening my mouth, I assume he wants me to taste it—after all, he's done it before. Instead, he presses his finger behind my ear, rubbing it into my skin like perfume. It takes me a second to register that the scene is not over. "I want you to walk out of here with my cum dripping down your legs, with it behind your ear like your own blend of perfume. Like I'm *marking* you as mine."

I laugh. "As if anyone will know—"

"I'll know. All night, as you talk to people, as that predatory professor tries to get in a last word," he says, his voice soft as he trails his finger into my still-open mouth. "I will know that my scent is all over you. Between your legs, on your neck, and on your breath," he finishes, reaching down and scooping up another finger of cum before placing it into my mouth.

My knees are shaking as he helps me straighten and smooth out *the* dress, and I look at myself in the mirror. I look positively half-fucked. Fixing my hair as quickly as I can, I wipe the mascara from my cheeks and swipe on some fresh lipstick. When I finish, I notice Chase watching me in the reflection of the mirror. His brows are furrowed, and his expression is reverential.

He may have been your first, Juliet, but I intend to be your last.

"Ready?" he asks, his smile cocky as he holds out a hand.

If I wasn't so observant, I might not miss the bob of

his throat, the way his eyes are scanning me for any trepidation, the way he seems to be offering something more than his hand.

"Yes, sir," I tell him, smiling as his eyes glaze over slightly.

————

After an hour of mingling, hanging on to Chase's arm, we make our way back to the valet line. His car is ready before I can ask about our plans for the rest of the evening, and he drives us toward my house as I tamp down my disappointment. Just as he pulls up to the house, he turns to face me.

"I'd invite you home tonight, but your brother is there, and I'd rather not have that conversation tonight."

My heart skips a beat at his words. "Yeah, we should probably tell him soon, though."

Chase nods once, his expression serious. "We should." He looks up at my house. "May I come in for a minute?" I nod, feeling excited, but he smirks knowingly. "Aftercare, Juliet. Remember?"

He climbs out of his side and opens my door, taking my hand and walking with me to the front door. I unlock it, and he comes inside, looking around for a few seconds before following me into the kitchen.

"I love this house," he murmurs, leaning against the counter.

I lean against the small island and narrow my eyes. "You do?"

"Yeah. This feels more like *home* than the castle ever did for me."

I swallow thickly, thinking of how much Dylan hated it. Thinking of Chase's stipulations.

They must be okay living in that house until the day you decide to sell it. And maybe that's never. And they have to be okay with that. Am I making myself clear?

"Are you okay?" he asks, walking over to where I'm standing.

"I'm fine," I tell him, my eyes fluttering closed as he trails his fingers over my neck.

"Go into your bedroom, Juliet. I'll check you over before I leave."

I walk across the kitchen to the hallway, and I feel his hand on my lower back as we enter my bedroom. My cheeks flush when I see the pile of clothes in the corner, the desk with scattered papers pertaining to my dissertation. My barely-made bed—I'd pulled the duvet over the rumpled sheets this morning, not bothering to properly make it. Plus, there are several water glasses on my bedside table.

"I should've tidied my room before you came over."

Chase chuckles. "You think I don't know that both you and your brother are two of the messiest people ever to exist?"

I snort. "That must bother you. His notorious piles in your pristine apartment."

I hear Chase laugh as he turns me around, running a hand down my back to my zipper, slowly unzipping the dress.

"I'm used to it. Doesn't bother me." I step out of the

shoes and dress, and I hear Chase lay the dress over the back of my desk chair. "On the bed."

I crawl over to the middle of the bed, clad only in my thong and strapless bra. Reaching up, I unpin my hair, letting it fall down my back as I stare at the floor.

"I'm really fine. You don't have to do this." Looking up at him, I'm startled to see the way he's staring at me incredulously.

"Parker, I take my role as your Dominant very seriously. That means ensuring your wellbeing at all times. I was rough with you earlier. Let me check you over. Please lay down on your stomach."

I do as he says, my cheeks heating as he inspects my backside. He rubs a hand over where he spanked me earlier, and seemingly satisfied, he grabs my ankles and rolls me onto my back. Crawling into bed next to me, I see his eyes scan my body—my neck, specifically. He runs a finger behind my ear, the hint of a smile playing at his lips.

"You did well tonight," he murmurs.

I preen at his praise. "Thanks."

"Your professor will leave you alone now," he says sternly, standing up.

"I know. You made it crystal clear."

He places his hands in his pockets, and my eyes graze over his evident erection. "And what, exactly, did I make clear?" He quirks a brow.

"I'm yours," I whisper. My eyes scan his body, and I suddenly feel hot and needy. "You're really going?" I ask, hating the way I sound desperate.

Chase smiles. "I don't have to. Not yet." I squeeze

my thighs together at his insinuation, and he doesn't miss the motion. His eyes darken as he drops to his knees.

"What are you—"

He pulls my hips down to the edge of the bed, wrapping my legs around his waist as a finger trails along the seam of my white lace underwear. He slowly pulls them off, and I blush when I realize how wet they are—from his cum, from my arousal. He doesn't say anything as he places both hands on my waist.

"One more taste for the night," he murmurs before dipping his head and laving his tongue up my slit in one fell swoop. I arch off the bed, moaning as I hear him inhale. "I don't think I'll ever get tired of how you taste, Juliet. It makes me feral. And our scents combined? It's like my own personal blend of heroin. Addictive, sweet, and agonizingly intoxicating." Another long lick and I'm whimpering. "You were such a good girl tonight. I think you deserve to come again, don't you?"

"Yes," I whisper, squeezing my eyes shut.

"Eyes open," he demands, and my eyes fly open. "There you go. I want you to see what you do to me," he growls, and I see one hand dip to his waist, the sound of his belt coming undone clinking through my bedroom.

"Oh fuck," I moan, watching as his hand quickly moves below my line of sight. Knowing he's finding his pleasure while his lips are on me—knowing that my taste undoes him like this... "Chase," I beg. "I need more."

"Tomorrow, love."

I gasp at the pet name. He's never called me anything but Juliet or Parker. His dipped head soon makes me forget my name, though, and thirty seconds later, I convulse against his face, riding his tongue as he sweeps it slowly—roughly—across my clit. I cry out his name, fisting his hair as I shake uncontrollably, bucking my hips up until it slowly dissipates. I hear Chase groan, and then he crouches over me as his load spills over my core in thick, hot jets. His face is slack, his eyes boring into mine as he finishes.

"Fuck," he hisses, collapsing next to me on the bed.

"Thank you," I tell him, covering my face.

I feel him pepper kisses along my jaw, my stomach, my inner thighs. A few seconds later, a warm washcloth is cleaning me up, and it feels incredible. I shiver as he runs it down to my feet, massaging them with the warm cloth.

I'm suddenly exhausted.

"Are you hungry?"

"No. Just tired," I tell him.

"Want me to start a bath for you?" he asks, already walking to my ensuite bathroom.

I open and close my mouth when I hear the water running. Walking back out, I see that he's already managed to buckle himself back into his pants.

I could get used to this.

"I should go," he says, bending down to kiss me softly on the lips. "What are you doing tomorrow?"

"I have to work on my dissertation tomorrow, and then I'm getting dinner with Jackson."

"What if I bring you lunch?" he suggests.

I grin. "I'd love that."

He smiles too, and it makes my stomach flutter. "Goodnight, Parker."

"I'll lock up," I say quickly, starting to get off the bed.

He holds a hand out. "I still have a key. I'll lock up. Go enjoy your bath."

He gives me a dazzling smile before exiting my bedroom. I hear him close the door, and then I collapse back onto the bed as the bath fills.

I roll onto my side, smiling like an idiot.

Oh, I am in so much trouble.

CHAPTER TWENTY-FOUR
THE UNCERTAINTY

CHASE

After leaving Juliet's house, I head back to my apartment. I can already feel the void of not having her around. Like a goddamn addict. I spent all week thinking about her, grateful for the daily check-ins, impatient for tonight... and all I could think about from the minute I saw her in that dress was ripping it off. I wasn't lying when I told her that she makes me feel feral. I've always been primal, but she turns me into a sex-crazed beast.

It's also more than that, though—and I have to push it down into the recesses of my mind so that I don't overanalyze.

And it's not that I avoided intimacy—it just never interested me. There's something to be said for the fact that I also care about her as a friend. I always have. I've always wanted to take care of her.

I don't half-ass anything.

Perhaps that's why I feel the need to give her every-thing—every fucking piece of my soul.

When I pull into my garage, I lock the vintage car up and take the elevator up to my apartment. I quickly check my appearance in case Jackson is still awake, and when the doors open, I make my way to the kitchen.

"Hey," Jackson says, nursing a cup of tea. He's sitting at the island, looking exhausted as hell, like usual.

"It's past your bedtime," I tease.

"It's only ten," he deadpans, glaring at me. "And where were *you* this lovely evening?"

"Gallery opening. New client. Though her husband is a fucking creep," I mutter.

"Our lives are so different," Jax jokes. "Tea?"

I shrug. I'd prefer scotch, but I also know that it's rare that we're able to talk like this with no distractions.

"Sure. I'm going to go change."

My feet clack along the marble as I walk to my bedroom, loosening my tie. After changing into sweat-pants and a T-shirt, I saunter back into the kitchen.

"Have a good night?" I ask, sipping the herbal concoction and trying not to grimace.

He nods but doesn't elaborate. We sip our tea in comfortable silence. I think about Juliet taking a bath —about how she mentioned telling Jackson about us. The thought makes me nervous as fuck. I'd like to think that Jackson would be happy for us, but he's also been a constant witness to my lifestyle—my parties, the women in and out of my bedroom, a new one every week. I grip the mug tightly as I think about how it would play out. Me asking about Juliet. Maybe broaching the subject. Would he be happy? Or would he tell me to fuck off? The last thing I want to do is for him to find out the wrong way—perhaps catching us somehow.

So, fuck it. Maybe I can lay the groundwork. It's not like I intend for her to go anywhere. I'm all in now—and it seems like she is, too.

"How's Juliet?" I ask casually, keeping my face neutral.

Jax shrugs. "She's fine. I guess she's seeing someone new. I'm happy for her."

I press my lips together. Okay, so he knows she's seeing someone. Maybe this will be easy, then.

"I didn't realize she would be up for dating so soon."

Jackson looks at me with a weary expression. "You know Jules. I'm sure she has her reasons."

I nod once. "Right. And I'm sure those reasons are fact-checked and peer-reviewed, too."

Jax laughs. "Of course." I feel him look at me as I sip my tea. "Why do you ask?" *Fuck.* There's a hint of suspicion in his voice.

Do I ask him? Tell him? How do I tell my best friend that I might be falling for his sister?

I school my face into something indifferent and hard. "She's grown up. Smart. Intelligent. It's hard for me not to notice," I finish, my heart pounding in my chest.

Jackson snorts. "What, you have a crush on my sister now?"

I shrug. "I was asking how she was, Jax." When I turn to face him, he's watching me with narrowed eyes.

"Do you?" he asks, his voice a little harder now.

"Do I what?" I ask, playing dumb.

"Do you like her?"

It's now or never...

"Maybe. But I wanted to talk to you first."

Jackson laughs again, and I feel my blood turn to ice as he continues. "No offense, but she's way too good for you."

I grind my teeth together. "Obviously." Before I can ask him more questions, Jackson sighs and stands.

"I need to get to bed." My eyes dart to his when he hesitates by the sink, his jaw feathering as he considers his next words. "There's something I want to talk to you about. Are you free for lunch tomorrow?"

Fuck. Lunch. Juliet.

I'll reschedule. This sounds serious. "Yeah. Here?"

He shakes his head. "No. Maybe we can do that pub we like in town?"

"Perfect. See you tomorrow."

After he walks out, I decide to forgo the tea for scotch. Sitting on my couch, I watch the city below me as I take small sips, considering Jackson's words.

No offense, but she's way too good for you.

Before I know it, I'm grabbing a second glass, and then a third, and then a fourth. By the time I'm sloshing the expensive whiskey as I pour, I decide that maybe Jackson is right. Maybe she is too good for me. I mean, she's bound to realize that soon, right? I may have money, but I'm still a Ravage. I've never been in a serious relationship. Why the *fuck* did I ever think she could be my first? Jackson knows me better than most people. I put feelers out and he shot me down.

Groaning, I lean back on the couch and stare up at the ceiling as the room spins.

I tried so hard to keep my distance from her. That's the most frustrating thing about this. I tried to get her to stay away, but she broke through my wall so much easier—and faster—than I ever thought anyone could.

But maybe there's room for growth here, too.

Maybe I can use the lunch with Jax tomorrow to prove to him that I *am* good enough for her. That I can prove it—that I never want to let her go.

I fall into bed a few hours later, dreaming of dark-blue velvet, long legs, and the smell of Juliet's arousal.

———

The next morning, despite my pounding head, I decide to focus my energy on Jackson. I text Juliet, asking if we can meet a little later than planned, and she agrees. I send a few more texts to Luna, readying the castle for an outlandish lunch in the gardens. It's sunny and warm, and it will be a nice place for her to take a break from her work. Maybe a little bit of fun as well. And then I can drive her home before her dinner with Jackson.

I ready the paperwork I've been planning to share

with Jackson—the new regulations and employee guidelines that Saint Helena Academy has sent through. It's official as of yesterday. I won't make any mention of why I did it, but I will be sure he understands that his job is, and always will be, secure.

Smiling and whistling, I meet Jackson at the pub at noon, the folder under my arm. I can tell instantly that he's nervous—his fidgeting fingers and the empty pint glass are two indicators. Slipping into the booth across from him, I'm fully prepared to tell him about acquiring Saint Helena, and if the conversation goes there, exactly how I feel about Juliet. But before I can get a word in, Jax lets out a heavy sigh and puts his face in his shaking hands.

"There's something I need to tell you," he says, his voice shaky.

I set the folder on the table. "You okay?"

He nods, running a hand over his face. "Fuck, why am I so nervous?" he asks, laughing.

"If you're here to tell me you're in love with me..." I joke, and he laughs again. It eases the tension somewhat.

He blows out a shaky breath. "I'm gay. Okay? I had this whole speech planned, but I'm so *fucking* nervous that I have to tell you now before I shit my pants," he continues, lips trembling.

"Thank you for telling me," I say carefully.

Jackson snaps his eyes to me. "You're not surprised?"

I shrug, taking a sip of the beer he already ordered

for me. "I've known you since you were fourteen. You think I didn't notice?"

Jackson looks flabbergasted, and I try not to smile. "But I—how did—" He runs another hand down his face. "I mean, *how* did you know?"

The lingering glances at other men.

The way his heart never seemed to be into sex and women like mine was.

There were numerous instances where he'd light up with a man and go lackluster with a woman.

But I don't say any of that.

"Do you remember what you said to me when we first met?" He shakes his head, visibly relaxing now that the cat is out of the bag. "I asked you if you knew who I was. You were being so goddamn nice to me, I assumed it was a prank. No one had ever treated me with respect, you know?" Jackson swallows, and I continue, finding my throat starting to constrict with emotion. "And you looked me right in the fucking eye and said, 'You're Chase.'"

Jackson laughs. "How meta of me."

I chuckle. "So I suppose it's the same with you. You're Jackson, and I always noticed how you were attracted to men. I'm observant. But of course, I didn't want to say anything, and it didn't matter to me."

Jackson nods once. "So you... it's not weird that I'm..." he trails off, flustered.

"Jackson," I say firmly, trying to reiterate my point. "First of all, thank you for telling me. I love you. I support you. Whenever you're ready to talk more about it, I will be here to listen. You're my best friend. Nothing will ever change that."

Jackson's eyes are brimming with tears. He nods again, taking a sip of his beer. "Well, that was easy."

I laugh. "You should talk to Juliet."

I realize my mistake the instant I say it.

"Jules?" he asks, brows raised.

I look down at the table, trying to make myself appear casual. "Yeah. I know she would want to know."

It's quiet for a minute as Jackson considers my words. I should have kept my goddamn mouth closed, because when I look back up at Jax, he's watching me with a wary expression.

"What's going on between you and my sister?"

Fuck.

Well, here goes nothing...

"We've been, uh, casually dating."

Jackson leans back and crosses his arms. "Ha ha. Very funny."

I grimace, taking another sip of my beer. "It's true, Jax."

My voice is soft enough that Jackson rears his head back and glares at me. "Stay the fuck away from her," he says, his voice like ice.

"Jax—"

He stands, pointing a finger into my chest. "No. I'm glad I told you about myself today, and thank you for the support, but don't fucking joke around with me right now, Chase."

I stand up, nostrils flaring. "Jackson, listen to me. It's real. I care for her. It's a very recent thing—"

"You're not joking." His face is white as he assesses me.

"No. I'm not joking. Please, hear me out—"

"No!" Jackson yells, and a few people look over at us. "I thought you maybe had a casual interest in her, which, by the way, I'd planned to extinguish as much as possible. But now you tell me that you're dating?" His face pales as he slides out of the booth. "It was you, wasn't it? The dress box and the black roses?" He's panting now, looking like he's either going to punch me or cry. "I'm only going to say this once and only once. You are not good enough for her. Stay the fuck away from her."

Something in my chest cracks in half. I'm desperate to lay it all on the line. I can't lose him. Not now, not after he looked so fucking happy a moment ago.

"I'm sorry. Please listen to me," I beg, holding my hands out. "She's more than a casual fling. I've cared about her for a long time, and I compare every woman to her. She's... different. She makes me feel something —fuck, I might even love h—"

Jackson steps forward and shoves me back. "No, you listen to *me*," he seethes, eyes glassy with rage and betrayal. "I know what you're like. A different woman every weekend, willing to suck your cock and then disappear forever. You think I don't see the headlines? I've been living with you for two years," he growls, breathing heavily. "And I've known you for twenty years.

I know how you are. People don't change overnight. Jules isn't like that. She might seem tough, but deep down, she's like me. Someone who desperately wants to be loved. And you? You're..." he trails off, glaring at me. "You're so fucking wrong for her. Just stay away from her." He grabs his phone and pockets it. "Great talk, by the way," he adds caustically, placing a twenty-dollar bill on the table before twisting around and walking out.

Guilt racks me then, and I have to sit down to steady myself. I put my face in my hands as I think about everything he told me and how I completely fucked it all up. He was opening up to me, and I ruined it.

I have to talk to Juliet.

Standing up, I glance down at the folder sitting on the table. Sighing, I pick it up and hope that I can tell him about Saint Helena soon.

CHAPTER TWENTY-FIVE
THE BREAK

JULIET

I'm pulling my hair into a messy bun when Dylan knocks on the open door of my office.

"Hi!" I chirp, unsure if I should stand and hug him or if I should stay seated. I decide to stand and hug him, and luckily, he hugs me back.

"Hey, Jules." When I pull away, he gives me a lazy smile. "Sorry to show up unannounced. I wasn't sure if you saw the editor's decision earlier this week or..." he trails off, referencing the paper we submitted together a couple of months ago.

I sigh. "Yes. I saw it. I'm sorry, it's been a crazy week, and I meant to reach out."

He shrugs and sets his bag down in my chair. "It's no problem. Are you free to talk about it now?"

"Yeah! Let me save this," I mumble, closing down

the rough draft of my dissertation that I have pulled up.

"How's it going?" he asks, dropping into the other chair across from me.

"Oh, you know. Working on a Saturday. And probably tomorrow. Hell, I'll be pulling seven-day weeks for the foreseeable future."

He laughs. "Tell me about it."

I smile as he pulls his computer out of his bag.

We're so much better as friends.

"Right, so the editor had some suggestions for the discussion portion. We also need to resubmit better-quality images before they can accept, and we'll need to reformat the abstract..."

I glance at the clock on my computer. I have three hours before I'm supposed to meet Chase at my house.

"Do you have time now?" I ask. "Might as well get this all done so we can resubmit. It'll be great to add to my CV if they accept it quickly. Maybe we can knock out the revisions today?"

"Yeah, that works for me."

I nod. "Great. Let me pull up the final paper, and we can go through each section together."

I hear his chair scrape against the floor as he comes around to my side of the desk. It feels nice—normal, even. He gives me a small smile that tells me he feels exactly the same way.

"Jules?" he says as I pull the document up.

"Yeah?" I turn to face him.

"I think you were right. About being in love. I think I was complacent. But I'm glad we realized that we're better off as friends. I'm really grateful for you."

I pull my lips to the side and bump his shoulder with mine. "You too."

———

Dylan is leaning over my shoulder, chewing on a french fry from the basket he procured from the cafeteria an hour ago when a knock startles me out of my concentration. My head snaps up, and my heart drops when I see Chase leaning against the frame. His expression is completely closed off, but his eyes are shifting between Dylan and me. His jaw flexes once, and I see one of his fists curl at his side.

"Am I interrupting?" he says, and to an outsider, his tone might not set up any alarm bells. But to me, he's using his Dominant voice. His blue eyes pierce into mine, and he holds my gaze for a second before looking away, expression stormy.

I glance at the clock on my computer and gasp, cupping my mouth. I was supposed to meet Chase at my house an *hour* ago. "Oh, fuck. I'm so sorry, Chase. Dylan and I were working on our paper, and I must've lost track of time."

Dylan stands, holding his hand out. "I'm Dylan."

My eyes move between them—and Chase glares at me as he shakes Dylan's hand. "Right. We actually met at the engagement party," Chase says, his voice low and lethal. "Chase Ravage."

"Oh shit, sorry. I forgot." Dylan gives me a knowing

smirk. "I was actually about to get going. I'll see you next week, okay, Jules?"

Chase's eyes narrow as he watches Dylan pack his things up. "Nice to see you, Declan."

"It's Dylan," I say, crossing my arms. *He knows that.*

"Of course," Chase says, watching as Dylan waves and walks out of the office. Chase snaps his eyes to me and closes the door a little too loudly.

I hold my hands up as he takes a step closer. "I'm sorry. We got a decision on our paper, and we needed to make revisions, and—"

"I'm only going to ask this once, and then I'll never ask again. Are you and he able to work as friends after being lovers for so long?"

His voice is dripping with jealousy, and I swallow before answering. "Yes. We work better as friends. He told me so earlier today."

Chase takes another step forward. "Second thing," he murmurs, inches away from me now as he eyes my messy desk. "When I ask you to meet me somewhere, I expect you to be there *on time*," he growls, his eyes darkening. "Both as your Dominant and your—" He snaps his mouth closed, and I see him curling his fists again as he takes a steadying breath.

His reaction hits a nerve. "I said I was sorry." My voice is steady, but it's edged with annoyance. "I wasn't standing you up. I got absorbed in my project and—"

"Right. With *Dylan*." His voice is dripping with derision. "Your life might be so much easier if you and I could discuss methods and research rather than safe words and best ways to cover up bruises," he adds, taking a step away.

I see the resignation written all over his face. "No. That's not it at all. I don't *want* to discuss those things with you. I like what we have. Dylan and I were great on paper. He's nearly perfect in every other way—"

Chase huffs a cruel laugh. "Right. How could I forget?"

I study the way he's looking anywhere but my eyes. The way he seems to almost be *in pain*.

"Chase, I'm falling for *you*," I admit, taking a step closer. "I don't want Dylan. I'm really sorry I missed our lunch date."

His jaw tics, but he doesn't look up at me. Instead, he runs a hand through his messy hair. How long was he pacing in front of my house, running a hand through his hair just like this?

My phone chimes.

"You should get that," he mumbles, sitting down in the chair by the door.

I nod as I check my text messages.

> Seriously, Jules? You and Chase? Wow. I truly thought that my best friend and my fucking sister would've had the balls to tell me about their secret affair. How long has this been going on?? You know what? I don't want to know. And I don't want to see either of you right now, so please leave me alone.

The blood drains from my face. My heart is

pounding when I look up at Chase. "Fuck. Jackson knows about us," I say softly, holding my phone out.

Chase doesn't take my phone. He watches me as his next words spill out. "I know. We talked about it earlier."

The room spins. "You—what?" I hiss. "I thought we agreed we would tell him together? Why would you do that?"

Chase stands abruptly, walking over to me and pressing the backs of my thighs against the ledge of my desk.

"Because you are driving me *fucking* crazy, Parker. Because I couldn't keep something this monumental from my best friend."

I see red. "You had *no* right to tell him," I retort, my voice breaking.

"He's my best friend," Chase says, looking slightly more unsure than he did a few seconds ago.

"And he's my brother," I grit out, curling my lips.

"He'll come around," Chase says, his voice low. Ashamed. Something in his expression tells me that perhaps he doesn't quite believe it.

Fuck.

Tears spring to my eyes. He reaches out for my face, but I push his hands away. "He's all I have left," I tell him, full-on sobbing. "In this instance, you were wrong."

His eyes flash, softening when they track a tear down my cheek. "Juliet—"

I shove him away, wiping my cheeks and opening

my office door. "Please, just go. I need to talk to Jackson."

Chase stiffens. "Parker, please, let's talk—"

"You can't storm into my place of work and piss all over any man that tries to talk to me. This isn't going to work if you keep underestimating me." My eyes sting with unshed tears as I look at him. "I don't know how else to tell you that I am falling in love with you. And that maybe I always have been in love with you. But you need to *trust me,* just like I proved that I trust you. I've let you take over seventy-five percent of my life already in the last week. The last ten years, if I'm being honest. But I'm not giving you the other twenty-five percent because it's for *me*. My work is for *me*. And my brother? Telling him about us? That was for *me* to do, not you. You can't keep making these calls about *my* life, Ravage."

Chase nods once, gripping the open door with his hand. "Got it. Thanks for clarifying." He's halfway out when he turns to face me. "I warned you. I told you I would be too much. That this? It would be *too* much for us to handle. I warned you that I would break you. That I'd consume you until there was nothing else left. I don't know how else to be, because I've never fucking felt like this before," he adds, his voice *so* soft. "Your brother was right. I'm not good enough for you, and I never will be."

"Chase—"

"I have a business trip this week, so I'll see you when I get back next weekend."

He turns and walks away before I can fully digest his words.

I clean myself up and glance at my phone again, seeing several texts from Chase—one of which includes what looks to be a picture of a romantic picnic lunch.

I groan as I sit, rubbing my face with both hands.

Jackson is mad at me.

Chase has every right to be mad at me, too—especially the way I berated him. But maybe it's good that we take some space. It started so quickly—we ignited like a match to a flame. Maybe taking a tentative step back is what we need. Besides, I have so much work, and I have to talk to Jackson...

Still, I can't help but feel like the best thing that ever happened to me just walked out of the door.

Maybe for good, apparently, if my brother had anything to do with it.

CHAPTER TWENTY-SIX
THE DRAGON

CHASE

I'm already nursing my second scotch when Miles bumps my elbow with his. We're 35,000 feet in the air, on our way to New York City, and we've been airborne for less than thirty minutes. I snap out of my daze and sit up, glancing over at him in the first-class seat next to me. Our father has a private jet, but the bastard next to me refuses to use it—citing environmental reasons.

At this point, I give zero fucks about how we get there.

"Are you going to mope all week?" Miles asks.

"Probably," I tell him, my voice flat.

"Goody. I love it when you're all melancholy and self-flagellating."

"Fuck off," I growl, indicating to the flight attendant that I'd like another. It's not like we have anywhere to be. I'm stuck here for five and a half more hours. I'll be sober by the time we land.

"Ah, so we're drinking ourselves into a stupor before noon, are we?"

"I thought I told you to fuck off."

"Very Charles Ravage of you, now that I think of it."

I close my eyes and set my glass down. *Fuck.* I know he's goading me, but still... it hits too close to home.

"I think it's very telling that I've never seen you this wrecked over a woman," Miles says, sipping his water.

"Yes, well, the other women weren't Juliet Parker. Also, yes, I'm a fucking idiot, but I almost feel worse about Jackson."

Miles is quiet as he flicks mindlessly through a fiction book he grabbed at the airport. I know him well enough to know that he's about to offer me very wise, older brother advice.

"What did Jackson say about it, exactly? He hasn't mentioned anything to me."

Of course, Jackson insisted on moving out, but I knew he made pennies at his job, and I couldn't ask him to move in with Juliet, either. We were wrong to keep our relationship from him, so I had Miles reach out to him and offer him a temporary room at the castle. It was the least I could do, since he refused my money when I offered to get him a suite at the Four Seasons.

"We had a good lunch, actually. One of the best we'd ever had. He... told me something, and it finally felt like I was seeing my *true* best friend, you know? Juliet and I had made tentative plans to tell him about our relationship together. Nothing set in stone, but I never would've told him without her. He pulled it out of me. One minute, we were talking about him, and the next, I was saying her name, and I guess he put two and two together. I couldn't lie to him. I'd never lie to him. And then he said he suspected when she got the black roses with the Diana dress, because obviously he's seen those fucking roses all around my apartment," I sigh, rubbing my face.

"Hold up, the *Diana* dress? Mom's dress? I thought it looked familiar on Friday night."

I wince. "Yep."

Miles lets out a loud breath. "Fuck. You really are a goner. Please tell me you didn't defile Mom's favorite dress?"

My lips twitch. "Don't worry. I'm having it professionally cleaned."

Miles sighs. "Naturally. So then what?"

The attendant brings a new scotch, but I push my drink away. His comment about our father had the impact he was hoping for.

"He berated me. For several minutes. Said I'd never be good enough for her and to stay away from her. I apologized, but it was too late. He hates me, and I lost my best friend."

Miles reaches over for my glass, taking a swig. I arch a brow as I continue. "I had a whole fucking thing set up for Juliet in the garden. We were supposed to meet at her house. I was anxious as fuck about everything with Jackson. She didn't show when we were supposed to meet, and then I remembered her saying something about working on her dissertation, so I drove to her office and saw her cuddled up with her ex."

Miles snorts. "Cuddled up?"

I frown. "Fine. Not cuddled, exactly, but way too fucking close. I don't think I've ever been that pissed off. But in the middle of talking, she got a text from Jackson."

"And she assumed you told him behind her back."

I nod. "Bingo."

"And now you're here with me."

"Second smartest brother," I murmur. "Obviously I am the smartest." He hits my shoulder, and I laugh. "I don't know. Jackson's words kept rolling through my head. That I wasn't good enough for her. And suddenly, I felt like a fucking idiot. Why was I there, staking a claim on her? Why did I think it could work between us when she's perfect, and I'm... me."

I stare down at my shoes as the words reverberate around our large seat cabins.

"Oh, buck the fuck up," Miles growls. I snap my head up to glare at him. He takes a delicate sip of *my* scotch and turns to look at me with a disbelieving smirk. "If you think that girl hasn't been in love with you for years, you're fucking delusional."

Something warm fills my chest at his words, and I suddenly want to hear all of his theories about this very subject.

"What makes you say that?" I ask, snatching my scotch back and shooting the rest of it.

Miles glowers at the empty glass before rubbing his

chin with his index finger and thumb. His gold cuff-links—engraved with the exact same 'R' as my signet ring—catch the light of the morning sun out of the airplane window. I begin to fiddle with my ring, adjusting myself in my seat when I think of the very same letter as a purple bruise on the inside of Juliet's thigh. *Fuck.* I was branding her as mine before I realized—or could admit—the extent of my feelings.

"Listen, I don't know her very well. But I saw the way she was searching for you all night at her engagement party. And the eager way she asked about you at your apartment two weekends ago. Plus, it takes some massive balls to come to the office and ask me for an invite to your hunting thing. She's been hard for your cock for a while."

I stop fiddling with my ring, turning to face my brother. "So it was you who gave her the invitation." He shrugs and opens his mouth, but I interrupt him. "That wasn't a question, by the way. I know it was you, so don't even try to fucking deny it," I add, narrowing my eyes at him.

Miles smiles innocently. "She came looking for the push. An excuse. I saw a fire behind her eyes that I've only ever seen in yours. So I nudged her. Do you blame me?"

I smirk. "Must you meddle in my love life?"

He grins. "That's what brothers are for. Especially brothers who can see what an idiot their younger brother is being. I'm still not sure what you're worried about. You guys spent all weekend at the castle, if Luna's reports are any indication. And yeah, she may be mad at you temporarily, but do you really think she's going to walk away now? She won't give up that easily. And if you think she will, you're underestimating her."

This isn't going to work if you keep underestimating me.

I stare at the seat in front of me, scowling. I see Miles pick his book back up, flipping page after page as we head east. I don't order another scotch, though I want one. Instead, I sip water and think about how I'm going to move forward. Last weekend changed everything for me—and I'm sick of fighting myself over something that feels right. But the thought of hurting her—or fucking up—is strong enough to make me want to rebuild my walls. The fear is potent enough to let her find someone else.

Anyone but me—isn't that what I'd told her all those weeks ago?

I close my eyes, thinking of someone else touching her the way she lets me touch her. Of disregarding her pleasure in favor of their own. Of not knowing the nuances of her life, her history, that house, her brother...

I know her.

It hits me then that perhaps I've been right for her all along.

That pushing her away only delayed the inevitable. We were two sparks circling each other for years, waiting for the blaze to peter out. Instead, we became engulfed in the flames.

There was never any other option for us. Even if she

ended up with someone else, I would've brooded about it for years, turning into a grumpy old man who let *the one* get away. Either that or I would've been alone with her again, waiting for that spark to catch, waiting to be consumed by her.

I was so worried about her ruining me that I didn't realize the truth. She did ruin me but in the best way. She pulled my walls down, brick by brick with her tenacity, her insistence on learning about being a submissive *from me.*

Now that I've had her, there was no fucking way I'd ever let her go.

Why I thought a taste would be enough is beyond me.

I scroll through my phone, stopping when a picture pops up on my feed of Juliet hunched over her desk, smirking at the camera. I sit up and zoom in, noticing *fucking* Dylan posted it from his account a few minutes ago. The caption: **Nearly done with this paper... almost time to celebrate.**

I pinch the bridge of my nose and resist the urge to throw my phone.

Almost time to celebrate...

Juliet and her ex-fiancé. Celebrating together.

"Motherfucker," I grit out, clenching my jaw.

"What's wrong?" Miles asks, and I jump, having forgotten he was sitting right next to me while I had my temper tantrum. I show him the picture, and he hands it back, shrugging. "Those two have about as much chemistry as two potatoes. I wouldn't worry about it."

"Yeah, but he's there, and I'm three thousand miles away. Proximity breeds familiarity."

Miles sighs and sets his book down, crossing his arms. "You're such a fucking dragon, brother."

I arch my brows and scowl at him. "How so?"

Miles shrugs. "You stockpile the things you love. Like it's fucking gold. Even as a kid, you always had to have the best. The best toys, the nicest clothes, and now, need I say more about your plethora of rare cars?"

I scoff. "That's a hobby."

"Sure. Let's call it a hobby, then. Is your hobby also dressing the woman you've loved for years in the most famous dress in the world?"

My jaw clenches as I consider his words. "Juliet isn't like other women—"

Miles laughs. "Trust me. I know. You've been unintentionally hoarding her away for years like a greedy reptile. And I don't even think you realize you're doing it."

"That's not true—"

"Every single woman you fuck looks a little bit more like Juliet Parker. Long brown hair, golden skin, light eyes... you have a type. Did you know that?" I scowl and pretend to pick lint off my pressed dress shirt. "Sometimes I wonder if the reason you asked Jackson to move in with you is because you hoped Juliet would visit more often."

"She hasn't," I blurt, scowling. "She's usually there when I'm away."

"Right. And that bothers you."

I look anywhere but at my brother as he continues.

As he unravels everything I've carefully hidden away. Every hope, every secret desire... it's all unspooling right now somewhere over Iowa. My heart races in my chest as the panic settles in.

"You compare every woman to her, keeping her high up on your reptilian pedestal. And you're content to leave her there to save her from yourself. But what you don't realize is that maybe you need to pull her down and tell her exactly how you feel. Because I think she likely has a very similar pedestal for you."

Images of a nine-year-old Juliet flash through my mind. Braces and frizzy hair. Cat headphones over her ears. She was so fucking wily and curious—always bothering Jackson and me. And then one day... she was fifteen. Leaving for homecoming in a dress that made me want to wring the neck of her fifteen-year-old date. And then every year after that got harder and harder... and my denial grew deeper and deeper. Until everything came to a head eight years ago. Until she offered me her *fucking* virginity. She trusted me enough.

I'm an idiot. I should've said yes.

I should've told her to walk into her room.

I should've quietly closed the door and stripped her bare and given her the fucking seven-course meal she always deserved for her first time.

I should've put my ego to the side, my worries and anxieties, and given her exactly what we both wanted.

But there's no use in ruminating on what should have been.

Maybe if I let go of everything I *think* should happen, I can give her exactly what she needs now.

Someone to treat her like a goddamn seven-course meal: check.

Someone who will love her with every cell in their body: check.

Someone willing to live in her house until the day *she* decided to sell it: check.

I'd live in that goddamn house for the rest of my life if it meant I could wake up with her next to me.

"Fuck," I murmur, running my hand down my face as I take a few steadying breaths. "I'm a fucking idiot."

Miles chuckles. "You're just now realizing that?"

I nod. "And now I'm gone for five days."

"So? She's not going anywhere. If you guys can put a stopper on your tension for eight years, you can wait five more days. But maybe now's the time to pull the romance card. Make sure she remembers that you're coming home to *her.*"

I crane my neck and look at him. "Why are you so good at giving advice?"

He gives me a shit-eating grin. "Because I'm your big brother, Chasey."

"Don't call me that," I grumble, frowning at his nickname for me. "And maybe take your own advice every once in a while, yeah?"

He laughs. "Right. The difference between you and me is that you have someone to go home to. I have no one."

"You'll find her," I assure him.

"It's too late now. Gotta find someone to fake it til I make it, according to Dad. No time for love and all that shit."

"Fuck Dad," I growl. "Seriously, fuck him. Is he the one putting the pressure on you?"

Miles shakes his head, grimacing before plastering a fake-as-fuck smile on his face. "It's fine. He's not wrong."

I open my mouth to argue that point when my phone chimes. Thank god for plane Wi-Fi. I glance down at the name, picking it up as I read my best friend's text.

> Last of my things are all moved out.
> Take care, Chase.

I groan and set my phone down. I see Miles lean over and read it in my peripheral.

"Looks like you're going to have to romance two people," he mutters, laughing. "I don't envy you."

I glare at him. "Wow, thanks."

Miles shrugs and gives me a cheeky grin. "I gave you my opinion. I never said it was going to be easy. Every dragon has to clean up the ashes from their fire at some point."

I ignore him for the rest of the flight, deciding on another two glasses of scotch as we descend into New York City.

It was going to be a long fucking five days.

CHAPTER TWENTY-SEVEN
THE EXPLANATION

JULIET

For the second time in a month, I am standing in Ravage Castle, this time before the double doors of the south wing. Straightening my spine, I wipe my sweaty palms on my corduroy skirt and look down at my boots as I take a steadying breath. Onwards and upward... isn't that the saying? Jackson might tell me to fuck off, and it would break my heart, but I had to try. We'd never gone this long without talking, and seeing as it's now Thursday evening, that means he's been giving me the silent treatment for five days. Rightfully so—I never intended for him to find out how he did.

I tamp down the anger at Chase as I reach forward and knock.

"Who is it?" Jackson asks from the other side of the door.

"Jax, it's me."

Please let me in.

Please let me explain...

"Go away, Jules. I'm busy, and I don't want to see you."

"Please let me come in. I wanted to tell you, I swear."

"But you didn't," he says, and I hear him unlock the door as he pulls it open.

I gasp when I look up at him. His hair is a mess, there are dark circles under his eyes, and he's wearing pajamas.

I push myself into the room as he scoffs, but he doesn't make me leave, so I set my purse down on the dining room table and glance around his living quarters. This wing is completely different from Chase's—it's modern, all black and white decorations, with pops of poppy red. Very modern and masculine. My eyes peer over the takeaway containers laying around, the dishes piling up in the small sink over in the kitchen, and the piles of clothes in each corner.

"I wasn't expecting company," Jackson mutters, crossing his arms. "I'm working," he says, and I see his laptop sitting on the couch next to a melting carton of mint ice cream—his favorite.

"Can we talk?" I ask, looking over at him with pleading eyes.

"I don't really have a choice, do I?" he adds, and his expression is cold. It makes my stomach drop. Jax and I have always been *so* close, and right now, the distance between us feels like the Grand Canyon. There's no warmth in his grimace—no teasing in the lilt of his voice.

"I'm sorry," I tell him softly. He opens his mouth, but I hold up a hand. "No, let me explain first, please?" He clenches his jaw and glares at me. I swallow thickly and continue. "I don't expect you to forgive me right away. I know... it's a lot to take in. Chase wasn't supposed to tell you," I add, trying to keep my voice calm. The betrayal of him telling Jackson still stings— but I don't need to pull Jax into the mix.

Jackson tilts his head and scowls. "Chase didn't tell me."

"What?" I ask, unsure if I heard him correctly.

Jax rolls his eyes. "He didn't tell me. We were out to lunch, and I guessed. I'm not an idiot, Juliet. He was gone last weekend—so were you. He was gone Friday night, as were you. The roses. The dress box. You're my sister, and he's my best friend. Honestly, you guys were painfully obvious about it all."

I swallow. "Yeah. We were," I tell him, my voice glum. "So he didn't tell you?"

Jackson shakes his head. "No."

I nod once. "Right. Okay." I sit and let out a heavy breath. "Are you hungry?"

Jackson shrugs. "I already ate. But there's some leftover pizza in the fridge. Help yourself," he says, his voice still detached and emotionless. He sits down and crosses his arms and legs as I walk over to the kitchen.

I subtly begin to tidy, trying to think through everything. Chase didn't tell Jackson. He didn't betray my trust. Instead, he planned a romantic picnic lunch and then walked in on me working with my ex. Why did I get so mad at him? It was all a terrible misunderstanding. Maybe if I worded what I was about to say carefully, I could ease Jackson into our relationship, too. I know deep down that he doesn't oppose us as a couple. But I have to come at it from his perspective. We were keeping something from him, and he feels betrayed.

I had to be fully honest.

I had to tell him things I wasn't even sure I'd admitted to myself.

These past five days away from us were good for him, I think. I know my brother well enough to understand his need to ruminate and sulk when he's angry. By now, he should at least be willing to hear me out. *Hopefully.*

By the time I'm done, the kitchen is clean, and I make my way back into the living room. I pluck the stray clothes lying around and set them by the front door, assuming the castle has someone to help with laundry. Next, I quickly gather the takeaway dishes and set them in the recycling bin. By the time I make my way back to the couch, Jackson is watching me suspiciously.

"I thought you were hungry."

I huff a laugh. "I am. But I couldn't eat with the moldy dishes taunting me."

I watch him carefully as his lips twitch. "It's been an eventful week," he retorts.

Grabbing two slices of pizza, I hand him a piece and sit on the other side of the couch. He eats it reluctantly, and I try to formulate what I'm going to say. Finally, dusting my hands off, I give him a no-nonsense look and take a deep breath.

"Do you want the long version or the abridged version?"

He huffs a laugh, and his pissed-off expression falters for a second. "The long version. Always." His scowl returns.

I nod once. "Okay. I'll start from the beginning. I think I've been in love with Chase since I was a teenager," I admit, looking straight at him. *Cut right to the chase, no pun intended.*

Jackson sits up. "Seriously? But you hated him for so long."

"Did I?"

Jackson opens and closes his mouth. "Jules, you would literally beg me to come to the house so that you didn't have to see him at the apartment. I assumed you two didn't get along, so I minimized interactions."

I smile when I think of how it might look to an outsider. "No. Let me explain. And please, let me finish before you judge me, okay?"

He presses his lips together and gestures for me to get on with it. I take another steadying breath. Here goes nothing.

"When I was eighteen, a few weeks before going off to college, I asked Chase to take my virginity."

"You did *what*?!" Jax hisses, his tone all authoritative and big-brothery.

"Let me finish," I beg him, realizing that my voice is shaking. "I made a list of all the pros and cons. I'd been thinking about it for a while—and he was always around, so it seemed obvious. I trusted him. He took such good care of us after Mom and Dad died," I add, my voice wobbling. "I know now that it wasn't right to ask him. To put him in that position."

Jackson makes a noise of disgust. "I can't believe he would sleep with y—"

"He didn't. He rejected me."

Jackson's face relaxes a bit. "Oh."

"Anyway, after he rejected me, we fought, and he made himself scarce in my life after that. And every time I saw him, I felt silly for wondering about him. For thinking of what it would be like to *be* with him. I missed his friendship, but it took me a long time to realize that I'd probably been in love with him. My heart broke for months after he rejected me."

Jax shifts uncomfortably, but he doesn't say anything as I continue.

"Anyway, then the engagement party happened, and he pulled me aside, and we fought—but Jackson, I felt more alive in those ten minutes than I ever had before. At my engagement party to another man, mind you. It made me realize that the time apart didn't tamp down my feelings for him. It only made them stronger."

Jackson hollows his cheeks as he narrows his eyes. "Really?"

I nod. "Yes. And in the middle of me yelling at him for paying for the engagement party, he let it slip that he was having a party at his apartment two weeks later."

Jackson sits up. "Wait. Is this why you broke it off with Dylan?"

"No. Of course not. That happened organically."

Jackson looks away and frowns. "Go on, then. I'm invested now." He gives me a chagrined grimace, and I try not to laugh.

"So I turned up at this BDSM party, completely out of my element, and Chase kicked me out."

Jackson chokes, and when he's done coughing, he's grinning. "Oh my god. You actually *went* to one of his parties?"

I arch a brow. "Of course."

"I'm glad he kicked you out," he adds, wrinkling his nose.

"Well, then we may want to skip over what happens next."

"Give me the abridged version," he says, turning to face me, though reluctantly.

"That night I was at the apartment with you and Miles, do you remember what Miles said? About Chase going hunting?"

"Yeah. I assumed it was some code word for something sexual."

I nod. "Yup. So, I showed up here the next morning, and well, one thing led to another..." I trail off, trying to think of how to phrase it without grossing my brother out.

"Jules, I *truly* don't want to know the rest. But thank you for explaining." I open my mouth, but he continues. "I didn't know... I had no idea you liked him in that way. I guess when I found out about the two of you last weekend, I assumed he coerced you into something."

I huff a laugh. "I coerced him, if anything."

He scowls, silent for a minute before speaking. "Are you happy? Does he make you happy?"

I swallow. "He does. And I am. I feel like I'm flying when I'm with him. It's uncontrollable, but it's thrilling, you know? And our chemistry is... off the charts."

My cheeks heat as Jax pretends to gag. "Okay, I can't hear any more. He said pretty much the same thing."

I perk up. "He did?"

"Yeah. How he's always compared other women to you, yada yada. But I was so angry, I wasn't really paying attention. It took me a few hours to cool down enough to text you."

I bite my lower lip. "I appreciate you listening to my explanation."

Jackson picks at the hem of his shirt, and I wait for him to say something. *Anything*. Finally, he sighs and looks up at me.

"It's going to take me a while to get used to it, but I suppose I can't stand in the way of true love."

My heart soars. "Really?"

He shrugs and gives me a small smile. "Yeah. Just... don't canoodle in front of me for a few months. My brain can't handle the two of you together yet, and I'm sure Chase is all fucking lovey-dovey with you."

I laugh and lean forward, taking his hands. "I think I love him, Jax."

Jackson gives me a resigned smile. "Yeah. He said that, too." My pulse races as he pulls his hands away. "I, um, actually have something to tell you too."

I sit up straighter. "Oh?"

He nods and runs a hand through his hair. "Yeah. And, well, I wasn't totally honest with you about why I'm such a mess this week." I look at him and hope my expression is neutral. He continues. "I, um, have been seeing someone. A man." He wrinkles his nose and looks away. "The guy from—"

"I know," I interrupt. I put a hand over my mouth. "Sorry. I just meant that I know who he is. Please go on."

Jackson stands, shaking slightly.

Oh, Jax...

"Anyway, at first, it was just as friends. But last week, he kissed me when he dropped me off, and I... *really* liked it, Jules. And I don't know—I'm not—well, I didn't think I was..." He takes a deep breath and pinches his nose. "No, I'm lying. I've known most of my life. But I wasn't ready to come out in high school. And in college, it was easier to play it off and to act straight. I knew I would probably come out eventually, but then Mom and Dad died—" His voice breaks, and my heart cracks as I stand up, walking over to where he's pacing. I take his hands again, and he gives me a grateful smile as he continues.

"Anyway, I've been carrying this baggage around that has prevented me from being free. My job. My kids. What I thought was *expected* of me. It meant that I never really felt free to be myself—especially in the confines of my job. You know how it is there."

"Jackson," I whisper, pulling him into a hug. "I'm so, so sorry. I'm sorry that you didn't feel supported."

His body shakes as he cries, clutching my jacket. "Maybe I could've saved myself from the pain and anguish had I come out sooner. I found a genuine connection with a couple of the women I'd dated in the past, but there was always something missing. Then I met Mark, and it was... similar to what you said about Chase. It was like fucking flying, Jules. Like my world was turned upside down. Like some animalistic, primal part of me was lit on fire. And that first kiss... and what happened next..." he trails off, and now he's sobbing. "I was *so* scared after. I'd just had the most amazing sex of my life, and I walked out. I apologized, and I told him that I wasn't gay. That I couldn't see him anymore. And I haven't heard from him since."

Tears stream down my face as I pull him closer. "Jax... I'm so sorry."

Jackson pulls away and wipes his face with the back of his palm, sniffing. "I really like him. I've spent all week trying to come to terms with it all, and I..." he trails off, looking away. Finally, he looks at me with glassy, bloodshot eyes. "I'm gay. I like men."

I grin. "I'm so proud of you, Jackson. Of realizing your truth. Of being courageous enough to admit it to yourself and to tell me. I'm honored to be the first to know."

Jackson gives me a timid smile. "Oh, um, actually... I told Chase first."

I huff a laugh and pull him into another hug. "That's fine. Thank you for telling me."

We stand there for several minutes, and by the time we pull apart, my heart is full again.

"You have to talk to Mark," I say, wiping my cheeks with the back of my hand.

He nods. "I know. But what if he doesn't want anything to do with me? He's so goddamn happy and confident about it all. This is all new for me."

For a second, I see my brother as the boy who taught me to ride a bike. The boy who tried so hard to fit in, even though people always loved being around him. The boy who always stood up for me, glaring at anyone who was mean to me. The young adult grappling with being my guardian after our parents died in the middle of finishing his college degree.

But right now, he's vulnerable. And scared. Maybe it's my turn to help him.

I shrug. "We're all on different journeys. I'm sure he'll understand if you tell him what you told me."

"Yeah. You're right." He looks around and laughs. "God, I'm a fucking mess. I've never been this much of a mess over anyone."

I smirk. "I understand that."

Jackson looks at me and gives me a small smile. "Thanks, Jules. For everything."

"You don't have to thank me. I'm your sister. I'll love you no matter what." I walk into the kitchen, grabbing another pint of ice cream from the freezer. "Now, why don't we sit down on the couch and finish this pint of ice cream together?"

Jackson preens. "I suppose."

As I sit next to him, holding out a spoon, he watches me carefully. "What?" I ask, taking a large spoonful and shoving it into my mouth.

He shrugs. "It's going to be weird to see you with Chase."

I laugh. "Why?"

Jackson's eyes rove over my face as he considers his next words. "I don't know. You're both very passionate. And Chase is... he's complicated."

I roll my eyes. "Trust me, I know. I'm still trying to decipher who he is under that hard exterior." I take another bite, swallowing quickly. "Though, underneath the facade, he's like..." I trail off, trying to think of how to phrase it.

"Fire?" Jackson suggests.

I nod. "Yeah. His heart is encased in stone, and he loves to push people away, but if you get inside, if you're lucky enough to crack it open, it's molten lava." Jackson chuckles as he takes a bite. "What?"

He shakes his head. "I should've seen it sooner."

I scowl. "Seen what?"

"The two of you. It actually makes perfect sense."

I try to hide my smile as I chew. "Yeah," is all I can think to say.

He turns to face me, a serious expression on his face. "Jules?"

"Hmm?" I ask, swallowing.

"Just promise me one thing."

"Of course. Anything."

He winces slightly, formulating his words for a few

seconds. "You guys are two of the most important people in my life."

My heart clenches. "Jackson—"

"No, I'm serious, Jules. Chase can be intense. I worry..." he trails off, sighing. "I know this sounds silly, but I worry about losing you to him. If push comes to shove, I will always take your side. I'm your brother. If you two broke up..." He stops talking, bobbing his head. "Just tread carefully. Okay? And know that if he hurts you, even a little bit, I will fuck him up."

I nod, trying to tamp down my smile. "I promise."

"He's gone this week, isn't he?"

"Yup. Shitty timing. I think he's back on Saturday."

Jackson's lips twitch. "Though it pains me to discuss my fuckboy best friend and my baby sister *in that way*, you should probably make amends."

I scowl down at the black leather couch. I know he's right. And I will make amends. But for now, I need some time to think things through.

"I will. Now, will *you* promise me one thing?"

Jackson gives me a sly smile. "Of course I'll be your maid of honor, but you should know that Chase is probably going to ask me to be his best man, so there will be a conflict of interest—"

I shove his shoulder playfully. "I'm serious, Jax." He nods once. "If I make amends, that means you have to make amends with Mark too. And, if things go well... I'd love to meet Mark. Officially, I mean."

Jackson inhales once, nodding slowly. "Yeah, okay. That's fair. He probably hates me, but you only live once, right? Maybe we can all get together this weekend if things work in our favor."

I nod. "Sure. That is, if Chase and I aren't lounging around naked in bed all weekend—"

The pillow hits my face before I finish speaking, and I giggle manically as I throw one back at him.

"Absolutely no sex talk about my best friend—" His nose wrinkles. "No, scratch that," he adds, shaking his head and giving me a look of disgust. "No sex talk with you in general. Please. For the love of God, or I'll ask one of my students to stab me in the eardrum with a pair of safety scissors."

I cackle. "Fine. That's fair." Just as I set the ice cream carton on the coffee table, a knock sounds on the door. "Expecting someone?" I ask, wiggling my brows.

Jackson looks at the door suspiciously. "It's probably Miles. He keeps trying to take me out as his wingman."

I snort as I walk to the door, expecting one Ravage brother...

And finding another standing at the other side of the door.

My heart starts to beat furiously as Chase stares at me, his mouth open in surprise.

"Parker," he growls, his hands in his pocket. He looks... nervous.

I cross my arms, though I'm not sure why. I've forgiven him. He didn't tell Jackson about us. Still... my feelings for him are potent, and I resist the urge to throw myself at him and also to shove him for not texting me good morning every morning like he had been all last week. I'm feeling a hundred different things at once, but most notably, relief that he's here. That maybe there's a way forward for us.

"Jules?" Jackson calls from behind me. I hear him get up off the couch, and Chase's eyes don't leave mine as Jackson pads closer. They darken slightly, roving over my lips briefly before they come back up to my eyes. "Who is—oh."

Jackson comes to my side, and I turn and walk over to the dining room table, grabbing my purse as Jackson lets Chase inside. When I turn back around, Chase is still watching me.

"I'll let you two talk," I tell them, giving Jackson a pointed look. My eyes flick to Chase's, and I nod once, though I'm unsure of what I mean to say with a single nod. I wasn't expecting to see him until Saturday. He must've come home a day early.

I brush past Chase as I go, and I feel the faintest brush of his fingers against mine, the softest touch of his thumb against my wrist. I look up at him, finding that he's smirking down at me with a knowing look.

Just as I close the door behind me, I hear Chase murmur an apology and Jackson's threatening response.

"If you hurt her, I won't hesitate to destroy you..."

I'm still grinning when I walk down the wide staircase to the first floor, nearly bumping into a brunette woman wearing a short plaid skirt and a white blouse. Her eyes are red, and she sniffs when she sees me. Her hair is pulled back into a braid, and she narrows her eyes slightly when I hold my hands up.

"Sorry," I tell her, giving her a small smile and continuing down the hall.

"We're all the same to him, you know," she calls out after me.

I turn around to face her. "Excuse me?"

She slowly saunters toward me, wearing five-inch pumps and, despite her puffy eyes, looking like she just stepped off a photo shoot.

"Chase Ravage. I assume you're here to see him? Unless Miles is taking submissive applications now."

My hackles rise. "I'm sorry, I don't know what you're talking about."

She shrugs, giving me a once-over. "You're his type. I would know," she adds, smiling softly and gesturing to her brown hair. "Just a warning... he'll lure you in with pretty words, but he'll never change. His *contract* guarantees it."

With that, she storms away, heels clacking against the floor. I take a deep breath as I attempt to shake off her words. I know she's probably one of his ex-subs, and perhaps she had words with him a minute ago, but the last thing she said snags on some small, insecure part of me.

He'll lure you in with pretty words, but he'll never change. His contract *guarantees it.*

I close my eyes as I imagine Chase going through his contract—and list of limits—with her. She was... stunning. And yet she still acted like a woman scorned.

I walk through the castle, flat boots thudding

against the marble. It's hard not to compare myself to someone like her, though, and once I'm inside my car, I grit my teeth and quickly pull out of the parking lot.

I knew he was experienced, and I'd be an idiot to think he hadn't had his fair share of other women.

You're his type. I would know...

Did Chase have a type? Was I his type? I'd never considered it, but now, as I drive away from the castle with burning eyes, I have to wonder if I can live up to the kinds of women he's used to—if I can live up to the kinds of *submissives* he's used to.

CHAPTER TWENTY-EIGHT
THE APOLOGY

CHASE

"Drink?" I ask Jackson, wandering over to the small bar set up in the dining area.

"Sure, make yourself at home," he chides, and I have to hide the smirk lifting my lips.

"It is my house," I add, pouring us both a hefty finger of whiskey. It's not my favorite—I prefer the smoky peat of scotch—but I know Jackson, and I know he's a massive lightweight, so hopefully this will help him get it all out of his system.

I am fully prepared to take a verbal lashing.

He takes the drink from me and watches me skeptically. I fucking hate this. Since he befriended me early on in high school, I don't think we've ever fought. Not once. Sure, we may argue and disagree about things, but never to this extent. I consider him my fifth brother. I don't know what I'd do without him, and I can only hope he feels the same way about me, because right now, he's looking at me like I'm a pile of shit.

Which I suppose I am.

I open my mouth to apologize again—as if my numerous texts and voicemails weren't enough—but he holds a hand up and takes a healthy swig of the whiskey.

"I won't pretend to know what my sister sees in you," he starts, grimacing as he takes another sip of his drink. "I love you. You're my closest friend. You've been there for me for everything. I know you'd lay your life down for me, and I hope you know that I'd do the same. But you have to know how much it scares me that your newest pursuit is my baby sister."

I'd expected him to say something like this, but it doesn't hurt any less. I craved his approval. It was strange, seeking it from my best friend—from someone I know so well—but that almost makes me want it more.

It also makes me feel ashamed because he's been there every step of the way. Every one-night stand for the last two years, and even before that. Every time I throw one of my parties and warn him that it might get rowdy. Every time he sees the way I casually check women out. The time he found one of my contracts and then quickly asked me to never bring it up again. He doesn't know *exactly* what my proclivities are, but he has some idea. I mean, fuck, an ex-sub had cornered me in the hallway just a minute ago, demanding to know why I'd ghosted her.

So, in a way, he's right to be worried about Juliet. I

don't blame him for wanting to keep his sister—his only living family—away from me. I can only imagine what he thinks of my dating life.

"She's not just a pursuit, Jackson," I tell him gently, trying to explain that she's so much more than that.

"Then why her? What does my sister mean to you? I've heard her version of the events, but I haven't heard it from you."

I sigh and shoot the rest of my drink, and Jax does the same. His neck is flushed, and I take our glasses to refill them. My hand is steady as I pour us another generous finger.

"Your sister was always off limits," I tell him slowly, handing him the glass of whiskey. I watch him as he takes a small sip, knowing that he's getting tipsy. I should cut him off after this one. "Which was fine—for a long time. She was six years younger than us. I didn't—*couldn't*—notice her until she was older. I wouldn't allow it. But I think I started to fall for her the summer before she went off to college."

Jax scoffs. "Right, when she proposed that you take her virginity," he says darkly, nose wrinkling.

I smirk. "She told you about that?"

He nods. "Unfortunately."

Chuckling, I continue, knowing I'm about to lay my life bare before him. "I don't think you realize what an enigma your family was for me, Jax," I murmur, looking down at my glass. "I was raised by Charles Ravage—a raging alcoholic who was a horrible, ruthless businessman. A man who didn't know how to be a good father, or a good husband. Our house was big, but it was cold. Devoid of love, of warmth, of the things that make a place a home. My brothers and I clung to each other, and if it weren't for us being close, we'd all probably be in jail, or worse. So when I met you, and got accepted into your family, it felt like I'd won the lottery. I had something my other brothers didn't have, though your family always tried to include them as well."

Jackson swallows, looking down, and I continue.

"I felt accepted with you. With your parents. With Juliet. The nights I came over for dinner. The weekends I stayed over. Those are some of my favorite memories of my childhood. And then, when your parents died, I knew I had to step in. Not just for you, but for Juliet. And it was in those moments—holding her while she cried, making her favorite breakfast, ensuring the very last thing she had to worry about was money... I realized I was doing it all for her. Yes, partly for you, but she was sixteen. A sophomore in high school. I knew you were grieving, but Juliet was..." I trail off, pulling my lower lip between my teeth.

"Broken," Jax offers.

I nod. "Yeah. Taking care of her gave me a purpose. I realized I enjoyed it—not *just* because of her, but because of a myriad of reasons I won't get into, and that led me into the BDSM lifestyle. By the time she came to me about taking her virginity, I was two years into exploring my kinks, and she was so... *is* so... perfect. Unblemished. I felt like a tainted rain cloud, always hovering, always ruining her lightness with my darkness. So I pushed her away. That night, and every day after that. I thought she was desperate, trying to check her virginity off a list, so I kept her at a distance so she wouldn't see how much I wanted her. I couldn't fathom that she wanted me, too."

Jackson sighs, cheeks flushed, and sets his empty glass down. And then, to my surprise, he starts to laugh.

Maybe the whiskey was a bad idea.

"Something funny?" I mutter, trying to dispel the irritation tainting my voice. I mean, I'd bared my soul to him, and he was laughing?

"Sorry. I'm just... if you guys get married, you'd be my brother. Legally."

I smile. "You'd officially be stuck with me."

He laughs harder. "Fuck my life," he wheezes, standing up and walking over to me, giving me a tight hug. He pulls away, glaring at me, the mirth suddenly gone from his expression. "I was serious earlier. I will destroy you if you hurt her. I will cut your beating heart right out of your chest, do you hear me?"

I frown. "Jesus, Jax."

He laughs again and hugs me. "I'm joking. You know I can't stand the sight of blood." Pulling away, he smiles. *Genuinely* smiles. "I'm happy for you. Truly. And her. But I'll tell you the same thing I told her. Never *ever* talk to me about your sex life."

I chuckle. "It's a deal."

We're both quiet for a moment as he looks around the living quarters, digesting everything that was said. Finally, Jackson looks at me with wide eyes.

"You owe me, right?" His voice is slightly slurred.

My mouth twists into a smile. "I suppose so."

He nods once, and then his expression is resolved. "Right. Thanks to you, I am now too drunk to drive. But I think..." he trails off, placing a finger on his lips. "I think I need to go do something."

I'm grinning by the time I'm pushing him into his bedroom, begging him to shower and offering to borrow Miles' driver to drive him to Mark's house.

CHAPTER TWENTY-NINE
THE AMENDS

JULIET

When I get home, I go on a long run, taking my favorite route along the ocean. The sun is setting, and I relish in the way my body moves me, the way my body supports me, mile after mile. I didn't bring my headphones, so I listen to the sounds my body makes. The way my body feels. Light puffs of air through my pursed lips. The soft pads of my shoes on the concrete sidewalk. The way my running shorts make a rustling sound with each movement. And then there are the internal sensations—my lungs burning slightly, but not uncomfortably, as I breathe heavily. My heart pulses in my veins. The sting of my calves when I go uphill.

I tune everything else out and *listen* to my body as I turn around, heading back home. By the time I open my front door, my legs are wobbly from overexertion, and my sports bra is soaking wet. I don't stop walking as I kick off my shoes, shed my clothes, and walk straight into my shower. I moan when the warm water hits my skin, genuinely smiling for the first time in days. I'm not worried about my dissertation, or Chase, or Jackson, or the woman at the castle.

Everything is going to be fine.

When I'm done shaving my legs, I turn my shower off and wrap a towel around myself, walking into my bedroom, still dripping wet. I stop walking when I see a note sitting on my pillow. Walking over slowly, I pick it up and read it, my heart pounding inside of my chest.

Parker,

I thought this list might help determine your next move, since you love data so much. If you wish to proceed, please go to your favorite coffee shop.

Pros: great sex, he's already best friends with your brother (yes, still), rich as fuck, knows your favorite color, flower, TV show, food, and smell, willing to grovel (but please don't mention this to anyone), will attempt to tame the jealousy, will always think you're the loveliest person I've ever fucking met, seven-course breakfasts every morning ;), but seriously, what do I have to do? Tell me, and it's done.

Cons: mediocre sex, seriously, is that what

*you want?, mediocre cars, mediocre dresses,
having to deal with your brother's annoying
best friend who will accept your rejection but
still wants to pay for your future wedding,
because he wants you to be happy...*

I'm swiping at my cheeks by the time I finish Chase's note. Laughing, I quickly change into a pair of ripped jeans and an old sweatshirt, sliding my feet into sandals before I throw my hair up into a wet bun. I grab my keys and drive to Perky Roasters, though seeing as it's nearly half past eight at night, I highly doubt it's open. Besides, how does Chase know my favorite coffee shop?

After I park, I walk into Perky Roasters, surprised to see it open.

"Hello?" I ask, looking around. A man walks to the register, smiling at me. He's young, and as my eyes adjust to the lighting, I realize all of the chairs are stacked and the tables wiped down. "Are you still open?" I ask, my voice unsure.

He shrugs. "It depends on if you're Juliet. If so, I was paid a hefty sum to stay open for you." He procures a cardboard cup. "Cappuccino with an extra shot?"

I take the coffee from him. It's still warm. "Um, thanks? Is there a note or anything?" I ask. *This is the strangest thing that's ever happened to me... but also the most romantic.*

He gives me a lazy, stoned smile. "Check the side of

your cup, lady." Then he turns and walks into the back, and I'm left wondering *who* is a lady and do I really seem *that* old?

I walk back to the privacy of my car, taking a delicious sip of coffee as the same scratched scrawl is written on the side of the cup.

> *You'll need your energy for tonight.*
> *And yes, I paid that kid five hundred dollars to stay open until you got there. Repeat after me: I don't half-ass anything. Not even an apology.*
> *Come to my apartment.*
> *PS: In case you're wondering, yes, I know your favorite coffee shop. Even when you thought I wasn't paying any attention to you, I couldn't look away.*
> *Xo*

My hand is shaking slightly as I take another sip of coffee, wondering how I'm going to quell my nerves enough to deal with romantic Chase. And with coffee fueling the adrenaline...

You'll need your energy for tonight.

I set my cup down and drive to his apartment in a daze, parking in Jackson's spot. I drink the rest of the coffee as I take the elevator up to *The Penthouse*, and as the doors slide open, I laugh when I see Miles standing against the foyer table, holding a black envelope.

"Did he put you up to this?" I ask, taking the envelope he's holding out for me.

"He certainly did," Miles grumbles, frowning. "First, he insists we leave New York early, and second, I'm told to wait here until you arrive—"

I cut him off and lurch forward, wrapping my arms around him in a tight hug. He goes still, and as I pull away, he's looking down at me with careful consideration.

"I'm not really the hugging type, Juliet," he grumbles, adjusting his tie as he takes a step back.

I smirk. "Right. Sorry. Thanks for this," I tell him, holding the envelope up.

"Oh, and Juliet?" Miles asks, crossing his arms. "I know I should give you the whole 'don't hurt him' speech, but we both know you're helplessly in love with him, so I suppose I'll save my speech for the wedding day."

His words send a cacophony of butterflies through me, and all I can do is nod before the elevator doors closed. I'm already ripping at the envelope. I expect to see an invitation, perhaps something pertaining to the castle, but all that's inside is a single, folded slip of paper. I unfold it as the doors open, walking quickly to my car before reading it.

Once seated, I squint down at what looks like a contract—and upon further inspection, is a revised copy of my original contract. Well, the abridged version at least.

Chase Charles Ravage and Juliet Marie Parker agree to the following, effective from today to the end of this calendar year, at which time this contract will end or (hopefully) be renegotiated. Any participant may also choose to end this contract before that time, for any reason (but the Dominant hopes this doesn't happen). Other terms to be agreed upon in person at The Black Rose.

I smile as I start my car, my heart beating in my chest as I turn right and head for The Black Rose. It's only a few blocks away, and as I pull up to the valet line, it doesn't surprise me that there's no one else waiting, and only one parking attendant. He smiles and opens my door, obviously expecting me, and I walk inside the very same restaurant from a few weeks ago. The arching pergola leading into the dining area is twinkling with lights, and I gasp when I see the main dining area empty save for one table—with a large bouquet of black flowers.

And sitting at the table is Chase, dressed impeccably in a black suit.

I cross my arms and stop walking a few feet away from the table. "Is sending me on a wild goose chase really how you're going to try and woo me?"

Chase smirks, watching me from his casual position. One leg is resting over the other, and his left arm is slung around the back of his chair.

"Truthfully, I only meant to do the pros and cons list. It spiraled out of control after that once Jackson and Miles got involved."

I open my mouth. "Oh?"

"Jackson was smart enough to suggest a caffeine boost, and Miles was dying to hand you another sealed envelope."

I scoff. "Very funny."

Before either of us can say anything else, Chase stands up and walks across the restaurant toward me. It reminds me so much of the times he marched across a room, furious and blazing with power. Tonight, he's relaxed, and... happy. His eyes are crinkled in the corners, and he's wearing a small smile as he stops an inch away from me. With one hand, he grips my waist, pulling me flush against his body.

"I'm sorry, Parker. For all of it. For rejecting you that night eight years ago. For talking to Jackson before talking to you. For being a jealous asshole with Dylan —though I can't promise that will change all that much. I did warn you that my one hard limit was sharing."

My lips twitch as I gaze into his eyes, my body bent at the waist. I place my hands on his chest, mulling over my words before they tumble out of my mouth.

"Well, then it's a good thing I'm yours and only yours."

His cocky expression flickers for a second, giving way to something vulnerable and open. But then he pulls me up to his lips, pressing his tongue into my mouth, and everything else falls away. I moan as both hands come to my waist, squeezing me and pulling me into his hard body. As his tongue sweeps into my mouth again, one hand comes to the back of my hair, and he fists it gently, growling into my mouth when I whimper.

"I had a whole dinner planned, but now I'm

thinking I want to eat you," he murmurs, breathing hard against my lips.

"Fine by me," I tease, smiling.

"As much as I want to devour you, it will be a long night. Let's eat. *Food,*" he clarifies.

Something warm lances through me at his words, and he pulls away, grabbing my hand and leading me to the circular table. It's simple—black tablecloth, pillar candles, and a bouquet of black roses. I feel thoroughly underdressed, but as Chase pulls my chair out, his hand comes to the inch of bare skin on my back between my jeans and my sweatshirt. I pull my hair out of my bun, letting it hang half-dry down my back. Chase pours me a glass of champagne—the fancy kind, I notice—and then we clink glasses.

"What are we celebrating?" I ask, taking a large sip of the delicious liquid.

"Our first date," he says, almost incredulously.

I frown. "No, this can't be our first date. I didn't dress up."

He laughs and then raises his brows, looking around. "You haven't given me a chance to tell you the next part of our date."

I look around suspiciously. "The next part?"

He nods. "In the back, there's an office. You may remember it from your engagement party. You'll find a dress—*if* you want to wear it. You already look perfectly ravishing in those jeans, Parker." His darkened eyes pierce into mine. *Oh, flirty Chase is dangerous. And smooth.* "Do you remember where it is?"

I open and close my mouth. "Yeah." I stand. "Be back in a minute."

I walk to the office he pulled me into a month ago, and there's a dress hanging from a hook on the wall. It's cream-colored and silk, elegant, and looks brand new. The thin straps hold up a low cowl neck, and the simple silhouette of the dress means it slips easily over my head. I forgo a bra and underwear, as the dress doesn't really allow for either. And there are pockets.

My favorite.

Shaking my hair out quickly, I use the tiny mirror on the wall to study my makeup-less face. I wish I'd thought of doing *something*, but it's fine. I see a pair of simple nude heels sitting in a box on the floor, so I step into them and look down at myself.

How Chase managed to get a dress that fit me perfectly is beyond me. Just as I turn to walk to the door, my eyes skim over a gold tube of Chanel lipstick. Smirking, I open it and use the mirror to apply the dark pink color. It compliments the dress, my hair, and my eyes perfectly. When I stand back, I'm impressed. It's simple and understated, yet I feel beautiful.

I exit the room and walk over to Chase, and his eyes slowly drag up my body, starting at my spiky heels and drifting up to my face and hair. He stands when I reach the table, and I try not to laugh. Always opening doors, always pulling my chairs out, always standing whenever a woman leaves or appears at a table... I'd bet money that he had some formal etiquette lessons growing up.

"Stunning," he murmurs. "Though, I want to point

out that I always think you're stunning, no matter what you wear."

"Thank you," I tell him as he walks around and pulls my chair out. And then the tiny, little voice from earlier pops into my head. *We're all the same to him, you know.* "I think I ran into one of your ex's at the castle earlier," I admit, looking up at his face as he sits down across from me.

He blows out a soft breath of air. "Ah, so I see you've been blessed with Clarissa's presence. Or was it Carissa?" My mouth drops open, and he grins. "I'm kidding. Clarissa came to me a few months ago after something traumatic happened to her. She sort of... imprinted on me. It happens sometimes. The experience is intense for some. Anyway, she must've figured out a way inside of the castle. We had some words, and I told her, like I have before, that it's over between us. She's angry with me, but she'll leave me alone now."

I run my fingers along the tablecloth as I take in his words. "How do you know? That she'll leave you alone now, I mean?"

He gives me a lopsided smile. "I told her that I was in a relationship. And that it was serious."

My cheeks burn as I look down, but I can't help but deny the way his words flood me with warmth.

"Why did you ask me to meet you at The Black Rose?" I ask, placing my elbows on the table and resting my chin on my clasped hands.

Chase's eyes twinkle as he leans back, sipping his wine. "Because it was the first time I realized how fucking much you drove me crazy."

I snort. "You mean the engagement party?"

"No, actually."

His answer catches me off guard. "But..." I trail off, frowning.

"Do you remember your graduation dinner, Parker?"

I inhale sharply. *My graduation dinner.* It was eight years ago, two months before I asked Chase to take my virginity. Jackson, Chase, and a few other people had thrown a surprise party for me here. I hardly remember the night—I was *so* tired because I'd been awake for two days trying to finish my finals and extra credit papers. But Chase had been there.

It was almost two years exactly after losing my parents.

"You probably don't remember what happened, do you?" he asks, a cocky smile on his full lips.

I shake my head. "No. I was exhausted—that whole week of graduation is a blur."

He nods, chuckling. "So you don't remember yelling at me about ordering for the table?"

I open and close my mouth, a sly smile creeping up on my face. "Maybe? Like I said, it's all a blur. Remind me of what happened, please?"

He laughs. "It was a perfectly enjoyable evening. I could tell you were tired, so when the server came to our table, I ordered one of everything. And I'll never forget the look you threw at me. It was pure outrage. You kept saying you were looking at the pesto pasta, and before I could explain, you went into a diatribe about how you weren't raised in a barn and how you didn't need me to mansplain the menu to you," he finishes, smirking.

I put my face in my hands. "Oh my god, I'm sorry. That sounds like something I would say."

When I lower my hand, Chase reaches out and takes my hand in his. "It's fine. I didn't take offense back then. As a matter of fact, I'd ordered you an extra serving of the pesto pasta without you knowing. And you were so tired that you fell asleep on my shoulder before dessert."

I bark a laugh. "No wonder I drove you crazy."

His thumb sweeps over the back of my hand, and he starts to rub small circles on my pebbled skin.

"Not in the way you think," he says slowly, looking at me through his lashes. "You were wearing this small, purple dress that barely covered your perfect ass, and I grumbled something to you about how the dress was too small," he starts.

I smile. "You were always complaining about my clothes."

"Oh, I loved the clothes, Parker. Too much."

My stomach drops and something hot flashes through me at his words. He continues.

"Your hair was wavy. Back then, it was shorter, and you had it tucked behind both ears. I was mesmerized. It was the first time I could see myself with you— kissing your delicate neck, running one of my hands up your decadent thighs," he murmurs, his eyes darkening. "You started fighting with me, and I was so fucking hard," he admits.

I laugh. "You were?"

He nods. "And then you fell asleep on my shoulder, and all I could smell was you. I carried you to Jackson's car, and I remember not wanting to let you go. I wanted to carry you all the way back to the castle and keep you there forever." He looks down. "Miles jokes that I'm a dragon guarding his golden hoard when it comes to you, and I'm now realizing how much I've always wanted to keep you for myself."

"So what took you so long?" I ask, my body heating under his gaze.

"You were off limits. Simple as that. And Jackson is my best friend. I didn't want to jeopardize it."

"Why did you, then? At the engagement party—at your apartment... the castle..." I trail off, everything sparking inside of me each time his thumb brushes a new circle on my hand.

His lips twitch, and he gives me a lopsided smile. "You wore me down."

I scoff. "Right. I wore you down. Because pinning me against the desk at my engagement party was *all* my fault," I chide.

He throws me one of those heart-stopping smirks. "I never said I wasn't attracted to you. I've always wanted you, Parker. In more ways than one. It was a matter of *when* my resistance would snap." My chest is rising and falling with each breath, and I feel *so hot* under his scrutinizing gaze. "I suppose it was always a matter of *when*. And I think, deep down, we both knew this would happen eventually. I certainly hoped it would, though I never could admit it out loud."

My heart is racing as he continues smirking.

"Chase," I start, feeling the emotion beginning to bubble up inside of me. "I—it was the same for me," I finish. "I never stopped thinking about you. And I think..." I trail off, closing my eyes briefly. *What if I tell him that I might love him, and he doesn't feel the same way?*

"Parker," he growls, and my eyes snap open. "Stop overthinking things. I've been waiting eight years for you. To *love* you. Don't you think it's about time someone did it properly?"

I open my mouth to reply, but just then, the server walks over with our first course. It's fresh tomato pasta with burrata, butter-fried sage, and flakes of parmesan. My mouth waters. I look up at him, my skin tingling.

I've been waiting eight years for you. To love *you.*

"Eat," he commands, using a spoon in one hand and a fork in his other to twirl his pasta. *Yeah, he definitely took etiquette classes.* "You need your energy. I don't plan on sleeping tonight," he adds, giving me a commanding, pointed look.

Oh.

I eat slowly, savoring the taste of the burrata, and watching Chase eat—though I've seen him eat numerous times—is foreplay all on its own. He eats elegantly, in a way only someone like him can. His eyes don't leave mine as he takes another bite, daring me to say something snarky. But I don't—I just watch him, soaking it all in. Studying the silk threading of his suit. The gold signet ring. The long fingers as they hold his utensils. The subtle scruff along his jaw. The way his throat bobs when he swallows. The dark-blue ring around his light-blue irises.

I've been waiting eight years for you. To love *you.*

"You're staring," Chase teases, smiling as he eats his chocolate cake.

I push my plate away. I've only taken two bites of the decadent cake, but I am stuffed. Chase's eyes flash when I place my hands in my lap.

"Come here," he directs.

I stand up and walk to his side of the table. Just as I ask where he wants me, he leans back and pushes his left sleeve up. His sharp gaze lands on me, and I take a steadying breath as he finishes. My subconscious lowers the wall I keep up, allowing him inside. Allowing him to tell me what to do next. It's strange... this feeling. Of letting go completely. He doesn't *control* me. He is *in control* of the situation, and for someone like me, it means no more overthinking. *Trusting* him completely.

I'd been doing more research this past week on the whole primal aspect of BDSM, and there was usually a natural tendency to freeze, fight, or run. I never experienced any of that with Chase. Not really—at least not for long. When he starts a scene, I go from fight or flight mode straight into a melted puddle. I am malleable. He consumes me, and I allow it. It's passionate and intense, and it's times like these that I feel myself drop right into subspace.

And since I assume he doesn't intend to chase me around the restaurant, I do the only other thing I can think to do.

I drop to my knees at his feet.

He chuckles. "Clever girl," he drawls.

Smiling, I place my hands on my legs.

This doesn't feel like a scene. It never does. It's not a contractual relationship between two civil people. It feels inescapable. *Undeniable*. Like it was always meant to be this way between us.

And it hits me at that moment. That maybe we're perfect together.

"We're alone now," Chase says, eating his cake. "I told the staff they must leave once they serve the cake."

"I see. And what is it that you would like me to do, sir?"

Chase looks over at me, an appreciative smile tugging at his lips. "Exactly what you're doing."

His praise makes my whole body warm with pride, so I watch him eat with a small smile. When he finishes, he pushes his plate away and looks at me with a heated gaze.

"Stand up."

I pull myself up, wobbling slightly in my heels. Chase appraises me with something soft and tender, and I swallow as his arm comes underneath the hem of my dress. His warm palm slides up my calf, eliciting a moan to escape my lips. Pressing me back slightly, my thighs hit the table. Before I can register what's happening, he lowers himself to the floor so that *he's* the one kneeling before me. I gasp when his hands come under my dress again, sliding up my thighs.

"What are you doing, sir?" I ask, my voice shaky as his calloused fingers come up between my thighs. The second they don't meet the hem of my underwear, his eyes flash, and he snaps them up to me, deliciously dark and hooded.

"Having my second dessert, Parker."

And then he tugs my dress up, leaning his head forward and latching on to my sex with his lips. I cry out as he grabs my ass, tugging me closer to his mouth. Eyes rolling, I drop my head back and use the table behind me to steady myself as he laves his tongue up and down my slit.

"Fuck," I mewl, my knees buckling as they attempt to hold me up.

"I never want to go this many days without tasting you, Juliet," he murmurs, using my first name as he whispers against my clit, his lips brushing the swollen nub. "Never again."

"Never again," I acquiesce, humming when he inserts one of his long fingers.

He presses his ring against my inner thigh, smiling.

Chase Ravage. Dominant. Possessive.

"*Mine*," I whisper, one of my hands coming to his hair, running my fingers through his short, soft hair. He groans when I curl my fingers, and his free hand squeezes my hip as his other hand pumps into me roughly.

"That's right," Chase growls. "I am yours. Check your hands, Parker," he adds, looking up at me between my legs.

I almost gasp at the openness I see—his messy hair, his wet mouth, his unguarded, darkened eyes...

"My heart," he adds, his voice softer. "You hold my heart in your hands, so please be gentle."

Fuck.

Me.

I gasp as he dives back in between my legs, pulling me closer to his mouth as his fingers dig into my hip and as his other fingers curl and pump into my cunt.

I fall over the edge seconds later, shattering on his tongue as my body convulses and shudders. If it weren't for his grip on my hip, I might've fallen over, and I cry out as he slowly draws the last of it out with his fingers, with the way his teeth so *gently* graze my swollen clit. I'm still shaking when he leans back on his heels, lifting his hand and tasting me on his fingers before pulling them out with a popping sound.

He places both hands on my thighs. "You're so beautiful when you fall apart," he murmurs, running a hand up my thighs. I shiver at his touch.

"You—you're—"

My words are failing me.

Chase chuckles and stands, pulling me off my leaning position against the table. "Let's go before I fuck you on the table," he says, his lips against my ear.

"I fail to see the problem with that..." I trail off, smirking.

His eyes look down at me with a dangerous glint. "Grab your things and let's go."

CHAPTER THIRTY
THE DEVOTION

Chase

After I've verified that my apartment is free from my older brother, I'm barely through the threshold of my bedroom when Juliet drops to her knees and pulls me forward by my belt buckle.

I grab her hands and give her a warning glare. "Not yet, love," I mutter, pulling her up. "But I appreciate the enthusiasm," I add, placing a kiss on her forehead. "I plan on taking my time with you tonight."

"Well, it's a good thing I'm fully caffeinated," she replies, her light green eyes boring into mine.

"We're still in the scene, Parker," I remind her, guiding her to my bed.

"Yes, sir," she says, her eyes slightly hooded as she sits down on the edge of my freshly made bed.

I growl with satisfaction. She's such a good girl, already broken in and ready to accept my whims. I've never spent more than a day with a submissive before, only getting tastes of other women, so I don't know if this is normal, or if it's because she truly wants to submit to me. Something tells me it's the latter. Tonight, and a few times at the castle, I'd seen the way her expression would go slack the instant I'd roll my sleeves up. She enjoyed fighting back, but times like tonight, when the stakes were higher, I knew she needed me to guide her. *Wanted* me to guide her.

I drop to my knees before her, and she gives me a questioning smile. Reaching for her foot, I pull her heels off slowly, letting them fall to the floor.

"I always assumed being a submissive meant I'd be worshipping *you,* Ravage," she says softly, using her nickname for me.

"A lot of people think being Dominant and being domineering are the same thing, but they're not. And I think you'll find that true Dominants want nothing more than to worship their submissives. After all," I add, bringing her ankle to my lips and placing a soft kiss on her skin. "I find my pleasure on the other side of yours," I continue. "There's a saying in our community: you are never more Dominant than when you are caring for your submissive."

Her throat bobs when I kiss her other ankle. After, I stand, and I know her big brain is processing all of this. It's not like Dominants have the best reputation in popular culture, so I'm sure she's mentally scouring the things she absorbed during her research to verify what I've told her.

"Take it off," I tell her, slipping a finger underneath the strap of her silk dress.

Her eyes bore into mine as she eases the dress off, and it falls to the floor in a silken heap.

Fuck.

I'll never get over the delirium that takes over whenever Juliet is naked before me.

"Another famous dress?" she asks, arching a brow and looking down at the off-white silk.

"Not famous, but special nonetheless," I admit, wondering if I should tell her.

Looking at me from under her lashes, she leans back on the bed until she's lying down, propping herself up on her elbows and crossing her legs at her ankles. My eyes slowly peruse her golden skin, soft yet muscled from running. Curvy, yet lithe. Her breasts are begging for me to touch them, and her cunt is still glistening with her arousal. I *need* to touch her. To feel her. To make up for lost time. And yet, I stay where I am, looking back at her face.

"Tell me," she says, interrupting my thoughts. "About the dress."

I suck in a breath, looking away. "I bought it for you."

She lets out a light, tinkling laugh. "I figured. But what makes it so special?" Her voice is gentle, open, and curious. But I know that once I tell her, she'll always know.

"I bought it for you for your engagement party to Dylan."

Her brows knit together, and she tilts her head

slightly. "But we hadn't spoken in months," she says cautiously.

I nod once. "That didn't mean I stopped thinking about you." Her eyes widen slightly, and I continue. "I saw it in a store, and it reminded me of you. The pockets..." Her lips twitch. "I'd heard about your engagement, and I was *so fucking close* to sending it to you. But then I saw you with him in Perky Roasters a few days before your engagement, and you looked so happy. You were laughing. Smiling. I didn't want to complicate things. So I never sent it."

Her eyes are flicking across my face, and she holds a hand up to her mouth. "You asked me why I was wearing black like I was going to a funeral."

"Yes. It was the first time I realized that you might not be as happy as I thought you were. It's why I tempted you with an invite to one of my parties."

She taps her lips as she considers me. My cock is so hard inside of my pants—and as my eyes do a slow perusal of her body, it starts to physically ache from not being inside of her tight heat.

"Did you want me there that night?"

I rock back on my heels. "I did. But I couldn't admit it to myself. I refused to believe you'd be interested in all of this," I tell her honestly.

"You idiot," she breathes, teasing me. "You could have led me off the side of a cliff and I would've followed you."

I smile. "I am an idiot, Parker. I should've said yes that night." She inhales sharply, her naked chest rising and falling. "I pushed you away for so long, but not anymore."

I unbutton my shirt as she pulls her lower lip between her teeth. "I love the dress," she admits, grinning.

Smirking, I pull my shirt off and start to undo my belt. "I knew you would."

"And how much did that scrap of silk cost?" she asks innocently, cocking her head.

I pull my pants down and watch the way her eyes take in my boxers and the hard, leaking shaft inside. I palm myself a couple of times, and her pupils bloom darker as she watches me.

"I can't remember," I lie. "Probably less than a million dollars."

She pushes up into a sitting position. "Can I touch you now, sir? Please?"

I'd planned on fucking her into my bed, but it's been almost a week since I've been inside of her, meaning I should probably take the edge off. It's going to be a long night. Epiphanies and telling her exactly how I feel notwithstanding, I want to show her how much I've missed her. I want to give her pleasure, dragging it out over and over again until her cunt is weeping. But right now, I want nothing more than to see those pretty, pink lips around my cock.

"You may," I tell her, walking closer. "Lie down."

She snaps her eyes up to mine. "But—"

I shoot her a warning glance, and she drops back onto the bed. "Turn around so that your head is hanging off the bed."

I see the instant she realizes that I'm about to fuck her mouth. Her lips part and she eagerly turns around, her neck and head hanging off the side closest to me.

God, she will be my undoing.

Just seeing her laying on my bed, perky tits bouncing as I slide my cock down her throat...

I remove my boxers and walk up to her. "Open your mouth, Parker."

She does as I say, and my bed is at the perfect height for me to slide right into her mouth. I hiss as her teeth graze the underside of my length, but after I take half a step closer, I'm able to slide in with less resistance.

"Okay?" I ask, my voice gravelly and hoarse. It feels so *fucking* good. She gives me a thumbs up. "You remember your non-verbal safe word?" I ask, trying not to smile when I imagine her humming the theme song to Wolverine with my cock down her throat. Another thumbs up. "Good girl. Now, take a deep breath," I instruct. Her eyes find mine as I pull out. She inhales, her tongue dancing over the head of my cock, and then I slam into her mouth, hitting the back of her throat.

"Fuck," I groan, wrapping a hand around her upside-down throat as I piston in and out of her hot, wet mouth. "You take my cock so well, Juliet."

She flattens her tongue, and I moan as my head drops forward, as I lean over her and rest my free hand next to her shoulder on my duvet. She gags a couple of times, but otherwise, she handles it like a champ. I haven't gone in fully, and I'm considering it as she reaches behind me, grabbing my hips and pulling me deeper, further down her throat.

"Yes, just like that," I hiss, fully fucking her mouth now. I move my hips slower so that she can catch her breath and *fuck me,* she looks so good taking me like this.

I never want to let her go, never want to give her up. If that means I have to hoard her all to myself like a fucking dragon, then so be it.

My balls begin to tighten as my cock hardens further. "Juliet," I gasp, her name falling from my lips like a prayer. "I'm close." My entire body goes taut as her mouth sucks me in tighter, hollowing her cheeks, and then I fall over the edge. "Fuck," I hiss, going still as my cock pulses down her throat. She swallows with every jet of cum I shoot into the back of her throat, and if I wasn't already in love with her, that act alone would convince me to worship her forever. I let out a final roar, placing both hands on the bed beside her as my cock bobs against her soft tongue. Slowly, I pull out, and she wipes her mouth with the back of her hand.

"You're going to kill me, Parker," I whisper, falling into the bed next to her.

"Not yet. I was told it would be a long, very exhausting night. I'm all hyped up on caffeine, you see," she taunts, crawling over to my lap and straddling me.

"Fuck," I murmur, my voice ragged. "If you ride me, I might spontaneously combust. I need a minute."

She gives me a Cheshire smile, large and mischievous. "Okay. But that was really hot, and I'm finding myself... *very* wet," she adds, sinking down to slide against my still-hard cock.

I run a hand over my face as I smile up at her.

"You're really going to ruin me forever, do you know that?"

"Not if you ruin me first," she says, sliding against my shaft again and smirking. "Now, which course is this?" I furrow my brows in confusion. "You mentioned earlier that your second dessert was me, so you owe me... five more courses, yes?"

Seven-course meal. Of fucking course.

I grin as I grab her hips and flip us both over so that I'm on top. "I am quite hungry."

CHAPTER THIRTY-ONE

THE BRUNCH

JULIET

"Stop fidgeting. You look beautiful," Chase murmurs, taking my hand underneath the table so that I stop adjusting my blouse and smoothing my hair.

"I don't think you realize how big of a deal this is, Ravage," I growl. "I've never met any of his significant others. *Ever.*"

Chase's lips twitch with a smile. "But you already met him."

I scoff. "Yes, briefly. But not as Jackson's *date*," I hiss, looking around my favorite brunch restaurant.

"And I have some idea, Parker. He is my best friend."

I look over at him, and he's sipping his coffee with his signature smug smile. "I know. I'm sorry. I want to get this right. Oh! And, not to mention, he's never seen us as—"

I go still, closing my mouth. *What are we, exactly?*

Chase leans closer. "Seen us as what, Parker?" he murmurs into my ear. "Do tell me what label you've given me today, because last night, while I was fucking your brains out, I believe you told me you loved me."

My cheeks burn at his words, remembering my admission in the throes of passion. "Yes, well, we've never introduced ourselves to someone else, so I'm unsure of—"

"How about we tell people we're dating, Parker?" I open and close my mouth, shocked at his admission. Chase Ravage doesn't *date.* He must be enjoying my shock, however, because he leans back and takes another sip of his coffee. "Or would you rather tell everyone about how I'm your predator and you're my prey?"

I inhale sharply as Jackson wanders into the restaurant, Mark trailing slightly behind him. Jumping up, I forgo formalities and hug both of them. Mark doesn't seem phased by my outward show of affection, only chuckling as he takes a seat next to Jackson. Chase is much more perfunctory, giving Mark a handshake instead and throwing Jackson a knowing smile.

We all sit down and say hello as the server brings us all menus, effectively silencing us as we peruse them. I keep sneaking glances at Jackson and Mark, but Chase pinches my thigh and grabs my hand, which catches Jackson's attention.

"I see you two have finally kissed and made up," he mutters, giving us a sly smile.

"Mmm, the same could be said for you, brother," I

retort, cocking my head and giving him a genuine smile.

"Oh, that's a story for another day," Mark murmurs to my surprise. "He recreated the scene from *Love, Actually*. The one where Keira Knightley's friend comes to the door? It was very sweet," he murmurs, looking over at Jackson, who is smirking, before turning back to us. His eyes flick to Chase and a look of confusion passes over his face. "Did you dye your hair?" he asks Chase. "I swear, you had blonde hair at the party—"

Jackson makes a subtle, slicing motion at his neck. "Different guy, remember?" he hisses quietly.

Mark laughs. "Right. Sorry. I forgot," he says, looking at me. "It's nice to see you again, Juliet."

I smile. "You too, Mark. And yes, this idiot next to me is the one who paid for that whole lavish ordeal," I explain, ignoring the way Chase is squeezing my thigh tightly.

I swear, the way he always has to be touching me —like he's worried I'll float away—makes me *dizzy* with lust and longing. I look over at him, and he's watching me with a darkened glower, his lower lip between his teeth. *Fuck.*

We all make small talk, and I observe how Jackson looks at Mark with a sated smile—which makes me endlessly happy. In fact, I've never seen him this happy, apart from when he's at work. Mark and Chase talk about The Black Rose, and I learn that Mark is currently going to school for his master's in theater.

They really are two peas in a pod.

Jackson and I order our usual brunch—chocolate

chip pancakes with a side of bacon. We've been coming here since we were kids, and as the server places our plates down, I look up at him and notice he's watching me with the same sad smile he always wears whenever he talks about our parents. I reach out for his hand, and he takes it.

"I think they'd be proud of us," I say, breathing slowly so that I don't cry. "Of you, especially."

He nods, batting away a stray tear, and Chase's hand never leaves my thigh.

After Chase and Mark finish their respectable eggs and hash, and after Jackson and I finish dipping our bacon into the maple syrup, we all talk for another hour. Jackson seems so... carefree. With his arm slung on the back of Mark's chair, I can tell by the way his eyes crinkle and the way his posture is relaxed that he's *truly* happy. Just as the server clears the table, Chase reaches into his blazer pocket and pulls out an envelope. I look up at him and tilt my head quizzically.

"Jax," Chase starts, unfolding the paper. "Ravage Consulting Firm recently acquired a new client. I'm now the biggest shareholder of Saint Helena Academy, which means I sit on their board of directors," he starts.

I look over at Jackson when I realize what Chase is doing. He looks confused, and his eyes dart between me and Chase.

"Saint Helena?" he asks, pushing his glasses up on his nose. "Why?"

Chase takes a deep breath, ignoring his question and diving right into the nitty gritty. "As a member of their board of directors, and as the new landlord of the property they lease, as well as their biggest investor, I now have a lot of sway with their policies. Most of the regulations were outdated—glaringly so—but since taking over, I've consulted with the biggest compliance firm in the country to create new policies." He pushes the piece of paper toward Jackson, who reads it slowly.

"Chase," he says, a look of puzzlement on his face. "How... why?"

Chase huffs a laugh, and I see him wipe his palms on his trousers. *He's nervous.*

"Because you're Jackson. And while I know I can't protect you from everything in this cruel world, I can and do have the financial means to ensure you can always stay safe at Saint Helena, if you choose to do so."

Jackson nods once, and Mark glances down at the letter, his eyes widening before looking up at Chase.

"This is a big deal," Mark mutters, smiling. He looks at Chase.

Jackson pushes away from the table and comes around to where Chase is sitting. Chase stands, and they hug for a long time. Mark winks at me when I look over at him, and it hits me suddenly that perhaps everything is going to be okay.

"I also spoke to my older brother, Malakai," Chase continues, subtly winking at me. "He's going to be accepting the position of headmaster starting this fall, so you will have a powerful ally as your boss."

"Great, more Ravage brothers to contend with," Jackson jokes, but he pulls Chase in for another hug.

Soon after that, Jackson and Mark leave, and I watch them walk away as I grin like a maniac.

"I'm glad he's happy," Chase says from next to me, laying down some cash before helping me out of my chair. "Mark seems nice."

I give him a conspiratorial smirk. "You pulled all the cards today," I tease, snuggling into his side as he wraps an arm around my shoulder and leads us outside. "Tell me more about Malakai. Or, actually, tell me more about all of your brothers."

We walk slowly to his parked car a couple of blocks away, and he sighs once before he speaks.

"Well, you know Miles. He's an asshole, but we're the closest because we work together."

"I'm excited for his impending wedding," I joke, and Chase huffs a laugh.

"Next is probably Liam. He lives a bit north of here and is a professor of Creative Writing. He's pretty reclusive, and as the oldest, does a shit job of being the wise old soul we all crave. But we talk a few times a month. Then there's Malakai, who is a pastor. He took everything wrong with our family and turned it around. I think he saw how we all turned out and decided to do the exact opposite of us." I laugh. "And Orion is the youngest. He's still in his twenties, still partying and drinking too much. He's unemployed at the moment, but we all try and watch out for him as best as we can."

"So you're all pretty close?"

He nods. "Yeah. I mean, as close as we can be, seeing as we're the offspring of Charles Ravage."

I brace myself for my next question. "And your father?"

Chase shrugs. "He's still licking his wounds, moving from estate to estate all around the world. I think he's currently holed up in Paris. Miles still speaks to him. And I think Orion still sees him sometimes. Because our mom remarried when Orion was still living at home, he didn't quite get the full Charles Ravage experience. His stepfather is a nice guy. He has a daughter—Layla—so Orion got some much-needed feminine energy." He pulls away from me and moves to unlock the car on my side. Today it's a new model, some fancy green Bentley SUV with gold accents. He opens my door and turns to face me. "But Liam, Malakai, and I all decided a long time ago to cut ties with him."

I slide into the buttery leather seat as he walks over to his side. Once he climbs in, I turn to face him.

"I've been meaning to ask you... why were your brothers at my engagement party?" I ask, smiling when he chuckles.

"I told Jackson that if I were going to pay for your engagement party and your wedding, the least he could do is invite them. I never expected all of them to show up."

He turns on some music as we drive back to his apartment. I've been there since Thursday night, and we've hardly left the bedroom. Tomorrow is Monday, though, and it's hustle time for my dissertation. I have a month until it's due, and then I can focus on everything else. Just as we pull into Chase's parking garage a few blocks away, I turn to face him.

"What happens if I get offered a position at a university in a different state this fall?" I ask, my hands nervously sliding along my jeans to dry them.

He pulls into one of his spots and cuts the engine. "Then you accept it. *If* the terms are all right with you, that is."

I worry my lower lip between my teeth as he opens his door and walks around to my side. When he pulls it open, I blurt the first thing I can think.

"But what happens to us? If I have to move to Wisconsin or Pennsylvania or somewhere like that?"

Chase hangs off my door, considering my words, and I can't help but admire the way his white dress shirt pulls tight across his chest and how the dark jeans, black blazer, and black leather boots all somehow complement his frame.

"According to Liam, that's a big possibility. As far as I know, and correct me if I'm wrong, but when it comes to academia, you can't really be picky about location."

He's not understanding my question...

I swallow. "I know. But what happens to *us* if I have to move to Wisconsin?"

"Then I guess we'll move to Wisconsin," he says simply, looking at me with tilted brows, looking at me confidently with those intense, light-blue eyes. "Parker, there is no version of my future without you in it. So if we have to move, we'll move."

"But your job—"

"I can do my job remotely," he tells me calmly, his lips lifting up into a small, comforting smile. "And fly into California when needed."

My heart is racing, and I want to be sure he knows what he's getting himself into. "But we've only been dating for... less than a week," I blurt.

Chase gives me one of his earth-shattering smiles, the kind that tugs at his dimples and makes him seem so fucking young.

"Right, but I've been loving you for eight years."

He grabs my hand and helps me out of the car. I love this—the way he's always caring for me, touching me, making sure I'm all right... I swallow the emotion creeping up my throat, waiting to burst out. Leading me to the elevator, I'm still ruminating on his words.

I've been loving you for eight years.
I've been loving you for eight years.
I've been loving you for eight years.

On the elevator ride up, Chase watches me. I know he's used to my mind working its magic, used to me overthinking every single thing. I grab his hand as we get to *The Penthouse*, squeezing it once in a silent thank you. As the doors slide open, he tugs me to the right, away from the kitchen and toward an area of the apartment that I haven't explored yet.

"Where are we going?" I ask.

"You'll see," he says, looking down at me mirthfully.

We turn a corner, and I take in the sun-filled courtyard before us. And inside the courtyard is...

"Mr. Rooster," I breathe, grinning as I open the door and walk outside.

A large rooster is prancing around the yard, and though I never imagined myself saying this about a rooster, I look at Chase and say, "He's beautiful."

Chase nods and walks up to the animal, patting his head. "He's a wild Kauai rooster," he explains. "No one wanted him after my father..." he trails off. "Anyway, he's been my buddy for years. Their normal lifespan is five to eight years, but I've had him for over a decade."

I take in the turquoise tail and the red and yellow feathers. "Does he have a name?"

Chase chuckles. "I've started calling him Mr. Rooster."

I turn to face him when Mr. Rooster crows—*loudly*. I jump, eyes wide, looking at Chase.

"I thought he didn't crow?" I ask, looking between the rooster and Chase.

Chase shrugs, looking at the fancy coop as a small hen comes wandering out into the open. She must be the same breed as Mr. Rooster—she has the same orange and turquoise feathers.

Chase puts his hands in his pockets and walks up next to me as I watch the two animals strut around their sizable courtyard.

"Turns out he just needed a hen. Hasn't stopped crowing since I introduced Mrs. Chicken. Roosters, unbeknownst to me, prefer to have a flock to care for. And to dominate," he murmurs. "Guess we have that in common," he adds, his smile broadening as he walks up and wraps his arms around me. "Why don't we go inside, yeah?" he purrs, his intention obvious.

I twist in his arms and grin, wrapping my hands around his neck. "Wherever I go this fall, we'll need to make sure we have room for them," I say, standing on my tippy toes and planting a kiss on Chase's lips.

"Already thought about it, Parker," he says against my lips.

"There's probably a lot we should talk about since we've only been dating for less than a week and we've both said 'I love you,'" I whisper. "It's like we're doing everything backward."

"I know. And I don't give a fuck about what order we do things in. Because right now, all I want to do is drag you into my bedroom and fuck you until you forget your name," he growls, pulling me behind him.

"Fine with me," I squeal, trailing behind him as he marches through his apartment with the kind of intention that makes everything inside of me coil with anticipation.

Yeah, I could get used to this.

EPILOGUE
THE MAZE

JULIET

Four Years Later

I wake up early as the sunrise bathes our room in a soft, pink light. Turning over, I find the other side of the bed cold, meaning Chase is already gone and has been for a while. Yawning, I roll over and check my phone, noticing a black envelope propped up against my bedside lamp. My heart beats faster as I sit up and rip it open, grinning as I take in my husband's perfect scrawl.

> Mrs. R
>
> Enjoy your breakfast, love. No need to go on a run or get dressed. You'll be running enough as it is, and you'll be naked within seconds of me finding you.

I know you have some papers to grade, so take your time this morning.

I'll be waiting at the front gate of the maze at 10:00.

Do NOT be late.

Welcome to The Hunt...

Mr. R.

I tamp down the thrill that runs through me at his words, glancing over to my dressing table where I see a silver tray of food and a steaming cappuccino. My eyes flick to the letter, to the way he used his—*our*—family crest to seal the wax. I'm both scared of what's to come and entirely aroused, but I push it all down in favor of the delicious breakfast he prepared for me.

After I'm done eating, I work through the essays I'd gotten back from my students. Hunched over my desk in my office, I keep a close eye on the time, pulling my silk robe tighter when a cool breeze flutters through my open window. It's sunny and cool today, the perfect spring day in Northern California. I'm on my second cup of coffee when I notice it's nearly nine thirty. Jumping up, I walk down the hall to our bedroom, shedding my robe and taking a quick shower.

I pull my hair back into a sleek ponytail—something I know Chase loves. The feel of him wrapping my ponytail around his fist is enough to elicit goose bumps. Pulling the silk robe back on, I go downstairs and make my way to the back garden. There is still dew on the grass, but the sun is already out and the warmth hits my skin perfectly. I use the stone pathway since I'm barefoot, and when I get to the entrance of the maze, I see another black envelope with a gold wax seal propped up against the slightly ajar iron gate.

Mrs. R,
I hope you weren't late, because you only get a five-minute head start.
I'm going to find you, so you better run...
Mr. R

I set the letter down and walk into the maze. My breathing is already heavy with excitement, and the space between my thighs is already slick. It's been a busy few months, with me settling into my tenured position at the local university, buying this house, and now, the next step in our relationship...

I swallow, my skin tingling with what the future holds.

We hadn't played outside of the bedroom in months, and we'd yet to take advantage of the final selling point of this property—a full-size hedge maze.

I wander between the hedges, my eyes snapping to every corner, every crevice, waiting for him to find me. I think back to a few days ago, discussing the maze and how to use it today. The way he had me pinned beneath him in our library... the way he uttered *exactly* what I wanted to hear...

"You know by now how to give up control, Juliet. So why would this be any different?"

"Yes, but all the books say—"

"My love, when have we ever done anything by the books? Stop overthinking things. You can't plan this. It's entirely out of our control. Now, I know you've been stressed about it all, so I have an idea if you'll allow me the satisfaction of helping you unwind."

I smile. "What's your idea?"

"Saturday is the day, yeah?" he asks, nuzzling his nose behind my ear and dragging it down to my chest, inhaling.

My eyes flutter closed. "Yes."

"Okay. Let me take the control from you, then. All you need to worry about is feeling, obeying... and running."

I shiver as the memory passes, turning a corner to find the next section empty.

Is he even here? Maybe he got held up on a work call —I know he and Miles are currently securing a big client. He's been down south all week because of it, and aside from a quickie last night when he got home, I'd barely touched him. I missed him. But I had to trust him. I *did* trust him. He knows how important today is. But where is he? He said he was going to give me a five-minute head start... surely it's been five minutes. Is he watching me? Lurking behind a corner somewhere? The thought makes me wetter, and I walk quicker to dispel some of the tension.

My hands are shaking as I turn the next corner, letting out a long, slow breath when it's clear.

Keep going, Juliet. Your predator is waiting.

———

Chase

At exactly five minutes past ten, I allow myself to enter the maze. My eyes flick over the opened envelope, and I straighten the collar of my white shirt as I walk between the narrow hedges. Every crackle, every rustle of leaves, has my eyes skating across my surroundings. I think I caught a whiff of her shampoo, but I can't be sure. Still, I follow the scent around the next corner, stiffening when I see her slowly approaching the next corner, her back to me.

My cock hardens inside of my pants, aching to be inside of her. I was wearing her favorite hunting outfit— just for her. *All for her.* Black pants, white button-up, sturdy, lace-up boots, and her new favorite accessory... black leather gloves. My eyes take in her long, silk robe. Her hair is pulled back into a ponytail. And she's barefoot —which she's learned before puts her at a disadvantage.

My lovely *prey*. My wife. She wants to be caught— and the hunter inside of me wishes for nothing more than to hunt her properly, to claim her in the ultimate way, ensuring she's full of my essence. And I'd fill her full of my cum—over and over and over.

Until today, there'd never been a good time to complete my ultimate fantasy, but now? I could fill her up and lock her legs shut. I knew how much she wanted this. We'd been planning it for weeks, but the body is fickle. Today... she'd be ripe and ready for the taking.

I take a step forward as she rounds the corner.

Normally when we play, I chase and she runs. But today, I want to stalk her. *Slowly*. Relishing in the way her chest rises and falls. Making her think—*just for a second*—that I'm not coming after her. Give her a false sense of safety. It would be in that moment that I would strike—that I'd claim her for myself. Her tongue would flick against the leather, and she'd taste it—moaning when she did. She *fucking* loved it when I touched her with the leather.

I'd acquired a healthy amount of leather accessories in the last four years, sometimes wearing them just to make her crazy.

Driving gloves.

A leather tie.

Leather shoes, and most recently, a black leather cuff bracelet and matching collar for her.

I adjust myself in my pants as I round the corner slowly. Juliet is about to round the next corner, but a twig snaps under my feet, and her eyes shoot over her shoulder as I duck behind a hedge. I can see her, but she can't see me—and my cock is *throbbing* as I see her swallow, following it down her throat to her flushed chest. She turns and quickly walks around the next corner.

I follow.

She's going quicker now—left, right, left, right... so predictable, my prey.

She must know I'm right on her heels. Must know that I am calculating her next turn. It's too predictable.

A thrill runs through me, and I crack my neck as she turns left on the next corner.

I go right.

Then left—curling my fists when I see her stumble into the same passage as me, looking over her shoulder for me.

Oh, little prey, I am right in front of you.

I let out a low growl, taking so much fucking pleasure when she visibly shivers and slowly turns to face me.

"There you are, love," I murmur, my voice thick and dangerous. Sliding my hand to my belt, I pull on the black leather riding crop—a surprise for her. I see her eyes widen as I run it over my hand smoothly before holding it up. "Your ass is mine today. As is your cunt. Do you understand?"

"Yes, sir," she says tightly, and I smile at the way her pupils are already blown out, making her eyes seem nearly onyx in color.

Seems making my wife wait this morning was a good call.

I discovered early on in our relationship that Juliet enjoyed when I tricked her—when I surprised her. And while we normally played without toys, today was different.

I also knew she was a masochist and enjoyed the pain almost more than the pleasure I gave her afterward.

It's a good thing I was a sadist.

I would always get so close to coming in my pants whenever I spanked her.

"Come here, my pretty, little prey," I command, taking a step toward her.

She cracks a grin, her nostrils flaring with excitement as she shakes her head. "Catch me," she taunts, and then she's gone.

I swear under my breath as I jog after her.

Seems like someone wants to be punished, I think, holding the riding crop in my hand as I turn the corner.

She's gone—probably two or three passages away. *Fuck.*

"That's okay," I yell. "You can run, but you can't hide," I tell her, hoping she can hear me. Hoping my words are making her wet and needy. I swish the riding crop against the hedge, sending a flock of birds up into the air. I grin when I hear her yelp of surprise to my right.

I place the crop back in its holster, and then I *run.*

———

Juliet

I don't know if I've ever been this turned on. I'm *dripping,* my wetness sliding down my legs, and my vision is blurry with lust and terror—two things that make it an extremely satisfying game for me. I hear another snap of his riding crop, and I know he's close. I want to stop—want to let him find me, but I also know how much better it is for him when I make him work for it. I learned early on that Chase prefers to *earn* his reward.

I turn the corner and cry out, my hand flying over my mouth when I see my husband waiting patiently for me at the other end of the passage.

He removes the riding crop from his holster—*that was new, dear god... I would never recover from seeing him use it*—and slowly stalks closer to me. I'm breathing so hard that my throat is burning, and my nipples are sensitive and aching for his mouth. So is the rest of my body.

Just as I take a step back to run, he lurches forward and grabs me by the front of my robe, pulling me against his warm, broad chest and glaring down at me with hunger and longing.

"I don't think so, Mrs. Ravage," he says, his voice husky.

"You don't know me very well then," I say sweetly, trailing a hand up his chest and ignoring the shudder of my body when his leather glove grazes my skin.

I pull away quickly, giggling as I run off.

He likes this. He never tolerated brats before me, but he loves it when I fight back.

I hear him let out a low growl behind me, hear the soft footsteps as he chases after me. And then a second later, they're gone.

But I know better than to assume he stopped pursuing me.

"Juliet," he calls out, the crack of the riding crop sounding from my right.

I move quicker, only to end up at a dead end.

Panicking, I turn and run the other way, only for Chase's arm to snap out from an adjacent passage, pulling me roughly into his body.

"Got you," he murmurs. "And I'm not letting you go this time."

Before I can act, he picks me up and tosses me over his shoulder.

"Let me go!" I scream, beating his back.

He runs a leather-clad hand up my thigh, chuckling when I gasp. *Screw him.* He knows how much I love those gloves, how much I love the buttery feel of the leather on my sensitive skin.

"Be a good girl and stop struggling," he tells me, twisting us further into the maze.

"Where are you taking me?" I ask, feeling all of the blood rush to my face from being upside down.

"You'll see."

A minute later, we entered a clearing. The middle of the maze, I realize. He sets me down, and I look around, stunned.

He must've been planning this all morning—or for weeks, perhaps. Before me is a large picnic blanket—more like a camping mattress due to the thickness and numerous pillows strewn over the soft fabric, but bigger. There's a table with water, food, and black roses and another table with an assortment of toys. Above it all is a trellis of wood, ivy climbing up and over the top to give the illusion of shade, though the sun is still behind the tall hedges. Before I can look at everything closer, Chase comes up behind me and runs the riding crop across my stomach.

"On the floor, Mrs. Ravage," he growls into my ear before walking me to the blanket and shoving me onto my hands and knees. Before I can protest, he crouches beside me and pulls my robe off completely, muttering praise as his fingers run along my spine before he runs the crop over my ass. "I can't fucking wait to see how pink I can make this ass," he murmurs. "Count for me, love," he says gently.

I fist the blanket underneath me in preparation. "How many?" I ask, breathless.

"Let's do four for now. One for every year of marriage," he adds, and my skin pebbles at the reverence in his voice. At the memory of him proposing after only dating for three months. At the way he couldn't wait to plan a proper wedding—and how he convinced me to marry him that night.

It was, and still is, the craziest thing we'd ever done.

A month later, we threw a lavish party at Ravage Castle, and it was everything I ever could've hoped for.

"My prey," he says softly. "Are you going to show me how sorry you are for running away from your predator?" he asks.

And because I apparently have a death wish—and I know how much we both enjoy my snark—I scoff and look over my shoulder.

"I'm never sorry, Mr. Ravage."

His pupils darken, and his jaw clicks as he fists the crop in his hand. Kneeling before me like this on one knee, I can see the outline of his thick cock running up his leg, and I lick my lips when he tilts his head, clearly annoyed at my utter defiance.

"You'll pay for that mouth, Juliet," he growls. "I'm doubling it."

Please do.

Holding me down with one hand, he raises the hand with the crop and brings it down on my bare ass. I scream. *Fuck, it hurts so much more than his hand, even more than the paddle, which* really *fucking hurts and leaves me bruised for days.*

"One," I cry out, keeping my voice even. I can't—won't—break on the first hit. Besides, he knows I'll use the safe word if I need to. Lord knows I've used it before.

I shift my hips, the slippery wetness between my thighs dripping onto the blanket underneath me.

Chase hits me with the crop again—twice—in quick succession. "Two! Three!" I gasp, blinking back the tears that are leaking from my eyes. My core pulses with arousal.

"Good girl," he murmurs, smoothing over where the crop is surely causing me to bleed. I can't think of why or how it would hurt so much otherwise. "So pink already. Such a beautiful, blooming color, love."

I hardly have time to take in his almost sweet words before he swings the riding crop down again, slightly gentler this time.

"Four," I breathe out, sniffling and shaking.

"You're so good, Mrs. Ravage. Taking my crop so well. I wish you could see how pretty your ass looks right now," he adds, removing his gloves. His free hand roves between my legs. I moan when he works a finger inside my dripping pussy. "Mmm. So ripe and ready for me, so fruitful and needy for my seed," he says, his voice wavering with the double entendre. We both know he loves to say things like this during a scene, but today, he means it.

Without warning, he brings the riding crop down on my ass with his other hand.

"Five," I moan. My heat grips him firmly as the pain dissipates.

I'm panting as I look up at him over my shoulder. His eyes flutter for a second before he nods and hits me again.

"Six!" I scream, fisting the fabric. He adds a second finger, curling them so that they're dragging against the front walls of my channel. He massages that spot, groaning when I squeeze him again.

"My wife likes it when I punish her," he murmurs, using his thumb to stroke my clit lightly.

"Yes," I whisper.

"Good. Keep counting, love."

I open my mouth and let out a guttural warble as he brings the crop down over the same spot again.

"Seven!"

I arch my back, writhing in pain. For a second, I consider using the word *yellow*—telling him to stop, telling him it's too much. But then he pushes his fingers deeper, swiping his thumb across my aching clit, and I moan with the flood of pleasure that flashes through me unexpectedly.

He knows.

He knows I'm on the brink, on the edge of my sanity.

"There we go," he says soothingly. "Can you take one more, Juliet?"

Suddenly and randomly, I grieve for the name he used to use for me. *Parker*. But once we were married, he refused to call me that since I took his last name. Something about how it was important that I was a Ravage—to him. So I let him call me Juliet, but right now, I miss the way he used to call me Parker.

"Yes," I whisper, knowing my face is wet with tears.

He plucks his thumb across my swollen nub again, and I whimper as he doles out the last of the punishing smacks. It cracks loudly in the air, and I gasp, pressing my body up to get away from the pain.

"Eight," I sob, and as I'm about to shout my safe word, as I try to tell him I cannot possibly take another one, he drops the crop to the ground and lays down next to me, pulling me tight into his body so that I'm lying sideways. His fingers are still buried deep inside of me, and he moves my hips away from him slightly so that the front of his trousers don't touch the sensitive skin where he spanked me.

"You're so good," he murmurs, and my eyes flutter closed as I grind against his fingers. I can hear and feel how wet I am, how close I am to the edge. "You always take your punishment so beautifully," he moans, and I hear the telltale click of his belt. I know, from experience, that he's close too. I also know that he's going to make himself come all over my ass so that he can fuck me properly, but today, I want all of him. Every single spent drop.

"Chase," I beg.

"That's not my name, is it?" he tells me, smacking my hip gently.

"Sir," I moan, writhing and riding his long fingers. "I want you to come inside of me. Please, please," I beg again, my voice breaking.

"Yeah?" Chase asks, his voice hoarse. He's close. I can hear him frantically stroking himself behind me. "You want me to fill you nice and full with my cum?"

"Yes," I gasp, rolling my hips.

"Since you asked so nicely," he growls, lifting my leg, removing his fingers, and thrusting deep inside of me in one fell swoop.

"Oh god," I utter, squeezing my eyes shut as my cunt clenches around him.

"I'll give you one more chance to say the right name," he warns, his voice low and threatening. "God is not the one with his cock buried deep inside of you, filling your tight cunt with my seed. Who is?" he asks, grabbing my hip with his free hand to drag me back onto his length.

"You, sir," I whisper. "Yes, fuck, Chase—"

"That's it, Parker. I want you to milk every last drop out of me."

The use of my old name on his lips makes me shatter around his cock, and I convulse against his chest as he roars, spilling deep inside of me. I see white as I rock against him, as my body shudders with pleasure. I feel the way I soak the hand still working my clit, hear his satisfied moan, and the way his cock jumps inside of me. I try to lower my leg, but he holds me tightly.

"Don't fucking move," he breathes, maneuvering out of me and carefully turning me so that I'm on my back. "Legs closed, love," he mutters, grabbing a nearby pillow and propping it up underneath my ass.

I laugh. "You realize this is an old wives' tale, right?"

He kisses me softly on the lips. "Yes, but why take a chance? You think I won't make you hold it all in? You're going to be so full of my cum by the time I'm done with you, Juliet."

My stomach swoops low at his words. "Promise?" I ask, reaching out for his face.

"I have one job," he murmurs, peppering kisses along my jaw. "And I never half-ass anything. Especially not the most important thing I'll ever do."

———

Chase

I sip my scotch as my wife dozes on the other side of the bedroom, her worn-out body prone on our large, four-poster bed. I have another business trip on Monday, so I am making up for lost time, and perhaps that meant I was a bit too rough with her. Still, she never used the safe word—and I know she's not afraid to, as she's used both *red* and *yellow* numerous times in the past. Her ass is still red, a dark bruise forming where I used the crop. Grimacing, I drain the last of my scotch and stand, walking into the bathroom.

When I emerge, Juliet is watching me with tired, hooded eyes.

"We should do some more of this," I tell her, holding up the tub of soothing lotion.

She nods lazily, still riding the high of our scene. The more intense our play is, the harder she feels it after—that hazy, happy feeling. Most nights, I lay awake and watch her, ensuring I can take care of her in every way imaginable. Today, especially, I am keeping a close eye on her. Making sure she's hydrated, fed, warm, comforted...

I finish rubbing the lotion into her bruise. "You should go back to sleep," I murmur. "It will help."

"What if it doesn't work?" she asks, her voice small.

I run my fingers through her long hair, pulling the covers over her so that she stays warm. "Then we'll try again next month. And the month after. Until you're swollen with the next Ravage heir, Juliet," I whisper, brushing her hair off her back. "And if it never works, then we will figure out our next step together. You know I'm open to anything. Adoption, too."

She smiles and lets out a contented sigh. *This* is the version of my wife that I love the most. Exhausted and boneless from giving her pleasure all day long, vulnerable, half-asleep, so *trusting* and willing to take my help and my tender words. It's this, when she gives into me fully, that I can see all the ways she's perfect for me. How we fit so fucking perfectly together.

It's why I married her three months after we

started dating. And I would've married her sooner if I could have. I would have agreed to it the day she came to Ravage Castle wanting to play.

She offered herself to me that day, and I took it all.

Just like a dragon hoarding his gold.

And now, she was ready to start our family.

Here, in Northern California, almost four years into her job as a professor, and six months after buying our dream house out in the middle of nowhere. Jackson had claimed their childhood home with his now husband, Mark, so it made sense for us to put down roots near her job. Besides, she'd always have the house to go back to, now that Jackson was living there.

I'm still not sure how everything turned out so perfectly, but it did.

And I'll forever be grateful for it. For *her*. For giving me a second chance.

"Chase?" she asks, reaching for my hand.

I lace my fingers with hers. "Yes, my love?" I lie down next to her so that we're facing each other.

"Tell me again," she says, smiling. Her voice is thick with sleep.

I pull her closer so that her body is pressed against mine, resting my chin on top of her head as my arms wrap around her chest.

I chuckle. "It was the pros and cons list that did me in officially," I joke, and she lets out a small huff of laughter.

"I'm serious. Tell me again what you wanted to do that night."

She likes to ask about that night when she's still in

a sub drop. I suppose making her ruminate over my words for eight years will do that to a person. I've since apologized a million times over.

"You know exactly what I wanted to do that night, Parker," I tell her, running my hand over her stomach and laying my palm flat against her skin.

And I tell her.

I don't leave out any details as I confide the deepest, darkest desires I had for her when she asked me to take her virginity. By the time I'm finished with the hypothetical scenario, she sits up and straddles me, sinking down on my hard cock and gasping as I twine my fingers with hers.

I don't ask to dominate her.

I let her take the lead as she rolls her hips, taking her own pleasure as I chase mine immediately afterward. And as my wife pants on top of me, I hold her close as she falls asleep. I wasn't lying when I told her that I was never going to let her go. She was mine, and she always would be.

The dragon and his princess.

———

Thank you so much for reading Prey Tell! Are you ready for Miles' story?

You can preorder it here:
mybook.to/MarryLies

If you want to sign up for Marry Lies release news and

updates, as well as receive excerpts and teasers before anyone else, **you can join my mailing list here:**

www.authoramandarichardson.com/newsletter

(You also get a free student/teacher novella as a thank you for joining!)

ACKNOWLEDGMENTS

First of all, thank you for reading. I LOVED every second of writing this book, and I hope it shows. I think this might be my favourite ebook I've ever written... from the angst, to the jealous/possessive hero... it's everything I adore about reading romance.

There are soooo many people I have to thank for this book! I'm going to start with my readers, who loved the woods chase scene in Savage Reign so much that several of you begged me for a full-length primal play book... so this one's for you guys.

To my husband, for helping me with so much of this book (not in *that* way... get your mind out of the gutter, lol). From the conception to the proofreading, you have been my rock.

To Britti Van and Amanda Anderson, for helping me with plotting the very early versions of this book. Brittni, so many of the one liners in this book are ideas you gave me, so thank you!

To Tori Ellis, for the outline help. I printed your suggestions out and used them every step of the way. I can't tell you how helpful your calls have been!

To Renee and Brittni for the alpha reading... my oh my it was fun having you along for this ride!

To Jon, Lo, and Kerrie, for the sensitivity reading. Your suggestions undoubtably made this book so much better. I will forever be grateful for your expertise.

To Jess, Jasmine, and Chanel, thanks for beta reading! You know I love you all.

To Emma, for the gorgeous cover.

To Rafa, for bringing Chase to life. I can't wait for your other images to bring the Ravage brothers to life!

To Michele, for the last minute proofreading. You are a lifesaver! Also, Mila and Lilith, for the screenshots. You guys are amazing and definitely went above and beyond to help me when I was in a pickle.

To my Keyboard Whores... you guys are the best and I'm so lucky to have such a wonderful, diverse group of author friends. Much of this book was written during our sprints, which is some days the only thing grounding me and making me feel a part of a community. I love you guys.

And to Amelia Wild... your innocuous post about Manacled led me down the rabbit hole of Dramione (Draco/Hermione) fan fiction. Chase Ravage's possessive traits are based on all of the different amalgamations of Draco Malfoy that I've read over the last six months, and it's because of you that my obsession is where it is now (i.e. I am obsessed)! Also, team #Dramione forever, but that's a given.

To my dark hearts, I wouldn't be here without you guys. Thanks for being so excited for this story.

ABOUT THE AUTHOR

Amanda Richardson writes from her chaotic dining room table in Yorkshire, England, often distracted by her husband and two adorable sons. When she's not writing contemporary and dark, twisted romance, she enjoys coffee (a little too much) and collecting house plants like they're going out of style.

You can visit my website here: **www.authoramandarichardson.com**

ALSO BY AMANDA RICHARDSON

CONTEMPORARY ROMANCE

Ravaged Castle Series (MF):

Prey Tell

Marry Lies

Ward Willing

Step Brute

Holy Hearts

Ruthless Royals Duet (Reverse Harem):

Ruthless Crown

Ruthless Queen

Savage Hearts Series (Reverse Harem):

Savage Hate

Savage Gods

Savage Reign

Darkness Duet (Reverse Harem):

Lords of Darkness

Lady of Darkness

Love at Work series (MF):

Between the Pages

A Love Like That

Tracing the Stars

Say You Hate Me

HEATHENS Series (Dark Romance, MF):

SINNERS

HEATHENS

MONSTERS

VILLAINS (coming 2024)

Standalones (MF):

The Realm of You

The Island

PARANORMAL ROMANCE

Shadow Pack Series (Paranormal Romance, under my pen name K. Easton):

Shadow Wolf

Shadow Bride

Shadow Queen

Standalones:

Blood & Vows (K. Easton)